10687573

CALGARY PUBLIC LIBRARY

OCT - - 2005

TROY

LORD OF THE SILVER BOW

www.**books**at**trans**world.co.uk

For more information on David Gemmell and his books, see his website at
www.booksattransworld.co.uk/davidgemmell

DAVID GEMMELL

TROY

LORD OF THE SILVER BOW

BANTAM PRESS

LONDON · TORONTO · SYDNEY · AUCKLAND · JOHANNESBURG

TRANSWORLD PUBLISHERS
61–63 Uxbridge Road, London W5 5SA
a division of The Random House Group Ltd

RANDOM HOUSE AUSTRALIA (PTY) LTD
20 Alfred Street, Milsons Point, Sydney,
New South Wales 2061, Australia

RANDOM HOUSE NEW ZEALAND LTD
18 Poland Road, Glenfield, Auckland 10, New Zealand

RANDOM HOUSE SOUTH AFRICA (PTY) LTD
Endulini, 5a Jubilee Road, Parktown 2193, South Africa

Published 2005 by Bantam Press
a division of Transworld Publishers

Copyright © David A. Gemmell 2005
Map by Hardlines
Part-title illustrations © John Bolton 2005

The right of David A. Gemmell to be identified as the author of this work has
been asserted in accordance with sections 77 and 78 of the Copyright,
Designs and Patents Act 1988.

All the characters in this book are fictitious, and any resemblance to actual
persons, living or dead, is purely coincidental.

A catalogue record for this book is available from the British Library.
ISBN 0593 052196 (cased)
0593 05220X (tpb)

All rights reserved. No part of this publication may be reproduced, stored
in a retrieval system, or transmitted in any form or by any means,
electronic, mechanical, photocopying, recording, or otherwise, without the
prior permission of the publishers.

Typeset in 11/14pt Sabon by
Falcon Oast Graphic Art Ltd

Printed and bound in Great Britain
by Clays Ltd, Bungay, Suffolk

1 3 5 7 9 10 8 6 4 2

Papers used by Transworld Publishers are natural, recyclable products made from
wood grown in sustainable forests. The manufacturing processes conform to the
environmental regulations of the country of origin.

Lord of the Silver Bow is dedicated with great affection to Lawrence and Sally Berman, two friends who have sailed the Great Green in storms and fair weather on their yacht, *Goli*. Their support and friendship during the last seven years has been beyond price.

ACKNOWLEDGEMENTS

My thanks to my test readers Lawrence Berman, Jan Dunlop, Tony Evans, Alan Fisher, Larry Finlay, Stella Gemmell and Steve Hutt. Special thanks to Lawrence who put together and largely wrote the scene detailing the sinking of Gershom's ship. Grateful thanks also to my editors, Selina Walker at Transworld UK and Steve Saffel at Del Rey US, who helped shape the novel and keep it focused, and to my copy editors Eric Lowenkron and Nancy Webber.

The Great Green

THRAKI

SAMOTHRAKI

IMBROS

Mt. Olympos ▲

LEMNOS

Troy ⦿ DARDANIA

TENEDOS

Mt. Ida ▲

THESSALY

Phthia

LESBOS

EUBOEA

KIOS

ITHAKA

Thebes • Aulis

KEPHALLENIA

• Athens

Mykene ⦿

Argos •

Pylos •

• Sparta

THERA

KO

KYTHERA

K R E T O S

Knossos •

Phaistos •

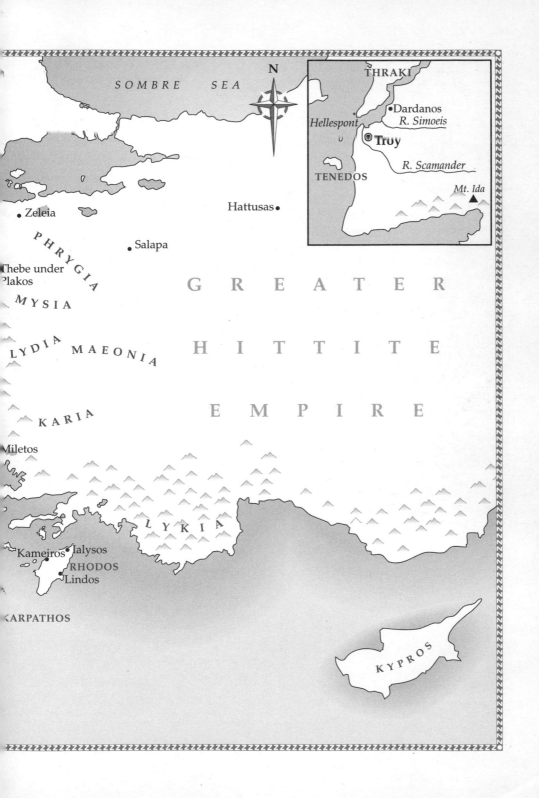

TROY

LORD OF THE SILVER BOW

PROLOGUE

To sleep is to die.

So he clung to the driftwood as the raging seas hurled him high, then plunged him deep into the storm-dark valleys between the waves. Lightning flashed, followed by deafening thunderclaps. Another wave lashed him, spinning the driftwood, almost tearing him clear. Sharp splinters pierced his bleeding hands as he tightened his grip. Salt spray stung his swollen eyes.

Earlier in the night, after ferocious winds had swept the galley against hidden rocks, splintering the hull, four men had grasped this length of shattered deck. One by one the storm had leeched away their strength then plucked them loose, their despairing death cries swept away by the wind.

Now only the man called Gershom remained – thanks to arms and shoulders strengthened by months of labour in the copper mines of Kypros, wielding pick and hammer, and bearing on his back sacks of ore. Yet even his prodigious strength was failing.

The sea lifted him once more, the length of decking pitching suddenly. Gershom hung on as a wave crashed over him.

The sea no longer felt cold. It seemed to him like a warm bath, and he could feel it calling to him. Rest now! Come with me! Sleep now! Sleep in the Great Green.

To sleep is to die, he told himself again, squeezing his bloodied hands against the jagged wood. Sharp, lancing pain cut through his exhaustion.

A body floated by head-down. A wave caught it, flipping the corpse. Gershom recognized the dead man. He had won three copper rings on the Bone Game the night before last, when the galley had been drawn up on a small stretch of beach below a line of towering cliffs. The sailor had been happy then. Three rings, though not a princely sum, was enough to purchase a good cloak, or hire a young whore for the night. He did not look happy now, dead eyes staring up at the rain, mouth slack and open.

Another wave crashed over Gershom. Ducking his head against the planking he hung on. The wave carried the dead man away, and Gershom saw the body sink below the water.

Lightning ripped across the sky once more, but the thunder did not come immediately. The wind eased, and the sea calmed. Gershom hitched himself across the driftwood, managing to lift his leg across the broken planks. Carefully he rolled to his back and shivered in the cold night air.

The rain was torrential, washing the salt from his face and eyes and beard. He stared at the sky. A shaft of moonlight showed through a break in the storm clouds. Looking left and right he could see no sign of land. His chances of survival were bleak. All the trade ships held to the coastline. Few ventured out into deeper water.

The storm had arrived with sickening speed, strong winds gusting down from the high cliffs. The galley had been making for a bay where they would shelter for the night. Gershom, rowing on the starboard side, had not been worried at first. He knew nothing of the sea, and thought this might be normal. Then, seeing the anxious looks on the faces of the rowers, he glanced back. The ferocity of the gusts increased, heeling the ship sideways, and driving it further from the shore. Gershom could see the headland which marked the entrance to the bay. It seemed so close. The rhythm of the rowers began to fail. Two oars crashed together on his side, throwing the line into disorder. One broke away. With the oars no longer working in unison the galley turned beam on to the wind, driven round by the rowers on the port side.

A large wave broke over the side, swamping Gershom and the starboard rowers. The heavily laden ship began to tip. Then it slid into a trough, and a second wave swamped it. Gershom heard a rending sound as planks gave way beneath the weight of the water. The sea surged in, and – driven down by the mass of its copper cargo – the galley sank within moments.

It occurred to Gershom, as he clung to the ruined decking, that he himself had probably mined some of the copper that doomed the ship he sailed on.

The stern face of his grandfather appeared in his mind. 'You bring your troubles on yourself, boy.'

That was certainly true tonight.

On the other hand, Gershom reasoned, without the back-breaking labour in the mines he would not have built the strength to endure the power of the storm.

No doubt it would have pleased his grandfather to see Gershom working the mine in those early days, his soft hands blistered and bleeding, to earn in a month what he would, at home, have spent in a heartbeat. By night, in a filthy dugout, he'd slept beneath a single threadbare blanket, as ants crawled upon his weary flesh. No servant girls to tend his needs, no slaves to prepare his clothing. No heads bowed now as he passed. No-one to flatter him. At the palace and the farms his grandfather owned all the women told him how wonderful he was, how masculine and strong. What a joy it was to be in his company. Gershom sighed. On Kypros the only available women for mine workers said exactly the same – as long as a man had copper rings to offer.

Lightning lit the sky to the south. Perhaps the storm is passing, he thought.

Thoughts of grandfather came again, and with them a sense of shame. He was being unfair to the man. He would not glory in Gershom's downfall. Any more than he would have taken pleasure from the public execution he had ordered for his grandson. Gershom had fled the city, heading out to the coast, where he took ship to Kypros.

He would have stayed on there had he not seen a group of Egypteians in the town a few days before. He had recognized two of them, both scribes to a merchant who had visited grandfather's palace. One of the scribes had stared at him. By now Gershom was thickly bearded, his hair long and unkempt, but he was not sure it was enough.

Gathering the last of the copper rings he had earned in the mine he had wandered to the harbour, and had sat on the beach, staring out at the ships in the bay.

A bandy-legged old man approached him, his skin leathery, his face deeply lined. 'Looking for sea work?' he asked.

'I could be.'

The man noted Gershom's heavy accent. 'Gyppto are you?' Gershom nodded. 'Good sailors, the Gypptos. And you have the shoulders of a fine oarsman.' The old man hunkered down, picked up a stone and hurled it out over the waves. 'Several ships looking for men.'

'How about that one?' asked Gershom, pointing to a huge, sleek, double-decked galley at anchor out in the bay. It was beautiful, crafted from red oak, and he counted forty oars on the starboard side. In the fading sunlight the hull had a golden gleam. Gershom had never seen a ship so large.

'Only if you yearn for death,' said the old man. 'It is too big.'

'Too big? Why is that bad?' Gershom had asked him.

'The great god Poseidon does not suffer large ships. He snaps them in two.'

Gershom had laughed, thinking this was a jest.

The old man had looked offended. 'You obviously do not know the sea, young fellow,' he said stiffly. 'Every year arrogant ship-wrights build larger craft. Every year they sink. If not the gods, then what could cause such catastrophes?'

'I apologize, sir,' said Gershom, not wishing to cause further offence. 'But that ship does not seem to be sinking.'

'It is the Golden One's new ship,' said the man. 'Built for him by a madman no-one else would employ. It won't have a full crew. Even the half-witted sailors around here have refused to serve upon it. The Golden One has ferried in seamen from the outer islands to man it.' He chuckled. 'Even some of them deserted as soon as they saw it – and they are known to be morons. No, it will sink when Poseidon swims beneath it.'

'Who is this Golden One?'

The old man looked surprised. 'I would have thought that even the Gypptos would have heard of Helikaon.'

'I think I have heard *that* name. Isn't he a warrior of the sea? Did he not kill some Mykene pirate?'

The man seemed satisfied. 'Aye, he is a great fighter.'

'Why do they call him the Golden One?'

'He is blessed with unholy luck. Every venture brings in riches, but I think he will have another name after *that* monstrosity sinks.' He fell silent for a moment. 'However, we are drifting with the wind now. Let us return to our course. You need a ship.'

'What would you advise, my friend?'

'I know a merchant who has a twenty-oar galley – the *Mirion* – heading for Troy the day after tomorrow. He is short of men. For ten copper rings I'll take you to him and offer a recommendation.'

'I don't have ten copper rings.'

'You get twenty for a voyage, half when you sign on. Give me that half, and I'll tell him you are a master oarsman.'

'It won't take them long to find out you lied.'

The old man shrugged. 'By then you'll be at sea and the merchant will still be on land. When you return you'll be a fine oarsman, and no-one will be the wiser.'

Gershom had heard of Troy, of its great golden walls and high towers. The hero Herakles was said to have fought a war there a hundred or so years ago. 'Have you been to Troy?' he asked the old man.

'Many times.'

'It is said to be beautiful.'

'Aye, it is good to look at. Expensive though. Whores wear gold, and a man is considered poor if he doesn't own a hundred horses. Copper rings won't buy you a cup of water in Troy. There's plenty of other stops on the way there and back, though, boy. There's

Miletos. Now *that* is a place for sailors. Big-titted whores who'll sell you their souls for a copper ring – not that their souls are what you'd be looking for. There's some of the prettiest land you'll ever see. You'll have the time of your life, boy!'

Later that day, after the old sailor had found him a place on the *Mirion*'s crew, Gershom had wandered down to the seafront to look at the ship. He knew nothing about such vessels, but even to his untrained eye it seemed to be lying low in the water. A huge man, bald-headed and with a forked black beard, approached him. 'Seeking a berth?' he asked.

'No. I sail the day after tomorrow on the *Mirion*.'

'She is overladen and there's a storm coming,' said the big man. 'Ever worked on a galley?'

Gershom shook his head.

'Fine craft – if the captain keeps her shipshape, clean of barnacles, and if the crew are well trained. The *Mirion* has none of these advantages.' The man peered at him closely. 'You should sail with me, on the *Xanthos*.'

'The Death Ship? I think not.'

The bald man's face darkened. 'Ah well, all men make choices, Gyppto. I hope you don't come to rue yours.'

Another crack of thunder boomed in the heavens. The wind picked up again. Gershom carefully rolled onto his stomach and gripped the edges of the driftwood.

To sleep is to die.

Part One

THE GREAT GREEN

I

The Cave of Wings

THE TWELVE MEN, IN ANKLE-LENGTH CLOAKS OF BLACK WOOL, STOOD
silently at the cave mouth. They did not speak or move. The early
autumn wind was unnaturally chill, but they did not blow warm
breath on cold hands. Moonlight shimmered on their bronze
breastplates and white crested helmets, on their embossed wrist
guards and greaves, and on the hilts of the short swords
scabbarded at their waists. Yet despite the presence of cold metal
against their bodies they did not shiver.

The night grew colder, and it began to rain as midnight
approached. Hail fell, and clattered against their armour. And still
they did not move.

Then came another warrior, tall and stooping, his cloak flapping
in the fierce wind. He too was armoured, though his cuirass was
inlaid with gold and silver, as were the helmet and greaves he wore.

'Is he inside?' he asked, his voice deep.

'Yes, my king,' answered one of the men, tall and broad-
shouldered, with deep-set grey eyes. 'He will summon us when the
gods speak.'

'Then we wait,' replied Agamemnon.

The rain eased away and the king's dark eyes scanned his
Followers. Then he looked into the Cave of Wings. Deep within he

could see firelight flickering on the craggy walls, and even from here smell the acrid and intoxicating fumes from the Prophecy Fire. As he watched, the fire dimmed.

Unused to waiting, he felt his anger rise, but masked it. Even a king was expected to be humble in the presence of the gods.

Every four years the king of Mykene and twelve of his most trusted Followers were expected to hear the words of the gods. The last time Agamemnon had stood here he had just interred his father and his own reign was about to begin. He had been nervous then, but was more so now. For the prophecies he had heard that first time had come true. He had become infinitely richer. His wife had borne him three healthy children, though all girls. The armies of Mykene had been victorious in every battle, and a great hero had fallen.

But Agamemnon also recalled the journey his father had made to the Cave of Wings eight years previously, and his ashen face on his return. He would not speak of the final prophecy, but one of the Followers told it to his wife, and the word spread. The seer had concluded with the words: 'Farewell, Atreus King. You will not walk the Cave of Wings again.'

The great battle king had died one week before the next Summoning.

A woman dressed all in black emerged from the cave. Even her head was covered by a veil of gauze. She did not speak, but raised her hand, beckoning the waiting men. Agamemnon took a deep breath, and led the group inside.

The entrance was narrow, and they removed their crested helmets and followed the woman in single file, until at last they reached the remains of the Prophecy Fire. Smoke still hung in the air and, as he breathed, Agamemnon felt his heart beating faster. Colours became brighter and small sounds – the creaking of leather, the shifting of sandalled feet on stone – were louder, almost threatening.

The ritual was hundreds of years old, based on an ancient belief that only on the point of death could a priest fully commune with the gods. So every four years a man was chosen to die for the sake of the king.

Keeping his breathing shallow, Agamemnon looked down at the slender old man lying on a pallet bed. His face was pale in the firelight, his eyes wide and staring. The hemlock paralysis had already begun. He would be dead within minutes.

Agamemnon waited.

'Fire in the sky,' said the priest, 'and a mountain of water touching the clouds. Beware the Great Horse, Agamemnon King.' The old man sagged back, and the woman in black knelt by him, lifting and supporting his frail body.

'Offer me no riddles,' said Agamemnon. 'What of the kingdom? What of the might of the Mykene?'

The priest's eyes briefly blazed, and Agamemnon saw anger there. Then it passed, and the old man smiled. 'Your will prevails here, O king. I would have offered you a forest of truth, but you wish to speak of a single leaf. Very well. Mighty still will you be when next you walk this corridor of stone. Father to a son.' He whispered something then to the woman, who held a cup of water to his lips.

'And what dangers will I face?' Agamemnon asked.

The old priest's body spasmed, and he cried out. Then he relaxed and stared up at the king. 'A ruler is always in peril, Agamemnon King. Unless he be strong he will be torn down. Unless he be wise he will be overthrown. The seeds of doom are planted in every season, and need neither sun nor rain to make them grow. You sent a hero to end a small threat, and thus you planted the seeds. Now they grow, and swords will spring from the earth.'

'You speak of Alektruon. He was my friend.'

'He was no man's friend! He was a slaughterer and did not heed the warnings. He trusted in his cunning, his cruelty and his might. Poor blind Alektruon. Now he knows the magnitude of his error. Arrogance laid him low, for no man is invincible. Those the gods would destroy they first make proud.'

'What more have you seen?' said Agamemnon. 'Speak now! Death is upon you.'

'I have no fear of death, King of Swords, King of Blood, King of Plunder. You will live for ever, Agamemnon, in the hearts and minds of men. When your father's name has fallen to dust and whispered away on the winds of time, yours will be spoken loud and often. When your line is a memory, and all kingdoms come to ashes, still your name will echo. This I have seen.'

'This is more to my liking,' said the king. 'What else? Be swift now, for your time is short. Give a name to the greatest danger I will face. '

'You desire but a name? How . . . strange men are. You could have . . . asked for answers, Agamemnon.' The old man's voice was fading and slurring. The hemlock was reaching his brain.

'Give me a name and I will *know* the answer.'

Another flash of anger lit the old man's eyes, holding back the advancing poison. When he spoke his voice was stronger. 'Alektruon asked me for a name, when I was but a seer, and not blessed – as now – with the wisdom of the dying. I named Helikaon, the Golden One. And what did he do . . . this foolish man? He sailed the seas in search of Helikaon, and brought his doom upon himself. Now you seek a name, Agamemnon King. It is the same name. Helikaon.' The old priest closed his eyes. The silence grew.

'Helikaon threatens me?' asked the king.

The dying priest spoke again. 'I see men burning like candles, and . . . a ship of flame. I see a headless man . . . and a great fury. I see . . . I see many ships, like a great flock of birds. I see war, Agamemnon, long and terrible, and the deaths of many heroes.' With a shuddering cry he fell back into the arms of the veiled woman.

'Is he dead?' asked Agamemnon.

The woman felt for a pulse, then nodded. Agamemnon swore.

A powerful warrior moved alongside him, his hair so blond it appeared white in the lamplight. 'He spoke of a great horse, lord. The sails of Helikaon's ships are all painted with the symbol of a rearing black horse.'

Agamemnon remained silent. Helikaon was kin to Priam, the king of Troy, and Agamemnon had a treaty of alliance with Troy, and with most of the trading kingdoms on the eastern coast. While maintaining these treaties he also financed pirate raids by Mykene galleys, looting the towns of his allies and capturing trade ships and cargoes of copper, tin, lead, alabaster or gold. Each one of the galleys tithed him their takings. The plunder allowed him to equip his armies, and bestow favours on his generals and soldiers. Publicly, though, he denounced the pirates and threatened them with death, so he could not openly declare Helikaon an enemy of Mykene. Troy was a rich and powerful kingdom, and that trade alone brought in large profits, paid in copper and tin, without which bronze armour and weapons could not be made.

War with the Trojans was coming, but he was not yet ready to make an enemy of their king.

The fumes from the Prophecy Fire were less noxious now, and Agamemnon felt his head clearing. The priest's words had been massively reassuring. He would have a son, and the name of Agamemnon would echo through the ages.

Yet the old man had also spoken about seeds of doom, and he could not ignore the warning.

He looked the blond man in the eyes. 'Let it be known, Kolanos, that twice a man's weight in gold awaits whoever kills Helikaon.'

'Every pirate ship on the Great Green will hunt him down for such a reward,' said Kolanos. 'By your leave, my king, I will also take my three galleys in search of him. However, it will not be easy to draw him out. He is a cunning fighter, and cool in battle.'

'Then you will make him less cool, my Breaker of Spirits,' said Agamemnon. 'Find those Helikaon loves, and kill them. He has family in Dardanos, a young brother he dotes upon. Begin with him. Let Helikaon know rage and despair. Then rip his life from him.'

'I shall leave tomorrow, lord.'

'Attack him on the open sea, Kolanos. If you find him on land, and the opportunity arises, have him stabbed, or throttled, or poisoned. I care not. But the trail of his death must not end at my hall. At sea do as you will. If you take him alive saw the head from his shoulders. Slowly. Ashore make his death swift and quiet. A private quarrel. You understand me?'

'I do, my king.'

'When last I heard Helikaon was in Kypros,' said Agamemnon, 'overseeing the building of a great ship. I am told it will be ready to sail by season's end. Time enough for you to light a fire under his soul.'

There was a strangled cry from behind them. Agamemnon swung round. The old priest had opened his eyes again. His upper body was trembling, his arms jerking spasmodically.

'The Age of Heroes is passing!' he shouted, his voice suddenly clear and strong. 'The rivers are all of blood, the sky aflame! And look how men burn upon the Great Green!' His dying eyes fixed on Agamemnon's face. 'The Horse! Beware the Great Horse!' Blood spurted from his mouth, drenching his pale robes. His face contorted, his eyes wide with panic. Then another spasm shook him, and a last breath rattled from his throat.

II

The God of the Shrine

i

THE GODS WALK IN TIMES OF STORMS. LITTLE PHIA KNEW THIS, FOR HER mother had often told her stories of the immortals: how the spears of Ares, God of War, could be seen in the lightning, and how the hammer of Hephaistos caused the thunder. When the seas grew angry it meant Poseidon was swimming below the waves, or being drawn in his dolphin chariot across the Great Green.

So the eight-year-old tried to quell her fears as she struggled up the muddy slope towards the shrine, her faded, threadbare tunic offering no protection from the shrieking winds and the driving rain lashing the coast of Kypros. Even her head was cold, for ten days earlier mother had cut away her golden hair in a bid to free her of the lice and fleas on her scalp. Even so Phia's thin body was still covered in sores and bites. Most of them were just itchy, but the rat bite on her ankle remained swollen and sore, the scab constantly breaking and fresh blood flowing.

But these were small matters, and did not concern the child as she pushed on towards the high shrine. When mother had taken sick yesterday Phia had run to the healer in the centre of town. Angrily he had told her to stand back from him. He did not visit those the gods had cursed with poverty, and had barely listened as she explained that mother would not rise from her bed, and that her body was hot, and she was in pain.

'Go to a priest,' he said.

So Phia had run through the port to the Temple of Asklepios, and queued there with others seeking guidance and help. The waiting people all carried some kind of offering. Many had snakes in wicker pots, some had small dogs, others gifts of food or wine. When at last she was allowed through the high doors she was met by a young man who asked her what offering she brought. She tried to tell him about mother's sickness, but he too ordered her away, and called out for the person next in line, an old man carrying a wooden cage in which two white doves were cooing. Phia didn't know what to do, and had returned home. Mother was awake, and she was talking to someone Phia couldn't see. Then she started crying. Phia began to cry too.

The storm came at dusk, and Phia remembered that the gods walked in harsh weather. She decided to speak to them herself.

The Shrine of Apollo, Lord of the Silver Bow, was close to the angry sky, and Phia thought the gods might hear her better if she climbed to it.

She was shivering now as the night grew colder, and worried in case the wild dogs roaming the hills caught the scent of the blood on her ankle. She stumbled in the darkness. Her knee struck a rock and she cried out. When she was small, and hurt herself, she would run to mother, who would hug her and stroke away the pain. But that was when they lived in a bigger house, with a flower garden, and all the uncles had been rich and young. Now they were old and grubby, and they did not bring fine presents, but only a few copper rings. They no longer sat and laughed with mother. Mostly they did not talk at all. They would come in the night. Phia would be sent outside, and they would leave after a short time. Lately no uncles had come at all. There were no gifts, no rings, and little food.

Phia climbed higher. On top of the cliff she saw the jagged stand of rocks that surrounded the shrine. Apollo's Leap, it was called, because, as mother had said, the golden-haired God of the Sun had once rested there, before flying back into the sky to his chariot of fire.

The child was almost at the end of her strength as she forced her way up the steep slope. Dizzy with fatigue, she stumbled into the rocks. Lightning lit the sky. Phia cried out, for the brilliant light suddenly illuminated a figure standing on the very edge of the high cliff, arms raised. Phia's legs gave way, and she slumped to the ground. The clouds broke then, the moon shining through. The god lowered his arms and turned slowly, rain glistening on his naked upper body.

Phia stared at him, eyes wide and frightened. Was it the Lord of the Silver Bow? Surely not, for this god's hair was long and dark, and Apollo was said to have locks fashioned from golden sunlight. The face was striking and stern, the eyes pale and hard. Phia gazed at his ankles, hoping to see wings there, which would mean he was Hermes, messenger of the gods. Hermes was known to be friendly to mortals.

But there were no wings.

The god approached her and she saw that his eyes were a bright, startling blue. 'What are you doing here?' he asked.

'Are you the God of War?' she asked, her voice trembling.

He smiled. 'No, I am not the god of war.'

A wave of relief swept over her. The mighty Ares would not have healed mother. He hated humans.

'My mother is ill, and I have no offerings,' she said. 'But if you heal her, I will work and work and I will bring you many gifts. All my life.'

The god turned away then, and walked back through the rocks.

'Please don't leave!' she cried. 'Mother is sick!'

He knelt down and lifted a heavy cloak from behind a rock, then, sitting beside her, he wrapped the garment round her shoulders. It was of the softest wool. 'You came to the shrine seeking help for your mother?' he said. 'Has a healer visited her?'

'He would not come,' she told the god. 'So I went to the temple, but I had no offerings. They sent me away.'

'Come,' he said, 'take me to your mother.'

'Thank you.' She tried to rise. Her legs gave way and she fell awkwardly, mud splattering the expensive cloak. 'I'm sorry. I'm sorry,' she said.

'It matters not,' he told her, then lifted her into his arms, and began the long walk back into the town.

Somewhere during that walk Phia fell asleep, her head resting on the god's shoulder. She only woke when she heard voices. The god was speaking to someone. Opening her eyes she saw a huge figure walking alongside the god. He was bald, but had a forked beard. As she opened her eyes the bearded one smiled at her.

They were approaching the houses now, and the god asked her where she lived. Phia felt embarrassed, because these were nice houses, white-walled and red-roofed. She and mother lived in a shack on the wasteland beyond. The roof leaked, and there were holes in the thin wooden walls, through which rats found their way in. The floor was of dirt, and there were no windows.

'I am feeling stronger now,' she said, and the god put her down. Then she led the way home.

As they went inside several rats scurried away from mother. The god knelt on the floor alongside her, and reached out to touch her brow. 'She is alive,' he said. 'Carry her back to the house, Ox,' he told his friend. 'We'll be there presently.'

The god took Phia by the hand, and together they walked through the town and stopped at the house of the healer. 'He is a very angry man,' Phia warned, as the god hammered his fist on the wooden door.

It was wrenched open and the healer loomed in the doorway. 'What in Hades . . . ?' he began. Then he saw the dark-haired god, and Phia saw his attitude change. He seemed to shrink. 'I apologize, Lord,' he said, bowing his head. 'I did not know . . .'

'Gather your herbs and medicines and come immediately to the house of Phaedra,' said the god.

'Of course. Immediately.'

Then they began to walk again, this time up the long winding hill towards the homes of the rich. Phia's strength began to fail again. The god lifted her. 'We will get you some food,' he said.

When at last they reached their destination Phia gazed in wonder. It was a palace, a high wall surrounding a beautiful garden, and there were red pillars on either side of a great entrance. Inside they walked upon floors decorated with coloured stones, and there were wall paintings in vivid colours. 'Is this your house?' she asked.

'No. I stay here when I am in Kypros,' he answered.

He carried Phia to a white-walled room at the rear of the house. There was a woman there, golden-haired and young, dressed in a robe of green, edged with gold thread. She was very beautiful. The god spoke to her, then introduced her as Phaedra. 'Give the child something to eat,' said the god. 'I shall wait for the healer and see how the mother is faring.'

Phaedra smiled at Phia and brought out some fresh bread and honey. After she had eaten Phia thanked the woman, and they sat in silence for a while. Phia did not know what to say. The woman poured herself a goblet of wine, to which she added water. 'Are you a goddess?' asked Phia.

'Some men have told me that I am,' replied Phaedra, with a wide smile.

'Is this your house?'

'Yes. Do you like it?'

'It is very big.'

'Indeed it is.'

Phia leaned forward and said in a low voice, 'I do not know which god he is. I went to the shrine and saw him. Is he the Lord of the Silver Bow?'

'He is a lord of many things,' said Phaedra. 'Would you like some more bread?'

'Yes, thank you.'

Phaedra told her to help herself, then fetched a pitcher of cool milk, and filled a cup. Phia drank it. The taste was sublime. 'So,' said Phaedra, 'your mother was ill and you went to the shrine for help. It is very high up there, and treacherous. And there are packs of wild dogs.'

Phia did not know how to respond, so she sat silently.

'That was very brave of you,' said Phaedra. 'Your mother is lucky to have you. What happened to your hair?'

'Mother cut it. I have fleas.' Again, she felt shame.

'Tonight I will have a bath prepared for you. And we will find some ointments for those bites and scratches on your arms.'

The god returned then. He had changed his clothes and was wearing a white, knee-length tunic edged with silver thread, his long black hair pulled back from his face and tied in a ponytail. 'Your mother is very weak,' he said, 'but she is sleeping now. The healer will come every day until she is well. You may both stay here for as long as you wish. Phaedra will find work for your mother. Does that answer your prayers, Phia?'

'Oh yes,' said the girl. 'Thank you.'

'She was wondering if you are Apollo,' said Phaedra, with a smile.

He knelt alongside Phia and she looked into his brilliant blue eyes. 'My name is Helikaon,' he said, 'and I am not a god. Are you disappointed?'

'No,' replied Phia, though she was.

Helikaon rose then, and spoke to Phaedra. 'There are merchants coming. I will be with them for a while.'

'You still intend to sail for Troy tomorrow?'

'I must. I promised Hektor I would be at the wedding.'

'It is the storm season, Helikaon, and almost a month at sea. That could prove a costly promise.'

He leaned in and kissed her, then walked from the room.

Phaedra sat down with Phia. 'Do not be too disappointed, little one,' said Phaedra. 'He *is* a god, really. He just doesn't know it.'

ii

Later, with the child bathed and in bed, Phaedra stood under the portico roof, watching the lightning. The wind was fresh and cool, gusting over the garden, filling the air with the scent of jasmine from the trees against the western wall. She was tired now and strangely melancholy. This was Helikaon's last night in Kypros. The season was almost over and he would be sailing his new ship hundreds of miles to Troy, and then north to Dardania for the winter. Phaedra had been anticipating a night of passion and warmth, the hardness of his body, the taste of his lips upon hers. Instead he had returned to the house with the half-starved, flea-bitten child of the toothless whore Ox had carried in earlier.

At first Phaedra had been angry, but now she was merely unsettled.

Sheltered from the rain Phaedra closed her eyes and pictured the child, her shaven head covered by bites, her face thin and pinched, her eyes huge and frightened. The little girl was asleep now, in the room next to her mother's. Phaedra had felt the urge to hug her, to draw her close and kiss her cheek. She had wanted to take away the pain and the fear from those large, blue eyes. Yet she had not. She had merely drawn back the coverlet to allow the skinny girl to clamber into the wide bed, and lay her head back on the soft bolster. 'Sleep well, Phia. You will be safe here.'

'Are you his wife?'

'No. He is one of my Gift-givers. I am like your mother – one of Aphrodite's Maidens.'

'There are no Gift-givers now,' said Phia, sleepily.

'Go to sleep.'

Of course there were no Gift-givers, thought Phaedra. The mother was ugly and thin, and old before her time.

As you are getting old, she thought. Though blessed with a youthful appearance Phaedra was approaching thirty-five. Soon her Gift-givers too would fall away. Anger touched her. Who cares if they do? I have wealth now.

And yet the sense of melancholy remained.

In the eighteen years since she had become a Follower of Aphrodite Phaedra had been pregnant nine times. On each occasion she had visited the Temple of Asklepios and swallowed bitter herbs to end the pregnancies. The last time had been five years ago. She had delayed for a month, torn between the desire to increase her wealth and the growing need to be a mother. 'Next time,' she had told herself. 'Next time I will bear the child.'

Only there had been no next time, and now she found herself dreaming of children crying in the dark, calling out to her. She would run around blindly trying to find them, and wake in a cold sweat. The tears would come then, and her sobs would echo the emptiness of her life.

'My life is *not* empty,' she told herself. 'I have a palace and servants, and wealth enough to live out my life without the need of men.'

Yet was it true, she wondered?

Her mood had been fragile all day, and she had felt close to tears when Helikaon said he was going up to the Shrine of Apollo. She had walked there with him once, a year ago now, and had watched as he stood on the very edge of the cliff, arms raised, eyes closed.

'Why did you do that?' she had asked him. 'The cliff could give way. You could fall and be dashed on the rocks.'

'Perhaps that is why,' he had answered.

Phaedra had been mystified by the answer. It made no sense. But then so much of Helikaon defied logic. She always struggled to understand the mysteries of the man. When he was with her there was never a hint of the violence men whispered of. No harshness, no cruelty, no anger. In fact he rarely carried a weapon when in Kypros, although she had seen the three bronze swords, the white-crested helm, the breastplate and the greaves he wore in battle. They were packed in a chest in the upper bedroom he used when on the island.

Packed in a chest. Like his emotions, she thought. In the five years she had known him Phaedra had never come close to the man within. She wondered if anyone did.

Phaedra stepped out into the rain, lifting her face to the black sky. She shivered as her green gown became drenched, the wind seeming icy now as it flowed across her wet skin. She laughed aloud and stepped back under cover. The cold stripped away her fatigue.

Lightning flashed, and she thought she saw a shadowy figure

dart past the screen of bushes to her right. Spinning round she saw nothing. Was it a trick of the light? Nervous now, she moved back into the house, pushing shut the door.

The last of Helikaon's guests had gone, and she walked upstairs to his apartment. The room was dark, no lamps lit. Entering silently she walked to the bed. It was empty. Moving to the balcony she looked down into the garden. There was no-one in sight. The clouds broke briefly, and the moon shone bright.

Turning back inside she saw a muddy footprint on the floor. Fear rose and she glanced around the room. Someone had been here. He had climbed through the window. Moving back to the balcony she glanced down once more.

A shadow moved, and she saw a hooded, dark-garbed man run for the wall. Then Helikaon emerged from behind a statue, a dagger in his hand. The man saw him and swerved away. He ran and leapt high, hauling himself onto the high wall, and rolling over to the open land beyond. The clouds closed in again, and Phaedra could see nothing.

Running out into the corridor she descended the stairs, arriving at the entrance just as Helikaon stepped inside. Pushing shut the door Phaedra dropped the locking bar in place. 'Who was he?' she asked. Helikaon tossed the bronze dagger to a table top.

'Just a thief,' he said. 'He is gone now.' Moving past her he walked to the kitchen, taking up a towel and drying his face and arms. Phaedra followed him.

'Tell me the truth,' she said.

Stripping off his tunic he continued to dry his body. Then he walked naked across the room and filled two goblets with watered wine. Passing one to her he sipped his own. 'The man was following me when I went to the shrine. I caught glimpses of him. He is very skilled, and held to the shadows. Ox and my men did not see him.'

'But you did?'

He sighed. 'My father was murdered by an assassin, Phaedra. Since then I have been . . . more observant of those around me, shall we say?'

'Do you have many enemies, Helikaon?'

'All powerful men have enemies. There are merchants who owe me fortunes. Were I to die they would be free of their debts. I have killed pirates who left behind brothers and sons who desire vengeance. But let us talk no more of it tonight. The assassin is gone, and you are looking beautiful.'

Had she been his wife she might have told him that she no longer desired to make love. But I am not his wife, she thought. I am Aphrodite's Child and he is my Gift-giver. Like the toothless hag in the upper back bedroom I am just a whore. Sadness flowed in her, but she forced a bright smile and stepped into his embrace. His kiss was warm, his breath sweet, the arms around her strong.

'Am I your friend?' she asked him later, as they lay together on her broad bed, her head resting on his shoulder, her thigh across his own.

'Now and always, Phaedra.'

'Even when I am old and ugly?'

He stroked her hair. 'What would you have me say?'

'The truth. I want to hear the truth.'

Leaning over her he kissed her brow. 'I do not give my friendship lightly,' he said, 'and it does not depend on youth and beauty. If we both live to be old and ugly I will still be your friend.'

She sighed then. 'I am frightened, Helikaon. Frightened of getting old, frightened of your being killed, or tiring of me, frightened of becoming like Phia's mother. A long time ago I chose this life, and it has brought me wealth and security. Now I wonder whether I made the right choice. Do you think I could have been happy wed to a farmer or a fisherman and raising children?'

'I cannot answer that. We make choices every day, some of them good, some of them bad. And – if we are strong enough – we live with the consequences. To be truthful I am not entirely sure what people mean when they talk of happiness. There are moments of joy and laughter, the comfort of friendship, but enduring happiness? If it exists I have not discovered it.'

'Perhaps it only comes when you are in love,' she suggested.

'Have you ever been in love?'

'No,' she lied.

'Nor I,' he replied, the simple words sliding like a dagger into her heart.

'What a sad pair we are,' she said, forcing a smile, and sliding her hand down over his flat belly. 'Ah!' she said, with mock surprise, 'there is one among us who does not seem sad. Indeed he is beginning to feel rampantly happy.'

Helikaon laughed. 'You do have that effect on him.' His hands clasped her waist, lifting her over him, then he drew her down and kissed her deeply.

III

The Golden Ship

i

THE STORMS OF THE PAST TWO DAYS HAD FADED INTO THE WEST, AND the sky was clear and blue, the sea calm, as Spyros rowed his passenger towards the great ship. After a morning of ferrying crewmen out to the *Xanthos* Spyros was tired. He liked to tell people that at eighty years of age he was as strong as ever, but it wasn't true. His arms and shoulders were aching and his heart was thumping as he leaned back into the oars.

A man was not old until he could no longer work. This simple philosophy kept Spyros active, and every morning, as he woke, he would greet the new day with a smile. He would walk out and draw up water from the well, gaze at his reflection in the surface and say: 'Good to see you, Spyros.'

He looked at the young man sitting quietly at the stern. His hair was long and dark, held back from his face by a strip of leather. Bare-chested, he was wearing a simple kilt and sandals. His body was lean and hard-muscled, his eyes the brilliant blue of a summer sky. Spyros had not seen the man before, and guessed him to be a foreigner, probably a rogue islander or a Kretan.

'New oarsman, are you?' Spyros asked him. The passenger did

not answer, but he smiled. 'Been ferrying men like you in all week. Locals won't sail on the Death Ship. That's what we call the *Xanthos*,' he added. 'Only idiots and foreigners. No offence meant.'

The passenger's voice was deep, his accent proving Spyros' theory. 'But she is beautiful,' he said, amiably. 'And the shipwright says she is sound.'

'Aye, I'll grant she's good to look upon,' said Spyros. 'Mighty pleasing on the eye.' Then he chuckled. 'However, I wouldn't trust the word of the Madman from Miletos. My nephew worked on the ship, you know. He said Khalkeus wandered about talking to himself. Sometimes he'd even slap himself on the head.'

'I have seen him do that,' agreed the man.

Spyros fell silent, a feeling of mild irritation flowering. The man was young, and obviously did not appreciate that the gods of the sea hated large ships. Twenty years ago he had watched just such a ship sail from the bay. It had made two voyages without incident, then had vanished in a storm. One man had survived. He had been washed ashore on the eastern mainland. His story was told by mariners for some years. The keel had snapped, the ship breaking up in a matter of a few heartbeats. Spyros considered telling this story to the young oarsman. He decided against it. What would be the point? The man had to earn his twenty copper rings, and he wasn't going to turn back now.

Spyros rowed on, the burning in his lower back increasing. This was his twentieth trip out to the *Xanthos* since dawn.

There were small boats all around the galley, stacked with cargo. Men were shouting and vying for position. Boats thumped into one another, causing curses and threats to be bellowed out. Ropes were lowered and items slowly hauled aboard. Tempers were short among both the crew on the deck and the men waiting to unload their cargo boats. It was a scene of milling chaos.

'Been like this all morning,' said Spyros, easing back on the oars. 'Don't think they'll sail today. It's one of the problems with a ship that size, getting cargo up on that high deck. Didn't think of that, did he – the Madman, I mean?'

'The owner is to blame,' said the passenger. 'He wanted the largest ship ever built. He concentrated on its seaworthiness, and the quality of its construction. He didn't give enough thought to loading or unloading it.'

Spyros shipped his oars. 'Listen, lad, you obviously don't know who you are sailing with. Best not say anything like that close to the Golden One. Helikaon may be young, but he is a killer, you know. He cut off Alektruon's head and ripped out his eyes. It's said he ate them. Not someone you want to offend, if you take my meaning?'

'Ate his eyes? I have not heard *that* story.'

'Oh, there's plenty of stories about him.' Spyros stared at the bustle around the galley. 'No point trying to push my way through to the stern. We'll need to wait awhile until some of those cargo boats have moved off.'

A huge, bald man, his black beard greased and twisted into two braids, appeared on the port deck, his voice booming out, ordering some of the cargo boats to stand clear and allow those closest to offload their cargo.

'The bald man there is Zidantas,' said Spyros. 'They call him Ox. I had another nephew sail with him once. Ox is a Hittite. Good man, though. My nephew broke his arm on the *Ithaka* a few years back and couldn't work the whole voyage. Still got his twenty copper rings, though. Zidantas saw to that.' He turned his face towards the south. 'Breeze is starting to shift. Going to be a southerly. Unusual for this time of year. That'll help you make the crossing, I suppose. If it does get under way today.'

'She'll sail,' said the man.

'You are probably right, young fellow. The Golden One is blessed by luck. Not one of his ships has sunk, did you know that? Pirates avoid him – well, they would, wouldn't they? You don't cross a man who eats your eyes.' Reaching down he lifted a water-skin from below his seat. He drank deeply, then offered it to his passenger, who accepted gratefully.

A glint of bronze showed from the deck and two warriors came into sight, both wearing breastplates, and carrying helmets crested with white horsehair plumes. 'I offered to ferry them out earlier,' muttered Spyros. 'They didn't like my boat. Too small for them, I don't doubt. Ah well, a pox on all Mykene anyway. Heard them talking, though. They're not friends of the Golden One, that's for sure.'

'What did they say?'

'Well, it was more the older one. He said it turned his stomach to be sailing on the same ship as Helikaon. Can't blame him, I suppose. That Alektruon – the one who lost his eyes – was a Mykene too. Helikaon has killed a lot of Mykene.'

'As you say, not a man to offend.'

'I wonder why he does it.'

'What? Kill Mykene?'

'No, sail his ships all over the Great Green. They say he has a palace in Troy, and land in Dardania, and somewhere else way north. Don't remember where. Anyhow, he is already rich and powerful. So why risk himself on the sea, fighting pirates and the like?'

The young man shrugged. 'All is never as it seems. Who knows? Maybe he is a man with a dream. I heard that he wants to sail one day beyond the Great Green, to the distant seas.'

'That's what I mean,' said Spyros. 'The edge of the world is there, with a waterfall that goes down for ever into darkness. What kind of idiot would want to sail off into the black abyss of the world?'

'That is a good question, boatman. A man who is not content, perhaps. A man looking for something he cannot find on the Great Green.'

'There you go! There's nothing of worth that a man cannot find in his own village, let alone on the great sea. That's the problem with these rich princes and kings. They don't understand what real treasure is. They see it in gold and copper, and tin. They see it in herds of horses and cattle. They gather treasures to themselves, building great storehouses, which they guard ferociously. Then they die. What good is it then?'

'And you know what real treasure is?' asked the young man.

'Of course. Most ordinary men do. I've been up in the hills these last few days. A young woman almost died. Babe breeched in the womb. I got there in time, though. Poor girl. Ripped bad, she was. She'll be fine, and the boy is healthy and strong. I watched that woman hold the babe in her arms and gaze down on it. She was so weak she might have died at any moment. But in her eyes you could see she knew what she was holding. It was something worth more than gold. And the father was more proud and happy than any conquering king with a vault of treasure.'

'The child is lucky to have such loving parents. Not all children do.'

'And those that don't get heart-scarred. You don't see the wounds, but they never heal.'

'What is your name, boatman?'

'Spyros.'

'How is it you are a rower and a midwife, Spyros? It is an unusual pairing of talents.'

The old man chuckled. 'Brought a few children into the world during my eighty years. Developed a knack for delivering healthy babies. It began more than fifty years ago. A young shepherd's wife had a difficult birth, and the babe was born dead. I was there, and picked up the poor little mite, to carry it away. As I lifted him he suddenly spewed blood, then started to cry. That began it, you know, the story of my skill with babies. My wife . . . sweet girl . . . had six children. So I knew more than a little about the difficulties of childbirth. Over the years I was asked to attend other births. You know how it is. Word gets round. Any girl within fifty miles gets pregnant and they'll send for old Spyros, come the time. It is strange, you know. The older I grow the more pleasure I get from bringing new life into the world.'

'You are a good man,' said the passenger, 'and I am gladdened to have met you. Now take up your oars and force your way through. It is time for me to board.'

The old man dipped his blades and rowed in between two long boats. Two sailors above saw the boat, and lowered a rope between the bank of oars. Then the passenger stood, and, from a pouch at his side, pulled out a thick ring, and handed it to Spyros.

It glinted in his palm. 'Wait!' shouted Spyros. 'This ring is gold!'

'I liked your stories,' said the man, with a smile, 'so I will not eat your eyes.'

ii

A loud crash from the deck above was followed by angry shouts. As Helikaon cleared the rail he saw that two men had dropped an amphora, which had smashed. Thick, unwatered wine had drenched a section of planking, its heady fumes lying heavy in the air. The giant, Zidantas, was grappling with the men, and other sailors were standing by shouting encouragement to the fighters.

The moment they saw Helikaon all noise ceased, and the crew returned silently to their work.

Helikaon approached Zidantas. 'We are losing time, Ox,' he said. 'And there is still cargo on the beach.'

As the morning wore on Helikaon remained on the high rear deck in full view of the toiling men. Tensions were still running high, and the crew remained fearful of sailing on the Death Ship. His presence calmed them, and they began to relax, the work flowing more smoothly. He knew what they were thinking. The Golden One, blessed by the gods, was sailing with them. No harm would befall them.

Such belief in him was vital to them. The greatest danger, he knew, would come if he ever started believing it himself. Men talked of his luck, and the fact that none of his ships had been lost. Yes, there was always luck involved, but, more important, at the end of every trading season those ships were checked by carpenters, drawn up on beaches and de-barnacled. Necessary repairs were undertaken. The crews were carefully chosen, and the captains men of great experience. Not one of his fifty galleys ever sailed over-laden, or took unnecessary risks in the name of greater profits.

With the storm past the sixty-mile crossing to the mainland

coast would be a gentle test for the new ship, allowing the crew to grow accustomed to her – and to each other. The boatman's comment about local sailors was correct. It had not been easy finding skilled men willing to sail on the *Xanthos* and they were still some twenty crew short. Zidantas had scoured the port seeking sailors to join them. Helikaon smiled. They could have filled the quota twice over, but Zidantas was a harsh judge. 'Better to be short with good men, than full with dross,' he argued. 'Saw one man. A Gyppto. Already assigned to the *Mirion*. If I see him in Troy I'll try again.'

'Gypptos are not used to galley work, Ox,' Helikaon pointed out.

'This one would be,' replied Zidantas. 'Strong. Heart like an oak. No give in him.'

A light breeze drifted across the deck. Helikaon walked to the starboard rail and saw that many of the small cargo boats were making their way back to the shore. The last of the trade items were being loaded now. By the port rail he saw the youngest member of his crew, the boy Xander, sitting quietly awaiting orders. Another child of sorrow, thought Helikaon.

Just after dawn that morning, as he had prepared to depart, Phaedra had come to him. 'You must see this,' she said, leading Helikaon through to the bedroom put aside for the sick woman. The child, Phia, had been given her own room, but had crept back to be with her mother. The two were fast asleep, the child's arm laid protectively across her mother's chest.

'Thank you for taking them in,' he had replied, as Phaedra quietly closed the door once more.

'You gave me all this, Helikaon. How can *you* thank *me*?'

'I must go. You understand that I meant what I told the child. They stay for as long as they wish.'

'Of course. It was lucky Phia found you. The healer said the mother would probably have been dead by morning.'

'If you need anything I have instructed Parikles to supply it.'

'You take care. Of all my lovers you are the most dear to me.'

He had laughed then, and drawn her into an embrace, lifting her from her feet and swinging her round. 'And your friendship is beyond price,' he said.

'Just as well my body isn't,' she responded. 'Otherwise I might have been living like Phia's mother in that hovel.'

Smiling at the memory he scanned the ship. The two Mykene passengers were standing on the port side. Both wore armour and had swords scabbarded at their hips. The elder of them, the chisel-bearded Argurios, stared up at him, his gaze openly malevolent.

You would like to kill me, Helikaon thought. To avenge Alektruon. But you will come at me face to face, Argurios. No dagger in the back, no poison in the cup. The young man beside Argurios spoke then, and the warrior swung to face him. Helikaon continued to watch him. Argurios was not a big man, though his arms were heavily muscled. They were also criss-crossed with many scars of combat. Stories of heroes were told in every port on the Great Green, spread by sailors who loved tales of combat and bravery. Argurios featured in many of those tales. He had fought in battles all across the western lands, from Sparta in the south to Thessaly in the north, and even to the borders of Thraki. All of the stories told of his courage, and not one spoke of rape, torture or assassination.

Helikaon's thoughts swung back to the man who had followed him in Kypros. He'd thought he had the assassin trapped at Phaedra's house. Zidantas and four other men were waiting beyond the wall. Yet he had avoided them all. Ox said he had disappeared, as if by magic. Helikaon did not believe in magic. The assassin was highly skilled – like the man who had killed Helikaon's father. No-one had seen him either. He had entered the palace, made his way to the king's apartments and cut his throat. He had also – inexplicably – sliced away his father's right ear. Then he had left. Not one of the guards had seen him. Not one of the servants had noted any strangers present.

Perhaps he too was being hunted by such a man.

He saw the fork-bearded Zidantas approaching, followed by two senior crewmen.

Zidantas climbed to the rear deck. 'We are ready, Golden One,' he said. Helikaon nodded. Ox swung away. 'Ready the oars! Stand by the sail!' he bellowed. 'Raise the anchors!'

The crew moved swiftly to their places, the anchor men fore and aft, hauling on the thick ropes, lifting the great stone anchors from the seabed.

Helikaon glanced at the young boy, Xander. He was looking frightened now, his eyes wide and staring. He kept glancing back at the shore.

'By the mark of One!' shouted Ox. The banks of oars lifted and dipped.

And the great ship began to glide serenely across the bay.

iii

For the twelve-year-old Xander the trip on the *Xanthos* represented the greatest adventure of his life. For as long as he could remember he had dreamed of sailing upon the Great Green. High in the Kypriot hills, as he tended his grandfather's goats, or helped his mother and sisters prepare paints for the pottery dishes they traded in the settlement, he would imagine being on a ship, feeling the swell of the sea beneath his feet. Often, as he wandered along the high ground he would stop, and stare longingly at the vessels heading south towards Egypt, or east to Ugarit – or even to Miletos and the legendary Troy with its towers of solid gold.

He remembered his father, Akamas, and the other sailors launching the *Ithaka*. He had stood with his grandfather on the beach as the galley floated clear, and watched the oarsmen take up their positions. His father was a great rower, powerful and untiring. He was also, as grandfather often said, 'a good man to have beside you in a storm'.

Xander recalled the last farewell with agonizing clarity. His father had stood and waved, his red hair glinting like fire in the dawn light. He had died days later in the battle with the savage Mykene pirate, Alektruon. Xander knew he had died bravely, defending his friends and his ship. The Golden One had come to their house in the hills, and had sat with Xander, and told him of his father's greatness. He had brought gifts for mother and grandfather, and had talked quietly with them both. In this he did them great honour, for Helikaon was the son of a king. He was also a demi-god.

Grandfather scoffed at the story. 'All these nobles claim descent from the gods,' he said. 'But they are men like you and me, Xander. Helikaon is better than most,' he admitted. 'Not many highborns would take the trouble to visit the bereaved.' He had turned away and Xander had seen that he was crying. And he had cried too. After a while grandfather put his arm round Xander's shoulders. 'No shame in tears, boy. Your father deserved tears. Good man. I was proud of him always. As I will be proud of you. Next year Helikaon says he will take you in his crew and you will learn the ways of the sea. You will be a fine, brave man, like your father, and you will bring honour to our family.'

'Will I be an oarsman, grandfather?'

'Not for a while, lad. You are too short. But you'll grow. And you'll grow strong.'

The year had dragged by, but at last the great new ship was ready, and the crew began to muster. Grandfather had walked with him to the port just before dawn, filling him with so much advice it seemed to be running out of Xander's ears. 'Look to Zidantas,' was one comment he remembered. 'Good man. Your father spoke well of him. Never shirk any duty Ox gives you. Do your best always.'

'I will, grandfather.'

The old man had gazed at the great ship, with its two banks of oars, and its colossal mast. Then he had shaken his head. 'Be lucky, Xander. And be brave. You will find that bravery and luck are often bedfellows.'

Xander had been rowed out to the ship just as the sun appeared in the east, its light turning the *Xanthos* to pale gold. It was a beautiful sight and Xander felt his heart surge with joy. This wondrous vessel was to be *his* ship. He would learn to be a great seaman, like his father. Grandfather would be proud of him. And mother too.

The small rowing vessel came alongside the ship, under the raised bank of oars. There were three other crewmen being ferried out, and they tossed up their sacks of belongings and scaled ropes to the deck. Xander would have done the same, but a sturdy rower moved alongside him. 'Up you go, shortshanks,' he said, lifting Xander up to the lowest oar port. He had scrambled through and fallen over a narrow rowing seat.

It was dark here below decks and cramped, but as Xander's eyes adjusted to the gloom he saw the oarsmen's narrow seats, and the planking against which they would brace their legs for the pull. Putting down his own bag he sat in a rowing seat and stretched out his legs. Grandfather was right. He was too short to brace himself. Next year, though, he thought, I will be tall enough. Gathering his bag he made his way to the upper hatch and climbed out.

There were already sailors on board, and two passengers, wearing armour. The eldest was a grim-faced bearded man with cold, hard eyes. Xander had seen men like them before. They were Mykene, the same race as the pirates who had killed his father. Their armies roamed the western lands, plundering towns and cities, taking slaves and gold. Mykene pirates often crossed the sea to raid settlements along the coastline. Grandfather hated them. 'They are a blood-hungry people, and they will one day come to dust,' he had said.

The main cargo hatch was open and Xander saw sailors carrying goods down into the hold: big clay amphorae, filled with wine or spices; large packages of pottery plates, bound in rawhide and protected by outer layers of bark. There were weapons, too, axes and swords, shields and helms. Seamen with ropes were hauling up other goods. Xander moved forward to peer down into the hold. It was deep. A man came up the steps and almost bumped into him. 'Be careful, boy,' he said, as he moved past. Xander backed away from the working crew.

He wandered to the deck rail, and stared back at the beach, where his grandfather still stood. The old man saw him and waved. Xander waved back, suddenly fearful. He was about to go on a voyage, and the immensity of the adventure threatened to overwhelm him.

Then a massive hand settled on his shoulder. Xander jumped and swung round. An enormous, bald-headed man with a forked black beard stood there.

'I am Zidantas,' he said. 'You are the son of Akamas?'

'I am Xander.'

The giant nodded. 'Your father spoke of you with some pride. On this voyage you will learn how to be useful. You are too small to row, and too young to fight. So you will help those who *can* do these things. You will carry water to the rowers, and perform any tasks asked of you. When my other duties permit I will show you how to tie knots, how to reef the sail, and so forth. Other than that you will keep out of the way and watch what men do. That is how we learn, Xander. It will be some time before we are ready to sail. It is taking far longer to load than we expected, and the wind is against us. So find somewhere out of the way and wait until the sail is set. Then come to me on the rear deck.'

Zidantas strode away, and the fear of the unknown returned to Xander. Too young to fight, Zidantas had said. What if they were attacked by pirates? What if he was to die like his father, or drown in the Great Green? Suddenly his tiny room at grandfather's house seemed a wonderful place to be. He looked over the side again, and saw grandfather walking away up the long hill.

Time passed, and tempers among the men grew short, as the difficulties of hauling goods aboard so high a vessel became more and more vexing. A boat rowed out to them bringing a long fishing net, and this was used to raise the more fragile cargo to the deck. Arguments flared and then two sailors dropped a large wine amphora. The clay shattered, and thick red wine flowed across the planking. A fight started then, when one of the two threw a punch at the other, calling him an idiot. The two men grappled. Zidantas stepped in, grabbing each by the tunic and dragging them apart. Other men had begun to shout encouragement to the fighters, and the atmosphere was tense.

Then, in an instant, all activity ceased and a silence fell on the crew.

Xander saw the Golden One climb over the side and step onto

his ship. He was bare-chested and wearing a simple leather kilt. He carried no sword or weapon, and yet his presence quietened the crew, and they shuffled back to work.

Xander saw him walk over to where Zidantas was still holding the two men, though they were no longer struggling. 'We are losing time, Ox,' he said. 'And there is still cargo on the beach.'

Zidantas pushed the men away. 'Clear up this mess,' he told them.

Helikaon glanced at Xander. 'Are you ready to be a sailor, son of Akamas?'

'Yes, lord.'

'Are you frightened?'

'A little,' he admitted.

'A great man once told me there can be no courage without fear,' said Helikaon. 'He was right. Remember that when your belly trembles, and your legs grow weak.'

IV

The Madman from Miletos

i

IT ALWAYS IRRITATED KHALKEUS WHEN HE HEARD HIMSELF DESCRIBED as the Madman from Miletos. He hated the simple inaccuracy of the statement. He wasn't from Miletos. To be called madman bothered him not at all.

He stood on the starboard side of the bireme's central deck, watching as sailors hauled up the great stone anchors. It was close to midday and, mercifully, the cargo was now loaded. Helikaon's arrival had brought a fresh sense of urgency to the crew, and the *Xanthos* was preparing to leave the bay.

A gust of wind caught Khalkeus' wide-brimmed straw hat, flipping it from his head. He tried to catch it, but a second gust lifted it high, spinning it over the side. The hat sailed over the shimmering blue water, twisting and turning. Then, as the wind died down, it flopped to the surface and floated.

Khalkeus stared at it longingly. His once thick and tightly curled red hair was thinning now, and sprinkled with grey. There was also a bald patch on the crown of his head, which would burn raw and bleed under harsh sunlight.

An oarsman on the deck below, seeing the floating hat, angled

51

his oar blade beneath it, seeking to lift it clear. He almost succeeded, but the wind blew again, and the hat floated away. A second oarsman tried. Khalkeus heard laughter from below decks, and 'catching the hat' quickly became a game, oars clacking against one another. Within moments the straw hat, hammered by broad-bladed oars, had lost its shape. Finally it was lifted clear as a torn and soggy mess and brought back aboard.

A young sailor pushed open a hatch and climbed to the upper deck, bearing the dripping ruin to where Khalkeus stood. 'We rescued your hat,' he said, struggling not to laugh.

Khalkeus took it from him, resisting the urge to rip it to shreds. Then good humour reasserted itself and he donned the sodden headgear. Water dripped down his face. The young sailor could contain himself no longer, and his laughter pealed out. The wide brim of the hat slowly sagged over Khalkeus' ears. 'I think it is an improvement,' said Khalkeus. The boy spun and ran back to the oar deck. The heat of the morning sun was rising, and Khalkeus found himself enjoying the cool, wet straw on his head.

On the rear deck he saw Helikaon talking with three of his senior crewmen. The trio looked stern and nervous. But then why would they not? thought Khalkeus. They were about to sail on a vessel designed and built by the Madman from Miletos.

Turning back from the deck rail he surveyed his great ship. Several members of the crew were looking at him, their expressions mixed. The new ship had been the subject of much mockery, and Khalkeus – as the shipwright – had been treated with scorn, and even anger. Now, however, they were to sail in the madman's vessel, and they were fervently hoping that his madness was, in fact, genius. For if not they were all doomed.

The two Mykene passengers were also looking his way, but they regarded him with studied indifference. Unlike the sailors, they probably did not appreciate that their lives now depended on his skills. Khalkeus wondered suddenly if they would care, even if the knowledge was imparted to them. The Mykene were a fearless race: plunderers, killers, reavers. Death held no terror for such men. He stared back at them. Both were tall and lean, cold and distant. The elder, Argurios, had a chisel-shaped black chin beard, and bleak, emotionless eyes. The younger man, Glaukos, was obviously in awe of him. He rarely spoke unless to reply to a remark from Argurios. Although they travelled now among peaceful settlements and quiet islands they were garbed as if for war, short swords and daggers belted at their sides, bronze-reinforced leather kilts about their waists. Argurios had a finely wrought leather cuirass, the shoulders and chest armoured by overlapping bronze discs. The fair-haired Glaukos had a badly shaped breastplate with a crack on the left side. Khalkeus reasoned that Glaukos was from a poor Mykene family, and had attached himself to Argurios in the hope of advancement. For the Mykene advancement always came through war, plunder and the grief and loss of gentler men. Khalkeus loathed the whole damned race!

If the ship does go down, he thought, that armour will plunge them to their deaths with satisfying speed.

He felt a flash of irritation at such a defeatist idea. My ship will not sink, he told himself. Then he repeated it in his mind over and over again. His heart began to pound and his fingers started to tremble. Turning to the deck rail he took hold of it, and stood very still, waiting for the panic to pass.

Ten years of failure and ridicule had damaged his confidence more than he had realized. Reaching into the pouch at his side he pulled forth a tiny piece of silver-grey metal, and ran his thick, workman's fingers over its glossy surface. He sighed. Here was the source of all his misery and the seed of all his hopes. Hidden within this one shard was a secret he believed could change not only his fortunes but the destiny of nations. How galling then that he could not discover it.

His gloomy thoughts were interrupted by the sound of a booming voice, calling out an order to the sixty oarsmen. Zidantas, the hulking Hittite who served as the Golden One's second in command, leaned over the rear deck rail. 'By the mark of One,' he shouted, sunlight gleaming from his shaved skull. From below deck came a responding call from the lead oarsman.

'Ready! Lift! Brace. And *pull*!'

Khalkeus took a deep breath. The oar blades sliced into the blue water and the *Xanthos* began to glide out over the sea.

The shipwright listened to the creaking of the wood, seeking to identify the source of every murmur, every tiny, muted groan. Swiftly he calculated once more the amount of rock ballast against the weight of the ship's timbers and decking, then leaned over the side to watch the prow cleaving through the gentle waves.

The oarsmen below the top deck began to sing, creating a rhythmic harmony between the smooth actions of their bodies and the chant of the song. There should have been eighty oarsmen, but not even the wealth and reputation of Helikaon, the Golden One, could attract a full crew to the Death Ship. He had heard the Kypriot carpenters whispering as they shaped the hull timbers. 'She'll sink when Poseidon swims.'

When Poseidon swims!

Why did men always have to hang a god's deeds on the simple forces of nature? Khalkeus knew why longer ships sank in storms, and it had nothing whatever to do with angry deities. The rise and fall of a ship in heavy water would cause extra – and uneven – pressure at the centre of the keel. Khalkeus had demonstrated this to Helikaon a year ago, as the two men sat on a jetty in the sunshine, overlooking the small Kypriot shipyard. Khalkeus held a long stick with both hands, then slowly bent it up and down, then side to side. Eventually the stick snapped. The longer the stick, the sooner it broke. When this happened to the hull of a ship in angry seas, he had explained, the results would be swift and terrifying. It would tear itself apart in a matter of moments.

The problem was further exacerbated, Khalkeus continued, by the manner of shipbuilding. Under normal circumstances the hull was pieced together first with planking and dowels. Only then would an inner frame be inserted to strengthen the structure. This was, in Khalkeus' view, idiotic. Instead, the frame needed to be established at the outset, then the timbers fastened to it. This would give added strength amidships. There were other innovations Khalkeus spoke of on that first meeting. A separate deck, on which the oarsmen could sit, leaving the top deck open, either for cargo or passengers; staggered oar stations, running in a zigzag pattern up and down along the hull; support fins bolted to the hull at the front and rear, so that when the ship was drawn up on beaches at night it would not tilt too violently. These, and more, Khalkeus had described.

Helikaon had listened intently and then asked, 'How big a ship could you build?'

'Twice the length of any galley now sailing the Great Green.'

'How many oars?'

'Between eighty and a hundred.'

After that the Golden One had sat silently, his blue eyes staring off into the distance. Khalkeus had thought him bored, and waited to be dismissed. Instead Helikaon had begun a series of more specific questions. What timber would be used? How tall and how thick would the mast need to be? How would Khalkeus ensure that such a large ship would sit well in the water, and retain manoeuvrability and speed? Khalkeus had been surprised. The Golden One was young, in his twenties, and the shipwright had not expected such a depth of knowledge. They talked for several hours, then shared a meal together, and the conversation continued long into the night. Khalkeus etched diagrams into wet clay, rubbed them away, and refined them, showing panels and support frames.

'How could such a huge ship be beached at night?' Helikaon had asked finally. 'And if beached how could it be refloated again come daybreak?'

'It could not easily be *fully* beached,' Khalkeus admitted. 'But that would not be necessary. Under most conditions it would be adequate to merely ground the prow, or the stern, on the beach, and then use stone anchors and lines to hold her in place for the night. That would allow the crew to land and prepare their cookfires.'

'*Most* conditions?' queried Helikaon.

And here was the crux of the problem. Sudden storms could arrive with great speed, and most ships would flee for the shore. Being small and light, galleys could be hauled up onto the safety of the sand. A ship the size and weight of that planned by Khalkeus could not be pulled completely from the water when loaded with cargo.

Khalkeus explained the problem. 'You would not want to half-beach a ship of this size during a storm. The thrashing water at one end, against the shingle or sand at the other, would tear her apart.'

'How then would you run from a storm, Khalkeus?'

'You would not run, Helikaon. You would either ride the waves, or seek shelter anchored in the lee of an island or an outcrop of rocks. The ship I propose would not fear storms.'

Helikaon had stared hard at him for a moment. Then he had relaxed, and given a rare smile. 'A ship to ride a storm. I like that. We will build her, Khalkeus.'

Khalkeus had been stunned – and suddenly frightened. He knew of the Golden One's reputation. If the new ship proved a failure Helikaon might kill him. On the other hand, if it was a success Khalkeus would be wealthy again, and could continue his experiments.

Khalkeus looked into the young man's eyes. 'It is said you can be cruel and deadly. It is said you chop the heads from those who offend you.'

Helikaon had leaned forward. 'It is also said that I am a demi-god, born of Aphrodite. And that you are a madman, or a fool. What does it matter what gossips say? Give me of your best, Khalkeus, and I will reward you, whether what you do is successful or not. All I ask of men who serve me is that they put their hearts into it. No more can be demanded.'

And so it had begun.

The wind picked up as the ship cleared the harbour, and Khalkeus felt the swell increase in power.

Once at sea the mast was raised, the crossbeam tied in place, and the sail released. A southerly breeze rippled the canvas. Khalkeus glanced up. A huge black horse, rearing defiantly, had been painted on the sail. The crew cheered as they saw it.

Khalkeus eased his way to the prow on unsteady legs.

Off to the port side a group of dolphins were leaping and diving, their sleek bodies glistening in the sunlight. Khalkeus looked up at the sky. Away to the north dark clouds were forming.

And the *Xanthos* clove through the waves towards them.

ii

Argurios of Mykene steadied himself on the shifting deck, and glanced across at the stocky, red-headed Khalkeus. Everyone said he was a madman. Argurios hoped this was not true. He dreamed of dying on a battlefield, cutting down his enemies and earning himself a place in the Elysian Fields. To dine in the Golden Hall, fashioned by Hephaistos, and sit alongside men such as Herakles, Ormenion and the mighty Alektruon. His dreams did not include slipping below the waves in full battle armour. Yet, if he had to die on this cursed boat, then it was only fitting that, as a Mykene warrior, he went to his death with his sword, helmet and breast-plate. So it was that he stood in the morning sunshine fully armed. He watched with interest as the crew moved smoothly about the deck, and noted the racks of bows and quivers of arrows neatly stored below the rails. There were swords too, and small, round bucklers. If the *Xanthos* was attacked the sailors would transform themselves into fighting men within moments.

The Golden One left little to chance.

On the high curve of the prow was a device Argurios had not seen on any other ship. It was a wooden structure, bolted to the deck in four places. It was a curious piece, seeming to have no purpose. A jutting section of timber rose from its centre, topped by what appeared to be a basket. At first he had thought it would be used to load cargo, but on closer examination he realized that the basket could not be lowered over the side. The entire piece was a mystery, which he assumed he would solve during the near month-long journey to Troy.

Argurios glanced towards the rear deck, where Helikaon stood at the great steering oar. It had been hard to believe that any man could have defeated Alektruon the Swordsman. He was a legend among the Mykene. A giant of a man, fearless and mighty. Argurios was proud to have fought alongside him.

Yet the full horror of the day was well known. Argurios himself heard the tale from the single survivor. The man had been brought back to Mykene on a cargo vessel, and was taken before Agamemnon the king. The sailor had been in a pitiful state. The stump of his wrist still bled, and there was a bad odour emanating from it. Skeletally thin, he had a bluish sheen to his lips and he could hardly stand. It was obvious to all that he was dying. Agamemnon had a chair brought for him. The story he told was stark and simple.

The mighty Alektruon was dead, his crew massacred, the legendary *Hydra* set adrift, its sail and decks ablaze.

'How did he die?' asked Agamemnon, his cold, hard eyes staring at the dying sailor.

Argurios remembered the man had shivered suddenly, as the harsh memories returned. 'We had boarded their vessel and victory was ours. Then the Golden One attacked. He was like a demon. It was terrible. Terrible. He cut three men down, then tore at Alektruon. It was a short fight. He plunged his blade into Alektruon's neck, then hacked his head from his body. We fought on for a while, but when it was hopeless we threw down our weapons. Then the Golden One, his armour covered in blood, shouted, "Kill all but one!" I saw his eyes then. He was insane. Possessed. Someone grabbed me and pinned my arms. Then all my comrades were hacked to death.'

The man had fallen silent.

'And then?' asked Agamemnon.

'Then I was dragged before Helikaon. He had removed his helmet and was standing there with Alektruon's head in his hands. He was staring into the dead eyes. "You do not deserve to see the Fields of Elysium," he said. Then he stabbed the blade through Alektruon's eyes.'

The warriors gathered in the Lion's Hall had cried out in rage and despair as they heard this. Even the grim and normally expressionless Agamemnon had gasped.

'He sent him blind into the Underworld?'

'Yes, my king. When the deed was done he hurled the head over the side. Then he turned to me.' The man squeezed shut his eyes, as if trying to block the remembered scene.

'What did he say?'

'He said: "You will live to report what you have seen here, but you will be a raider no longer." Then, at his command, two men stretched my arm over the deck rail, and the Golden One hacked my hand away.'

The man had died two days after telling his story.

The defeat of Alektruon had tarnished the Mykene reputation of invincibility. His death had been a sore blow to the pride of all warriors. His funeral games had been muted and depressing. Argurios had gained no satisfaction there, despite winning a gem-encrusted goblet in the javelin contest. There was an air of disbelief among the grieving fighting men. Alektruon's exploits had been legendary. He had led raids from Samothraki in the north, all the way down the eastern coast as far as Palestine. He had even sacked a village less than a day's ride from Troy itself.

News of his defeat and death had been met with incredulity. Word had spread through the villages and towns, and people had gathered in meeting places and squares to discuss it. Argurios had the feeling that in years to come all Mykene would remember exactly what they were doing the moment they heard of Alektruon's passing.

Argurios gazed with quiet hatred at the Golden One. Then he sent a silent prayer to Ares, the God of War. 'May it fall to me to avenge Alektruon! May it be my sword that cuts the heart from this cursed Trojan!'

iii

The wind stayed favourable, and the *Xanthos* sped across the waves. Slowly the green island of Kypros faded from sight. On the rear deck, alongside Helikaon, stood the powerful figure of

Zidantas. At fifty he was the oldest man in the crew, and had sailed these waters for close to thirty-five years. In all that time, through storms and gales, he had never once been wrecked. Almost all his childhood friends had died. Some had drowned when their vessels foundered. Others had been murdered by pirates. Two had succumbed to the coughing sickness, and one had been killed over a lost goat. Zidantas knew he had been lucky.

Today he was wondering whether his luck was running out. The *Xanthos* had set sail just before midday, and, though the friendly, southerly wind was in their favour now, Zidantas was worried.

Usually a vessel from Kypros, travelling north, would leave no later than dawn, cross the narrowest section of open sea to the rocky coastline of Lykia, and then find a sheltered bay for the night. All sailors preferred to beach their vessels at dusk, and sleep on dry land. The crew of the *Xanthos* offered no exceptions to this rule. They were brave men, and daring when circumstances demanded it, but all of them had lost friends or kinsmen to the capricious cruelty of the sea gods. They had waved goodbye to comrades setting sail on calm waters beneath a blue sky, never to be seen again in this life. Ferocious storms, treacherous coastlines, pirates, and rocky shoals, all took their toll on the men who lived and worked upon the Great Green.

Out of sight of land the crew grew silent. Many of the rowers emerged from the lower deck to stand at the rail and gaze out over the sea. There was little conversation. Like Khalkeus they began to listen to the groaning of timbers, and to feel the movement of the ship beneath them. And they gazed with fearful eyes around the horizon, seeking any sign of anger in the skies.

Zidantas both shared and understood their fears. They had heard sailors from other vessels mocking this new ship, and issuing dire warnings about the perils of sailing upon it. The Death Ship they called her. Many of the older members of the crew could also recall other large ships being built and sailing to their doom. Zidantas knew what they were thinking. The *Xanthos* feels fine now, but what will happen when Poseidon swims?

He gazed at the silent men and felt a sudden surge of pride.

Zidantas never sailed with cowards. He could read a fighting man, and had always cast his eye over a crew before joining it. These men were fearful now of the unknown, but if a storm did break, or pirates appeared, they would react with courage and skill. As they had on the *Ithaka* the day Alektruon attacked.

The memory of that day haunted him still, and he sighed.

White gulls swooped overhead, wheeling and diving above the black horse sail. The wind picked up. Zidantas glanced at the sky. Sudden storms were notorious during the autumn months, and few trading ships ventured far once summer was over. 'If the wind changes,' he said.

'There was a storm two days ago,' said Helikaon. 'Unlikely to be another so soon.'

'Unlikely – but not impossible,' muttered Zidantas.

'Take the oar, Ox,' Helikaon told him, stepping aside. 'You'll feel more at ease with the ship under your control.'

'I'd feel more at ease back home, sitting quietly in the sunshine,' grumbled Zidantas.

Helikaon shook his head. 'With six young daughters around when do you have the chance to sit *quietly* at home?'

Zidantas relaxed, and gave a gap-toothed grin. 'It's never quiet,' he agreed as he glanced over the side, reading the swell of the sea. 'She's smoother than I thought she would be. I would have expected more roll.' Zidantas curled his massive arm over the steering oar. 'I'd be happier, though, had we waited for tomorrow's dawn. We have left no room for error. It tempts the gods.'

'You are a Hittite,' replied Helikaon. 'You don't believe in our gods.'

'I never said that!' muttered Zidantas, nervous now. 'Maybe there are different gods in different lands. I have no wish to cause offence to any of them. Nor should you. Most especially when sailing a new ship.'

'True,' answered Helikaon, 'but our gods are not quite as merciless as yours. Tell me, is it true that when a Hittite prince dies they burn twenty of his soldiers along with him to guard him in the Underworld?'

'No, not any more. It was an old custom,' Zidantas told him. 'Though the Gypptos still bury slaves with their pharaohs, I understand.'

Helikaon shook his head. 'What an arrogant species we are. Why should a slave or a soldier still serve a master after death? What possible incentive could there be?'

'I do not know,' answered Zidantas. 'I never had a slave, and I am not a Hittite prince.'

Helikaon moved to the deck rail and glanced along the line of the ship. 'You are right. She is moving well. I must ask Khalkeus about it. But first I will speak to our passengers.' Helikaon leapt down the three steps to the main deck, and crossed to where the Mykene passengers were standing.

Even from his vantage point on the rear deck, and unable to hear the conversation, Zidantas could tell the elder Mykene hated Helikaon. He stood stiffly, his right hand fingering the hilt of his short sword, his face impassive. Helikaon seemed oblivious of the man's malevolence. Zidantas saw him chatting, apparently at ease. When at last Helikaon moved away, seeking out Khalkeus at the prow, the bearded Mykene stared after him with a look of anger.

Zidantas was worried. He had argued against the decision two days ago when Helikaon had agreed to allow the Mykene to take passage to Troy. 'Let them take the *Mirion*,' he said. 'I've been watching them overload her with copper. She'll wallow like a drunken sow. They'll either be sick the whole voyage, or end up dining with Poseidon.'

'I built the *Xanthos* for cargo *and* passengers,' Helikaon had said. 'And Argurios is an ambassador heading for Troy. It would be discourteous to refuse him passage.'

'Discourteous? We've sunk three Mykene galleys now. They hate you.'

'*Pirate* galleys,' corrected Helikaon. 'And Mykene hate almost everyone. It is their nature.' His blue eyes had grown paler, his expression hardening. Zidantas knew that look well, and it always chilled his blood. It brought back memories of blood and death best left locked away in the deep vaults of the subconscious.

The *Xanthos* powered on. Zidantas leaned in to the steering oar. The ship felt good beneath his feet, and he began to wonder if indeed the Madman from Miletos might have been right. He fervently hoped so.

Just then he heard one of the crew shout: 'Man in the water!'

Zidantas scanned the sea to starboard. At first he saw nothing in the vast emptiness. Then he caught sight of a length of driftwood, sliding between the troughs of the waves.

A man was clinging to it.

V

The Man from the Sea

GERSHOM NO LONGER HAD ANY LASTING SENSE OF WHERE HE WAS, nor of the links between dreams and reality. The skin of his shoulders and arms was blistered by the sun, his hands clenched to the wood in a death grip he could no longer feel. Voices whispered in his mind, urging him to let go, to know peace. He ignored them.

Visions swam across his eyes: birds with wings of fire; a man carrying a staff that slithered in his hands, becoming a hooded serpent; a three-headed lion with a scaled body. Then he saw hundreds of young men cutting and crafting a great block of stone. One by one they laid their bodies against it. Slowly they sank into the stone as if it were water. At last all Gershom could see were hands, with questing fingers, seeking to escape the tomb of rock they had crafted. And the voices continued ceaselessly. One sounded like his grandfather, stern and unforgiving. Another was his mother, pleading with him to behave like a lord, and not some drunken oaf. He tried to answer her, but his lips were cracked, his tongue nothing but a dried stick in his mouth. Then came the voice of his little brother, who had died last spring. 'Be with me, kinsman. It is so lonely here.'

He might have given in then, but the driftwood tilted and his bloodshot eyes opened. He saw a black horse floating over the sea. After a while he felt something touch his body, and opened his eyes. A powerful bald-headed man with a forked beard was floating alongside him. Gershom recognized him, but could not remember from where.

'He is alive!' he heard the man shout. 'Throw down a rope.' Then the man spoke to him. 'You can let go now. You are safe.'

Gershom clung on. No dream voices were going to lure him to his death.

The driftwood thumped against the side of a ship. Gershom looked up at the bank of oars above him. Men were leaning out of the ports. A rope was tied round his waist, and he felt himself being lifted from the water. 'Let go of the wood,' said his bearded rescuer.

Now Gershom wanted to, but he could not. There was no feeling in his hands. The swimmer gently prised his fingers open. The rope tightened and he was lifted from the sea, and pulled over the deck rail, where he flopped to the timbers. He cried out as the raw sunburn on his back scraped against the wood, the cry tearing the dry tissue of his throat. A young man with black hair and startlingly blue eyes squatted down next to him. 'Fetch some water,' he said.

Gershom was helped to a sitting position, and a cup was held to his mouth. At first his parched throat was unable to swallow. Each time he tried he gagged.

'Slowly!' advised the blue-eyed man. 'Hold it in your mouth. Allow it to trickle down.'

Swirling the liquid around his mouth he tried again. A small amount of cool water flowed down his throat. He had never tasted anything so sweet and fulfilling.

Then he passed out.

When he awoke he was lying under a makeshift tent, erected near the prow. A freckle-faced youngster was sitting beside him. The boy saw his eyes open, and stood and ran back along the deck. Moments later his rescuer ducked under the tent flap and sat beside him. 'We meet again, Gyppto. You are a lucky fellow. Had we not been delayed we would certainly have missed you. I am Zidantas.'

'I . . . am . . . grateful. Thank . . . you.' Heaving himself to a sitting position Gershom reached for the water jug. Only then did he see that his hands were bandaged.

'You cut yourself badly,' said Zidantas. 'You'll heal, though. Here, let me help.' So saying he lifted the leather-covered jug. Gershom drank, this time a little more deeply. From where he sat he could see along the length of the ship, and recognized it. His heart sank.

'Yes,' said the giant, reading his expression, 'you are on the *Xanthos*. But I know the hearts of ships. This one is mighty. She is the queen of the sea – and she knows it.'

Gershom smiled – then winced as his lower lip split. 'You rest, fellow,' Zidantas told him. 'Your strength will soon come back, and you can earn your passage as a crewman.'

'You . . . do . . . not know me,' said Gershom. 'I am . . . no sailor.'

'Perhaps not. You have courage, though, and strength. And, by Hades, you sailed a piece of driftwood well enough.'

Gershom lay back. Zidantas spoke on, but his voice became a rhythmic murmur and Gershom faded into a dreamless sleep.

ii

Helikaon stood at the steering oar, adjusting his balance as the great ship clove through the waves. The dolphins had returned, leaping and diving alongside the vessel, and he watched them for a while, his normally restless mind relaxed and at peace. Only at sea could he find this exhilarating sense of freedom.

On land there were so many tedious distractions. With more than fifty ships in his fleet there were constantly problems to solve. Authorizations for repairs to galleys, reports to read from his captains, meetings with his senior scribes and treasurers, checking the tallies of cargo shipped against the goods or metals received in exchange. His lands too needed supervision, and though he had good men marshalling his horse herds, and patrolling his borders, there were still matters only he could resolve. His heart lifted as he thought of young Diomedes. His half-brother was almost twelve now, and within a few years would be able to take on real responsibility. The blond-haired boy had begged to be allowed to sail on the *Xanthos*. His mother had forbidden it.

'I am the king,' Diomedes had said. 'People should obey me.'

'You *will* be king, and people *will* obey you,' Helikaon had told him. 'But for now, little brother, we must *both* obey the queen.'

'It is not fair,' complained Diomedes. 'You sailed with Odysseus on the *Penelope* when you were young.'

'I was three years older than you. However, the next time I see Odysseus I will ask him if you can sail with him one day.'

'Would you do that? Oh, that would be wonderful. You would allow that, wouldn't you, mama?'

The slender, golden-haired queen, Halysia, gave Helikaon a look of affectionate reproach. 'Yes,' she said. 'If Odysseus will have you.'

'Oh, he will,' said Diomedes, 'for I am just as brave as Helikaon.'

'Braver,' Helikaon told him. 'When I was your age I was frightened of everything.'

'Even spiders?'

'Especially spiders.'

The boy sighed. 'Oh, Helikaon, I wish I could come to Troy with you. I'd like to meet great-uncle Priam, and Hektor. Is it true you are going to marry the beautiful Kreusa?'

'No, it is not true. And what would you know about beautiful women?'

'I know they are supposed to have big breasts and to kiss men all the time. And Kreusa is beautiful, isn't she? Pausanius says she is.'

'Yes, she is beautiful to look at. Her hair is dark and long and she has a pretty smile.'

'Then why won't you marry her? Great-uncle Priam wants you to, doesn't he? And mother says it would be good for Dardania. And you said we both had to obey mother.'

Helikaon had shrugged, and spread his hands. 'All this is true, little brother. But your mother and I have an understanding. I will serve her loyally in all matters. But I have decided to marry only when I meet a woman I love.'

'Why can't you do both?' asked the boy. 'Pausanius has a wife and two mistresses. He says he loves them all.'

'Pausanius is a rascal,' said Helikaon.

Queen Halysia had stepped in to rescue him from the boy's questioning. 'Helikaon can marry for love *because* he is not a king, and does not have to consider the needs of the realm. But you, little man, *will* be a king, and if you are not a good boy I shall choose a wife for you who is dull and cross-eyed and buck-toothed . . . and bandy-legged.'

Diomedes had laughed, the sound rich and full of life. 'I shall choose my own wife,' he said, 'and she will be beautiful. And she will adore me.'

Yes, she will, thought Helikaon. Diomedes would be a good-looking man, and his nature was sweet and considerate.

The wind was picking up and Helikaon leaned in to the steering oar. His thoughts turned to Priam's favourite daughter. Kreusa was – as he had told Diomedes – very beautiful. But she was also greedy and grasping, with eyes that shone only when gold was reflected in them.

But then, could she have been any different, he wondered, raised as she was in a loveless palace by a father who considered nothing of worth, save that which could be placed upon his scales.

Helikaon had no doubt that it was Priam who had ordered Kreusa to flatter and woo him. The lands of Dardania, directly north of Troy, had never been rich. There were no mines supplying mineral wealth in gold, copper, silver or tin. But Dardania was fertile, and its grasslands fed horse herds of surprising strength and endurance. Corn was also plentiful. Helikaon's growing wealth as a merchant prince had also financed the building of ports, allow-ing access to the trade goods of Egypt and all the lands to the south and west. Dardania was growing in wealth, and therefore power. Of course Priam would seek an alliance with his northern neighbour. No doubt in a few years Priam would seek to marry one of his daughters to Diomedes. Helikaon smiled. Perhaps strange little Kassandra, or gentle Laodike. The smile faded. Or even Kreusa. The thought of his little brother wed to such a creature was dispiriting.

Perhaps I am being unfair to her, he thought.

Priam had little time for most of the fifty children he had sired on his three wives and thirty concubines. Those he drew close had been forced to prove their value to him. His daughters were carelessly sold to foreign princes in exchange for alliances; his sons laboured either in his treasuries, or in the priesthood or the army. Of them all, he lavished what passed for affection on only two: Kreusa and Hektor. His daughter understood the secrets of gathering wealth; Hektor was unbeatable upon the battlefield. Both were assets that needed to be maintained.

It even seemed to amuse the old man that many of his children plotted his death, seeking to overthrow him. His spies would report on their movements, and then, just before they could act upon their plans, he would have them arrested. In the last three years Priam had ordered the deaths of five of his sons.

Pushing aside thoughts of Priam, Helikaon gazed up at the sky. It was a cloudless brilliant blue, and the southerly breeze remained strong and true. Mostly, as summer ended, the prevailing winds were from the northwest, making the crossing a hard day's work for the oarsmen. Not today. The *Xanthos*, sail billowing, cut through the waves, rising and falling with grace and power.

Helikaon saw Khalkeus pacing up and down the main deck, one hand holding his straw hat in place. Occasionally the pitch of the ship would cause him to stumble and grab for a deck rail. He was a landsman, and completely out of place at sea – which made it all the more strange that he should have designed and built a ship of such beauty.

Up at the prow, Zidantas left the makeshift tent where the shipwrecked man had been carried and made his way to the rear deck.

'Will he live?' asked Helikaon.

'Yes. Tough man. He'll survive – but it's not him I'm worried about.'

Helikaon looked the giant in the eye. 'You are always worried about something, Ox. You are never happy unless there is a problem to grind your teeth over.'

'Probably true,' admitted Zidantas, 'but there's a storm coming.'

Helikaon swung to gaze back towards the south. Zidantas' ability to read the weather bordered on the mystical. The southern sky was still clear, and, at first, Helikaon thought the Ox might – at last – be wrong. Then he concentrated on the line of the horizon behind them. It was no longer clean and sharp, signalling rough water. He glanced at the black horse sail. The wind was still fresh and favourable, but it was beginning to gust. 'How long?' he asked. Zidantas shrugged.

'We'll see it before we see land, and it will be upon us before we beach.'

The stocky figure of Khalkeus came marching towards them, head down. He climbed the three steps to the rear deck. 'I have been thinking about what you said,' he told Helikaon. 'I think the fins may be the answer. As you know . . .'

'Fins?' queried Zidantas.

The shipwright stared at him coldly. 'Interruptions are irritating. They disturb the flow of my thoughts. Kindly wait until I have finished.' He leaned forward for extra emphasis, but his hat flopped down over his eyes. Angrily he wrenched it from his head, and swung back towards Helikaon. 'As I was saying . . . you know I had deep planking bolted to the hull, fore and aft, to help keep the ship upright when beached?'

'A sound idea,' said Helikaon.

'Indeed so. However, it is serving a separate and wholly beneficial purpose while at sea. The jut of the fins is countering the shallow draught. I should have realized it when I was designing them. I might have extended them further. They should also make it easier for the steersman. It is my understanding you have to aim the boat at a point above – or below, depending on the current and the wind – the point at which you wish to beach. My feeling is the boat will sail straighter, with less drift. Very pleasing.'

'Well, let's hope they also add some speed,' said Zidantas. 'There is a storm coming up behind us. It would be nice to beach before it hits.'

'Oh, you can't do that,' said Khalkeus.

'We can't beach?'

'Of course you could. But then the storm you speak of would wreck the *Xanthos*.'

'It can't wreck us on land!'

Helikaon cut in. 'What Khalkeus is saying, Ox, is that we cannot *fully* beach the *Xanthos*. She is too large. We don't have the men to haul her completely out of the sea, and if we did, we couldn't float her again.'

'Exactly!' said the shipwright.

'Surely we can get enough of her on the sand,' insisted Zidantas.

'If the storm is a violent one the ship would break up,' said Helikaon. 'Half on solid ground, half being thrashed around on the water. The stresses would crack the hull.'

'Then what *do* we do?' asked Zidantas.

'You need to ride the storm – or find a sheltered edge of land,' Khalkeus told him.

'Ride it! Are you mad?'

'Apparently I am,' answered Khalkeus. 'Ask anyone. Even so I have better things to do than swap insults with an imbecile.' With that he strode from the rear deck.

The giant took a deep breath, and held it for a moment. 'There are times when I imagine myself taking my club to that man.' He sighed. 'We could make for Bad Luck Bay, drop anchor offshore, and use the oars to stop us being driven onto the beach.'

'No, Ox. Even with a full crew that would be nigh impossible,' said Helikaon. 'Fighting a storm for an hour would exhaust them. What if it lasts all night? We'd be hurled onto the beach and wrecked.'

'I know – but then we'd survive, at least. There aren't any other choices.'

Helikaon shook his head. 'There is one. As Khalkeus said, we will ride it.'

'No, no, no!' said Zidantas, leaning in close and dropping his voice. 'The *Xanthos* is untried in heavy weather. She is a good ship, right enough, but my back is already aching. This is going to be heavy, Helikaon. Like a hammer.' He paused. 'And the crew won't stand for it. They are already frightened. Running for the beach may break up the ship, but they know they'll live. There's no way even *you* could convince them to turn *into* the storm.'

Helikaon looked at his friend, and saw the fear in his large, honest face. Zidantas adored his six daughters, and had spoken often in the last year of leaving the sea and watching them grow. Helikaon had given him a share in all profits, and Zidantas was now a rich man. There was no longer any need to risk his life on the Great Green. It was a difficult moment. Zidantas was too proud to speak the truth from his heart, but Helikaon could read it in his eyes. The big Hittite was as terrified as the crew would be.

Helikaon could not look at Zidantas as he spoke. 'I must ride this storm, Ox,' he said at last, his voice gentle. 'I need to know if the *Xanthos* has a great heart. So I am asking you to stand beside me.' He glanced back at the giant.

'I'll always be there when you need me, Golden One,' said Zidantas, his shoulders sagging.

'Then let us rest the crew for a while. Then we'll put them through some gentle manoeuvres. By the time the storm is apparent to them we will be too far from land for them to do anything but follow orders and ride it out.'

'We have a lot of new men aboard,' said Zidantas. 'You are taking a huge risk. A clash of oars as we turn, or panic among the oarsmen, and we'll be swamped.'

'You chose this crew, Ox. You never hire cowards.' He gave a broad grin. 'It'll be something to tell your grandchilden. We swam with Poseidon on the greatest ship ever built.'

The forced humour was wasted on Zidantas. 'I'll look forward to that,' he muttered despondently.

Helikaon glanced along the lines of the *Xanthos*.

And hoped the Madman from Miletos was right.

VI

Poseidon Swims

i

XANDER HAD BEGUN TO DOZE IN THE SUNSHINE. A SAILOR TRIPPED over him, and cursed. Xander muttered an embarrassed apology and climbed to his feet. Then he realized someone was calling his name. He spun round, and almost fell as the ship pitched. He saw it was Zidantas summoning him, and ran to the rear deck.

'Take water to the rowers,' said the big man. 'It'll be damn hot down there. Tell Oniacus to rest the men, and allow them on deck in sections of twenty.'

'Sections of twenty,' repeated Xander.

'Well, go on then, boy.'

'Yes, Zidantas.' He paused. 'Where will I find water?'

'There are full skins on hooks at the centre of both the oar decks.'

Xander moved down to the hatch, opened it and clambered down the vertical steps. It was gloomy and hot here. With the ship under sail now he saw that the rowers had lifted their oars, locking the handles into leather loops. Finding the water skins he unhooked one then carried it to the first rower on the port side, a broad-shouldered young man with thickly curled black hair.

'Where is Oniacus?' he asked, as the sailor pulled out the wooden plug and hefted the water sack. He drank deeply.

'That would be me.'

'Zidantas says to rest the men and allow them on deck in twenty sections.'

'Sections of twenty,' corrected Oniacus.

'Yes.'

'You are sure of the orders? We don't normally rest this close to land.'

'I am sure.'

The man grinned at him. 'You'd be Xander. Your father spoke of you. Said when you were seven or eight you took on a pack of wild dogs.'

'It was one dog,' said Xander. 'It was attacking our goats.'

Oniacus laughed. 'You are very honest, boy. And I can see your father in you.' He passed the water sack back to Xander. Then he called out, 'We're going to see some sunlight, lads. Every third man aloft – and make sure those oars are sheathed tight.' Men began to ease themselves from the rowing benches and make their way to the hatches. Oniacus remained where he was. 'Take water to the men remaining,' he told Xander.

The boy struggled along the cramped and shifting deck, offering drinks to the sweating crewmen. Most thanked him, some joked with him. Then he came alongside a thin, older man, who was pricking blisters on his hand with a curved dagger blade. His palms were sore and bleeding. 'They look painful,' said Xander. The rower ignored him, but took the water sack and drank deeply.

Oniacus appeared alongside, carrying a bucket on a rope. Leaning out of the oar port he lowered the bucket into the sea, then drew it up. 'Put your hands in this, Attalus,' he said. 'The salt water will dry out those blisters, and the skin will harden in no time.' The sailor silently bathed his hands then leaned back. Oniacus dipped thin strips of cloth in the water. 'Now I'll bind them,' he said.

'They don't need binding,' replied the rower.

'Then you are a tougher man than me, Attalus,' said Oniacus

amiably. 'At the start of every new season my hands bleed, and the oar handle feels as if it's on fire.'

'It is unpleasant,' agreed the man, his tone softening.

'You can always try the straps. If they don't work for you, then remove them.'

The rower nodded, and offered his hands. Oniacus wrapped the wet cloth round Attalus' blistered palms, splitting the cloth and knotting it at the wrists. 'This is Xander,' he said, as he applied the bandages. 'His father was my friend. He died in a battle last year. Fine man.'

'The dead are always fine men,' said Attalus coldly. 'My father was a drunken wretch, who broke my mother's bones. At his funeral men wept at the loss of his greatness.'

'There is truth in that,' agreed Oniacus. 'However, on the *Ithaka* – as on the *Xanthos* – there were only fine men. Ox does not choose wretches. He has a magic eye which sees our hearts. I have to say that sometimes it is infuriating. We are sailing short-handed because of it. Ox turned away at least twenty yesterday.' Oniacus swung to Xander. 'Time for you to return to your duties,' he said.

Xander hung the near-empty water sack on its hook and climbed to the upper deck. Helikaon called him over. He lifted a wax-sealed jug, broke the seal and filled two copper cups with a golden liquid. 'Take these to our Mykene passengers,' he said.

Xander carried the cups carefully down the steps and across the shifting deck. It was not easy retaining balance, and he was pleased that not a drop of the liquid was spilled. 'The lord Helikaon asked me to bring these to you,' he said. The man with the cold hard face took them from him without a word of thanks. Xander scurried away without looking him in the eye. He was the most frightening man Xander had ever seen. From the other side of the deck he watched them salute the Golden One and drink. They were standing close to the deck rail and Xander found himself hoping the ship would pitch suddenly and throw them both over the side. Then he noticed that the older warrior was looking at him. He felt a stab of fear, wondering if the evil one could read his mind. The Mykene held out the goblet, and Xander realized he was supposed to retrieve them. Swiftly he crossed the deck, collected the goblets and took them to Zidantas.

'What should I do now?' he asked.

'Go and watch the dolphins, Xander,' said Ox. 'When you are needed you will be summoned.'

Xander returned to where he had left his small bag of possessions. Inside there was a block of cheese and some dried fruit. Hungry now, he sat and ate. The grumpy old shipwright came past at one point, and almost trod on him.

The boy found the next two hours fascinating. Helikaon and Zidantas shouted out orders and the *Xanthos* danced upon the waves. The port-side rowers would lean in to their oars just as the starboard men lifted theirs from the water. The *Xanthos* would lurch and spin, changing direction, then surge forward once more as both banks of oars bit into the waves. Xander loved every minute of it – especially when the younger Mykene warrior fell to his knees and threw up. The older one, with the hard face, looked somewhat green, but he held grimly to the deck rail, staring out at sea. At last the manoeuvres were over and Zidantas called out for the men to rest.

The wind was gusting a little now, rippling the black horse sail. Xander glanced towards the south. The sky was darker there. Many of the oarsmen had climbed to the upper deck. Most, like him, also stared towards the south. Some of them gathered together and Xander heard someone say: 'Poseidon swims. We'll be lucky to make land before the storm hits.'

'It's that cursed Gyppto,' said someone else. Xander stared at him. The speaker was a wide-shouldered man, with thinning blond hair and a straggly beard. 'Poseidon took him once, and we thwarted him.'

This was a disquieting thought, and it frightened Xander. Everyone knew Poseidon could be an angry god, but it had not occurred to him that an immortal might have wanted this stranger to be swallowed by the sea. The conversation continued. Other men joined in. Xander could feel their fear as they discussed how best to placate the god. 'Need to throw him back,' said the man with the straggly beard. 'It's the only way. Otherwise we'll all be dead.' There were some grunts of agreement, but most of the men stayed silent. Only one spoke against the plan. It was the curly-haired lead oarsman, Oniacus.

'A little early to be talking about murder, Epeus, don't you think?'

'He is marked by Poseidon,' replied Epeus. 'I don't want to kill anyone, but the man is beyond saving. If the god wants him he will take him. You want us to be dragged down with him?'

Xander saw that the two Mykene warriors were also listening to the men, but they kept their own counsel. As the wind picked up, and the ship began to pitch more violently, Xander moved away from the crew and made his way to the rear deck. The man with the straw hat was there, talking to Zidantas and the Golden One. Xander waited at the foot of the steps, unsure now of what to do. He didn't want to see the injured man thrown over the side, but, equally, he did not want to incur the wrath of Poseidon. He tried to think of what his father might have done. Would he have thrown the man back into the sea? Xander didn't think so. His father was a hero. The Golden One had said so. Heroes did not murder helpless men.

Xander climbed to the stern deck. The Golden One saw him. 'Do not fear a little breeze, Xander,' he said.

'I am not frightened of the wind, lord,' said Xander, and told him what he had heard from the oarsmen. Before the lord could reply, a group of sailors began to gather below them. Xander turned and saw two seamen half dragging the shipwrecked man through the throng.

'Poseidon is angry!' shouted the burly Epeus. 'We must give back what we stole from him, Golden One.'

Helikaon moved past Xander and stared down at the sailors. He raised his hand and there was instant silence, save for the howling of the wind. For a moment Helikaon did not speak, merely stood. 'You are a fool, Epeus,' he said finally. 'Poseidon was not angry. But he is angry *now*!' He pointed at the troublemaker. '*You* have brought his fury down upon us.'

'I have done nothing, lord!' answered Epeus, his voice suddenly fearful.

'Oh, but you have!' roared Helikaon. 'You think Poseidon is such a weak god that he could not kill a single man who has been in the sea for two days? You think he could not have dragged him down in a heartbeat, as he did with others of his crew? No. The great God of the Sea did *not* want him dead. He wanted him *alive*. He wanted the *Xanthos* to rescue him. And now you have assaulted him, and are threatening to kill him. You may have doomed us all. For now, as all can see, Poseidon swims!' Even as he spoke the sky grew darker. Thunder boomed.

'What can we do, lord?' shouted another man.

'We cannot run,' Helikaon told them. 'Poseidon hates cowards. We must turn and face the great god like men, and show that we are worthy of his blessing. Take in the sail! All oarsmen to the lower deck, and await command. Do it now! And swiftly.'

The men scattered to obey him, leaving Gershom sitting, bewildered, on the deck. Zidantas leaned in to Xander. 'Help him back to the midships. There will be less heave and pitch there. Tie yourselves to the mast. We are in for a wild ride.'

Xander scrambled down to the deck, which was now pitching and twisting under his feet. He fell, then rose and took Gershom by the arm. Helping him to stand he led the way forward. It was almost impossible to stay upright, and they stumbled several times before reaching the mast. Xander looped a trailing rope round Gershom, tying it tight. Then he glanced around for something to tie to himself. There was nothing. The storm swept down on them, the wind howling, rain lashing the decks. Xander clung on to the rope round Gershom. The big man reached out with a bandaged hand, and drew him close. Above the howling of the wind Xander heard Zidantas bellowing orders to the oarsmen. The ship swung, then rocked wildly as a huge wave crashed against the hull. Slowly the *Xanthos* turned into the storm. Another massive wave struck the beam, washing over the main deck. Xander almost lost hold of the rope as his body was gripped by the wave and dragged sideways. Gershom cried out as his injured hand gripped the boy's tunic, holding him in place.

A scream came from above. One of the sailors tying the sail had been dislodged. Xander saw him fall. His body smashed into the deck rail on the starboard side, tearing a section loose. Then he was gone. Darkness descended. Afternoon passed into evening and then into night. Xander clung to the rope as the storm lashed the great ship. He held on as tightly as he could, but after a while his fingers were numb, and his strength began to fail. Only Gershom's powerful grip kept him from being swept away. The darkness was interspersed with brilliant flashes of lightning, followed by thunderclaps so loud Xander felt they would tear the ship apart. The deck heaved, one moment tilting up, throwing him back, then plunging down, causing him to spin forwards. Cold, wet and terrified, he prayed for life.

Ever more weary, the boy clung on. The *Xanthos* was heading into the storm now, climbing the waves, then sliding into the troughs. Water cascaded over the prow. Suddenly the ship lurched, as the tiring port-side rowers momentarily lost their rhythm. A roaring wall of water ripped across the *Xanthos*. It struck Xander, lifting him and dashing his body against the mast. Half stunned, he lost hold of the rope and was torn from Gershom's grip. The great ship pitched sharply and Xander slid across the wet deck. Lightning lit the sky. He saw he was sliding inexorably towards the hole in the ruined deck rail. His hands scrabbled for something to cling on to.

As the opening yawned before him he caught a glimpse of shining bronze. The Mykene warrior, Argurios, seeing his plight, had let go of the rail and hurled himself across the deck. His hand grabbed Xander's tunic, then the two of them spun towards the gaping hole. At the last moment Argurios grabbed a trailing rope. Xander felt the deck slip from under him, and was now directly over the raging sea. He looked up and saw the Mykene was also off the deck, hanging on the rope, his face twisted in a grimace of pain. Xander knew that, in all his armour, Argurios could not save them both. At any moment the Mykene would just let go, and Xander would be doomed.

But he did not let go. The *Xanthos* leapt and pitched. Argurios was thrown against the side. Xander's tunic started to rip.

Then the wind began to die down, the rain eased, and moonlight broke through the clouds. Two sailors left their positions of safety and braved the tilting deck. Xander saw Oniacus grab Argurios, hauling him back to safety. Then Attalus reached down, gripping Xander's arm, and dragging him to the deck.

Huddled against the deck rail Xander began to tremble. His hands wouldn't stop shaking. The Golden One appeared alongside him, patting him on the shoulder. He moved to where Argurios was now standing, kneading his fingers. Xander saw there was blood on Argurios' hand.

'That was bravely done,' said Helikaon.

'I need no praise from you,' replied Argurios, turning away and rejoining his companion.

Zidantas crouched down beside Xander. 'Well, lad, did you enjoy your first storm?'

'No.'

'You enjoyed surviving it, though?'

'Oh, yes.' The trembling began to pass. 'I thought I was going to die.'

'You were lucky, Xander. There was only one life lost.'

'Was it Epeus?'

'No. A young Lykian called Hippolatos. Good lad.'

'I don't understand. If Poseidon was angry with Epeus, why would he kill Hippolatos?'

'Life is full of mysteries,' Zidantas told him.

As the seas continued to calm, a ragged cheer went up from the crew. Helikaon walked among them and they gathered round him.

'Poseidon has blessed the *Xanthos*,' he called out. 'We swam with him and he read the courage in your hearts. Every man among you will receive double payment.' Now the cheers rang out even louder and a mood of exultation swept the ship.

Xander did not feel exultant.

Helikaon came to him then. He crouched down alongside the

trembling boy. 'The world is full of fear, Xander,' he said, 'but you were a hero today.'

'I did nothing, lord.'

'I saw you. You first tied Gershom to the mast. Not yourself. You put his survival before your own. Your father would be proud of you. As I am. And you saw two other heroes. Gershom clung to you, though his hands were torn and bloody. Argurios risked his life so that you would not die. There is greatness in both these men, and in you.'

ii

Gershom sat in the bow of the *Xanthos*, knees drawn up, a ragged piece of cloth round his raw shoulders and sore arms. The storm had passed now, and, though the moon was shining in a star-filled sky, he still trembled occasionally. Sudden shivers would rack his frame. Squinting through swollen lids, his eyes were fixed on the approaching land, willing it to come closer more quickly. Never had he been so anxious to feel steady ground under his feet. Close by, Zidantas was leaning over the side, staring intently down at the clear dark water below the prow. Beside him a crewman garbed only in a black loincloth was plunging a long notched pole into the sea, and calling out the depth. And the *Xanthos* inched forward.

'How long will we be ashore?' Gershom asked, hoping Zidantas would say several days.

'Just overnight,' replied Zidantas shortly. Without looking to the rear of the ship, he signalled twice with his right arm to the helmsman, and Gershom felt the great ship adjust fractionally in her course. He had been told there were dangerous shoals in these waters and he stayed silent, unwilling to break the concentration of the experienced seamen. He could see most oars were held high; only six dipped regularly in and out of the water as the *Xanthos* crept towards the safety of the shore.

To starboard was a tall island, its top shrouded in lush vegetation, its cliffs white with seabirds and their droppings. As the ship drew abreast of the isle, Gershom could see it screened the entrance to a great bay. The sight of it made him catch his breath, and next to him he heard the boy Xander gasp.

The bay was large and almost circular. Around it grey and white cliffs towered high and jagged. At the centre of the cliffs, directly ahead of them, two tall peaks of bluish rock stood sentinel, shining in the moonlight. At their base a glittering silver waterfall ran down through a riot of greenery, then appeared as a small river. Gershom could make out a cluster of buildings rising steeply in a jumble of white walls and red roofs, and at the top a fortress looked out over the sea. The river mouth divided the wide strip of white beach neatly in half. Other ships were already drawn up on the strand, and campfires were burning on the beach.

The boy glanced at him, mouth open.

'It's beautiful!' he said, his eyes alight with wonder.

Gershom smiled at him and felt his spirits lift. This child had travelled on the Great Green for only one day, had survived a violent storm, had looked certain death in the eye – yet here he was, undeterred, looking forward to his next adventure, eyes wide with anticipation.

'Where are we? What is this place called?' asked Xander.

Zidantas took his eyes off the water at last and stood up straight, his hands easing the small of his back. 'We're clear now,' he said to the crewman, who nodded, then returned back down the ship, pole in hand. Zidantas swung to the boy. 'The locals call it the Bay of Blue Owls,' he said. 'Others call it Bad Luck Bay.'

'Why do you come here if it's bad luck?' Gershom asked, thinking, *I've seen enough bad luck without seeking it out.*

Zidantas smiled without humour. 'It's never been bad luck for us, Gyppto. Just for other ships.'

Gershom could see the shore quite clearly now. Most of the ships were beached together to the right side of the river, but three black ships lay to the left, far from the others. He saw Zidantas' expression grow darker as he gazed at the black galleys. 'You know them?' he asked.

'Yes, I know them.'

'Rival traders?'

Leaning in close so that the boy could not hear, Zidantas whispered, 'They trade in blood, Gyppto. They are pirates.'

Xander had climbed to the topmost point of the high, curved prow. 'Look at all those people,' he shouted, pointing to the beach.

There was a crowd around a score of stalls set up on the sand; small fires had been lit and more were sparking to life even as he watched. Gershom almost believed he could smell roasting meats. His shrunken stomach gripped him painfully for a moment.

'Yes,' said Zidantas, 'it's a busy little place. This kingdom grows rich on the tolls the Fat King levies. But he keeps the bay safe for all ships, and – mostly – for sailors from every land. Good and bad. You'll meet all sorts here. They come to do a little trading, a little whoring.' He dropped a wink at Xander, who blushed. 'But mostly they come for safe anchorage for the night. The storm will have washed all sorts of flotsam into Bad Luck Bay tonight.'

At a call from Helikaon the bald-headed giant hurried back along the deck to the helm. Seconds later the ship started to turn sharply, until her nose was pointed once more towards the open sea.

'What's happening? Why aren't we beaching?' Xander asked anxiously, returning to stand beside Gershom.

Gershom could not answer him.

'Reverse oars,' came the booming command from Zidantas.

The *Xanthos*, uncertainly at first, began to back towards the beach. Zidantas and two crewmen lifted the steering oar clear of the water, sliding it back along a groove fashioned in the rear deck rail.

Thirty oars dipped into the wine-dark water, the men began to chant lustily, and the stern of the *Xanthos* surged towards a wide stretch of sand. Close by was a single galley, with huge crimson eyes painted on the bow. Men were stretched out on the sand around it, but many of them stood as the *Xanthos* approached.

The water was almost still near the shore and the pointed stern of the ship clove the gentle swell like an axe. Gershom grabbed on to the side. The thirty oars dipped in and out of the water relentlessly, the pace and volume of the men's chanting increasing, the white line of beach hurtling towards them . . .

Gershom held on tight and closed his eyes.

'Hold!'

There was a moment of silence as the chanting stopped, the oars poised in the air, then the stern of the *Xanthos* slid onto the beach, hurling sand and pebbles up on either side with a gritty roar as its timbers scraped over the stony waterline. It ground to a halt. There was a moment's pause, the ship shifted a little to one side, then settled.

A great cheer arose, both from the crew and from the men on the beach. Xander and Gershom had both been thrown to the deck but Xander jumped straight up again and joined in the cheering.

He turned to Gershom, his eyes alight. 'Wasn't that exciting?'

Gershom decided to stay where he was for a bit. Much as he wanted firm ground under his feet, he feared his legs would not carry him there just yet.

'Yes,' he said breathlessly. 'Exciting is the very word.'

There was a bustle of movement on board as men hurried to disembark, laughing and joking with one another as the fears of the day drifted away like ocean spray. The oarsmen were shipping their blades, quickly drying them and stowing them before snatching up their belongings from under the rowers' benches. Helikaon was the first over the side and Gershom could see him inspecting the planking on the hull. The hold doors were raised in the centre of the deck and Zidantas and the grumpy shipwright Khalkeus both quickly disappeared into the bowels of the ship, no doubt checking for damage.

The crewman were streaming off the *Xanthos*, shinning down ropes onto dry land.

'Come on, Gershom!' Xander had collected his own small leather bag. The boy was dancing impatiently from foot to foot. 'We've got to go ashore!' Gershom knew he was in agony lest he miss something.

'You go. I'll be a moment.'

Xander stood in line behind several sailors waiting to disembark.

When his turn came, he climbed over the deck rail, took hold of the rope and, hand over hand, lowered himself to the beach. He ran off without a backward glance to where the men of the *Xanthos* were already building a fire. The great ship was quiet and Gershom was alone on the deck. He closed his eyes and relished the moment of peace.

A shout disturbed him, and he opened his eyes with a jolt.

'Ho, Helikaon! You can always tell a man of Troy because he presents his arse to you first! Never seen it done with a ship, though.'

A ruddy-faced man in a saffron-coloured tunic was striding down the beach to the *Xanthos*. He was not tall, but wide and muscular, and his curly beard and long hair were tawny and unkempt. His tunic was dirty and his leather sandals old and worn, yet he wore an elaborately crafted belt decorated with gold and gems, from which hung a curved dagger. Helikaon's face lit up at the sight of him.

'You ugly old pirate,' he called out in greeting and, patting the hull of the *Xanthos* with evident satisfaction, Helikaon waded to the shore and threw his arms round the newcomer.

'You're lucky I'm here,' said the man. 'You'll need all my crew as well as your own to get this fat cow off the beach come daybreak.'

Helikaon laughed, then turned to gaze with pride at the great ship. 'She rode the storm, my friend. Fearless and defiant. She is everything I dreamt of.'

'I remember. To sail beyond Scylla and Charybdis, across uncharted oceans all the way to the end of the world. I'm proud of you.'

Helikaon fell silent for a moment. 'None of it would have come to pass without you, Odysseus.'

VII

The Lost Hero

ODYSSEUS LOOKED AT THE YOUNG MAN, AND WAS AMAZED TO FIND HE
was at a loss for words. His sudden embarrassment was covered by
the arrival of several members of his crew, who rushed forward and
gathered around Helikaon. They clapped him on the back or
embraced him, then drew him back to where other men waited to
greet him.

Odysseus gazed back at the great ship, and remembered the little
raven-haired child who had once told him, 'I will build the biggest
ship. And I will kill sea monsters, and sail to the end of the world,
where all the gods live.'

'They are said to live on Mount Olympos.'

'Do any of them live at the end of the world?'

'A terrible woman, with eyes of fire. One glance at her face and
men burn like candles.'

The child had looked concerned. Then his expression hardened.
'I won't look at her face,' he said.

Time flew faster than the wings of Pegasus, thought Odysseus.
He suddenly felt old. At year's end he would be forty-five. He drew
in a deep breath, his mood becoming melancholy. Then he saw a
young lad running from the *Xanthos*. He was looking around,
awestruck, at the fires and the stalls and the throngs of people.

'Where do you think you are going, little man?' asked Odysseus sternly.

The tawny-haired youngster looked at him. 'Is this your beach, sir?' he asked.

'It might be. Do you not know who I am?'

'I do not, sir. I have never sailed before.'

Odysseus kept his expression fierce. 'That is no excuse, boy. Was I not described to you in tales of wonder? Were the legends of my life not told round your cookfires?'

'I don't know,' answered the boy honestly. 'You haven't told me your name.'

'I am the king of Ithaka – the *warrior* king of Ithaka. The greatest sailor in all the world. Does that offer a clue?'

'Is this Ithaka?' asked the lad.

Odysseus shook his head. 'No, this is not Ithaka. I can see your education has been sadly lacking. Go on, now. Enjoy the delights of Blue Owl Bay.'

The boy swung away, but then turned back. 'I am Xander,' he said. 'I am a sailor too.'

'And a good one. I can tell. I am Odysseus.'

Xander stood very still, staring at him. 'Truly?'

'Indeed.'

'I *have* heard of you. Grandfather says you are the greatest liar in all the world, and you tell the best stories. He told me the one about how your ship was lifted by a great storm and left on a mountainside, and how you cut the sail in half and tied it to the oars and flapped them like wings so that the ship flew back to the sea.'

'For a while, though, we were lost in the clouds,' said Odysseus, 'and I had to be lowered on a rope to guide us back to the water.'

The boy laughed. 'I am sailing with the lord Helikaon,' he said. 'We went through a great storm, and I nearly fell over the side.'

'I sailed with Helikaon once,' Odysseus told him. 'He was about your age. I used my magic to teach him how to fly.'

'He can fly?'

'Like an eagle. Perhaps I'll tell you about it later. But for now I need to piss, and I hate to be watched, so be away with you.'

The boy ran off. Odysseus, his good humour returned, strolled along the beach. He sat down on a jutting rock and looked back to where Helikaon was surrounded by crewmen from the *Penelope*. They were – he guessed – talking about old times.

Old times.

It was twenty years since Odysseus had first laid eyes on Helikaon. *Twenty years!* Sometimes it seemed merely a few trading seasons had passed. Odysseus had been young, and at the height of his strength, and he remembered vividly the first time he had trodden the steep path to the hilltop fortress of Dardanos. The rocky fastness had become the capital of Dardania under Anchises the king, Helikaon's father. He was said to be wealthy with ill-gotten gains and, more importantly to Odysseus the trader, had a beautiful young wife. Thus he climbed the steep rock-strewn hill accompanied by three crewmen and two donkeys laden with rare perfumes, jewels and gold, rich textiles and trinkets such as might appeal to a woman of taste.

At the fortress gates he had joked with the royal guard while weighing up the defences. The gates were thick, but far too broad, a foolish vanity on the part of the king no doubt. But the walls were high and well made, blocks of limestone fitted cunningly together without mortar. The guards at the gate looked well fed and alert. They eyed him curiously, which was only to be expected. He had already made a name for himself, even in this distant northern domain.

Suddenly an excited young voice behind him cried, 'Sir, sir, is that your ship?'

He swung round and saw a boy of seven or eight with night-dark hair and brilliant blue eyes. The boy was pointing down to the beach where the *Penelope* had been drawn up, looming large over the fishing boats around her.

'What if it is, you ugly little dwarf?' he growled.

The boy was taken aback but he stood his ground. 'I'm not a dwarf, sir. I'm a boy. I am Aeneas, the son of Anchises, the king.'

Odysseus glared at him. 'Expect me to believe that? You don't look like any boy I've ever seen. All the boys I've met have had four arms. Don't try to fool me, lad. You'll regret it.' He placed his hand on his dagger and stepped forward menacingly.

The boy was uncertain still – until he saw the wide grins on the faces of the palace guards and laughed.

'My father told me Odysseus of Ithaka would be our honoured guest and that he is a fine teller of tall stories. Will you tell me about the boys with four arms, sir? How many heads did they have?'

Odysseus gave him a grudging smile. 'We'll see, lad,' he said. 'We'll see.'

At that moment a harassed-looking middle-aged woman appeared behind the lad.

'Aeneas, where have you been? I thought I'd never find you. I've been all the way down to the beach looking for you. Come. Come here. Your mother wants you. You're a bad boy,' she added as an afterthought.

She grabbed his arm and pulled him up the path towards the royal apartments. Aeneas grinned over his shoulder at Odysseus then suffered himself to be dragged up the stone steps to a side balcony where a slender, beautiful, dark-haired woman in blue robes waited. She knelt down to embrace the boy, who, glancing at Odysseus again, rolled his eyes.

Odysseus met the king in Anchises' *megaron*, the great stone hall where he received guests and ordered his daily business. The man was pale-skinned and grey-haired, his ice-blue eyes resting coolly on the trader as if he were no more than a palace servant.

Odysseus was well used to jumped-up brigands like this. He liked to think he was flexible in his dealings and he had an arsenal of weapons to call on, ranging from outrageous flattery through charm to scarce-concealed threats. This king, though, was cool and remote, and the trader found him hard to read. They discussed the state of trade on the local coasts, sipping well-watered wine, and Odysseus told a couple of stories to make Anchises laugh. But his best stories – even the one about the virgin and the scorpion – scarcely creased the king's stern features and his eyes remained cold.

Odysseus was almost relieved when Aeneas, barefoot and dressed in a linen tunic, came running into the *megaron* and skidded to a halt in front of the king.

'Have I missed everything, father? Am I too late?'

'Missed what? What are you talking about, Aeneas?' asked Anchises impatiently, his icy eyes turning to the dark-haired woman who followed the boy into the chamber.

'The stories, father. Of wild beasts and two-headed boys and adventures on the high sea,' he said, his face creased into a frown of anxiety. 'I had to do my lessons,' he explained to Odysseus, who watched him with amusement.

'I'm tired, lad, and I've run out of stories for the day.'

'Come, Helikaon, don't trouble your father and his guest,' said his mother and she took him gently by the arm. She was a woman of fragile beauty with delicate pale skin and, Odysseus thought, eyes which seemed to gaze on a different horizon. It was a look he had seen before, and he regarded the young queen with renewed interest.

'I have told you before,' said the king, harshly, 'to call him by the name I gave him. Aeneas. It is a proud name.'

The queen looked frightened and began to stammer an apology. Odysseus saw the boy's expression change, then he pulled away from his mother and said: 'I'm going to build the biggest ship in the world when I'm older. I am to be a great hero. The gods told mother.'

A pretty frown creased the woman's brow. She knelt before her son and embraced him again as Odysseus had seen her do on the balcony. She looked into the boy's eyes as if searching for something there. Odysseus was impressed with the lad. He was very young, and yet he had sensed his mother's distress, and had spoken to distract his father's anger.

'I know the hearts of men and heroes, boy,' he said, 'and I think your mother is right.'

'Go now,' said the king, and flicked his fingers at mother and child, as if dismissing servants.

In the three days the *Penelope* spent in Dardania the child had followed Odysseus around like an exuberant shadow. Odysseus tolerated his company. The boy was sharp, intelligent, curious about the world around him, friendly to all comers, yet reserving an independence of thought the trader found unusual. He was fascinated by ships and he extracted a promise from Odysseus to return to Dardania one day and take him on a voyage on the *Penelope*. The trader had no intention of keeping his word, but it satisfied the boy, who stood on the beach on the last day waving the trading ship goodbye until it disappeared over the horizon. That same summer Anchises' wife died, in a mysterious fall from a cliff. Sailors gossiped about the tragedy. One story had Anchises, known to be a cold-hearted king, hurling his wife to her death. Others said she killed herself after years of suffering at Anchises' hands. A few told more elaborate tales, saying that the queen had been possessed by Aphrodite. Odysseus dismissed that one out of hand. The idea of the Goddess of Love falling for a dry, dull brigand like Anchises was laughable. No, he had seen the queen's eyes. She had been swallowing opiates. Many highborn women belonged to mysterious sects, taking part in secret revels. When young – around twelve – Odysseus had risked execution in order to spy on one such gathering in Ithaka. The women there had behaved with glorious abandon, dancing and singing, and flinging their clothes to the ground. At one point a small goat had been brought into the clearing. The women had fallen upon it with knives, hacking it to pieces, then smearing themselves with its blood. Odysseus had been shocked and terrified, and had crept away.

Anchises' wife was said to be a priestess of Dionysus, and in that role would have experienced no difficulty in acquiring narcotics. They had undoubtedly unhinged her.

Odysseus stopped in Dardania several times over the following seven years, but they were overnight rests only. He saw nothing of the king or the boy and had no interest in them, until one day on the isle of Lesbos he got into conversation with a Kretan trader who had recently sailed to the Dardanian coast.

He told Odysseus the king had married again.

'A dull and unpleasant man,' Odysseus said musingly, 'yet I suppose even a cold fish like him must have a wife.'

'Yes,' said the Kretan, 'and the new queen has given birth to a son and heir.'

'A son?' Odysseus remembered the small black-haired boy on the beach waving as if his arm would fall off. 'He has a son. Aeneas. I had not heard he was dead.'

'As good as,' replied the Kretan. 'Almost a man and yet frightened of everything, they say. He stays in his room all day. The king has no time for him. As I wouldn't,' he concluded.

Odysseus had no reason to return to Dardania, but questions about the boy had lodged in his mind from that moment. He could not shake them free, and found himself, a month later, walking the steep path again to seek audience with Anchises. This time his reception at the gates was hostile, and he was left kicking his heels for several hours outside the king's *megaron*. He was fighting mad by the time Anchises deigned to receive him. Quelling his anger with difficulty, he accepted the wine cup the king offered and enquired after Aeneas.

The king's stern face darkened. His eyes turned away. 'You are here to sell me something, no doubt, and I am in need of a supply of tin.'

After lengthy dickering, they reached agreement. Odysseus returned to the *Penelope* with the intention of leaving at dawn, but was surprised to get a late-night request from the king to see him again.

The *megaron* was icy, almost in darkness, lit by the light of a single fire, and Anchises virtually invisible in the shadows of his great carved chair. He gestured Odysseus to a seat and offered him a wine cup. The wine was warmed but the trader shivered and pulled his woollen robe closer round him.

'His mother killed herself,' Anchises said suddenly. 'The boy has not been the same since. The stupid woman told him she was the goddess Aphrodite, and that she was going to fly back to Olympos. Then she leapt from the cliff. He saw her and tried to follow, but I grabbed him. He refused to believe she was insane. So I took him to the body, and he saw the ruins of her beauty, broken bones jutting from her flesh. He has been . . . useless to me since. He is frightened of everything. He speaks to nobody and goes nowhere. He will not ride a horse, nor dive or swim in the bay. So I have a proposition for you.'

Odysseus raised his eyebrows in question.

'He is fifteen now. Take him with you,' said the king.

'I am in no need of crew. Especially cowards.'

Anchises' eyes narrowed, but he swallowed his anger. 'I will see you are well recompensed.'

'You will pay for his keep and for the extreme inconvenience of having such a milksop aboard my ship?'

'Yes, yes,' Anchises said impatiently. 'I will make it worth your while.'

'The Great Green is a dangerous place, King. Your son might not survive the experience.'

Anchises leaned towards him and Odysseus saw his eyes glitter in the firelight. 'That thought is in my mind. I have another son now. Diomedes. He is everything Aeneas will never be. He is fearless and bright and born to be king. Now, should a tragedy occur while you are at sea I will reward you richly, in order that you might organize a suitable funeral. Do we understand one another?'

From a table at his side he took a cloth bundle and thrust it at Odysseus. The trader opened it and found a wondrous belt made of fine leather and gold rings, encrusted with amber and carnelian, and a curved dagger inlaid with ivory. He examined them critically. 'This is a good piece,' he said grudgingly, drawing the dagger.

'And we have an understanding?' the king pressed.

'You want me to take your son and . . . make a man of him,' said Odysseus, enjoying the spasm of irritation that creased the king's features. 'In order to succeed he must, of course, risk many perils. Danger is the seed from which courage grows.'

'Exactly. Many perils,' the king agreed.

'I shall speak to the boy tomorrow.'

Odysseus had returned to the *Penelope* with his booty, and had thought long about the king's request. The man wanted his own son murdered, and Odysseus loathed him for it.

Towards midnight he stripped off his tunic and jumped from the deck of the *Penelope* into the dark sea below. He swam across the moonlit bay, the cool water helping clear his mind. The vile king had dragged a sensitive child down to see the shattered corpse of his mother. Was it any wonder his heart was scarred?

Odysseus swam to a point below a high ledge on the cliff path. The water was deep here, and there were few rocks. The swim was enjoyable, but he was no nearer a decision when he returned to the *Penelope*.

Dressed in an old threadbare tunic he met Aeneas in the early morning, in the flower garden at the side of the palace overlooking the sea. When Odysseus last walked in the garden it had been a riot of greenery, grown with much care and attention despite the ever-present winds and the salt air. Since then all effort to keep it flourishing had ceased and the garden was the same as the rest of Anchises' palace grounds, rock-strewn and barren.

Aeneas had grown a lot during those years, but he was now, at fifteen, still below average height, blue-eyed and slender. He wore a knee-length white tunic and his long dark hair was bound back with a strip of leather. Odysseus noticed he kept far from the cliff edge and didn't so much as glance at the *Penelope* in the bay far below.

'So, lad, we have much to catch up on,' the trader began. 'Have you fulfilled your ambition yet?'

'What ambition is that, sir?' The youth turned ice-blue eyes on him and Odysseus felt his blood run cold. Under the bland reflective surface of those eyes, he sought for a spark of the bright child Aeneas had been.

'Why, to build the biggest ship in the world. Don't you remember?'

'I was just a boy then. Children have strange ideas.' Aeneas turned away.

Odysseus' anger, never far below the surface, rose again at the coldness in the young man's voice.

'They tell me you're frightened,' he said conversationally. 'Frightened of heights. Well, that's not unreasonable. Your mother threw herself off a cliff. You saw it. So you're frightened of heights. I understand that.'

If he'd hoped for a response from the youth he was disappointed.

'But,' he added, 'I hear you're picky about your food like a little maiden. Frightened you'll swallow a fishbone and choke, frightened you'll eat bad shellfish and die. You won't ride your horses any more, frightened, I suppose, that you'll fall off. You scarcely leave your room, I'm told.' He leaned in to Aeneas. 'What sort of life are you living, boy? What do you do in your room all day? Embroidery – like a girl? Is that it? Are you a girl in disguise? Do you dream of the day some ugly man decides to stick his cock up your arse?'

And then he saw it, for a fraction of a heartbeat. A glint in the eyes, the beginnings of anger. It was instantly snuffed out.

'Why do you insult me?' asked Aeneas.

'To make you angry. Why did you stifle it?'

'It serves no purpose. When we lose control we . . .' He hesitated. 'We make mistakes,' he concluded, lamely.

'We throw ourselves from cliffs. Is that what you mean?'

The boy reddened. 'Yes,' he said, at last. 'Though I ask you not to mention it again. It is painful to me still.'

Odysseus sighed. 'Sometimes pain is necessary, lad. The gods gave me a great gift, you know, for reading the hearts of men. I only have to take one glance to know whether he is a hero or a coward.'

'And you think me a coward,' said the youngster, anger once more seeking to take hold. 'My father tells me daily. I am a milk-sop, a useless creature. I have no need to hear it from a foreign sailor. Now are we done?'

'You are none of those things. Listen to me! Five years ago we hit rocks on the *Penelope*. Her hull was breached and she was shipping water. She rolled on the Great Green like a hog in a swamp. Her speed was gone and she almost sank. We kept her afloat and made it to port. Then she was repaired. I didn't judge her as a bad ship.

She was damaged in a storm. I judge her by how she sails when her hull is sound. You are like that ship. Your heart was breached when your mother died. And from the heart comes courage.'

The boy said nothing, but Odysseus saw that he was listening intently.

Odysseus moved away from the cliff edge and sat down on a grassy bank. 'There is no courage without fear, Aeneas. A man who rushes into battle fearlessly is not a hero. He is merely a strong man with a big sword. An act of courage requires the *overcoming* of fear.' Raising his hand, palm outwards, he instructed the boy to do likewise. Then he reached out and pressed his palm to the boy's. 'Push against my hand,' he said. Aeneas did so. Odysseus resisted the push. 'Now this is how courage and fear work, lad. Both will always be pushing. They are never still.' Dropping his hand he looked out over the sea. 'And a man cannot choose to stop pushing. For if he backs away the fear will come after him, and push him back another step, and then another. Men who give in to fear are like kings who trust in castles to keep out enemies, rather than attacking them on open ground, and scattering them. So the enemies camp round the castle, and now the king cannot get out. Slowly his food runs out, and he discovers the castle is not a very safe place to be. You built a castle in your mind. But fear seeped through gaps in the walls, and now there is nowhere else to hide. Deep down you know this, for the hero I see in you keeps telling you.'

'Perhaps there is no hero inside me. What if I am as my father tells me?'

'Oh, there is a hero, boy! You still hear his voice. Every time your father asks you to ride a horse, or do some daring thing, the hero in you longs to obey him, yearns for a smile from him, or a word of praise. Is that not so?'

The boy's head dropped forward. 'Yes,' he admitted.

'Good! That is a beginning. Now all you need to do is seek out that hero, boy, and embrace him. I can help you. For I know his name.'

'His name?'

'The hero inside you. You want to know his name, so that you can call for him?'

'Yes,' answered Aeneas, and Odysseus saw the desperation in his eyes.

'His name is Helikaon.'

The boy's face crumpled and Odysseus saw tears begin to fall. 'No-one calls me that any more,' he said. Then he angrily brushed the tears away. 'Look at me! I cry like a child!'

'Damn, boy! Everyone cries at some time. I wept for weeks when my son died. Blubbed until I had no strength left. But we are losing the breeze here. You need to find Helikaon.'

'And how do I do that?'

'Why, you sally out from the castle and scatter your fears. He will be there waiting for you.'

'Speak plainly, for there are no castles.'

Odysseus felt sympathy for the youngster, but he realized that the damage caused to him by years of abuse from his father could not be undone with a few fanciful notions. In truth, he thought, it will take years. And Odysseus did not have years to spend on a boy with a crippled heart.

Equally he could not take him on the *Penelope* and kill him – no matter what riches Anchises dangled before him.

So he had decided on one last gambit. 'If I asked you to dive from this cliff to the sea, a hundred feet or more below, you wouldn't do it, would you?'

'No,' replied Aeneas, his eyes wide with fear, even at the thought.

'Of course not. It is a long way down, and there may be hidden rocks there that would dash a man to pieces. Yet that is where Helikaon waits for you, lad. So I am going to give you a reason to make that dive.'

'Nothing will make me do that!' said Aeneas.

'Perhaps not. But I am going to jump from this cliff into the sea. I cannot swim, so if you do not come for me I will drown.'

'You cannot do this!' said Aeneas, surging to his feet as Odysseus rose.

'Of course I can. Helikaon and I will be waiting, boy.' Then, without another word, he ran to the cliff edge.

Even now, so many years later, Odysseus felt a shiver run through him at the memory. He had looked up at this ledge the night before. It had not appeared *so* high. But as he had reached it and looked down it seemed to him that the sea was an awesome distance below him. The *Penelope* suddenly appeared to be a toy ship, crewed by ant figures.

Though he would never admit it to anyone else, Odysseus was suddenly terrified.

'Please don't do it!' shouted the boy.

'Have to, lad,' answered Odysseus. 'When a man says a thing, he needs to find the nerve to follow it through.'

Taking a deep breath he flung himself out into the clear air. Cartwheeling his arms to stay upright he plunged down, the drop seeming to take for ever. Then he hit the sea with all the grace of a pig on a pond.

Rising agonizingly to the surface, his body awash with pain, his lungs on fire, Odysseus pretended to flounder, splashing his arms at the water. Glancing up he saw the youngster standing high above him. He felt foolish now. There was no way a frightened boy could make that leap, and Odysseus felt he had only made matters worse for the lad. However, he had told him he could not swim, and now felt obliged to continue the charade for a little while. Letting out his breath Odysseus sank below the surface, holding out for as long as he could. Then he came up, took several breaths – still splashing like a drowning man – and sank again. As he surfaced he looked up one last time.

And saw the sleek form of Aeneas high in the air above him, arms stretched out, his body framed against the brilliant blue of the sky. The dive was beautiful to behold – and Odysseus almost forgot his pretence. As Aeneas surfaced and swam towards him Odysseus went down again. This time a strong young arm grasped his wrist, hauling him up.

'Take a deep breath,' ordered the youngster, then dragged him back towards the *Penelope*. Ropes were thrown down and the two climbed on board.

Standing dripping on the deck, puffing and blowing, Odysseus looked round at his amused crew.

'This is Helikaon, lads,' he cried, gesturing at the youth. 'He is a prince of Dardania. He saved my life!'

The first mate, Bias – a heavily scarred, dark-skinned man with grizzled hair – clapped Helikaon on the back. 'I saw the dive. It was incredible. Well done, lad.'

Odysseus walked over to Helikaon, throwing a brawny arm round his shoulder. Then he leaned in. 'How did it feel to make that dive?'

'I feel . . .' Helikaon struggled for words. 'I don't know how I feel.'

'Exultant?' offered Odysseus.

'Yes, that is it. Exactly.'

'You scattered your enemies, Helikaon. I cannot tell you how proud I am of you. You found the path to the hero. You will never lose it again.' Swinging towards the crew he called out, 'Oarsmen to your places, and ready the sail. The Great Green awaits.'

'I don't understand,' said Helikaon.

'Ah, lad, did I not tell you? Your father thought a sea voyage would be good for you. So now you are a member of my crew. I think you will enjoy it.'

Alone now on the beach Odysseus smiled at the memory. He saw Helikaon rise to his feet and look around. Odysseus waved, and the Golden One walked over to him.

'Planning your next outrageous adventure?' Helikaon asked.

Odysseus grinned. 'I was remembering the day I watched a young prince fly like an eagle over the sea.'

VIII

Blue Owl Bay

i

XANDER FELT LIKE ONE OF THE HEROES OF LEGEND, THE MEN grandfather spoke of round the night fire before he and his sisters fell asleep. He had crossed the world to a foreign land, a place of enchantment and mystery, where there were different stars shining. And he had met the legendary Odysseus. It was like a wonderful dream.

All along the Bay of the Blue Owls Xander could see handcarts, full of dried driftwood, being hauled onto the beach. There was the smell of roasting meats, and the music of lyres and pipes could be heard round many of the fires. He saw the black-bearded Gyppto, Gershom, move away from the *Xanthos* men, and sit down with his back to a rock. He had an old piece of cloth round his shoulders, and he was shivering. Xander ran to him. 'Can I fetch you something?'

Gershom smiled. 'More water would be good. My throat feels as if I have swallowed a desert.' Xander moved off, and returned with a water skin. Gershom drank sparingly. Then he lay back on the sand and fell asleep.

Xander sat alongside him for a while as the night wore on. He stared up at the bright stars. He couldn't actually tell if they were different or not, but guessed they must be. When Gershom started to snore Xander rose from the sand and began to explore. Along the shoreline there were scores of stalls and carts, full of merchandise: jewellery, clothing, pots, jugs, protective amulets, and weapons. Elsewhere there were traders who had set out items on blankets in the sand. There were soothsayers and seers, astrologers and mystics, reading fortunes and making predictions. Everywhere Xander looked there was something exciting to see. He moved through the throng, wide-eyed and full of wonder.

He gazed for a while at a display of dazzling jewellery, earrings, bracelets and copper rings inset with coloured stones. On the next stall were pots and cups, but these were of poor quality. Not nearly as good as those mother made. He pointed this out to the stall-holder, an angry little man who swore at him. Xander danced away as the man threatened to cuff him. He was not frightened. Xander was a hero who had braved a storm, and felt no fear of a pottery man.

He paused at a clothing stall. It was a jumble of sandals, cloaks, and thigh-length chiton tunics of hard-wearing linen. Hanging lanterns illuminated the wares. Xander reached out and lifted a small sandal. 'Five copper rings they should go for,' said a round-faced woman, with missing front teeth. 'Yet I am feeling generosity tonight, for those who passed through the storm. So I thought four rings? However, I see how you look at them, little sailor, and it warms my heart. So for you I shall make them virtually a gift. A mere three copper rings.'

'I don't have any copper rings,' he said.

'No rings,' she repeated, then leaned towards him. 'But you are a pretty boy, and I know a man who would buy you those sandals if you were nice to him. Would you like to meet him?'

A giant figure moved alongside Xander. 'No, he would not,' said Zidantas. He took the sandal from Xander's hand and examined it. 'It would bind to his foot in the first rain. He might as well wear sandals made of clay.'

The woman swore at Zidantas, who laughed. 'Come away,

Xander. If you need sandals there is a stall on the far side with items of quality. But first let us eat.'

At a food stall they were each given a bowl of stew and a piece of flat-baked bread. Then Zidantas walked away to a rocky section of the beach, away from the revellers, and sat down. They ate in silence. Xander had not realized how hungry he was. Finishing the stew and the bread he rushed back to another stall, received two honey-baked pies and took one to Zidantas. The giant grinned. 'I like them well enough, but they make my teeth ache. You eat them both.'

Xander needed no further urging, and devoured them, finally licking the honey from his fingers. 'This is a wonderful place,' he said.

Zidantas brushed crumbs from his forked beard. 'Yes, it is a good bay, and the Fat King feeds sailors well.'

Xander glanced around, and saw Helikaon some distance away, chatting and laughing with sailors from another ship. 'The Golden One has many friends,' said Xander.

'Odysseus is a good friend to have,' replied Zidantas.

Xander saw soldiers in strange conical helmets and leather breastplates moving through the throng. They were carrying stout clubs.

'Is there going to be a fight?' he asked.

'There are usually one or two before the night wears out,' Zidantas told him. 'Unavoidable when you have strong drink, loose women and several hundred sailors. The soldiers will stop them soon enough. They'll crack a few skulls.'

'Will people be killed?'

Zidantas shrugged. 'I've known some who died here. Skulls of clay. Mostly there'll just be head pain and misery.'

Xander looked back at the group around Helikaon. 'Why is Odysseus a good friend to have?' he asked.

Zidantas laughed. 'Your mind flits like a butterfly, boy. You should get some sleep. It will be a long day tomorrow.'

'I am not tired, Zidantas, truly I'm not. And I don't want to miss anything.' Close by he saw a seer, examining a sailor's hand,

and heard him making predictions about the man's future wealth.

'How does he know all that?' he whispered.

'He doesn't.'

'Then why are people giving him copper rings?'

Zidantas laughed. 'Because they are idiots. Because they are gullible. Because they are sailors.'

'You are a sailor,' Xander pointed out.

'Yes, but I am an *old* sailor. And they could build palaces with the number of rings I have given to those who promised to read my future.'

'Can I ask another question?'

'You are like a ship with a cargo of questions. I have a daughter like you. Little Thea. Always wants to know answers. Where do the clouds come from? How does the rain get up into them? I come to sea to get away from that, lad.'

'Is that why you come to sea? Truly?'

Zidantas laughed. 'No, I was jesting. I miss my girls – especially Thea. Always cries when I put to sea. She'll be waiting on the beach with her mother when we sail back. She'll skip and wave, and run into the surf.' He chuckled. 'All the ages of children are wonderful to behold – but five is the best, I think. Now what was your question?'

'The sea is blue,' said Xander. 'So why is it called the Great Green?'

'Now *that* is a question every sailor asks when he first puts to sea. I asked it many times myself, and was given many answers. When Poseidon became God of the Sea he changed its colour because he preferred blue. Others say that out where the sea is deep, and no ships sail, it shines like an emerald. A Gyppto merchant once told me the Great Green referred originally to a massive river in their lands. The Nile. It floods every year, ripping away vegetation. This is what turns it green. He said that when men first sailed upon it they called it the Great Green, and the name came to mean all the water of the earth. The answer is that I don't know. I like the sound of it, though. There is a majesty to it, don't you think?'

'Yes,' agreed Xander. 'It is a wonderful name.'

Zidantas' smile faded, and Xander saw him looking at a group of six men some distance away. They were standing together, and staring towards where Helikaon sat with Odysseus and his crew. The newcomers were clustered around a tall, broad-shouldered warrior. He looked a little like Argurios, with a jutting chin beard and no moustache. But this man's beard and hair seemed almost white in the moonlight. As Xander watched he saw the white-haired young warrior shake his head, then move away with his men. Beside the boy Zidantas relaxed.

'Who were they?' asked Xander.

'Mykene traders. Well, that's what they call themselves. They are raiders, lad. Pirates.'

The curly-haired oarsman, Oniacus, moved across to where they sat. He smiled at Xander and ruffled his hair, then squatted down alongside Zidantas. 'Kolanos is here,' he said.

'I know. We saw him.'

'Should I send some men back on board to fetch weapons?'

'No. I doubt Kolanos will want trouble in the Fat King's bay.'

'The Golden One should sleep on the *Xanthos* tonight,' said Oniacus. 'Kolanos may not seek an open fight, but rely instead on a dagger in the dark. Have you warned Helikaon?'

'No need,' said Zidantas. 'He will have seen them. And I will keep watch against assassins. Stay alert, though, Oniacus. And warn a few of the tougher men. Keep it from the others.'

Zidantas rose and stretched, then he wandered off. Oniacus grinned at the now nervous Xander.

'Don't worry, little man. Zidantas knows what he's doing.'

'Are those men our enemies?' asked Xander fearfully.

'In truth they are everyone's enemies. They live for plunder. They rob, they steal, they kill. Then they brag about their courage and their bravery and their honour. But then the Mykene are a strange race.'

'Argurios is a Mykene – and he saved my life,' said Xander.

'As I said, boy, they are a strange people. But that was a brave deed. You can't say they lack courage. Everything else, charity, compassion, pity, but not courage.'

'Courage is important, though,' said Xander. 'Everyone says so.'

'Of course it is,' agreed Oniacus. 'But there are different kinds. The Mykene live for combat and the glory of war. I grieve for them. War is the enemy of civilization. We cannot grow through war, Xander. It drags us down, filling our hearts with hatred and thoughts of revenge.' He sighed. 'Trade is the key. Every race has something to offer, and something they need to buy. And, as we trade, we learn new skills from one another. Wait until you see Troy, then I'll show you what I mean. Stonemasons from Egypte helped craft the great walls and the towers, and the statues at the Scaean Gate; carpenters from Phrygia and Nysia fashioned the temple to Hermes, the God of Travellers. Goldsmiths from Troy travelled to Egypte and taught other craftsmen how to create wondrous jewellery. And as the trade increased so did the exchange of knowledge. Now we can build higher walls, stronger buildings, dig deeper wells, weave brighter cloths. We can irrigate fields and grow more crops to feed the hungry. All from trade. But war? There is nothing to be said for it, boy.'

'But war makes heroes,' argued Xander. 'Herakles and Ormenion were warriors, and they have been made immortal. Father Zeus turned them into stars in the night sky.'

Oniacus scowled. 'In a drunken rage Herakles clubbed his wife to death, and Ormenion sacrificed his youngest daughter in order that Poseidon might grant fair winds for his attack on Kretos.'

'I'm sorry, Oniacus. I didn't mean to make you angry.'

'You are just young, Xander. And I am not angry with you. I hope you never see what war makes men do. I hope that the current peace lasts all your lifetime. Because then we will see great things. All around the Great Green will be happy people, content and safe, raising families.' Then he sighed again. 'But not while killers like Kolanos sail the waters. Not while kings like Agamemnon rule. And certainly not while youngsters admire butchers like Herakles or Ormenion.' He glanced back at the crowd around Helikaon. 'I am going to have a word with a few of the lads. Don't you say anything to anyone.'

With that Oniacus ruffled the boy's hair again and moved off towards the *Xanthos'* crew.

Xander sighed. He didn't want to be a hero now. There were evil men on this beach, murderers who used daggers in the dark. Rising to his feet he followed Oniacus, and sat down alongside some of the crew. They were chatting and laughing. Xander looked at them. They were big men and strong, and he felt more confident in their company. Xander stretched himself out on the sand, his head resting on his arm. He fell asleep almost instantly.

ii

Had it not been for the two years she had spent on the isle of Thera, the flame-haired Andromache might have had no real understanding of just how boring life could be. She pondered this as she stood on the balcony of the pitiful royal palace overlooking the Bay of Blue Owls. She could not recall being bored as a child, playing in the gardens of her father's fine palace in Thebe Under Plakos, or running in the pastures, in the shadows of the hills. Life then had seemed carefree.

Puberty had put paid to such simple pleasures, and she had been confined to the women's quarters of the palace, behind high walls, under the stern gaze of elderly matrons. At first she had railed against the oppressive atmosphere, but she had succumbed, at last, to the languorous lack of pace, and the calm, almost serene, surroundings. Her three younger sisters eventually joined her there. Prettier than she, they had been dangled before prospective suitors, in order to become breeding cows for princes of neighbouring realms; items to be traded for treaties or alliances. Andromache herself, tall and forbidding, her piercing green eyes – intimidating, according to her father – extinguishing any possible fire in the heart of a would-be husband, had been presented for service of another kind. Two years ago, when she was eighteen, father had sent her to become a priestess on Thera.

It was not an act of piety. The temple required virgins of royal blood to perform the necessary rites, and kings received golden gifts for despatching daughters to serve there. Andromache had been 'sold' for two talents of silver. Not as much as father had received for the two daughters married into the Hittite royal line, and considerably less than the sum promised for the youngest sister, golden-haired Paleste, upon her wedding to the Trojan hero, Hektor.

Still, father had been pleased that this plain girl with the cold green eyes had proved of some service to the kingdom. Andromache recalled well the night he had told her of her fate. He had called her into his private chambers, and they had sat together on a gilded couch. Father had been out hunting that day, and he stank of horse sweat, and there was dried blood upon his hands. Never an attractive man – even when bathed and dressed in finery – Ektion looked more like a goatherd than a king on this occasion. His clothes were travel-stained, his weak chin unshaved, his eyes red-rimmed from weariness. 'You will travel to Thera, and train as a priestess of the Minotaur,' said Ektion. 'I know this task will be arduous, but you are a strong girl.' She had sat silently, staring at the ugly man. The silence caused his temper to flare. 'You only have yourself to blame. Many men prefer plain women. But you made no effort to please any of the suitors I found for you. Not a smile, not a word of encouragement.'

'You found dull men,' she said.

'From good families.'

'Well, father, no doubt you will grow rich anyway, selling my sisters.'

'Now that is what I mean!' Ektion stormed. 'Everything sounds ugly when it comes from your mouth. Your sisters will find joy in their children and the wealth of their husbands. Little Paleste is already betrothed to Hektor. She will live in the golden city of Troy, wed to their greatest hero. He will adore her, and she will be happy.'

'Which was, of course, your prime concern, father,' she said, her voice gentle. He stared hard at her. 'What will I do on Thera?' she asked.

'Do? I don't know what the women do there. Placate the angry god. Make sacrifices. Sing, for all I know! There are no men there.' She heard the malice in that last sentence.

'Well, that will be a blessing,' she said. 'I am already looking forward to it.'

It was not true, but she enjoyed the look of anger that flashed from father's eyes.

Her heart had been heavy the day the trade ship anchored in the circular bay of Thera. A life of dull banishment was about to begin.

But Andromache could not have been more wrong. Within days her life had expanded beyond measure. She learned to shoot a bow, to ride half-wild ponies, to dance in the revels of Artemis, drunk and full of joy. In short, to express herself without fear of complaint or censure. Without the restrictions of a male-dominated society, the women of Thera revelled in their freedom. Each day there was some new entertainment, foot races or archery tournaments. There were treasure hunts and swimming competitions, and in the evenings discussions on poetry, or storytelling. Every few weeks there was a feast offering tributes to one of the many gods, where strong wine was drunk, and the women danced and sang, and made love.

The priestesses of Thera also maintained the Temple of the Horse, conducting ceremonies of sacrifice to the dread Minotaur, seeking to soothe his troubled soul. Their work was vital. Two centuries ago he had burst his chains, and hot lava had spewed from the earth. The top of the mountain exploded, and Apollo, god of the sun, was so distressed that the world remained dark for three days. Poseidon also, in his anger at the Kretans, who were charged with appeasing the Minotaur, sent a tidal wave across the Great Green, destroying the olive orchards and the wine harvests of Kretos, laying salt upon the earth to prevent any new growth. At the time Kretos was a great power, but the Kretans were humbled by this savage display of godly rage.

Now two hundred priestesses kept the Minotaur subdued – though he still occasionally wrenched at his chains, causing the earth to tremble. On one occasion the western wall of the long dining room had split, shattering the mural upon it.

Despite these occasional crises Andromache enjoyed her two years of freedom. Then, one day in midsummer came dreadful news. Her sister Paleste – the sweetest of girls, with a smile to melt the coldest heart – had caught a chill, which turned into a fever. She had died within days of falling ill. Andromache could scarcely believe it. Of all the sisters Paleste had been the strongest and most vibrant. She had been pledged to wed the Trojan prince, Hektor, in the autumn, to secure an alliance between Thebe and Troy. Graciously – father wrote – the Trojan king, Priam, had agreed that Andromache could replace Paleste and marry Hektor.

Thus, at twenty, and set for a life without men, Andromache had been forced to leave Thera, and her beloved companions, and journey to Troy to wed a man she had never seen.

No more would she ride bareback over the Theran hills, or dance and sing in the Dionysian revels. No more would she draw bow to cheek and watch the shaft fly straight and true, or swim naked in the midnight seas around the bay. No more would she feel Kalliope's passionate embrace, or taste the wine upon her lover's lips.

Andromache felt anger rise, and welcomed it, for it briefly extinguished the boredom. In Troy she would become a breeding cow, and lie on a wide bed, legs spread to receive the seed of a grunting, sweaty man. She would swell like a pig, then scream as the infant clawed its way out of her. And why? So that her father's greed could be satisfied.

No, she thought, not just his greed. In this violent and uncertain world a nation needed allies. The Egypteian pharaohs constantly waged war on the Hittite peoples, and the Mykene raided wherever they perceived weakness. Her father was greedy, but without treaties and alliances his lands would be devoured by one of the great powers. Little Thebe Under Plakos would be safer under the protection of Troy and its fabled cavalry.

She gazed down on the beach, seeing the fires lit, and hearing the faint swell of music on the dusk breeze. Down there was a freedom she would never again experience. Ordinary people living ordinary lives, laughing, joking, loving.

A thought came. Delicious and tempting. Soon the ship would arrive to take her to Troy. Until then she was – if matters were handled with care – still free. Moving across the small apartment she took her hooded cloak of dark green wool and swung it round her shoulders. It complemented her gold-embroidered, olive-green gown. Tying her red hair back from her face with a strip of leather she walked from her room and along the silent corridor beyond, then slipped down an outside stairwell to a walled garden. There was a guard at the gate. He bowed when he saw her, pulling the gate open as she passed.

There was a breeze blowing over the cliffs as Andromache made her way to the main gate, and the steep road leading to the beach. Two more guards saw her. They did not know her, and neglected to bow, merely standing aside as she walked out onto the road.

How easy it was, she thought. But then who would have imagined that a king's daughter, and a priestess of Thera, would have any desire to leave the safety of the palace and walk among the hard and violent men of the sea.

It was a sobering thought. There was no bodyguard to protect her, and she carried no weapon. The thought of danger did not make her pause. Instead it quickened her heart.

The music grew louder as she approached, and she saw men and women dancing together drunkenly. Off to one side people were fornicating. She gazed down at the closest couple. The man's buttocks were pounding up and down, and she could see the thick shaft of his penis spearing into the girl he was riding. Andromache looked at her. Their eyes met. The girl grinned and raised her eyebrows. Then she winked at Andromache, who smiled back at her and walked on.

Moving through the packed stalls she saw that they were mostly covered with cheap and ill-made items. A man approached her, lifting his tunic and waggling his manhood at her. 'How much for a ride, girl?' he asked. Andromache stared hard at the stiffening penis, then transferred her green gaze to the man.

'The last time I saw something that small it was crawling out of an apple,' she said. Peals of laughter came from two women close by.

'It's getting even smaller now!' one of them called.

Andromache walked on, easing her way through the throng. Some distance away a crowd was gathering round a man standing on an empty stall. Great cheers went up as he raised his arms.

'Want to hear a true story?' he bellowed.

'No, we want to hear one of yours,' yelled someone in the crowd. The man's laughter boomed out.

'Then I'll tell you of a dread monster, with only one eye. Tall as ten men, and teeth sharp and long as swords.'

And the crowd fell silent.

iii

Helikaon always enjoyed the performances Odysseus gave. He did not just recount tall tales, but acted them too. As now, with four men lifting the wooden stall, heaving it back and forth to represent a tilting deck. Balanced upon it, Odysseus roared out a tale of a mighty storm that carried the *Penelope* to an enchanted isle. In the background some of the *Penelope*'s crew banged drums to imitate thunder, while others whistled shrilly at intervals. Helikaon had not heard this story before, and settled back to enjoy the surprises. Odysseus suddenly leapt from the stall. 'And we were upon a strange beach,' he said, 'and just beyond it the tallest trees I ever saw, twisted and gnarled. Just when we thought we were safe there came a terrifying voice.'

From the back of the crowd six of the *Penelope*'s crew all cried out in unison: 'I smell blood!' A flicker of enjoyable panic swept through the throng. The timing had been perfect.

' 'Twas a massive creature, with a single eye in the centre of its head. Its teeth were long and sharp. It ran from the trees and

111

caught one of my men by the waist, hauling him high. Then those terrible teeth ripped him apart.'

At that moment Helikaon saw several of Kolanos' crew working their way through the throng, moving ever closer to him. His eyes scanned the crowd, and he picked out Zidantas, Oniacus and several of the *Xanthos*' men, also manoeuvring their way towards him, while keeping wary eyes on the Mykene.

Odysseus was in full voice now, recounting the adventure with the Cyclops. Sweat gleamed on his face, and dripped from his beard. The audience was entranced, the performance – as always – boisterous, energetic and captivating.

Helikaon looked around. None of the Fat King's soldiers were close by. The Mykene were apparently unarmed, but one of them was wearing a jerkin of leather, which could conceal a knife. The chances were the Mykene would do nothing. The Fat King was merciless with any who broke his laws. Much of his wealth came from the ships that beached upon his bays, and the main reason they chose to stay was the reciprocal guarantee of safety for their crews and cargoes.

Even so it made sense to be cautious. Helikaon eased his way back into the audience, then cut to the left, seeking to circle the crowd and link with Zidantas.

Then he saw the woman.

She was standing just back from the gathering, dressed in a long cloak of green and an embroidered gown. It was difficult by fire and moonlight to see the colour of her hair, but it was long, thickly curled, and drawn back from her face. And such a face! She looked like a goddess. Not pretty, but awesomely beautiful. Helikaon's mouth was dry. He could not stop looking at her. She saw him, and he felt the power of her eyes. The look was cool, and yet strangely challenging. He swallowed hard, and stepped towards her. In that moment her expression changed, her eyes flickering beyond him. Helikaon spun. The man with the leather jerkin was behind him, a knife in his hand. The assassin darted forward. Swaying aside from the thrusting blade, Helikaon grabbed the attacker's wrist, pulling him away from the crowd, then stepped in and smashed a head butt to the man's nose. Stunned, blood pouring from his nostrils, the assassin fell back. Helikaon followed in, butting him again. The assassin's knees gave way and he dropped to the sand, the knife slipping from his fingers. Helikaon swept it up, plunging the sharp blade into the man's throat, then ripping it clear. Blood spurted through the air.

With Odysseus' tale still captivating the audience, no-one in the crowd had seen the brief exchange. The body lay, blood gushing at first, then pumping more slowly as the man died. Rising to his feet Helikaon looked around for further attackers, but it was Zidantas who emerged from the crowd.

'I am sorry,' he said, looking crestfallen. 'I should have been by your side. They played it neatly, though. We were watching the wrong men.'

Helikaon stood silently, looking down at the dead man. The man was young, his hair curly and dark. Somewhere there would be a wife, or a lover, and parents who had nurtured him. He had played games with other children, and had dreamed of a future bright with promise. Now he lay here on the sand, his life ended. Helikaon's thoughts were bleak.

'Are you all right?' asked Zidantas.

Helikaon turned back to where the woman had been standing. But she was gone. He shivered. Then the familiar post-battle head pain began, a throbbing ache emanating from the back of his neck and spreading up over the crown of his head. He realized Ox was looking at him, an expression of concern on his face.

'I am fine, Ox.'

Zidantas looked unconvinced. Oniacus pushed through the crowd to join them.

'The Mykene have returned to their galleys,' he said. Then he saw the dead man and swore. 'I am sorry, lord, I should have been here. They fooled us by—'

'I have already explained,' snapped Zidantas. 'Still, no harm done. One less Mykene in the world. All in all a good night.'

Thunderous cheering broke out as Odysseus finished his tale. Oniacus swore. 'I missed the ending,' he complained.

113

'So did he,' said Helikaon, pointing to the corpse. 'Let us move away.' Tossing the dagger alongside the body he walked back to the *Xanthos* campfire. Behind them someone shouted, and a crowd gathered round the corpse. Helikaon picked up a water jug and drank deeply. Then he poured water over his hands, washing the blood clear. In the firelight he saw that more blood had spattered over his tunic.

Odysseus wandered over to the fire. He was carrying a linen cloth, and wiping sweat from his face. He slumped down alongside Helikaon.

'I am getting too old for these athletic performances,' he said. 'I need to have a strong word with those sheepshaggers who held the stall. Damned if they weren't trying to toss me onto the beach.'

He did look tired. Helikaon threw his arm round the older man's shoulder. 'There will be gloom over the whole world if you ever stop telling your tales.'

'Aye, it was a good audience tonight. I used to tell that story with two Cyclops. Strange how one works better. More . . . more terrifying, and yet, somehow, pathetic.' He leaned in close to Helikaon. 'I take it the dead man was one of Kolanos' crew?'

'Yes.'

'Never liked Kolanos. Was at a feast with him one time. Never heard him fart at all. Can't trust a man who doesn't fart at a feast.' Helikaon laughed aloud. 'Don't treat him lightly, though, lad,' Odysseus continued. 'He is a man of great malice. Back in Mykene he is known as the Breaker of Spirits.'

'I will be wary, my friend. Tell me, while you were performing did you happen to see a tall woman in a green cloak? Looked like a goddess?'

'As a matter of fact, I did. Standing off to my right. Why? Did she rob you?'

'I think she did. She stole my wits.'

Odysseus leaned forward, took the water jug and drank deeply. Then he laid it down and belched loudly. 'Men should always be careful when choosing women. Or we should follow the Gypptos and have a score or two. Then one or two bad ones could pass unnoticed.'

'I think Penelope would be interested to hear you voice that opinion.'

Odysseus chuckled. 'Aye, she would. She'd cuff me round the head. But then I was lucky, lad. There is no woman on this green earth better than my Penelope. I couldn't imagine sharing my life with anyone else. You might find that with Kreusa.'

Helikaon looked at his friend. 'Not you too? Is there no-one who hasn't heard about Priam's matchmaking?'

'I heard you refused her. And that Priam is none too happy with you, lad.'

'His unhappiness concerns me not at all. And as for Kreusa . . . I recall you struggling to find something pleasant to say about her. What was it in the end? Ah yes. "She has a nice speaking voice."'

'Well, she does,' said Odysseus, with a wide smile. 'She is also wonderful to look upon. Dazzling, in fact. And she's not weak. However, I take your point. Not a woman I'd risk a storm to sail home to. Ah well, you should marry her, then build yourself a few more palaces around the Great Green, and set convivial wives in each of them. Gyppto women are said to be the best. You could build a great palace. Labour is cheap. You buy slaves by the hundred, I'm told.'

Helikaon shook his head. 'I want no more palaces, Odysseus.' He rubbed at his eyes as the headache worsened.

'A shame Phaedra wasn't a king's daughter,' continued Odysseus. 'Now *there's* a woman to gladden any man's heart.'

'She has many virtues.'

'But you are not in love with her?'

Helikaon shrugged. 'I am not truly sure what that means, my friend. How does one tell?'

Odysseus draped the towel over his shoulders and stretched his back. 'You remember practising with wooden swords? All the moves, the blocks, the counters, getting your footwork right, learning how to be in balance always?'

'Of course. You were a hard master.'

'And you recall the first time you went into a real fight, with blood being shed and the fear of death in the air?'

'I do.'

'The moves are the same, but the difference is wider than the Great Green. Love is like that, Helikaon. You can spend time with a whore, and laugh and know great pleasure. But when love strikes – ah, the difference is awesome. You will find more joy in the touch of a hand, or the sight of a smile, than you could ever experience in a hundred nights of passion with anyone else. The sky will be more blue, the sun more bright. Ah, I am missing my Penelope tonight.'

'The season is almost over, and you'll be home for the winter.'

'Aye, I am looking forward to that.' Lifting a water jug Odysseus drank deeply.

'Diomedes asked to be remembered to you,' said Helikaon. 'He is hoping you will let him sail with you when he is older.'

Odysseus chuckled. 'He's a fine, brave little lad. How old is he now?'

'Twelve soon – and not so little. He will be a fine king one day, if the gods will it. I feared he might be like my father, cold and unfeeling. Thankfully he has his mother's spirit.'

'You surprised me that day, Helikaon,' said Odysseus. 'But it was a good surprise, and one that did you credit.'

Before Helikaon could respond several soldiers in conical helmets and bronze breastplates approached the fire. The first bowed low. 'My lord Helikaon, the king requests you to join him.'

Helikaon rose. 'Tell him it is an honour to be invited. I will be there as soon as I have returned to my ship and donned garments suitable for a king's palace.'

The soldiers bowed again, and departed. Odysseus pushed himself to his feet. 'Take Argurios and his companion with you,' he said. 'I am sure they would wish to meet the king.'

'I do not feel like the company of Mykene, Odysseus.'

'Then do it for your old mentor.'

Helikaon sighed. 'For you I would walk into Hades. Very well. I shall spend the evening being bored by them. But do something for me, would you?'

'Of course, lad.'

'See if you can find that goddess. I would like to meet her.'

'She's probably a Lykian whore who'll give you the pox.'

'Find her anyway. I should be back before dawn.'

'Good. I shall enjoy standing in line to speak to her as she ruts with my sailors.'

IX

Andromache's Prophecy

i

ODYSSEUS WATCHED HELIKAON WALK BACK TO THE *XANTHOS*. THE giant Zidantas went with him, keeping a wary eye out for more Mykene assassins. Helikaon grasped a trailing rope and drew himself up onto the ship.

There will be more violence tonight, Odysseus thought.

The idea that Helikaon might be killed caused him to shiver. He had come to love the boy during his two years on the *Penelope*. The first few weeks had been difficult. Odysseus had no moral qualms about killing for profit. He had, in his time, been a raider and a plunderer. But the thought of murdering the young prince was abhorrent to him. Instead he had watched the boy with an increasingly paternal eye, revelling in the lad's new-found freedom, and feeling pride as the youngster steadily overcame his fears. Day by day he had stared them down. Climbing the mast in high winds to help draw up the sail, his face grey, his terror palpable; standing defiantly, sword in hand, as the pirate ship closed and the raiders leapt over the side, screaming their battle cries. Then hurling himself into the fray when every instinct screamed at him to run below and hide. Most of all, though, it was the rowing that won the hearts of the crew. The skin of Helikaon's hands was soft, and whenever he took his turn at the oars his palms would bleed. He never complained, merely bound the torn flesh and rowed on. Odysseus had convinced himself that the boy's father would put aside all thoughts of murder, once he saw the fine young man he was becoming.

Until the day the assassin Karpophorus took passage on the *Penelope*.

Now there were more assassins waiting. Odysseus gazed again at the high cliff road. Should he have been more direct with his warning? Should he have mentioned the blood price Agamemnon had placed on Helikaon's head?

The answer was no. Odysseus was a man without enemies, and that was rare in these harsh and bloody times. He never openly took sides, remaining neutral, and therefore welcome in any port. It was not always easy. When Alektruon had told him he was hunting down the Golden One, Odysseus had been sorely tempted to send a warning. Yet he had not. Happily it had all turned out well. Alektruon was dead, which was no loss to the world, and Odysseus had won a splendid blue cloak at his funeral games, outshooting Meriones with the bow. But now Helikaon dead was worth twice a man's weight in gold. There were kings who would sell him out for less than that.

After a while he saw Helikaon climbing down from the great ship. He was wearing a dark blue knee-length tunic, and a short sword was scabbarded at his waist. Zidantas was carrying an enormous club. Odysseus smiled. Ah, he understood then, he thought, with relief. Helikaon and Zidantas moved off towards where Argurios and Glaukos were sitting by the *Xanthos* fire. Odysseus watched as the two Mykene rose and accompanied Helikaon. Both were wearing their armour, swords sheathed at their sides.

A young man, with long golden hair, moved across Odysseus' line of vision. A pretty woman was holding his hand and smiling up at him. Suddenly he swept his arm round the girl's waist and drew her to him. She laughed and tilted her head back, accepting his kiss. Odysseus smiled.

As a child he had dreamed of being handsome and graceful like that boy, with the kind of looks men envied and women grew giddy to gaze upon. Instead he was stout and stocky, with too much body hair. It now grew in reddish tufts even on his shoulders.

No, the gods, in their infinite wisdom, had decided Odysseus would be ugly. There must have been great planning involved in the scheme, he decided, for they had accomplished their task with genius. His arms were too long, his hands too gnarled, his legs as bandy as a Thessalian pony rider's. Even his teeth were crooked. And Penelope had laughingly pointed out once that one of his ears was bigger than the other. Having created such a mismatch, at least one of the gods had taken pity on him. For he had been blessed with a gift for storytelling. He could spin a tale of dazzling complexity, and read an audience as well as, if not better than, he could perceive the subtle shifting of the trade winds. Wherever he beached his ship crowds would gather, and sit around waiting for the moment when he deigned to perform. Sometimes he would tell them he was tired, or claim that they knew all his tales now anyway. Then they would clamour and beg. At last he would sigh, and the performance would begin.

There was a magic to the stories. Odysseus was aware of it, though why the enchantment worked was beyond his understanding. They were fictions, and yet they led to truths. His second in command, Bias, had strutted like a peacock after Odysseus told a crowd that he had hurled the javelin that broke the wing of a demon pursuing their ship. After that Bias spent much of his spare time on land practising with the javelin. He became so proficient that he won a slave woman in the funeral games held for Alektruon.

Last summer, when the *Penelope* had been attacked by pirates, the crew had fought like heroes in an effort to live up to the stories Odysseus told of them. After the victory they had gathered round him, bragging of their courage, and anxious that he should include this latest adventure in his next performance.

But the magic of what Odysseus called the 'golden lie' had worked best with Helikaon. He had joined the *Penelope*'s crew as a frightened youth. The men, however, reacted to him as the young hero who had dived from a cliff to rescue their leader. They loved him and expected great deeds from him. He in turn supplied those deeds, living up to their expectations. The great fiction became the great truth. The lie of courage became the reality of heroism. Helikaon, the ship's mascot, became Helikaon the adventurer. The frightened boy became the fearless man.

Odysseus lay back on the sand, staring up at the stars. The gifts he received for storytelling had begun to exceed the amount he earned from trading on the Great Green. Last year, at the court of Agamemnon, in the Lion's Hall, he had spun a great epic tale of a mysterious island, ruled by a Witch Queen who turned his men into pigs. He had made that story last throughout a full evening, and not one listener had left the hall. Afterwards Agamemnon gave him two golden cups, inset with emeralds and rubies. The same night Agamemnon had stabbed to death a drunken Mykene nobleman who doubted him.

How curious, he thought, that a man who told huge lies would be paid in gold and gems while another who offered the truth would receive a dagger through his eye.

After a performance he was always unable to sleep, despite the heavy weariness that sat upon him like a bear. He rolled to his side, then sat up. Eventually he walked down to the water's edge, and squatted down to sculpt a face in the wet sand. As always he tried to capture the beauty of his wife, Penelope. As always he failed. He used the flat of his dagger to mould the features, the long, straight nose and the full lips, then the point of the blade to create the impression of hair. Suddenly a long black worm pushed up through the sculpture. Odysseus leapt back. The lugworm slithered across the face in the sand, then burrowed deep once more.

Odysseus laughed at himself for being so startled by a harmless sea worm.

Then a story began to form in his mind. A woman with snakes for hair, living on a secret isle, shrouded in mist. The *Penelope* would have stopped at the isle, seeking fresh water. One of the crew would go missing. The others would hunt for him. They would find only his bones . . . No! I've done that too often, he thought. They would discover . . . He had been turned into a statue. He had gazed upon the face of the snake-haired woman and his flesh had become stone. Odysseus smiled.

He glanced up the steep mountain trail. 'Be lucky, boy!' he whispered.

ii

When the fight began Andromache had turned swiftly from the violence and walked away through the deserted stalls. Once hidden she had glanced back to see one man dead, the other standing over him, a bloody knife in his hand. She was shocked, though not as shocked as she might have been had she not seen men die before. Father had a habit of killing criminals personally, having them dragged into the royal courtyard and forced to kneel before him. Then he would try out the various weapons in his armoury. The axe was a favourite. Father bragged he could hew the head from a man in a single stroke. He never had while Andromache was forced to watch. Usually two blows were necessary. As a child she had wondered why the victims never struggled when they were brought forward. Some begged, others wept, but she could recall no-one who sought to run.

At least what she had just witnessed here tonight had been a fight. An assassin had tried to commit murder, and had died. Andromache shivered. At first the man with the long dark hair had seemed more of a poet or a bard than a warrior. She could still picture his eyes. They were bright blue and beautiful. Yet he had proved to be as savage as any Mykene reaver, making no attempt to subdue his attacker, merely ripping his life away. But those eyes . . .

Think of something else, you stupid girl, she chided herself.

She wandered among the stalls. A mangy dog growled at her. Andromache snapped her fingers at it, and it ran away for a few steps, then stared back malevolently. She cut to the right, heading down through the rocks to sit by the sea's edge. Removing her sandals, she dipped her feet into the water, then stared out over the dark sea. Loneliness closed in on her, and she longed to be able to climb aboard a ship and say to the master: 'Take me to Thera. Take me home.'

Had she been marrying anyone but Hektor she would have been welcomed back to the temple with open arms. They would have applauded her courage, and made jokes about the stupidity of men. However, Hektor was the son of Hekabe, queen of Troy, the single largest benefactor of the Temple of the Horse. Under no circumstances would the sisterhood do anything to cause offence to such a great power. No, they would greet Andromache warmly, then place her on the next ship for the eastern mainland, probably under guard. She thought then of Kalliope, picturing her not at their tearful farewell, but at the Feast of Demeter the previous autumn. She had danced under the stars, her naked body glistening in the firelight. Tall and strong and fearless. *She* would not suffer them to send Andromache to a loveless marriage.

Which was another reason Andromache could not go back. Of all the women on Thera Kalliope was the most content there. Her loathing of men meant the island was the one place in all the world where she could be at peace; where her laughter could ring out and her soul soar free. Andromache's return, and the consequent turmoil, could lead to Kalliope's expulsion from Thera.

A cool wind blew over the sea, and Andromache gathered her cloak about her. Time drifted by. She knew she should return to Kygones', the Fat King's, palace, but she was loth to forsake the freedom the beach offered.

'You do not belong here,' said a man's voice. She glanced round, an angry retort on her lips. Then she saw it was the storyteller. In the moonlight his ugliness seemed almost otherworldly. She could imagine Dionysian horns sprouting from his head.

'Where do I belong?' she countered.

'Why, in one of my tales, of course. My friend was right. You do look like a goddess. You're not, are you?' He sat down on a nearby rock. The moon was full now, and she saw that his face, while ugly, had a boyish charm. 'I am Odysseus,' he said. 'And you haven't answered my question.'

'Yes, I am a goddess,' she told him. 'I'll leave you to guess which one.'

'Artemis the Huntress.'

'Not Aphrodite then? How disappointing.'

'I don't know much about how the gods *really* look,' he admitted, 'but I think the Goddess of Love would have bigger tits. And her eyes would be warm and beguiling. No, I think Artemis suits you. Tell me you can shoot a bow.'

Andromache laughed. 'I can shoot a bow.'

'I knew it! One of those flimsy Egypteian pieces, or a real Phrygian bow, of horn and wood and leather?'

Andromache smiled. 'On Thera we had both, and, yes, I preferred the Phrygian.'

'I have a bow no-one else can string,' he told her. 'It makes me laugh to see strong men grow red in the face trying. It is a powerful weapon. I once shot an arrow into the moon. It had a rope attached and I used it to draw my ship from the beach.'

'That was a long rope,' she observed.

Odysseus laughed. 'I like you, lass. Where are you really from, and what are you doing here, walking among whores and sailors?'

'How do you know I am not a whore?'

'If you were a whore you still wouldn't be here, for there's not a man could afford you. Well, save Helikaon perhaps. So what are you?'

'How would you define a whore?' she countered.

'Ah, a game. I love to play games. Very well . . . what is a whore? A woman gifted with the talent to make a hard man soft; a priestess of Aphrodite, the delight of sailors who miss their wives and their homes.'

'It is not a game,' said Andromache sharply. 'A whore is a woman who offers her body to a man she doesn't love for copper, trinkets or gifts. Not so?'

'I prefer my version, but then I am romantically inclined. However, yes, both definitions are sound,' he agreed.

'Then I am a whore, for my body is being offered to a man I do not love for riches and security,' she said.

'Ah,' cried Odysseus. 'You should have asked what is the difference between a king's daughter and a whore. I would have answered: "The price." So who is the lucky fellow?'

Andromache stared into his ugly face and considered telling him to be on his way. Yet there was something comfortable about his company, and she felt at ease with him. 'Hektor of Troy,' she said at last, and saw his eyes widen.

'You could do worse. A good man is Hektor.'

'By which you mean he drinks wine until he falls over, belches at table, and rushes off to fight wars and gain glory. May the gods save us all from *good* men. Are you married, Odysseus?'

'I am indeed. I am also the most fortunate man on the Great Green, for my wife is Penelope. And she loves me.' He chuckled. 'Whenever I say that I am filled with wonder. I find it incomprehensible that she should.'

'Then you are, as you say, fortunate. But then I expect sailors only marry for love. It makes them far richer than kings.'

'Well, yes, I suppose it does. I should point out, though, that I *am* a king.'

'Who shoots arrows into the moon?' she said, smiling.

'I know I don't *look* like a king, but I truly am. My kingdom is the isle of Ithaka, and Penelope is my queen. And before you ask, no, we did not marry for love. My father arranged the match. We only met on our wedding day.'

'And you fell in love the moment your eyes met, I suppose?'

'No. I think she loathed me on sight. Not hard to see why. The first few months were . . . shall we say scratchy? Then I fell ill with a fever. Almost died. She nursed me. Said I talked in my delirium. She never told me what I said, but somehow, after that, things were different. We started to laugh together, then take long walks along the cliffs. One day . . .' he shrugged. 'One day we just realized we loved one another.'

Andromache gazed at the ugly man, seeing him anew. There was a touching honesty behind the tall tales, and a charm that slipped almost unnoticed past her defences. 'You saw the attack on Helikaon?' he said suddenly.

For a moment she did not know what he meant, then remembered the knifeman rushing forward. 'The fight, yes. Helikaon is the man with the long black hair?'

'He is a close friend of Hektor. He could tell you far more about him than I could.'

'Why did the assassin want him dead?'

Odysseus shrugged. 'Too pleasant a night to spend telling boring stories about traders and pirates and old grudges. Ask me something else.'

'Was Helikaon the friend who said I looked like a goddess?'

'Yes. Never seen him so smitten. Having met you, of course, I can understand it.'

She leaned towards him. 'Let us not play this game any longer, Odysseus. I know what I am. Tall and plain, and a breeding cow for a Trojan prince. I need no false flattery.'

'And I offer none. You are not pretty, it is true. But, for what my opinion is worth, I agree with Helikaon. You are beautiful.'

'He said that?'

'He said you were a goddess. I am just adding a little colour to the mural.' She noticed he kept glancing back up towards the cliff path.

'Am I boring you, king of Ithaka?'

He chuckled and looked embarrassed. 'No, not at all. It is just . . . I am waiting for Helikaon to return.'

'You think there will be another attempt on his life?'

'Oh, almost certainly.' She saw him take a deep breath, and then relax. Following his gaze she looked up to see a group of men carrying a body down the path. 'They didn't succeed, though,' he said happily.

'Is he your son . . . or your lover?' she asked.

'My son died,' he said. 'And, no, Helikaon is not my lover. My tastes have never strayed in that direction. Which, when I was young, annoyed me. I felt I was missing something vital that all my friends enjoyed. No, I think of Helikaon almost as a son. Or perhaps as a younger version of the man I would like to have been. If that makes any sense.'

'You would like to have been handsome?'

'Indeed! Like a young god!'

'And would Penelope have loved you any more?'

He sighed. 'You are a shrewd woman. Will you tell me your name?'

'Andromache of Thebe.'

'Ah! I know your father, Ektion. Can't say that I like him much.'

Andromache's laughter pealed out. 'No-one likes father. There is nothing in his life of worth – except that which can be traded for silver.'

'You'll meet a lot of men like him. Your new father, King Priam, is such a man. Don't you find it odd that such men can sire wonderful children? Hektor is generous and brave. Young Paris is gentle and studious. Even strange little Kassandra has no meanness of spirit. And your father sired you, Andromache, and I see in you a great soul.'

'Perhaps you mistake intelligence for spirituality, Odysseus.'

'No, lass, I don't make mistakes about people. I have two gifts that have served me well. I can spin a yarn, and I can read the hearts of men and women. You are like my Penelope. You are, as you say, intelligent. You are also warm and open and honest. And you have courage and a sense of duty. My father once said that if a man was lucky he'd find a woman to ride the storm with. You are such a woman. Hektor is very lucky.'

'His luck is not my concern,' she said. 'What of mine?'

'Let us find out,' he said, rising to his feet.

'And how will we do this?'

'We'll seek out Aklides. Best soothsayer in Lykia. Well . . . when he's not drunk or drugged. He's from the desert country beyond Palestine. Lot of soothsayers come from the desert. He'll read your future.'

'Yes, and tell me I'll have nine children and be rich and happy and live long.'

'Are you frightened of a soothsayer, Andromache of Thebe?' he chided.

'I am frightened of nothing, Odysseus of Ithaka.'

'Then come with me.' He held out his hand, and she allowed him to draw her to her feet. Together they walked through the stalls and along the beach, past fornicating couples and drunken sailors, past campfires around which men were singing lusty songs. At last they reached a small tent below the cliffs. There was a long queue. Odysseus suggested they wait a little while longer, and perhaps find something to eat. Andromache had no wish to return to the palace just yet, and so agreed. They moved to a series of food stalls, Odysseus piling a prodigious amount of meat and bread onto a wooden plate. Andromache chose a small pie, filled with honey-soaked fruit, and together they returned to sit on a small wall near the water's edge.

They chatted then. Andromache talked of Thera, and the Temple of the Horse, though she did not mention Kalliope, or any of her friends there. Instead she explained to him the rituals that were said to keep the Sleeping God calm. Odysseus was as good a listener as he was a storyteller, prompting her with questions that showed his interest. 'I was on Thera once,' he said, 'long before it was decided that only women could placate the Minotaur. Strange place. All that rumbling below the ground, and the hissing of acrid steam from vents in the rock. I was glad to be back on the *Penelope*. Tell me, do you believe in the Minotaur?'

'An odd question from a man who has seen so many monsters and demons.'

'That would be my point, lass. I have never seen a single one. But in my travels I have seen hot springs, and lava pools. Not one of them boasted a minotaur. Have you ever glimpsed it?'

'No-one sees it,' said Andromache, 'but you can hear it rumbling and growling below the ground, pushing up, trying to escape. The older priestesses swear the island was smaller years ago, and that the straining beast is lifting it out of the sea.'

'So, you *do* believe in it?'

'Truly I do not know. But something makes that noise, and causes the ground to tremble.'

'And you placate it with what?'

'Songs to calm its troubled heart, offerings of wine. Prayers to the great gods to keep it calm. It is said the Kretans used to sacrifice virgins to it in the old days, forcing them to enter the deeper cracks in the rock and walk down to its lair. They did not appease him, for the Minotaur almost broke free many years ago.'

'My grandfather told me of it,' said Odysseus. 'How the sun fled for many days. And how rocks and ash fell from the sky, covering many of the eastern islands. There is an old sailors' legend about the sea rising up to the sky, and the sound of an army of thunders. Like to have seen it. Great story in that. Did you know that your new mother spent three years on Thera, and that part of her bridal dowry was a massive donation to build the Temple of the Horse?'

'Yes. They speak of Hekabe with great reverence there.'

'Strong woman. Intelligent like you. Beautiful as a winter morning and terrifying as a tempest. I think you'll like her.'

'You sound a little in awe of her, king of Ithaka,' said Andromache, with a smile.

He leaned forward and gave a conspiratorial grin. 'She has always frightened me. Don't know why. I think she even frightens Priam.'

The sky began to pale. The night was almost over and Andromache could hardly believe she had spent hours in the company of a stranger. She yawned and rubbed at her tired eyes.

'I think you are getting a little weary of waiting,' said the ugly king, pushing himself to his feet and walking back to the now shrinking queue. Approaching the men in the line he said: 'Now, lads, I have a beautiful woman with me who needs her fortune told. Would any object if we stole in next?'

Andromache saw the men turn to stare at her. Then Odysseus dipped his hand into the pouch by his side, and produced copper rings which he dropped into their outstretched palms.

After a short while a man came out of the tent. He did not look happy. Odysseus beckoned Andromache and stepped forward, lifting the tent flap and ducking inside. Andromache followed him. Inside the tent a middle-aged man was sitting on a threadbare blanket. Two lamps were burning, and the air was stiflingly hot and acrid. Andromache sat down and looked at the seer. His right eye was like an opal, pale and milky, his left so dark it seemed to have no pupil. The man's face was strangely elongated and thin, as if his head had been somehow crushed.

'And what have you brought me this time, Odysseus?' he asked, his voice low and deep.

'A young woman who wishes to know her future.'

Aklides sighed deeply. 'I am tired. Dawn is approaching and I have no time to count babies and offer platitudes to maidens.'

'Then do it for your old friend,' said Odysseus, opening his pouch once more, and this time producing a ring of bright silver.

'I have no friends,' muttered Aklides. His one good eye fixed on Andromache. 'Well, give me your hand and let us see what there is to see,' he said.

Andromache leaned forward, placing her slender fingers in his greasy palm. His hand was hot and she flinched as his fingers closed around her own. He closed his eyes and sat silently, his breathing shallow. Then he jumped, and a low groan rattled from his throat. His face spasmed, and he jerked his hand back, his eyes flaring open.

'Well?' asked Odysseus, as the silence lengthened.

'Sometimes it is best not to know the future,' whispered Aklides.

'Come, come, Aklides! This is not like you,' said Odysseus, an edge of anger in his voice.

'Very well. You will have one child. A boy.' Aklides sighed. 'I will volunteer nothing. But ask me what you will.'

'Will I know love?' asked Andromache, her voice betraying her boredom.

'There will be three loves. One like the Great Green, powerful and tempestuous, one like the Oak, strong and true, and one like the Moon, eternal and bright.'

'I like the sound of tempestuous,' she said, her tone sarcastic. 'Who should I look for?'

'The man with one sandal.'

'And the Oak?'

He gave a thin smile. 'He will rise from the mud, his body caked with the filth of pigs.'

'I shall look forward to that with great anticipation. And the Moon?'

'He will come to you with blood and pain.'

'What nonsense,' snapped Andromache. 'Take back your silver, Odysseus.'

'I speak only the truth, priestess of Thera,' said Aklides. 'I was content tonight, but now your visit means I shall never be content again. Through you I have seen the fall of worlds, the deaths of heroes, and I have watched the ocean touch the fire-red sky. Now leave me be!'

Andromache stepped out into the night. The stocky figure of Odysseus joined her. 'He is usually more entertaining than that,' he said.

Ahead on the sand she saw one of the Fat King's sentries making his rounds, his wooden club on his shoulder, his conical, bronze-edged helmet and cheek guards gleaming in the moonlight. Suddenly he stumbled, as the strap on one of his sandals broke. Angrily he kicked it off, then strode on.

'Such a pity,' said Andromache drily. 'There he is, the tempestuous love of my life, and we never met.' She gave a theatrical sigh. 'Should I call out to him, do you think?' She swung towards Odysseus. 'I thank you for your company, king of Ithaka. You are a fine friend on a starry night. But now I must return to the palace.'

'I would be happy to walk you there,' he said.

'No, you wouldn't. Save the lies for an audience, Odysseus. Let us have a pact, you and I. The truth always.'

'That will be hard. The truth is often so boring.' He grinned then, and spread his hands. 'But I cannot refuse a goddess, so I will agree.'

'You want to walk me back to the palace?'

'No, lass, I am dog tired now and just want to wrap myself in a blanket by a fire.'

'That is better, and how it should be between friends. So goodnight to you, Tale Spinner.' With that she looked up at the distant fortress, and, heavy of heart, set off for the cliff path.

X

The Fat King's Feast

i

AS HE WALKED SLOWLY UP THE HILL ROAD TOWARDS THE FORTRESS
town Helikaon could not stop thinking about the tall woman he
had seen while Odysseus performed. The way she stood – elegance
and confidence sublimely in harmony; the way her eyes met his,
defiant and challenging. Even her expression as she saw the man
attack him had not shown fear. Her eyes had narrowed, her face
becoming stern. Helikaon's heart beat faster as he conjured her
face in his mind. Beside him Zidantas trudged on in silence, his
huge, nail-studded club resting on his shoulder. Argurios and
Glaukos were a little way back.

The walk was perilous at night, despite the many lamps lit, and
left in crevices in the rock wall. The drop was sheer to the left, the
path rocky and pitted. Helikaon gazed out over the bay below, his
heart swelling as he looked down upon the sleek lines of the *Xanthos*.
From here he could also see the distant, now tiny form of Odysseus.
His mentor had walked to the water's edge and was digging away at
the sand with his dagger. Helikaon knew what he was doing. He had
seen it often during the two years he had spent on the *Penelope*.
Odysseus was shaping the face of his wife in the sand.

Behind him Helikaon heard Glaukos mutter an oath as he tripped over a rock.

The Mykene warriors had seemed surprised when he had invited them to meet the king. The courtesy had evidently been unexpected and Argurios had almost thanked him. Helikaon smiled as he recalled the moment. The Mykene's tongue would have turned black, he thought, if forced to utter a pleasantry.

Argurios moved alongside him, moonlight gleaming on the elaborately embossed bronze discs of his cuirass. 'This king is a friend of yours?' he asked.

'All reasonable men are my friends, Argurios.'

Argurios' expression hardened. 'Do not bait me. It would not be wise.'

'Why would I bait you?' answered Helikaon coldly. 'All reasonable men *are* my friends, for I seek no enemies. I am a trader, not a plunderer.'

Argurios looked at him closely. 'You are a man who has earned the hatred of all Mykene. You should understand there will be great joy when your death is announced.'

'I don't doubt that,' replied Helikaon, pausing in his stride and turning towards the warrior. 'There is great joy in Mykene when *anyone* suffers or is dispossessed. You are a people who thrive on murder and the sorrow of others.'

Argurios' hand grasped the hilt of his sword. For a moment Helikaon believed he was about to challenge him. Then Argurios spoke, his voice shaking with suppressed anger. 'The Law of the Road forbids me to rise to that insult. Repeat it on the beach and I will kill you.' With that he strode off, Glaukos running to catch up with him. Zidantas moved alongside Helikaon and sighed.

'What merry company you have chosen for us,' he said.

'I didn't choose them, Ox. Odysseus suggested we bring them.'

'Why?'

'Perhaps because somewhere ahead on the road will be Mykene killers seeking my blood.'

'Oh that makes wonderful sense,' muttered Zidantas. 'We are facing murderers so Odysseus gets us to bring them

134

reinforcements. Let's just go back to the beach. We can return with more men.'

'You know, Ox, in some ways you are just like the Mykene. You take no interest in other cultures. No, we are not going back to the beach. We will walk on – and see what transpires.'

'This is not a good place for a fight,' Zidantas pointed out. 'One wrong step and a man would be pitched over the side. It is a long way down.'

Helikaon did not answer. Increasing his pace, he kept close to the Mykene. Up ahead the path twisted to the left. Steps had been cut into the stone. At the top, Helikaon knew, the road widened. There were several caves there where armed men could hide.

'Soon?' whispered Zidantas.

'At the top of these steps, I would think. Do not attack them, Ox. Wait and see what happens first.'

Keeping close behind the two warriors they climbed the steps. Up ahead Argurios reached the top and suddenly paused. Helikaon came alongside him. Standing before them were six warriors, all clad in leather breastplates and carrying short swords. They did not rush in, and seemed confused and uncertain. One of them looked at Argurios. 'Step aside, brother, for our business is not with you.'

'I would do that gladly, idiot!' snapped Argurios. 'But you know the Law of the Road. If a man walks in company with other travellers then he is obliged to face dangers alongside them.'

'That is a Mykene law for Mykene travellers,' argued the man.

'I am in the company of Helikaon,' said Argurios. 'Now I loathe him as much as you do, but attack him and I will, by the law, be obliged to fight alongside him. You know me, and you know my skills. All of you will die.'

'We have no choice,' said the man. 'It is a matter of honour.'

Argurios' sword rasped from its scabbard. 'Then die as a man of honour,' he said.

'Wait!' said Helikaon, stepping forward. 'I wish for no blood to be shed here, but if a fight is necessary, then let us settle it with single combat.' He pointed at the warrior standing before

Argurios. 'You and I, Mykene. Or any of your comrades you care to choose.'

'I will fight you, Vile One!' said the man.

Helikaon drew his sword.

Raising his blade, the warrior attacked. Helikaon stepped in, blocking a thrust, and hammered his shoulder into the warrior's chest, hurling him back. The Mykene charged again, his sword hacking and slashing. Helikaon blocked and countered with ease. The man was not skilled with a blade, and tried to compensate by sheer ferocity. Helikaon waited for the right moment, then blocked a wild cut and grabbed the man's sword wrist. Curling his leg behind the knee of his opponent he threw him from his feet. The man landed heavily on his back. Helikaon's sword touched the fallen man's throat. 'Is it over?' he asked.

'Yes,' answered the man, hatred in his eyes. Helikaon stepped back and turned towards the others.

'You heard him,' he said, sheathing his sword. 'It is over.'

A movement from his left caused him to turn sharply. The man he had spared had risen silently to his feet and was rushing at him, sword raised. There was no time to draw his own blade. Then Argurios leapt between them, his sword slashing through the attacker's neck. The man fell back with a gargling cry, blood spraying from his open jugular. As the dying warrior's body spasmed Helikaon turned to the five remaining men. 'Return to your ship,' he ordered them. 'There is only death here for you, with no hope of victory.'

They stood very still, and Helikaon saw they were preparing themselves to attack. Then Argurios spoke.

'Sheathe your swords! It would weigh heavily on my heart if I were forced to kill another Mykene. And carry this treacherous creature with you,' he said, pointing to the corpse. Helikaon saw the men relax. They scabbarded their blades and shuffled forward, lifted the dead man, and made their way back to the steps.

Argurios, coldly furious now, marched to confront Helikaon. 'Did you know they would be here? Is that why you invited me, Trojan?'

'Firstly, Argurios, I am a Dardanian. As an ambassador to this side of the Great Green it might be worthwhile for you to understand that not all who dwell in these lands are Trojans. There are Maeonians, Lykians, Karians and Thrakians. And many more. Secondly, is it likely that I would have walked this path with two Mykene warriors had I known there were six more waiting to kill me?'

Argurios let out a long sigh. 'No, you would not,' he admitted. He looked into Helikaon's eyes. 'You have been blessed with luck twice tonight. Such good fortune cannot last.'

ii

The contradiction that was Kygones the Fat King sat on a high-backed chair, his skeletal frame clad in a simple, unadorned tunic. He was picking at his meal, his wary eyes scanning his guests. The two Gyppto ambassadors had hardly touched the food, and were locked in conversation, their voices low. The merchant from Maeonia was eating enough for three, shovelling the food into his cavernous mouth as if he hadn't eaten for weeks, gravy from the meat staining his several chins. The Dardanian prince, Helikaon, was sitting silently beside the fork-bearded Zidantas, and the two Mykene warriors with them had helped themselves to cuts of beef, ignoring the finer delicacies on display: the honey-dipped sweetmeats, the peppered sheep's eyes, the seared kidneys, marinated first in wine.

Helikaon also ate sparingly, and seemed lost in thought.

The king cast his weary gaze over the other guests, most of them merchants from outlying lands, bringing gifts of silk, or glass, or – more important – objects of gold and silver.

Kygones scratched at his pockmarked face and eased himself back against the chair, wishing the time to pass. A servant moved alongside him, filling his goblet with clear water. The king glanced at the man, and nodded his thanks. There was a time when Kygones would have sold his soul for the chance to be a palace servant; to be sure of at least one meal a day and to sleep under a roof, away from wind and rain.

The interminable banquet finally came to a close. Servants carried away the dishes and replenished the wine cups, and Kygones clapped his hands for the entertainment to begin. Female dancers from Kretos moved across the mosaic floor of the *megaron*, swaying rhythmically to the music from several lyres, their bodies slim and lithe, their naked breasts firm. Oil glistened on their skin. The dance grew wilder, the women twirling and leaping. The guests banged the table in time to the music. Kygones closed his eyes, his mind drifting back through the years. His father had assured him that hard work and dedicated service would lead to happiness for any peasant. Like most youngsters he had believed his father, and had toiled on the small farm from dawn to dusk every day. He had seen his mother age before his eyes, watched two brothers die, seen his three older sisters sold into servitude, and finally witnessed his father being murdered by Gypptos during the third invasion. That was when Kygones discovered the real secret of success.

It lay not in scratching at the land with sharpened sticks, but in grasping a sword in a strong hand.

The music faded, the women moving gracefully away. Acrobats replaced them, and jugglers, and finally a bard from Ugarit, who told a tale of magical beasts and heroes. It was a dull tale, and Kygones found himself wishing he had invited Odysseus to the feast.

The two Gypptos rose as the bard was still speaking, bowed low to Kygones and left the *megaron*. The bard's voice faded away as the men walked past him, and Kygones saw that the display of bad manners had unnerved the man. Lifting his hand he urged the storyteller to continue, his own thoughts meanwhile straying to his departing guests.

The Gypptos were an odd pair. They had arrived with gifts: a gold-inlaid ivory wrist band and a jewel-encrusted dagger. And though they spoke of trade and shipments of spices, they were not merchants. Kygones had waited to hear the real reason for their visit, and had suppressed a smile when the older one finally said, 'There is one small matter, King Kygones, that my master instructed me to make known to you.' He had spoken then of a criminal who had escaped justice in Egypt, following the slaying of two Royal Guardsmen. There followed a description of the man, tall, wide-shouldered, dark-bearded. 'He has no skills, save that he is a fighting man, and so may seek to join your army. My master, realizing that to apprehend him would put you at some inconvenience, has instructed me to say that there is a reward offered for his capture. Five gold ingots.'

'A big man, you say?'

'Indeed.'

'I shall instruct my captains to look out for him. He has a name?'

'He would not use it. We located a ship's captain who sailed to Kypros with someone of his description. This man called himself Gershom.'

'Then perhaps you should be seeking him in Kypros.'

'Indeed we are, and in every other land.'

The bard concluded his tale, which was greeted by polite, if unenthusiastic, cheers. He bowed to the assembly and, red-faced, left the *megaron*.

Kygones rose from his chair, thanked his guests for honouring him with their company, signalled to Helikaon and the Mykene to follow him, and walked back through the palace to his private apartments. There he wandered onto a high balcony and stared out over the dark sea. The night breeze was cool and refreshing.

'You seem a little weary, my friend,' said Helikaon. Kygones swung to greet him.

'Battles are less tiring than feasts,' he said. He looked at the two Mykene behind the Golden One. The first was lean, fierce-eyed and battle-hardened. The second was younger, and there was weakness in his eyes. He listened as Helikaon introduced them, then bade them sit. The room was large, with several couches, and two open balconies allowing the night breeze to dissipate the fumes from the lamps on the walls. 'I have heard of you, Argurios,' he said, as his guests settled themselves. 'You held a bridge during the war with the Myrmidons. Seventeen men you killed that day.'

He noted with satisfaction the surprise on the man's face. 'I had not thought the story would have travelled so far,' said Argurios. 'And it was only nine. The others were merely wounded and removed from the fighting.'

'Tales of heroes are often exaggerated,' said Kygones. 'You are a close companion, I understand, of King Agamemnon.'

'I have the honour to be a Follower.'

'You are the second Follower to grace my beach. The lord Kolanos is here also. You are friends?'

'Most friendships are forged in battle. I have never fought along-side him,' replied Argurios.

'I am told he is now considered the first of Agamemnon's Followers, and that the king places great trust in him.'

'All the Followers are trusted,' said Argurios. 'They gain their positions through their loyalty to the king, and their services to the land.'

Kygones nodded. 'I understand,' he said. You do not like him, warrior, he thought. Is it jealousy, or something else? The king sat down on a couch, beckoning his guests to seat themselves. Argurios and Helikaon moved to couches set against the walls, while Glaukos sat with his back to the door.

'Two of Kolanos' crew died tonight, one on the beach, and one on the path to my palace,' said the king.

Argurios remained silent. Kygones turned his attention to Helikaon. 'I have reprimanded the captain of the guard. He did not allocate enough men to patrol the beach. And now I have a small favour to ask of you, Helikaon, my friend. The intended bride of Hektor has been waiting here for almost ten days. I would dearly like to see her on a ship to Troy.'

Helikaon looked surprised. 'I thought she was already there.'

'Well, she is here,' said Kygones, 'and I pity Hektor. The time she has spent with me has felt like a season. By the gods she has a tongue on her that could cut through stone. I am amazed that Priam should have sought such a harridan for his eldest son. You'd have to be drunk or drugged before you climbed aboard that mare. Can you take her off my hands?'

'Of course, my friend. Though I had heard the girl was charming and shy.'

'Taleste might have been. But she died. Now Hektor has been offered the sister, Andromache. The words *charming* and *shy* do not apply.' Kygones chuckled. 'She was a priestess on Thera. I have heard stories about those women. They are not lovers of men, that's for sure.'

'We have all heard stories about *those* women,' said young Glaukos harshly. 'If true they should be sealed alive in weighted boxes and hurled into the sea.'

Kygones masked his surprise at the man's vehemence. 'An interesting thought,' he said, after a while. 'Tell me, should the same punishment be meted out to men who seek their pleasures among other men?'

'I was not talking about men,' said Glaukos. 'It is a good woman's duty to receive sexual pleasure from her husband and no other.'

Kygones shrugged and said nothing. The man was an idiot. He returned his attention to Helikaon. 'That is a fine sword you are wearing.'

Helikaon drew the blade, reversed it, and offered it to Kygones. There were no embellishments on the reinforced hilt, but the blade was beautifully fashioned, the balance perfection. Hefting it, Kygones stepped back, then slashed it through the air twice. 'Magnificent. One of the best I have held,' he said. He tested the edge, then examined the bronze blade under lamplight. His warrior's eye noted the sheen. Bronze swords were notoriously treacherous. Too soft and they would bend out of shape in a fight. Too hard and they would shatter on impact. But this blade seemed different. 'Crafted by a master,' he said. 'I have never seen the like before.'

As Kygones had anticipated, Helikaon was too sharp not to know what was expected of him. 'I am glad that you like it, my friend, for I brought it with me as a gift for you,' he said smoothly.

Lifting the scabbard from the loop at his belt he passed it to the king.

Kygones chuckled. 'You know the way to an old soldier's heart. Here!' he called to Argurios. 'A warrior such as yourself will appreciate this weapon.' Flicking his wrist he tossed the blade through the air. Argurios caught it expertly, and Kygones noted the gleam of pleasure in the man's eyes as he felt the balance of the blade.

'It is superb.' The Mykene's voice was awestruck.

'Who knows,' said Kygones, retrieving the blade, 'I might be using it before long. But for now I will rest.'

The men bowed and walked to the door. 'Ah!' the king called out. 'A moment of your time, Helikaon.'

Argurios and Glaukos left the room. Helikaon waited in the doorway. Kygones indicated he should shut the door and come back inside. 'Sit down, and let us talk awhile.'

'I thought you were tired, my friend.'

'The company of Mykene always tires me.' Lifting a pitcher of water he filled his goblet. 'They are an unpleasant people altogether. Hearts like lions, minds like snakes. Which is why I wanted to speak to you privately. Although Argurios strikes me as a better man than most of his race.' Kygones looked closely at his guest. Helikaon's face was pale, and there were lines of tension around his eyes. 'Are you ill, my friend?'

'No. A little head pain. It is already passing.'

Kygones poured a fresh goblet of water and passed it to Helikaon. 'Usually I have twice as many soldiers on hand when there are ships beached. However, the Hittites requested five hundred fighting men four days ago and my troops are spread thin.'

'Five hundred? There are fears of an Egypteian invasion?'

'It has already happened. A Gyppto army is moving up through Palestine. They have pushed north. Hektor and a thousand Trojan cavalry have joined the Hittites to confront them. The fat Maeonian merchant saw them pass three days ago. Interesting times lie ahead. The world is about to change, I think. Too many kings. Too many armed men with no employment. The Hittite empire is in its death throes. Something will replace it.'

'Not Egypte,' said Helikaon. 'They are wondrously equipped for desert warfare, but their troops are too lightly armed for battle in northern climes. And Hektor will not be defeated. The Trojan Horse are invincible in battle.'

'What of the Mykene?'

Helikaon looked surprised. 'The Mykene empire is in the west. They do not have the ships, or the men, to invade the east.'

'Agamemnon is a man of new ambitions. However, that is not my most pressing problem at the moment. My immediate concern is the sea. The trading season is almost done, but I am wondering whether the Gypptos will try to land a force on my coast. It would be a fine diversion. To offset this threat I could use . . . say . . . ten galleys until the spring.'

Kygones smiled inwardly as he saw the Golden One's expression change, his eyes narrowing, his mind weighing the cost. He wouldn't want to lose the friendship of a powerful king, but equally he would have no wish to find himself at odds with the power of Egypt. As a trader he needed access to Egypteian ports to sell cargoes of olive oil, decorated copper vessels, and Mykene jars. From those ports he would load Egypteian wares, like gold, salt, alabaster and papyrus. Kygones leaned back. He knew what Helikaon was thinking. Such a raid, with its attendant disadvantages, was extremely unlikely, while leasing galleys and crews to Kygones would provide income during the lean winter months, when trading on the Great Green was minimal.

'Ten would not be enough to prevent an invasion,' Helikaon said, suddenly.

'I have hired others. That is why Kolanos is here. His three galleys are now part of my fleet. I have other captains sailing here for the winter.'

'I will *sell* you ten ships,' said Helikaon. 'They will then be yours to command as you see fit. I will buy them back in the spring for the same price – as long as they are undamaged. You must supply your own sails. The Black Horse of Dardanos will not be seen to take part in any war.'

'And the crews?'

'They will be like the Mykene, mercenaries. Your treasury will pay them fighting wages. One hundred copper rings for each man.'

'Pah! What if there is no fighting? Fifty rings a man.'

'Ten ships, ten crews, one hundred rings a man. Come, come, my friend, you know this is fair. You just cannot resist haggling.'

'Fair? Why don't you just rip the shirt from my back and steal my boots too?'

'I gave you those boots last spring.'

Kygones laughed. 'So you did. Damned good boots they are too. Very well, Helikaon, I will agree to seventy rings a man. But only because I like you.'

'What are you paying the Mykene?'

'Sixty.'

For a while Helikaon said nothing, his face becoming mask-like, showing no emotion at all. Kygones cursed inwardly. He had spoken without thinking. The amount was correct, but it was too low, and had aroused the Golden One's suspicions. Then Helikaon appeared to relax. He shrugged. 'Friends must not fall out over such matters,' he said. 'Seventy rings it is. I will send the galleys from Troy.'

'Excellent! And now I really will take to my bed,' said the king. 'May your travels be blessed with fine winds and fair skies.' As Kygones spoke he realized he actually meant it. He had always liked Helikaon.

Such a shame then that he had to die tonight.

XI

Swords in the Moonlight

i

LEAVING THE APARTMENTS OF KYGONES, HELIKAON WALKED BACK through the *megaron*, where the remains of the food were being cleared away. He looked around for Zidantas, then summoned a servant. 'Did you see my companion, the big man with the forked beard?'

'No, lord.'

Moving on, he asked several others. Finally a stoop-shouldered servant with watery eyes supplied an answer. 'I saw him talking to Captain Galeos, then he left.'

'Where will I find Captain Galeos?'

Following the man's directions, Helikaon left the *megaron* and emerged onto an outside terrace. The night air was crisp with the promise of rain, and a cool wind was blowing from the sea. Helikaon paused to stand by the walkway rail and gaze down at the beach. Fires were still burning, but most of the sailors, who would be working hard from dawn's first light, were now asleep. Many of the stalls were covered by canvas sheets, their owners, wrapped in blankets, sitting by them, watching for thieves. As he stood, breathing in the sweet air, Helikaon thought through the events of the night.

145

It had been surprising that the Mykene had tried to kill him on the Fat King's beach. Kygones was not a forgiving man. Transgressors had their throats cut. The second attack, so close to the palace, bordered on the stupid. Or at least that was what he had thought.

Now he knew otherwise. Kygones had hired the Mykene to patrol his waters, and he had done so cheaply. In the moment that Kygones let slip the price, Helikaon knew he was betrayed. Mykene fighting men like Kolanos did not sell their services without receiving a good blood price. They would earn more by piracy and raiding. They had accepted sixty rings because there was something larger and more valuable offered to balance the fee.

His own life.

Everything fell into place then. The loss of five hundred men to the Hittite army would not have depleted Kygones' force so greatly as to reduce the number of men patrolling the beach. And even if it had, there would still have been soldiers around the crowd when Odysseus told his tale. In fact there had been none.

Also there had been too few torches on the cliff path, and no soldiers there either.

Kygones needed no extra galleys. He had merely delayed Helikaon so that Argurios and Glaukos would return without him. There was now no need to find the captain of the guard. Helikaon knew what had happened. Zidantas had been told Helikaon was staying the night at the palace. Ox had therefore returned to the beach.

The crowning moment of the betrayal had been when Kygones deprived Helikaon of his only weapon. He felt his anger rise – not at Kygones, but at himself. How could he have been so foolish? All the clues had been there, and he had not seen them. He stood for a while, until the anger passed, and he began to think more clearly. Kolanos would have sent more men to wait on the cliff path, so either he remained where he was until the dawn, or he found another way down. At first the thought of staying at the palace seemed the more obvious solution. Surely Kygones would not risk angering Troy by *actively* participating in the death of one of its allies. Yet, as he thought it through, he realized he could be killed in the palace, and his body dumped on the cliff path. Kygones might already have issued orders to trusted men.

Once on the beach, surrounded by his own men, Helikaon would be safe. But how to get there?

ii

The Mykene warrior Kolanos had never been a patient man. The night was almost gone, and his men had not returned. So, donning sword and helmet, he walked swiftly along the beach, following the line of the cliffs towards the path. The moon emerged from behind a thin screen of clouds. He saw then that his tunic was spattered with blood, spray patterns dotting the pale fabric. There was blood also on his hands. Pausing, he scooped up some sand to rub them clean.

Most of the sailors on the beach were asleep, save for a few sitting around fading campfires playing knucklebone dice. To his right was the *Xanthos* campfire. He saw Argurios sitting there, staring out at the sea.

Anger flared. He had never liked the man. His notions of honour were ludicrous. Enemies were to be killed by whatever means. How he could have defended Helikaon was a mystery Kolanos would never understand. When Agamemnon heard of it he would be furious. And Kolanos would ensure the king *did* hear of it. Argurios might revel in his role as a Follower now, but he would be stripped of that honour. With luck, depending on Agamemnon's mood, he might also be declared outside the law, his estates forfeit, a blood price on his head. Irritation touched him then. That would be too much to hope for. Argurios, for all his stupid clinging to the rituals of the past, was still a Mykene hero.

Kolanos strode up the cliff path. Near the top, almost within sight of the palace gates, he found the five men he had assigned to kill Helikaon. They were half hidden in the shadows of a deep cleft in the rock. Kolanos approached them. The bulky form of Habusas the Assyrian stepped into the moonlight. 'No sign of him, lord,' he said.

'Has anyone passed?'

'A few sentries. Some whores.'

Kolanos moved back into the shadows. Habusas followed him, keeping his voice low. 'Maybe he stayed the night.'

'If he does Kygones will have him killed, and his body thrown to the beach. Let us hope he comes. I want to see the bastard's face when my knife rips out his eyes.'

'Someone coming!' whispered one of the men. Kolanos peered through the gloom. A soldier wearing a conical helmet and carrying a club on his shoulder was strolling down from the palace.

'Go and ask him about Helikaon,' ordered Kolanos.

Habusas called out to the man, then walked across. They spoke for a little while, then Habusas returned.

'He said the Trojan went back to the king's apartments. That's all he knew.'

Kolanos glanced at the sky. There was no more than an hour of darkness left. 'We'll wait a while longer,' he said.

Time drifted by. Kolanos' irritation grew. Had Kygones changed his mind? Had he decided not to kill Helikaon?

Then Habusas lightly tapped his arm and pointed up the trail. A man wearing a dark chiton had emerged from the palace gates, and was beginning the walk down to the beach.

'Grab him and pin his arms,' said Kolanos, drawing his knife.

As the figure came closer Habusas stepped out, blocking the way. Other men moved around the startled newcomer, hustling him to stand before Kolanos.

His dark hair was close-cropped, his face heavy and fleshy. Kolanos swiftly sheathed his blade. 'Where did you get that tunic?' he asked roughly, recognizing the gold embroidery round the neck and sleeves. Instead of answering, the man turned to run. Habusas and two of the Mykene grabbed him and hauled him back to face Kolanos.

'I asked you a question. Answer it!'

'From the Trojan prince, lord.'

'Why did he give you his garment?'

'We exchanged clothes. I am a soldier of the king. He said he wanted to play a joke on his friends, and borrowed my uniform and my club. He said I could come down to the beach tomorrow and he would return everything.'

Bile rose in Kolanos' throat. Stepping back he looked at Habusas. 'Send this man to the beach. By the fast route.'

The Mykene dragged the struggling soldier to the cliff edge. In desperation he clawed at them. Habusas punched him twice, half stunning him. Kolanos ran in, knife in hand, and plunged the blade through the man's chest, then dragged it clear. Mortally wounded, the soldier fell to his knees. The Mykene rushed in and kicked him from the cliff edge. His body plummeted down to the rocks below.

The sky was growing lighter now.

'No more knives in the dark,' said Kolanos. 'We will take him at sea.'

iii

Helikaon stepped off the cliff path and strode across the rocky sand. He was tired now, but lifted by the fact that he had fooled the Mykene. Kolanos himself had been waiting there in the dark, with five of his men. It was a great compliment that they believed such force would be necessary.

The conical helmet slid sideways on his head, for he had not tightened the chin straps, and the bronze-reinforced leather breastplate was too large, chafing the skin of his shoulders. He felt clumsy as he walked across the beach towards the *Xanthos* fire. Then he stumbled, the strap of his right sandal snapping. Kicking it clear, he walked on.

Most of the men were asleep when he approached. Pulling off the helm, he tossed it to the sand, then unbuckled the breastplate. Oniacus saw him. 'You were better dressed when you set out,' he volunteered.

'Long day tomorrow – you should be sleeping,' Helikaon told him, then strolled off to the *Xanthos*. He climbed onto the rear deck. Two men were sleeping there, a third keeping watch. Helikaon opened a deck hatch and stepped down into the stygian gloom below. He found his chest more by feel than sight and lifted the lid. Reaching in, he felt around for a spare tunic, then returned to the upper deck and removed the soldier's calf-length linen garb. Donning his own clothes once more, he looked back at the palace.

It was a surprise that Kygones should have betrayed him. Not that they were friends, but the business they conducted together was profitable, and for the Fat King to collude in his murder he must have been offered a huge sum. No pirate could have afforded to bribe the king – not even Kolanos. No, the riches would have been promised on behalf of Agamemnon. Helikaon could make no sense of it. More than a year had passed since he had killed Alektruon, and he had done nothing since to offend the Mykene king. However, the reason for Agamemnon's new enmity was secondary now. The real question was: how many other kings on the trade routes had been offered a fortune to conspire in his death? How many pirate chiefs? Or assassins?

His own father, Anchises, had been slain by such a man. And mutilated. The killer had slashed a sharp blade across the king's throat, and then cut off his ear. How he had entered the palace remained a mystery. No guards reported seeing a stranger, though one man said he saw a shadow move on the high eastern wall. He assumed it was a trick of the light.

Even now, nine years later, Helikaon still had agents scouring the towns and cities of the Great Green seeking clues to the assassin and the man who hired him.

Movement caught Helikaon's eye. The Mykene galleys were being pushed back into the water, and he saw the blond Kolanos standing on the beach. The Mykene looked up, and their eyes met.

'Enjoy your day, Golden One!' shouted Kolanos. 'It will be one to remember!'

Helikaon ignored him, and continued to watch as the Mykene crewmen swarmed aboard their vessels. The three black galleys were long and sleek, each with fifty rowers positioned on the upper decks. Bronze-headed rams had been fitted to the prows. Kolanos was the last to wade out into the surf, and haul himself aboard his ship. Huge red eyes had been painted on the timbers of the upcurved prow, giving the galley a demonic appearance.

As the ships moved out into the bay, the rowers leaned in to their oars and the crews began to dismantle the masts. Helikaon knew then that they would be waiting for the *Xanthos* outside the bay. Galleys were more manoeuvrable in battle with their masts down. And they wanted him to know, otherwise they would have left their masts up until they were out of sight.

It was a challenge, and one that could not be ignored.

Kolanos had every reason to believe the day would be his. The Mykene galleys were smaller and faster than the *Xanthos*, and he had three times as many fighting men.

But he did not know of the genius of Khalkeus, the Madman from Miletos.

The sun cleared the eastern cliffs, turning the sky to coral and gold.

Striding back along the central deck, Helikaon climbed to the stern and gazed down on the beach, scanning the faces of his men.

Where in Hades is Ox? he thought.

XII

The Gathering Storm

i

AN HOUR EARLIER ANDROMACHE HAD CLIMBED THE LONG CLIFF PATH, thinking of the seer who had predicted her destiny. Odysseus was right: the man had not been entertaining. Yet how had he known she was a priestess of Thera? Perhaps, she thought, I should have called out to the man with one sandal. She smiled. To discover what? That he was a farmer's son from the low country, or married with seven noisy children? She walked on, her spirits lighter. The conversation with Odysseus had been more than pleasant. It was like water on a parched tongue to meet someone of wit and intelligence, who was also warm and amusing. The Fat King had a mind like a dagger, but there was no humanity in him – or none that she could perceive.

As she climbed the path she found herself thinking of the blue-eyed man who had been attacked. He was about to speak to her when the knifeman charged in. Andromache wondered what he was going to say. Would it have been a gentle greeting, or merely a coarse request for sex on the sand? She would never know.

At the top of the stone steps she saw blood on the rocks. There was a smeared patch on the edge of the path, above the drop to the rocks below. Andromache ignored it and continued on to the fortress gates.

Once through, she climbed the stairs to the apartments she had been allocated. Her slim, dark-haired servant girl, Polysia, was waiting inside. In the torchlight she looked strained and nervous, and her relief at seeing Andromache was palpable. She ran forward. 'Oh, where have you been? I was worried sick. I thought you had been abducted!'

'I went for a walk on the beach,' said Andromache.

'You shouldn't have. There has been murder tonight.'

Andromache nodded. 'I know. When men are gathered together is there not always a murder, or a fight, or a rape?'

Polysia's brows creased. 'I don't understand. Knowing that, why did you go?'

Andromache moved to the table and filled a clay goblet with wine and water. 'Why not? I cannot change the world of men, and I have no wish to hide in a cave.'

'I would have been in such trouble had you gone missing. The king would have had me whipped . . . or killed.'

Andromache put down her wine, walked over to the girl. A wisp of dark hair had fallen over her brow. Andromache brushed it back from her face, then leaned in and kissed her on the lips. 'But I haven't gone missing,' she said. 'I am here, and all is well.' Polysia blushed. 'And now you can go to your bed,' Andromache told her. 'I shall sleep for a while.'

'Would you like me to stay with you?'

'Not tonight. Go now.'

When Polysia had left Andromache walked to the balcony and gazed down on the beach below. Already the sky was lightening. She saw the three Mykene galleys being pushed out, men clambering aboard. Removing her clothes, she laid them over the back of a chair then climbed into the bed. Sleep came swiftly, and she dreamt of Kalliope. They were swimming in the bay at night. It was a good dream. Then Kalliope began to call her Princess, which was strange, for they were all princesses on Thera.

*

'Princess!'

Andromache's eyes opened, and she saw Polysia by the bedside. Through the open balcony she could see the sky was clear and blue, the sun bright. Andromache struggled to sit, her mind disoriented. 'Fetch me some water,' she said. Polysia did so, and she drank deeply.

'There is terrible trouble,' said Polysia. 'The king is furious, and there are soldiers on the beach.'

'Slow down,' Andromache urged her. 'What trouble?'

'More killings. One of the palace guards was stabbed and thrown from the cliff, and a sailor has been horribly mutilated. They cut off his head, someone told me.'

'This is truly a savage place,' whispered Andromache. Rising from the bed she walked naked to the balcony and breathed deeply. The air was fresh and cool.

'You should come in. Someone might see you.'

Andromache turned. The dreams of Kalliope still burned in her, and her body felt warm and uneasy. 'And what would they see?' she asked the servant girl.

Once again Polysia blushed. 'You are very beautiful,' she whispered.

Andromache laughed. 'Yesterday I was plain, and now everyone is telling me I am beautiful.' Drawing Polysia to her feet she kissed her again. This time the girl's lips parted, and the kiss was deep.

Then someone began pounding at the door. 'Are you dressed?' came a man's voice. She recognized it as Kygones'.

'Wait a moment,' she called. Polysia helped her into her long green gown, then the servant ran to the door, opened it, and stepped back, head bowed.

Kygones entered. His face was pale and tension clung to him like a cloak. 'You will be leaving for Troy today,' he said. 'Gather your belongings and I will take you to the beach.'

'It should be an exciting walk,' she said. 'I understand someone is killed every few moments on your beaches.'

His face hardened. 'Last night was exceptional,' he said. 'We are not savages here.'

'But someone was beheaded, I understand.'

'Be ready as soon as you can,' he said, then stalked from the room. Andromache turned back to Polysia.

'I think you would enjoy life on Thera,' she told her.

'I wish you were not leaving,' answered the girl sadly.

'Perhaps we will meet again. I hope so. Now help me gather my belongings, Polysia. The king is impatient.'

ii

Kygones was in no mood for conversation as he walked down the hill path alongside Andromache. Twenty soldiers followed them, two of them carrying the chests containing Andromache's clothes. As he walked Kygones kept his hand on the hilt of the bronze sword Helikaon had given him. He was hoping it would not be necessary to use it.

How, in the name of Zeus, had the Golden One known the assassins would be waiting?

The Fat King wished he had never listened to Kolanos, nor allowed thoughts of Agamemnon's gold to tempt him. The gold was worth more than two years of trading with Helikaon's ships, and the Golden One's death would not severely affect his profits. Someone else would have inherited the ships, and they would still use Blue Owl Bay. It had seemed so simple. Keep his soldiers back and allow Kolanos to kill Helikaon on the beach. When that failed he had invited the Golden One to the palace. Surely the assassins on the cliff path could kill him. But no. That left only the trip back to the beach.

Kygones had even managed to divest Helikaon of his sword – and still he had evaded assassination. The king shivered, and wondered if the gods themselves were protecting the Golden One.

The biggest question, however, and the one that filled his mind as he walked to the shore was: does he know?

And then there were the other deaths. The palace guard's murder was senseless. It took no great wit to realize that Kolanos, or one of his men, angry at missing the chance to kill Helikaon, had vented his fury on the poor unfortunate who had changed clothes with him.

But the headless corpse. That was another matter entirely. The body had been covered in cuts and burns, and had been disembowelled before the beheading. The wrists were bound, the skin around the binding ripped and torn, showing how the tortured man had writhed and struggled in his agony.

It was an act of barbarity that even Kygones found hard to take. Kill a man, yes, but torture and mutilation? No civilized man should involve himself in such vileness. What would be the effect on Helikaon, he wondered? He glanced back at his soldiers. They had been warned to watch for any sign of hostility.

The beach was still crowded, but there was little movement, and the mood there was sombre. Word had obviously spread. Kygones struggled to stay calm as he approached the *Xanthos*. Helikaon was standing talking with the Ithakan king, Odysseus. In the background Kygones could hear the sound of hammers and saws coming from the great ship. He looked up, but the decks were too high to see where the noise originated. Helikaon and Odysseus ceased their conversation as Kygones came closer.

The king looked into Helikaon's eyes and shuddered inwardly. His gaze was cold, and it seemed to the king that the temperature dropped as those eyes met his.

'I regret the death of your man,' said the king. Helikaon did not reply for a moment, and the silence grew. Kygones saw that he was staring intently at Hektor's bride-to-be. 'Allow me to introduce Andromache, daughter of the king of Thebe Under Plakos.'

'*You* are to marry Hektor?' he said.

'That is my father's command,' she replied. He fell silent again, and Kygones pressed on.

'You agreed last night to offer her passage to Troy.'

Helikaon did not look at the king. His gaze remained locked on the face of Andromache. 'You must travel with Odysseus,' said Helikaon. 'Three warships are waiting outside the bay. They will seek to finish what they began last night.'

Kygones spoke again. 'Kolanos is . . . a savage. He is no longer part of my fleet.'

And still the Golden One failed to respond. Instead he turned away to stare out to sea. Then followed a moment so bizarre that Kygones' stomach turned. The prince knelt down by a blood-drenched sack in the sand. Opening it he lifted forth a severed head. It had been mutilated, the eyes gouged out. Congealing blood covered the stump of the neck, and stained Helikaon's hands. 'You remember my friend, Zidantas,' he said, his voice conversational and calm, his expression unchanged. Shifting his hold, he held the head against his chest. The movement caused a severed vein to open. Blood dripped sluggishly onto his blue tunic, but he did not seem to notice. In the silence that followed Kygones could hear his own heart beating. Then Helikaon spoke again. 'Zidantas came to this place in good faith, seeking rest for the night. He came to this bay because it is well known that King Kygones keeps it safe. His soldiers patrol it. They are everywhere, preventing fights. Not last night, though. Last night this good man was lured away from your palace. Then he was tortured. Then he was killed.'

Kygones' throat was dry. He licked his lips. 'I explained about the lack of soldiers,' he said. 'And I share your pain at the loss of a crewman. However, think of Andromache, my friend. This grisly display must surely be upsetting for her.'

Helikaon seemed puzzled. 'Are you upset, goddess?' he asked. 'Does the sight of my friend, Zidantas, cause you distress?'

'No,' she answered calmly. 'I did not know him. He must have been a good man, though, for his loss to hurt you so.'

Kygones saw the softness of her words breach Helikaon's defences. A muscle in the prince's cheek twitched as he fought for control. Lifting the head to his face he kissed the brow, then returned it to the bloody sack. 'Yes, he *was* a good man,' he said. 'Father to six daughters. He was loyal and he was brave, and he deserved better than to die like this, murdered by Mykene savages.'

'Yes, he was murdered by savages,' said a voice. 'Do not seek to brand all Mykene with this monstrous act.'

Kygones swung to see the warrior Argurios moving through the crowd.

'You are not welcome here,' said Helikaon. 'I see your friend Glaukos has left with Kolanos and his murderers. Perhaps you should have joined them. Then we could have met at sea, and you could have tried for your revenge.'

'It is true that I wish to avenge Alektruon,' said Argurios. 'But I would do it facing you, sword to sword. I am no back-stabber, Helikaon. And no torturer either.'

'Ah,' said Helikaon, 'a good man, then, and a hero. Perhaps you would like to accompany us as we hunt down Kolanos and bring him to justice. We will not have far to go.'

Kygones saw Argurios' expression harden. 'Kolanos deserves to die,' he said, 'but I cannot raise my sword against another Follower. I will, however, report this atrocity to my king. You should remember, though, Helikaon, that Kolanos is not the first to sever a head and put out the eyes.'

Helikaon nodded. 'There is truth in that, though it is a Mykene truth, and that means it is twisted beyond recognition. Alektruon was a barbaric murderer, killed cleanly in single combat, following an unprovoked attack on a neutral vessel. Zidantas was a sailor, overpowered and tortured. His hands were bound. The blood upon his face shows his eyes were gouged out while he still lived.' Helikaon paused, then spoke again. 'Last night you proved your honour and saved my life. For that I am in your debt. Therefore you are safe, Argurios. However, as I said before, you are not welcome here.'

Kygones looked at the Mykene warrior, who was standing stiffly, his hand upon his sword. Then he spun on his heel and stalked away.

Helikaon swung back to Kygones. 'This is no longer a safe haven for honest sailors,' he said. 'My ships' captains will be instructed to avoid your bays.' With that he took up the blood-drenched sack and strode to the *Xanthos*.

Kygones felt sick. The loss of income from Helikaon's fifty ships would be a huge blow to his treasury. Within a year he would be unable to pay his mercenaries, and that would mean the bandits in the high country would begin once more to raid caravans passing through his territory. More loss of income.

Men from the *Xanthos* and the *Penelope* moved forward to push the great ship from the beach. As it floated clear the last of the crew swarmed up the ropes, and the rowers took up their positions. The mysterious hammering continued. As the *Xanthos* inched back, then swung, Kygones saw that several wooden structures were being added to the decks. But by now the king didn't care what they were building. He felt as if he had been stabbed, and his lifeblood was flowing to the beach.

Odysseus spoke then, his words cold. 'Ithakan ships will beach here no more either, Kygones. When word gets out others will come to the same conclusion.'

Kygones did not reply and Odysseus strode away. All along the beach there was an unusual lack of activity. No other ships were being launched. They all knew what was about to take place beyond the bay.

And they would wait until the battle was over.

iii

Andromache remained silent as she walked alongside Odysseus. The interplay between the men had been fascinating to observe, and there were undercurrents she could not identify. Kygones had been nervous when he approached Helikaon. Why should that be? Although she disliked the Fat King, he was not a timid man, nor one easily frightened. On the walk to the beach he was tense, and had warned his men to watch for signs of hostility. Why would he expect hostility? It was not his soldiers who had attacked Helikaon. Odysseus too seemed different today. Sadder and older. She glanced at him as they walked to the remains of the *Penelope*'s campfire. He looked fearful, his face pale, his manner subdued.

There was a group of men round the fire as they approached, and a tawny-haired young boy, his face ashen, his eyes wide. Odysseus knelt down by him.

'The *Penelope* is a good ship, Xander. A ship of legend. You will be able to tell your grandchildren you sailed on her.'

The boy looked up. 'Why did they do that to Zidantas?'

'Listen to me, lad. You could spend a lifetime trying to understand the works of evil men. Their joys are not ours. They love to inflict pain, create suffering, cause harm and death. It empowers them, for beneath the skin they are empty and worthless. Zidantas will walk the Elysian Fields in eternal sunshine. For the gods love a good man.'

'I just want to go home,' said the boy miserably.

'Me too,' Odysseus told him. 'But for now go and get yourself some breakfast, and bring me a slab of sweet pie from the stall yonder.'

Two soldiers arrived and laid Andromache's chests down on the sand. She thanked them and they moved away. Then Odysseus turned and watched the *Xanthos* sailing across the bay.

He wandered down to the shoreline. Andromache joined him there, and they stood in silence for a while, watching the new sun reflected in fragmented gold on the blue of the sea.

'What is wrong, Odysseus?' she asked him. 'Is it the coming battle? Do you fear for your friend?'

Odysseus shivered suddenly. 'I am filled with fear, but not for his safety. Helikaon is a fighter, but there are depths to the man which should never be plumbed.'

'I do not understand you.'

He sighed. 'Sometimes when a fear is voiced the gods are listening, and they make it real. So let us wait and see whether my fears are groundless.'

Andromache stood with him as the *Xanthos* was eased back from the bay into deeper water. After a while Xander returned with a slab of pie. Odysseus thanked him. When the boy had gone the Ithakan king stood silently. 'Why *did* they do that to his friend?' asked Andromache.

'To make Helikaon angry, to rob him of reason. To draw him out in a rage.' He swore softly. 'Mostly, though, Kolanos did it because he likes to inflict pain. He is a wretch.'

'It seems to have succeeded. Helikaon does seem . . . broken by the loss.'

'It won't succeed. I know Helikaon. When he sails out his mind will be calm.' He forced a smile. 'He called you goddess again.'

'I know. It surprises me that I have not heard his name before.'

'Ah, you probably have. Helikaon is what his friends call him. His name is actually Aeneas, and he is a prince of Dardania.'

'You are right, Odysseus, I have heard that name. The man who didn't want to be a king.'

'Far more to it than that,' said Odysseus. 'Less about what he might have wanted, and more about honouring his father. Not that the bastard deserved such a son. Anchises was a vile man. Should have been born with scaled skin like a lizard. He had dispossessed Helikaon, and had named his other son, Diomedes, as his heir.'

'Why?'

'A long story. I'll tell you about it on the voyage to Troy. However, Anchises was murdered on the night we sailed into his bay. Helikaon had been a crew member on the *Penelope* for two years, and we had just beached below his father's fortress. The assassin struck that night. With the king dead and the named heir still an infant the situation was rife for civil war. A nation can have only one king. And you know what would happen in most kingdoms?'

'The child and his mother would be killed,' said Andromache. 'Or men loyal to the queen would try to assassinate Helikaon.'

'Exactly. Some of the queen's followers arrived on the beach, intent on killing him. Other loyal men gathered round to stop them. The men of the *Penelope* had weapons in their hands. They would have fought for Helikaon, for they loved him. Still do. There should have been a battle.' Odysseus chuckled. 'By the balls of Ares, you know what he did? At seventeen! He ordered everyone to sheathe their weapons, approached the men who had come to kill him, and told them to take him to the queen. She was in her apartments, surrounded by loyal guards. She was terrified, for Halysia – though a sweet girl – is not a strong woman. Helikaon told her the child would be safe, and that she would not be harmed. He then pledged to follow his father's wishes, and swore allegiance to Halysia and Diomedes. He was standing there unarmed, completely in her power, and yet he had won. His authority had overwhelmed them all. That and the sincerity he radiated. Over the next few months he reorganized the kingdom, appointing new counsellors to serve the queen. No battles, no civil war, no killings. Unusual, you agree?'

'Yes it is,' she said. 'Why did he do it?'

'You must ask him that. He might even tell you.' Odysseus moved to the shoreline and sat down on a rock. 'There'll be no ships sailing for a while,' he said. 'So we will breakfast here.' He began to eat the pie Xander had brought.

'Tell me of Helikaon,' said Andromache, seating herself close by. 'Does he have children?'

Odysseus chuckled. 'You mean is he wed? No. He is waiting for love. I hope he finds it.'

'Why would he not? He is young and rich and brave.'

'Yes, he is brave, but love requires a different kind of courage, Andromache.'

She smiled. 'That makes no sense to me.'

Odysseus shrugged. 'There is one act a warrior prays he will never be forced to submit to, and yet must if he is to know love.'

'This is another riddle, and I am not good with riddles,' she said.

'Few are. Warriors fear surrender. They are proud and defiant. They will fight to the death for what they believe in. They will struggle to conquer. Love is not about conquest. The truth is a man can only find true love when he surrenders to it. When he opens his heart to the partner of his soul and says: "Here it is! The very essence of me! It is yours to nurture or destroy." '

Andromache looked into the face of the ugly king, and felt a great warmth for him. 'Ah, Odysseus,' she said. 'Now I see why Penelope loves you.'

He reddened. 'I talk too much,' he grumbled.

'You think Helikaon is frightened to love?'

'He is a fine man. But he was once a child of tragedy and sorrow. It left its mark on him.'

They stood in silence for a while. Then Andromache said, 'He is a friend of Hektor, you said.'

'More than that. They are closer than brothers. For a year Helikaon lived in Troy, building his fleet. He stayed with Hektor. Even rode with the Trojan Horse once, so I'm told. They are a sight to see. Best horsemen anywhere. You like horses?'

'I love to ride.'

'Then you will adore living with Hektor. No-one knows more about horses, or breeds finer mounts. Horses are his passion.'

'Now that is a disquieting thought,' she said, drily.

Odysseus laughed. 'And following on from your comment last night: Hektor doesn't get drunk, and only belches to be polite. As to rushing off to wars, I never met a man who likes war less, or does it better. Left to himself Hektor would stay on his horse farm and never ride to battle.'

'You like him.'

'Aye, I do, Andromache. In a violent world he is the bright morning after a storm. He will do his best to make you happy.'

'My happiness is not in the gift of others. I will be happy, or I will not be happy. No man will supply it, or deprive me of it.'

'You live by a hard philosophy, Andromache. You are right, though, in that not one of us is responsible for the happiness of others. Ironically, we can be responsible for another's *un*-happiness.' He glanced out to the bay, to see the *Xanthos* moving out onto open sea.

'I think they will rue what they did to Zidantas,' he said. Then he sighed. 'We may all come to rue it.'

XIII

The Ship of Flames

i

ON THE DECK OF THE *XANTHOS* THE CREW WERE WORKING FEVERISHLY.
Four more of Khalkeus' new weapons had been carried from the
hold in sections and were now, under the watchful eye of Oniacus,
being bolted to the deck. Men not working on construction were
donning leather breastplates and helmets, and gathering up bow,
quiver and sword. Helikaon buckled on his bronze armour. Out of
the corner of his eye he saw a powerful black-bearded figure
approach. His heart lifted, and for a moment he thought it was
Zidantas. Then, as the harsh realization of Ox's death struck him
anew, his stomach twisted. The Egypteian, Gershom, moved alongside him.

'You should have stayed ashore,' said Helikaon, more harshly
than he intended. 'Only fighting men are needed here.'

The man's dark eyes flashed with anger. 'I am no sailor,
Helikaon, but you will find I know how to fight.'

'Show me your hands.' Gershom held them out. Both were
bandaged, and there was blood seeping through the linen. 'You
couldn't grip a sword.'

'No,' admitted Gershom. 'But by your leave I will carry the club

164

of Zidantas. I knew him only a day, but he came into the sea for me and I owe him. And Oniacus tells me that Zidantas always stood by you in a fight.'

Helikaon nodded. 'Yes, he did.' He took a deep breath. 'It will be as you say, Gershom. Remain close to me.' Then he called out to Oniacus. The black-haired oarsman ran to the rear deck.

'You know what to expect outside the bay?' asked Helikaon.

'Poseidon's Trident, I would think,' answered Oniacus.

'That would be my guess also,' Helikaon agreed. 'Kolanos will have the command ship, so he will be the first prong, and furthest from us. As soon as we are in sight of him I want oars at six. We will close on him at maximum speed.'

Oniacus looked worried. 'That will leave both the other galleys with sight of our beams,' he observed. 'If they come at us fast we could be breached.'

Helikaon ignored the comment. 'I want men with ropes and hooks at prow and stern, along with ten of our best fighters, ready to grapple.'

Oniacus nodded. 'You think the Crippled Swan will work against *three* enemies?'

'No. We'll need to take out at least one with the Fire Hurlers. Concentrate on the command ship. It must be forced back, otherwise we could be rammed on two sides. I think the *Xanthos* could withstand it, but each of those galleys carries more than fifty fighting men. If they all close with us we'll be outnumbered more than two to one.'

'I'll be on the prow weapon myself. I won't miss, Golden One.'

Oniacus had been the most proficient of the men trained secretly in Kypros on the new weapons. The men chosen had been the steadiest and least excitable. It was vital, Helikaon knew, that no careless sailor was put in charge of *nephthar*. The acrid, foul-smelling liquid was highly flammable, and almost impossible to douse once lit. It burned even more brightly when water was added to it. The *Xanthos* carried eighty clay balls, wax-sealed, filled with the precious liquid. Each ball, the size of a man's head, cost the equivalent of five good horses, eight oxen, or twenty untrained slaves. And an accident could turn the *Xanthos* into a ship of flame.

'Make sure the men know exactly what we plan,' Helikaon warned. 'We won't know until the last moment which galley we'll Swan. I don't want to see our oars splintered as we turn, or a *nephthar* ball dropped.'

'Yes, lord,' answered Oniacus.

Helikaon walked back to where the nail-studded club of Zidantas had been laid by the steering oar. Hefting it, he passed it to Gershom.

'Find yourself a breastplate and helmet,' he said, 'and then return here.'

Gershom moved away and Helikaon turned to the steersman, the straggly-bearded Epeus. 'Where is your shield?'

'I forgot it, lord.'

'Fetch it now,' ordered Helikaon, stepping in and laying his arm over the oar. 'You'll be the man every Mykene bowman will try to bring down.'

'They'll not hit me,' replied Epeus, with a wide smile. 'A seer told me last night that I'd live to be eighty years old, with ten sons and thirty grandchildren.'

'May he be proved right,' said Helikaon. 'Now get your shield.'

As the steersman ran down to the main deck Helikaon stared out over the bay, and the open sea beyond. The sky was blue and clear, the sea calm, the winds light. The Mykene galleys were not in sight yet. He guessed that one would be just beyond the headland to the south, the other two behind the outer island, one to the west, the other north. They would come at the *Xanthos* in a trident formation, knowing that no matter how manoeuvrable the ship might be she could not protect her beams from a three-pronged attack. The object would be for one – perhaps two – of the galleys to ram the *Xanthos* amidships, breaching the hull. Once she was caught, and taking on water, the other galleys could close in and their warriors swarm aboard. Kolanos knew his ships would be faster than the heavier *Xanthos*, but he would not know of the Fire Hurlers, nor of the supply of *nephthar* they could deliver.

Epeus returned, a tall, curved shield strapped to his left arm. It was of black and white cowhide, edged with bronze, and would stop most shafts. Behind him came Gershom. The man was heavily muscled, and, though not as large as Zidantas, he looked as if he would have little difficulty wielding the heavy club. Thoughts of Zidantas weighed heavily on Helikaon's heart as the ship moved across the bay.

Argurios was right. Had it not been for the mutilation of Alektruon's corpse, Zidantas would probably have been alive now. Guilt tore at him. In all his life he had known three true friends: Odysseus, Hektor and Zidantas. Now one of them was gone.

Gershom's voice cut through the darkness of his thoughts. 'What is the Crippled Swan?' he asked.

'A manoeuvre to swing the ship. Imagine a swan with a broken wing trying to take off from a lake. It spins round and round. With a well-trained crew a galley can do the same. If it works, follow me, for I will be boarding one of their vessels, and the fighting will be fierce.'

'I will be alongside you, Golden One.'

Helikaon glanced back towards the beach. He could see the now tiny figure of Odysseus standing at the water's edge, the beautiful Andromache beside him. Andromache's face appeared in his mind. Odysseus often told stories of men who fell in love in an instant. Helikaon had not believed in such miracles. Love, surely, had to grow, through understanding and fellowship, mutual trust and the arrival of children. Now he was not so sure.

Last night the sight of her alone had struck him like a thunder-bolt. Today, even while suffering the loss of his friend, he had gazed upon her and felt a longing he had never before experienced. A sudden and embarrassing thought came to him. He looked at Gershom.

'Were you close enough on the beach to hear my conversation with the Fat King?'

'Yes.'

'Do you recall what I called the woman with him?'

'You called her goddess.'

Helikaon swore.

'She had a hard face,' said Gershom.

'Not hard. Strong. She is a woman of passion and also compassion. Intelligent, courageous and fiercely loyal.'

'You know her then? I thought she was a stranger to you.'

'My soul knows her.'

Slowly the *Xanthos* slid past the island at the mouth of the bay. Ahead, about half a mile to the west, Helikaon saw the Mykene command ship of Kolanos, the painted red eyes on the prow seeming to stare malevolently at the *Xanthos*. 'You see him, Oniacus?' Helikaon called out.

'I do, lord,' Oniacus shouted back. Helikaon scanned the *Xanthos*. Four men stood by each of the five Fire Hurlers. Archers knelt close by. Small copper braziers full of burning coals had been set near the deck rails, and the bowmen were busy tying oil-soaked rags around their shafts.

'Ready the *nephthar*!' ordered Helikaon. Each crew sprang to action, two men drawing back the weapons and hooking trigger ropes over jutting release bars. Then they carefully eased the large wax-sealed clay pots into the firing baskets.

The *Xanthos* moved out onto open sea. From the south another galley emerged from behind the headland, oars cutting into the water as it surged towards them. Helikaon glanced to his right. The third galley came into sight from the north, sunlight gleaming on the bronze ram beneath its prow.

'Ready oars!' bellowed Helikaon, transferring his gaze west to the Mykene command ship. It was beating towards them at speed some quarter-mile ahead. 'Oars six!'

The *Xanthos* leapt forward as the sixty oars cut into the still blue water. Picking up speed, the ship headed directly for Kolanos and his blood-eyed command galley. The enemy vessel from the south was closing, but the *Xanthos* moved beyond it.

Fire arrows sailed overhead. Several burning shafts struck the deck. Crewmen covered them with wet cloths, beating out the flames. The galley from the north was being rowed hard, hurtling towards the starboard beam. It would strike like a spear through the heart, the bronze ram splintering the hull. Helikaon stood grimly, watching the advancing ship.

All depended now on the skill of the *nephthar* crews.

In that moment a great calm descended on the Dardanian prince. It seemed that time slowed. Beside him, armed with the nail-studded club of Zidantas, stood the powerful form of Gershom. There was no fear apparent in the man.

Oniacus shouted out a command and a Hurler on the starboard side was released, the wooden throwing arm snapping upright. The *nephthar* ball sailed through the air, shattering on the deck of the advancing Mykene vessel. Another ball followed it. It struck true, breaking into shards and spraying acrid liquid over the port-side oarsmen. Archers on the *Xanthos* dipped their shafts into the fire braziers, then loosed flaming arrows, which arched across the sky to the galley's deck.

A fire began, spreading along the planks with impossible speed. Flames erupted everywhere. One of the rowers, who had been doused with *nephthar*, was beating at his blazing tunic, but then his hands began to burn. Two enemy crewmen hurled buckets of water on the flames. The result was devastating. With a great whoosh the fire billowed higher. Men ran back in panic from the oars and the galley slewed to port.

As the *Xanthos* glided by, archers sent bronze-tipped shafts into the panicked crew of the enemy ship. The Mykene, many of them with their clothes aflame, leapt into the sea. Even here the fires continued to burn. Two more clay balls struck the centre of the galley's deck. *Nephthar* had flowed down to the hold, and the deserted ship wallowed on the sea, fire burning through its timbers.

The other four Hurlers let fly – this time at the command ship of Kolanos. Three of the balls flopped into the sea, but one hit the port side, spraying its contents over the rowers. More fire arrows flew through the sky. One shaft landed on the deck, and Helikaon could see crewmen beating at the flames with blankets and cloaks. These too began to blaze.

Then the command ship veered away, and fled the fight.

Helikaon was about to order his rowers to give chase when an arrow flew past him, thudding into the deck rail. Glancing back he saw the last of the galleys closing from behind. Anger ripped through him. There was no time to pursue the fleeing Kolanos.

'Crippled Swan starboard!' he yelled. The rowers on the port side plunged their oars deep into the water, then lifted them clear, while to starboard the crew rowed with all their might. The *Xanthos* lurched, then swung swiftly. The pursuing galley powered on, seeking to use its ram as the *Xanthos* showed her beam. But the galley's captain misjudged the speed of the turn, and as the two ships came together they were almost head on. The starboard *Xanthos* rowers dragged in their oars. The Mykene were not quick enough, and many of their oars were snapped and shattered as the ships ground together. Several men at the prow of the *Xanthos* hurled grappling lines down, hooks biting into the deck rails of the galley below. Other men towards the stern did the same. Hauling on the ropes they drew the ships together.

Helikaon donned his bronze helm and ran down the centre deck to where the toughest of his crew waited, swords in hand. Clambering over the rail Helikaon shouted: 'For Zidantas!' Then he leapt down to the Mykene deck below. Enemy crewmen, armed with swords, axes and clubs, rushed to meet the invaders. Helikaon hammered his blade across the face of the first, shoulder charged another man to the deck, then leapt forward to drive his sword through the chest of a third. A fourth attacker aimed a blow at his head – but a huge club swept him from his feet. Gershom surged into the mêlée, the club of Zidantas thundering against bronze armour and hurling men to the deck. More *Xanthos* warriors clambered down to the galley, and the fighting was brutal and bloody. Helikaon killed another crewman. The battle was fierce now. Three warriors rushed at him. He parried a sword thrust from the first – then his foot slipped on the blood-smeared deck. As he fell he threw himself forward, rolling into the legs of another attacker, knocking the man from his feet. Twisting onto his back he blocked a plunging sword, and hacked a blow at the man's legs.

A slim crewman from the *Xanthos*, carrying two curved daggers, charged in, slicing a blade through the attacker's throat. Helikaon surged to his feet. Gershom was to his right, the crewman to his left. Mykene warriors rushed at the three.

Helikaon charged to meet the new threat. Gershom and the crewman leapt forward with him, and together they clove into the Mykene ranks, cutting and killing.

Helikaon saw the Mykene Glaukos, sword in hand. Fury swept through him and he cut down the opponent facing him, and ran at the Mykene warrior. Arrows began to rain down from the decks above.

As Helikaon reached Glaukos he heard someone shout: 'We surrender! Throw down your weapons, lads! For pity's sake! We surrender!' From all around came the clatter of weapons hitting the deck.

Glaukos stared hard at Helikaon for a moment. Then, seeing the men all around him had ceased to fight, he dropped his sword to the deck. Helikaon looked at the young man, and saw the hatred in his eyes.

'You sailed with Zidantas,' said Helikaon. 'You knew what they had done to him. Yet you joined them. I should gut you like a pig. But I will not. I will take you to where Argurios waits.'

Glaukos did not reply. Helikaon swung away from him. The slim crewman who had come to his rescue was cleaning his dagger blades. Helikaon approached him. The man was not young, in his forties at least.

'My thanks to you. What is your name?'

The man's eyes were dark, his expression calm. 'I am Attalus.'

'You fought bravely, and I am in your debt, Attalus.'

Turning away from the man Helikaon shouted instructions to the crew. 'Fetch rope! I want all prisoners tied to the deck rails. And throw out lines for any of the other crew who are still in the water.'

Crewmen swarmed down from the *Xanthos* and the Mykene were herded along the deck, their wrists roped to the rails. Then Helikaon ordered the body of Zidantas to be lowered to the galley. Wrapped in a bloodstained blanket, it was laid at the centre of the deck. Helikaon removed the mutilated head from the sack and placed it at the severed neck. Then he took a golden ring from the pouch at his side, and placed it in Zidantas' mouth – a gift for the Ferryman of Hades, to carry him across the dark river.

There was silence as he knelt by the body. After a moment, he rose and ran his eyes over the prisoners.

'This was Zidantas,' he said. 'Some of you knew him for a brief time. Some of you may even have been the men who overpowered him, and dragged him to your camp. He was a good man, father to six daughters. He sailed the Great Green for longer than most of you have lived. He was a Hittite, and we shall send him to his gods in the Hittite manner. All of you will attend the ceremony, and during it you will have time to consider your part in his murder.'

ii

Argurios sat alone on the beach for a while, lost in thought. The actions of Kolanos were yet another stain upon the honour of the Mykene. The torture and murder of Zidantas had been sadistic and unnecessary. And yet it would not be Kolanos alone who suffered for the events at the Fat King's bay. When Agamemnon learned that Argurios had saved the Golden One he would be furious. Argurios found himself wishing he had never agreed to walk with Helikaon. Had he remained on the beach then the assassination might have succeeded, and a good man like Zidantas would even now be preparing to sail home to his wife and daughters.

And how could young Glaukos have made such a decision, aligning himself with savage murderers?

It was a mystery to Argurios, and it saddened him.

Just then he saw the boy Xander nervously approaching him. He was carrying a wooden bowl in one hand, and a cheese-topped loaf in the other. 'I thought you might be hungry, sir,' he said.

Argurios stared hard at the freckle-faced boy, then nodded. 'I am hungry.' Taking the bowl he began to eat. It was a thin stew, but the spices were pleasantly hot on the tongue. The bread too was fresh. He looked up and saw the boy still hovering. 'There was something else?' he asked him.

'I wanted to thank you for saving me.'

Argurios had always been uncomfortable around the young, even when young himself. Now he did not know what to say. He looked at the boy. He was pale, and obviously frightened. 'Do not fear me,' said Argurios. 'I do not harm children.'

'I wish I had never come here,' said Xander suddenly. 'I wish I'd stayed at home.'

'I have had such wishes,' Argurios told him. 'Childhood is secure, but when the child becomes a man he sees the world for what it is. I grieve for Zidantas too. Not all Mykene are like the men who killed him.'

'I know that,' said Xander, sitting himself on the sand at Argurios' feet. 'You saved me. And you nearly died doing that. I was terrified. Were you?'

'Death holds no terror for me, boy. It comes to all men. The lucky ones die heroically, and their names are remembered. The unlucky ones die slowly, their hair turning white, their limbs becoming frail.'

Argurios finished the stew and the bread. Leaving the empty bowl on the rock beside him he stood, took up his helmet and walked over to where the men of the *Penelope* were gathered, watching the bay, wondering which ship, or ships, would return victorious.

Odysseus was sitting apart from his men, talking to the green-garbed Andromache. She was a striking woman. Argurios was even more uncomfortable around women than he was around children, but he needed to speak to Odysseus. As he walked forward he realized young Xander was beside him. The boy looked up and smiled cheerfully. Argurios was tempted to scowl at him, and order him gone, but the openness of the smile disarmed him.

He approached Odysseus, who glanced up, and gestured for him to sit. Then he introduced Andromache. Argurios struggled for something to say. 'I am sorry you had to witness such a grisly scene,' he said, recalling the moment Helikaon had drawn the head from the sack.

'I have seen severed heads before,' she replied coolly.

Argurios could think of no way to prolong the conversation. Nor did he wish to. He turned his attention to Odysseus. 'My mission is to Troy,' he said. 'May I sail upon the *Penelope*?'

'Don't know as I have room this trip,' said Odysseus coldly.

'He saved my life,' said Xander suddenly.

'Did he now? There's a tale I'd like to hear.'

Argurios had turned on his heel and was walking away. 'Wait, wait!' said Odysseus. 'Let me hear what the lad has to say. Go on, boy. Tell us this tale of daring.' Argurios paused. He had no wish to remain with the hostile Ithakan, but equally he needed passage to Troy. Ill at ease he stood as Xander blurted out the story of the storm and the broken rail, and how he had swung over the raging sea. Odysseus listened intently, then looked Argurios in the eye. His expression was more friendly now. 'You are a surprising man, Argurios. There will always be room on the *Penelope* for surprising men. It will be cramped, though.'

'That does not concern me.'

Someone called out, and men on the beach came to their feet.

Out in the bay they saw the *Xanthos* easing her way through the shallows. She was towing a war galley. Mystified by this turn of events Argurios wandered down to the sea's edge and stared out at the oncoming ships. The crew of the galley were lining the rails. As they came closer Argurios realized there were around fifty men roped and tied. He saw Glaukos bound at the prow.

The *Xanthos* began to turn, heading out into the deeper water of the bay.

'What is he doing?' asked Argurios. Odysseus did not reply, but the Mykene warrior saw that his expression was sorrowful, and his eyes had a haunted look. Concerned now, Argurios swung back to watch the ships. Once into the deeper water the *Xanthos* let slip the towing ropes and the galley slowly settled. The *Xanthos* pulled away.

Then Argurios saw something dark fly up from the *Xanthos* to crash upon the deck of the galley. Several more arced through the sky. The bound men began to shout and cry out, and struggle at the ropes. A score of fire arrows flashed from the *Xanthos*.

A great whoosh of flame billowed up from the galley. Screams followed, and Argurios saw Glaukos begin to burn. Fire swept over his tunic and armour, then his hair was ablaze. Now the screams were awful to hear, as men burnt like candles all along the deck. Black smoke billowed over the sea. Argurios could not believe what he was watching. At least fifty helpless men were dying in agony. One man managed to free himself and leap into the sea. Amazingly, when he surfaced the flames were still consuming him.

All along the beach there was silence, as the stunned crowd watched the magical fires burning the galley and its crew.

'You asked me what I feared,' said Odysseus. Argurios saw that he was talking to Andromache. 'Now you have seen it.'

'This is monstrous,' said Argurios, as agonized screams continued to echo from the stricken ship.

'Aye, it is,' agreed Odysseus sadly.

Black smoke was swirling now over the doomed galley, as the *Xanthos* slowly made her way back out to sea.

XIV

The Song of Farewell

AS THE LONG AFTERNOON WORE ON THE *XANTHOS* CONTINUED TO prowl the coastline towards the south, seeking the galley of Kolanos. Gershom stood at the prow, his bandaged hands still burning from the vinegar and olive oil salve Oniacus had applied. Alongside him Oniacus was staring at the southern horizon, seeking sign of the ship they were chasing. The quiet crewman, Attalus, was beside him. Twice they had caught glimpses of the galley in the far distance, but a mist had now fallen over the sea, and visibility was growing poorer by the moment. 'We have lost him,' said Oniacus, and Gershom believed he heard relief in his voice.

He glanced back towards the helm where Helikaon stood at the steering oar. No-one was with him, and the rowers were working silently. There had been no songs that day, no laughter or idle chatter as the *Xanthos* powered on in search of its prey. At first Gershom had thought the sombre mood had been caused by the death of Zidantas, but as the day wore on he realized there was more to it. The crew were tense and uneasy. Gershom struggled to find reasons for their disquiet. Did they fear another battle? It seemed unlikely, for he had seen them fight, and they were not fearful men. Also they had taken very few losses in the sea battle. The steersman, Epeus, had been shot through the back, but had held

176

the *Xanthos* on course until they boarded the enemy galley. Then he had collapsed and died. Three other men had been killed, but two of them were new crewmen, apparently, and had not been aboard long enough to forge deep friendships. The lack of victory joy made no sense to the powerful Egypteian.

Finally he swung towards Oniacus. 'You Sea Peoples celebrate victory in a most strange fashion,' he said. 'Whenever *we* win a battle there is song and laughter. Men brag of their heroic deeds. They feel good to be alive. Yet I feel I am on a ship of the dead.'

Oniacus looked at him quizzically. 'Did the sight of those burning sailors not touch you at all, Gyppto?'

Gershom was baffled. How could anyone mourn the deaths of enemies? 'They attacked us,' he said. 'We triumphed.'

'We *murdered* them. Cruelly. They were men of the sea. They had families and loved ones.'

Gershom felt anger touch him. What nonsense was this? 'Then they should have stayed home with their *loving* families,' he said. 'And not set out to torture an honest man to death. When a lion attacks you don't stop to consider whether he has cubs to feed. You just kill him.'

'Can't argue with that,' agreed Attalus.

Oniacus cast them both an angry look. 'The man who killed Ox is Kolanos. He is the one who should have suffered burning. We should have sunk the galley and freed the crew.'

Gershom laughed. 'Free them? So they could attack again? Had they captured the *Xanthos* would they have let you go?'

'No, they would not,' said the curly-haired oarsman. 'They would have killed us. But that is what separates the evil from the righteous. When we behave like them we become like them. And then what is our justification for being? By accepting their moral standards we discard our right to condemn them.'

'Ah, we are talking philosophy then,' said Gershom. 'Very well. Once, a long time ago, there was a rebellion in Egypt. The pharaoh captured the ringleaders. His advisers urged him to kill them all. Instead he listened to the grievances of the men who rose against him, and sought to address them. They were all released.

The pharaoh even lowered the taxes in the rebellious areas. He too was a man of philosophy. A few years later the rebels rose again, and this time defeated and slew the pharaoh in battle. They also slaughtered his wives and his children. He had reigned for less than five years. One of the ringleaders then became pharaoh in his place. He too suffered insurrections, but he crushed them, killing all who went against him. Not only did he kill them, but all their families too. He reigned for forty-six years.'

'What point are you making, Gyppto? That savagery is the way forward? That the most ruthless men will always succeed and those with compassion are doomed?'

'Of course. It *is* a sound historical argument. However, my point would be that the danger lies in the extremes. A man who is *always* cruel is evil, a man who is *always* compassionate will be taken advantage of. It is more a question of balance, or harmony, if you will. Strength and compassion, ruthlessness allied sometimes to mercy.'

'Today was more than ruthless,' said Oniacus. 'I never thought Helikaon to be so vengeful.'

'It was more than revenge,' said Attalus.

'How so?'

'We could have burned them at sea, then set out more swiftly in search of Kolanos. Instead we towed the galley back into the bay, so that all could witness the horror. Every sailor on that beach will carry the story. Within a few weeks there will not be a port on the Great Green that has not heard the tale. *That*, I think, was the point of it.'

'So that the whole world can know that Helikaon and his men are savages?'

Attalus shrugged. 'If you were a Mykene sailor, would you want to go against Helikaon now?'

'No,' admitted Oniacus, 'I wouldn't. Equally I don't believe many men will want to serve with him either. When we put back into Troy I think a number of the crew will choose to leave his service.'

'Will you?' asked Gershom.

Oniacus sighed. 'No. I am Dardanian and Helikaon is my lord. I will remain loyal.'

It was warm, a light breeze blowing from the south. Dolphins were once more swimming alongside the ship, and Gershom watched them for a while. The mist grew thicker, and they heard Helikaon call out for the oarsmen to slow their pace. Leaving Attalus at the prow Oniacus strode back along the deck. Gershom followed him, moving past crewmen still manning the fire throwers. The two men climbed the steps to the stern deck. Helikaon's face was an expressionless mask.

'We need to find a beach, Golden One,' said Oniacus. 'It will be dusk soon.'

For the next hour the *Xanthos* crept along the cliff line, finally angling into a deep, crescent-shaped bay. The beach beyond was deserted, and Helikaon told the Fire Hurler crews to step down, and stow the *nephthar* balls. Once this had been done, the *Xanthos* was beached, stern on.

Helikaon ordered some twenty of the crew to remain on board, just in case the Mykene galley found the same bay, though Gershom sensed he did not expect such an eventuality.

Ashore, several fires were lit, and groups of sailors moved off inland in search of extra firewood and fresh water. Gershom stayed aboard. His hands were still too sore to grip the trailing ropes and climb down to the sand. Even so, he felt his strength beginning to return. Helikaon too remained on the *Xanthos*. As the evening wore on, and the cookfires were lit, the atmosphere remained muted.

By the time the mist had cleared, and the stars were bright in the night sky, one or two of the sailors had fallen asleep. Most remained wakeful, however, and Gershom, who had dozed for a while on the rear deck, saw that they were gathered in a large group, and were talking in low voices.

Helikaon brought Gershom some food, a round of cheese and some salt-dried meat. He was also carrying a water skin. 'How are your hands?' he asked.

'I heal fast,' said Gershom, taking the food gratefully. The cheese was full flavoured, the meat spiced and hot upon the tongue. Helikaon stood at the stern, gazing down on the beach and the gathered men. Gershom watched him for a while, remembering the sight of him leaping down onto the enemy deck. For the crew it would be the memory of the burning men that remained from that battle. For Gershom it was the sight of the young prince, in battle armour, cleaving his way through the Mykene ranks. His sword style had been ruthlessly efficient, his attack unstoppable. He had radiated a sense of invincibility. This, more than anything else, had cowed the Mykene into surrender.

'I fear your crew are unhappy,' said Gershom, breaking the silence.

'They are good men, brave and honest. Zidantas was a fine judge. He only hired men with heart. Tonight they will be thinking of him. As I am.'

'They will be thinking of more than that, I think.'

Helikaon nodded. 'Yes, more than that,' he agreed. 'You fought well today, Gershom. Zidantas would have been proud of the way you wielded his club. If you wish to stay in my service you can.'

'I was thinking of leaving the ship in Troy.'

'Many will,' said Helikaon. 'You, however, ought to think about the wisdom of such a decision.'

'Why would it not be wise?'

Helikaon turned away from the beach and Gershom felt the power of his gaze. 'What crime did you commit in Egypt?'

'What would prompt such a question?' Gershom was evasive.

'You are a careful man, Gyppto, and that is a virtue I admire. Now, however, is not the time to be secretive. The Fat King told me that in every port Egyptian ambassadors have sought news of a powerful, black-bearded runaway who might be calling himself Gershom. There is a great sum in gold for the man, or men, who deliver him to justice. So, I ask again, what was your crime?'

Gershom's heart sank. He had not realized – though he should have – that his grandfather would go to such lengths to capture him. 'I killed two Royal Guardsmen,' he said.

'Were they seeking to arrest you?'

'No. I saw them attacking a woman and moved in to stop them. They drew swords. So I killed two of them. I was drunk, and not in control of myself. I regret it now, of course.'

'If they were attacking a woman you were right to oppose them.'

'No, I was not. She was a slave, and if Guardsmen choose to rut with slaves that is no crime. The woman was in the wrong for resisting them.'

'So you fled.'

'The sentence for the crime would have been the loss of my eyes, and then to be buried alive. No embalming, no walking with Osiris in the Fabled Land, no future among the stars. Yes, I fled. But it seems there is no safe refuge on the Great Green.'

'You will be safer among my crew in Dardania. We will winter there.'

'I will think on your offer, Helikaon. And I thank you for making it.'

Helikaon sighed. 'No need for thanks, Gershom. Many crew will leave when we reach Troy. I can't afford to lose another good fighting man like you.'

'I am sure you could convince them to stay on.'

Helikaon gave a rueful smile. 'Only by telling them the truth, and I cannot afford that.'

'You'll need to explain that riddle,' said Gershom.

'Perhaps I will – when I come to know you better.'

'So, what happens now?'

'We have lost Kolanos, and the season is almost over. I will resume the hunt in the spring. Though it takes all my life I will find him one day. Or he will be delivered to me.'

'No force under the stars is more powerful than hatred,' said Gershom.

'Hatred has no virtue, and yet men can never be free of it,' replied Helikaon bitterly. 'But even knowing that, I shall not rest until Kolanos is dead. Such evil cannot be allowed to pass unpunished.'

'You will send out assassins?'

'No, I will find him myself.'

Helikaon fell silent. 'What are you thinking?' asked Gershom.

Helikaon took a deep breath, then let it out slowly. 'I was think-ing of my father the last time I saw him. He was killed by an assassin. The killer had cut off his ear. Why, I do not know.'

'You never found out who ordered it?'

'No. I still have men searching. There is a reward for inform-ation. Yet nothing has surfaced. It will, though, one day. Then, like Kolanos, the man who ordered my father's death will die. This I have sworn.'

Just then a man on the beach began to speak in a loud voice. Gershom moved to the stern rail and looked down. It was Oniacus. 'Hear our words, O Hades, Lord of the Deepest Dark,' he shouted, 'for some of our friends now walk your lands in search of the Elysian Fields!'

The crew began to chant.

Helikaon climbed the rail and lowered himself to the beach. The men remaining on the ship gathered around Gershom, and they too began to chant. The sound was mournful, a song of death and farewell. When it was over Gershom saw Helikaon move to the centre of the circle of men on the sand. He began to speak of Zidantas, of his courage, of his love of family and crew, of his loyalty and the greatness of his spirit. After him came Oniacus once more. He spoke also of Zidantas, and of Epeus and the other dead men, but his stories were smaller and more personal: of the Ox's generosity and sense of humour, of Epeus' love of gambling. More men told stories, and at the conclusion of each the crew chanted: 'Hear our words, O Hades . . .'

It occurred to Gershom then that somewhere along this coastline there was another crew, probably chanting the same words, and speaking of the deaths of friends who had died attacking the *Xanthos*.

Easing his way through the crowded men at the rail he moved to a place amidships and settled down on the deck. Lying back, he stared up at the stars.

Do the gods listen, he wondered? Do they care at all about the small lives of those who worship them? Does golden Osiris weep for our losses? Does Isis mourn with us? Or this Greek deity, Hades? Or Jehovah, the grim god of the desert slaves? Or fire-breathing Molech of the Assyrians?

Gershom doubted it.

Part Two

THE GOLDEN CITY

XV

The City of Dreams

i

HELIKAON'S GRIEF DID NOT LESSEN AS THEY TURNED ABOUT AND SAILED north along the coast. Rather he could feel it swelling inside him, clawing at his heart. There were times when he felt he could not breathe for the weight of it. As the *Xanthos* clove through the waves alongside Blue Owl Bay once more the memories came back with increased sharpness and the loss of Zidantas threatened to overwhelm him.

The power of his grief was a shock to him. Zidantas had been a good friend and a loyal follower, but Helikaon had not realized how much he had come to rely on the man's steadfastness and devotion. All his life Helikaon had been wary of intimacy, of allowing people close, of sharing inner thoughts and dreams and fears. Ox had never been intrusive, never pushed to know what he was feeling. Ox was safe.

Odysseus had once told him that a man could not hide from his fears, but had to ride out and face them. He could not be like a king trapped within his fortress. Helikaon had understood. It had freed him to become the Golden One, the Prince of the Sea.

And yet, he knew, only a part of him had sallied out. The fortress was still there in his mind, and his soul remained within it.

What was it the old rower, Spyros, had said about children who suffer tragedy? They get heart-scarred. Helikaon understood that too. When he was small his heart had been open. Then his mother, in a dress of gold and blue, a jewelled diadem upon her brow, had flung herself from the cliff top. The little boy had believed she was going to fly to Olympos, and had watched in silent horror as her body plummeted to the rocks below. Then his father had dragged him down to the beach to gaze upon her broken beauty, her face shattered, one eye hanging clear. His father's words remained carved in fire on his heart. 'There she lies, the stupid bitch. Not a goddess. Just a corpse for the gulls to pick at.'

For a little while the child's wounded heart had remained open, as he sought to gain comfort from Anchises. But when he spoke of his feelings he was silenced, and shouted at for his weakness. He was at first derided and then ignored. Maids and servants who treated him with kindness or love were said to be feeding his weakness and replaced by cold, hard harridans who had no patience with a grieving child. Eventually he learned to keep his feelings to himself.

Years later, under the guidance of Odysseus, he had learned to be a man, to laugh and joke with the crew, to work among them and share their lives. But always as an outsider looking in. He would listen as men spoke with feeling of their loved ones, their dreams and their fears. In truth he admired men who could do this, but had never found a way to open the fortress gates and take part himself. After a while it did not seem to matter. He had mastered the art of listening and the skills of conversation.

Odysseus – like Zidantas – never pressed him to express his feelings. Phaedra had, and he had seen the hurt in her eyes when he evaded her questions, when he closed the gates upon her.

What he had not realized, until now, was that Ox had not been kept outside the fortress of his heart. Unnoticed, he had slipped inside, to the deepest chambers. His murder had sundered the walls, leaving Helikaon exposed just as he had been all those years ago when his mother, in drugged despair, had ended her life on that cliff.

Adding to the pain was the fact that his mind kept playing tricks on him, refusing to accept that Ox was dead. Every so often during the day he would look around, seeking him. At night he would dream of seeing him, and believe the dream was reality and reality the dream. Then he would awaken with a glad heart, only for the horror to wash over him like a black wave.

The sun was setting and they needed to find somewhere to beach the *Xanthos*. Helikaon ordered the crew to keep rowing, seeking to put distance between himself and the awful memories of Blue Owl Bay.

The ship moved on, more slowly now, for there were hidden rocks, and Oniacus placed men at the prow with sounding poles calling out instructions to the rowers. Helikaon summoned a crewman to take the steering oar and walked to the port side, where he stood staring out over the darkening sea.

'I will kill you, Kolanos,' he whispered. The words did nothing to lift his spirits. He had butchered fifty Mykene sailors, and that act of revenge had offered no relief to his pain. Would the death of Kolanos balance the loss of Ox?

A thousand men like Kolanos, he knew, could not replace a single Zidantas. Even if he slaughtered the entire Mykene nation nothing would bring back his friend.

Once again the pressure grew in his chest, a physical pain beginning to swell in his stomach. He drew in slow, deep breaths, trying to push away the despair.

He thought of young Diomedes, and his mother, Halysia. For a moment sunshine touched his anguished soul. Yes, he thought, I will find peace in Dardania. I will teach Diomedes to ride the golden horses. Helikaon had acquired a stallion and six mares from Thessaly four years ago, and they were breeding well. Strong-limbed and sleek, they were the most beautiful horses Helikaon had ever seen, their bodies pale gold, their manes and tails cloud white. Their temperaments also were sound: gentle and steady and unafraid. Yet when urged to the run they moved like the wind. Diomedes adored them, and had spent many happy days with the foals.

Helikaon smiled at one memory. In that first season, four years ago, eight-year-old Diomedes had been sitting on a paddock fence. One of the golden horses had approached him. Before anyone could stop him the boy had scrambled to the beast's back. The mare, panicked, had started to run and buck. Diomedes had been thrown through the air. He might have been hurt had not Ox been close by. The big man had rushed in and caught the boy. Both had tumbled to the ground laughing.

The smile faded and a stab of pain clove through Helikaon, so sharp that he groaned.

The crewman, Attalus, was close by. He glanced over, but said nothing.

Then Oniacus called out from the prow. Helikaon strolled to where the man was standing. Off to starboard there was a narrow bay. There were no ships beached there. 'Bring us in,' Helikaon ordered.

Later, on the beach, he wandered away from the fires and climbed up through a shallow wood to the top of the cliffs. There he sat, his thoughts whirling.

He heard movement behind him, and surged to his feet. He saw Attalus moving through the trees, two bulging water skins hanging from his shoulders. The crewman paused.

'Found a stream,' he said. 'You want water?'

'Yes. Thank you.' Helikaon took one of the skins and drank deeply. Attalus stood silently waiting. 'You don't say much,' Helikaon observed.

The man shrugged. 'Not much to say.'

'A rare trait for a sailor.'

'Hot food is ready,' said Attalus. 'You should come and eat.'

'I will in a while.' In that moment, in the quiet of the woods, Helikaon felt the urge to talk to this taciturn man, to share his thoughts and feelings. As always he did not. He merely stood quietly as Attalus strolled away with the water skins.

Helikaon remained on the cliff top for a while, then returned to the campfire. Taking a blanket he lay down, resting his head on his arm. Muted conversations flowed around and over him.

As he lay there he pictured again the face of Andromache, as he had seen her in the firelight. She too was heading for Troy. The thought that he might see her there lifted his spirits.

And he slept.

ii

Xander was embarrassed. For the third time that morning he had been sick, vomiting over the side. His head throbbed, and his legs felt unsteady. The *Penelope* was much smaller than the *Xanthos* – just half her length and very cramped, so there was nowhere to go to hide his shame. The rowers' benches were on the main deck and, once the ship was under oars, there was only a narrow passage between the ranks of oarsmen to walk from one end of the ship to the other. Unlike on the gleaming new *Xanthos*, the oak planks of the deck looked worn and chipped, and some of the oars appeared warped by the sun and the salt sea.

The mood was gloomy on the tiny foredeck, where he had been told to wait with the other passengers until they reached Troy. On the first day Xander had been excited at the prospect of sailing with the legendary Odysseus, but that excitement had passed swiftly, for there was little for him to do. He watched the land glide by, and listened to the conversation of those around him. Andromache had been kind to him, and had talked with him of his home and his family. Argurios had said nothing to him. In fact he said little to anyone. He stood at the prow like a statue, staring out at the waves. The old shipwright, Khalkeus, was also gloomy and quiet.

Even the nights were sombre. Odysseus told no tales, and the crew of the *Penelope* kept to themselves, gambling with dice bones, or chatting quietly to friends. The passengers were left largely to their own devices. Andromache would often walk along the beaches with Odysseus, while Argurios sat alone. Khalkeus too seemed glum and low of spirit.

One night, as they sheltered from heavy rain under overhanging trees back from the beach, Xander found himself sitting with the shipwright. As always, the man seemed downcast. 'Are you all right?' Xander asked.

'I am wet,' snapped Khalkeus. The silence grew. Then the older man let out a sigh. 'I did not mean to sound so angry,' he said. 'I am still suffering from the results of my actions. I have never had deaths on my conscience before.'

'You killed someone?'

'Yes. All those men on the galley.'

'You didn't kill them, Khalkeus. You were on the beach with me.'

'How pleasant it would be if that simple statement were true. You will find, young Xander, that life is not so simple. I designed the Fire Hurlers, and suggested to Helikaon that he should acquire *nephthar*. You see? I thought they would be a protection against pirates and reavers. It never occurred to me – stupid man that I am – that they could be instruments of murder. It should have. The truth is that every invention leads men to say: can I use it to kill, to maim, to terrify? Did you know that bronze was first used to create ploughs, so that men could dig the earth more efficiently? It did not take long, I suspect, before it was used for swords and spears and arrowheads. It angered me when the Kypriots called the *Xanthos* the Death Ship. But what an apt name it proved to be.' He fell silent. Xander didn't want to talk about burning men and death, so he too sat quietly as the rain fell.

By the twentieth day of the journey Xander thought he might die of boredom. Then the sickness had begun. He had woken that morning with a bad headache. His mouth was dry, his skin hot. He had tried to eat a little dried meat, but had rushed away from the group to throw up on the sand.

The day was windless, and a thick bank of mist around the ship muffled the sounds of the oars and the creak of wood and leather. Time crawled by and the *Penelope* seemed suspended in time and place.

Seated beside him, the old shipwright Khalkeus stared at his hands, turning and turning his old straw hat, mashing the battered brim, and occasionally muttering to himself in a language Xander did not understand. The lady Andromache was facing away from him, looking towards their destination.

An image flashed unwanted into the boy's mind of the blazing ship, the sound of the screams and the roar of the flames . . .

He dismissed the image and determinedly thought of his home and his mother and grandfather. Though the sun was obscured by mist he guessed it was well after noon and he imagined his grand-father sitting in the porch of his small white house, shaded by purple-flowering plants, eating his midday meal. The thought of food made his stomach twist.

Delving into his pack he brought out two round pebbles. One was blue speckled with brown like a bird's egg. The other was white and so translucent he could almost see through it.

'Are you going to eat them, boy?'

Xander swung round to see Khalkeus gazing at him.

'Eat them? No, sir!'

'I saw you looking in your bag and thought you were hungry. When I saw the pebbles I thought you might eat them. Like a chicken.'

'Chicken?' the boy repeated helplessly. 'Do chickens eat pebbles?'

'They do indeed. It helps to grind the grain they eat. Like mill-stones in the granary of their bellies.' The old man bared his few remaining teeth, and Xander realized he was trying to be friendly.

The boy smiled back. 'Thank you. I didn't know that. I picked the pebbles up on the beach before I left home. My grandfather told me they are round and shiny because they have been in the sea for hundreds of years, rolling around.'

'Your grandfather is right. He is obviously a man of intelligence. Why did you choose those two? Were they different from the rest of the stones around them?'

'Yes. The rest were just grey and brown.'

'Ah, then these pebbles are travellers, like you and me. They long ago left the seas where they were first made and they have travelled the world. Now they mix with pebbles of a different sort and home is but a dim memory.'

Xander had no answer to this baffling comment, so he changed the subject. 'Are you going to live in Troy?' he asked.

'Yes. I shall purchase a forge and return to my true calling.'

'I thought you were a builder of ships.'

'Indeed, I am a man of many talents,' said Khalkeus, 'but my heart yearns to work metal. Do you know how we make bronze?'

'No,' said Xander, nor did he want to. Bronze was bronze. It didn't matter to Xander whether it was found in the ground, or grew from trees. Khalkeus chuckled.

'The young are too honest,' he said, good-naturedly. 'Everything shows in their faces.' Reaching into his pocket he produced a small blue stone. Then he drew a knife of bronze from the sheath at his side. The blade gleamed in the sunlight. He held up the small stone. 'From this,' he said, 'comes this,' and he held up the knife.

'Bronze is a stone?'

'No, the stone contains copper. First we remove the copper, then we add another metal, tin. In exactly the right amount. Eventually we have a workable bronze. Sometimes – depending on the quality of the copper – we get poor bronze, brittle and useless. Sometimes it is too soft.' Khalkeus leaned in. 'But I have a secret that helps to make the best bronze in all the world. You want to know the secret?'

Xander's interest was piqued. 'Yes.'

'Bird shit.'

'No, really I would!'

Khalkeus laughed. 'No, boy, *that* is the secret. For some reason if you add bird droppings to the process the resulting bronze is hard, but still supple enough to prevent it shattering. That is how I made my first fortune. Through bird shit.'

The curious conversation came to an end when the lookout, high on the crossbeam of the mast, suddenly cried out and pointed to the south. The boy jumped up eagerly and peered in the direction the man indicated. He could see nothing except for the endless bank of blue-grey mist.

Then he heard another shout and saw Odysseus gesturing to him from the aft deck. His heart lifted, and with wings on his feet he ran down the deck to where the trader waited.

'We'll be on the beach at Troy shortly, lad,' Odysseus said. He was swigging mightily from a water skin, and liquid gushed down his chest. 'I want you to stick with Bias. Once the rowers have stowed their oars, the mast will be dismantled, for we will remain in the city for a few days. Bias will show you how we take down the mast and stow it safely. Then I want you to ensure the passengers have left none of their belongings on the *Penelope*.'

Xander was daunted by the trader's stern manner. 'Yes, sir.'

For the first time in days he suddenly felt anxious. He had never been to a city. He had never been anywhere larger than his own village until Bad Luck Bay. Where would he go once they reached Troy? Where would he stay? He wondered if he could remain on the *Penelope*. Surely someone would have to keep watch, he thought. 'What do I do when we reach the city? It is said to be very big, and I do not know where to go.'

Odysseus frowned down at him. 'Where do you go, lad? You're a free man now. You'll do what sailors do. Troy is rich in fleshpots and taverns, as in everything else. Now get about your duties.'

Crestfallen, Xander reluctantly turned away. 'Wait, boy,' said Odysseus. Xander swung back to see the ugly king smiling at him. 'I am jesting. You'll stay with us until we leave. If Helikaon hasn't come by then I'll see you safely back in Kypros. As for seeing the city . . . well, you can come with me, if you have a mind. I have much business to attend to and many people to visit. Perhaps you will even meet the king.'

'I should very much like to go with you, sir,' said Xander eagerly.

'Very well. Walk with Odysseus and you will breakfast with peasants and dine with kings.' He smiled. 'Look, there she is,' he said. 'The city of dreams.'

The boy peered ahead through the bank of mist but could still see nothing.

'Look up,' said Odysseus.

Xander looked up and fear lanced through him. Far to port and high in the sky above the mist he could see what appeared to be flames of red and gold. He saw high towers and roofs gleaming with molten bronze.

'Is it on fire?' he asked fearfully, an image of the flaming ship again invading his head.

Odysseus laughed. 'Have you not heard of the city of gold, boy? What do you think they mean? Troy's towers are roofed with bronze and the palace roof is tiled with gold. It sparkles in the sunlight like a painted trollop, luring fools and wise men alike.'

As the ship drew closer and the mist started to clear Xander got his first glimpse of the great golden walls, higher than he had ever dreamed, and stretching far into the distance. They sat atop a high plateau and he found himself craning his neck to see the gleaming towers. He could count three along the wall that faced the sea, all dwarfed by a single one to the south. The battlemented walls shone like copper and Xander could believe the entire city made of metal, shining like freshly burnished armour.

'There must be many great warriors living there,' he said.

'Aye,' said Odysseus. 'This is horse country and the home of horse tamers. The Trojan Horse – the city's cavalry – is legendary and its leader is the king's eldest son Hektor. He is a great warrior.'

'Do you know him?' Xander wondered if he would meet the king's warrior son.

'I know everybody, boy. Hektor . . .' He hesitated, and Xander saw that Andromache had moved up the deck to stand quietly beside him. 'Hektor is a fine rider and charioteer, the best you will ever see.'

'It is so beautiful,' said the boy suddenly.

Odysseus took another deep drink from his water skin and wiped his mouth, absently brushing drops from his tunic. 'Do you know what an illusion is, boy?'

'No, I don't think so,' said Xander uncertainly.

'Well, an illusion is a story, a tall tale if you like. It's a bright shining story that masks a hidden darkness. Troy is a city of illusion. Nothing is what it seems.'

Xander could now see the land stretching out around the high plateau. It was green and lush and he could make out the moving dots of horses and sheep on the low hills. Between the plateau and the sea, in front of the city walls, lay a massive town. Xander could make out individual buildings of many colours and even people walking in the streets. A wide road wound down from the great south tower of Troy, eventually reaching the beach where many hundreds of ships were pulled up and there was a riot of activity as they were loaded and unloaded.

Seeing the crowd of boats, Odysseus growled to Bias, 'This cursed mist has made us too late to get a good berth. By Apollo's golden balls, I've never seen the bay so full. We'll be halfway up the Scamander before we can get some sand under her keel.'

But at that moment a large ship started to pull away from the beach and Bias gave a quick command to the helmsman. The *Penelope* turned and headed for the strand, passing close to the departing ship, a wide low cargo vessel with purple eye markings and a patchwork sail.

'Ho, *Penelope*!' A powerful dark-haired man dressed in black waved from the other ship.

'Ho, *Phaistos*! You're setting sail late in the day!' called Odysseus.

'Kretan ships sail the seas when men of Ithaka are tucked up safe in their beds!' shouted the man in black. 'Sleep well, Odysseus!'

'Good sailing, Meriones!'

The sun was passing down through the sky by the time Xander had his feet safely on the sand of Troy. He was struggling with several heavy bags. There was his own small sack of belongings, an embroidered linen bag Andromache had entrusted to him, and two large leather satchels crammed to the brim, their drawstrings straining, which Odysseus had told him to carry. He looked up at the city looming above him and wondered how he would ever carry everything up to its heights. His legs felt unsteady, his head was aching, and dizziness ebbed and flowed over him. Dropping the bags to the sand he sat down heavily.

The beach was bustling with activity and noise. Cargoes were being unloaded and piled onto carts and donkeys. Xander saw bales of bright cloth, piles of pottery packed with straw, amphorae great and small, livestock in wooden crates. Odysseus he could see further up the beach, arguing with a thin man in a grey loincloth. Both men were shouting and gesticulating, and Xander wondered nervously if there would be more deaths. But Andromache stood quietly by the two and seemed unconcerned. She was now garbed in a long white robe, a white shawl round her shoulders, and a thin veil covering her head and face.

Finally Odysseus slapped the man on the back and turned to Xander, gesturing to him to join them. He struggled over, the leather satchels banging awkwardly against his legs. Odysseus pointed to a battered two-donkey carriage standing nearby. 'Is that a chariot?' asked Xander.

'Of a sort, lad.'

The wooden carriage was two-wheeled, and there were four seats, two on either side of its U-shaped structure. The thin man stepped onto the driving platform and took up the reins.

'In there, lad. Quickly,' ordered Odysseus.

Xander climbed in, dragging the bags and satchels after him and piling them at his feet. Odysseus handed Andromache into the cart and she sat beside the boy. He had never been so close to her before, and he could smell the fragrance of her hair. He awkwardly shifted away, trying not to touch her. She turned and he could see her smile at him under the veil. The small silver sea horses weighting the ends tinkled together as her head moved, and he could feel the gauzy softness of the cloth against his shoulder.

'Whose chariot is this?' he asked. 'Does it belong to Odysseus? Has he bought it?'

'No,' she said. 'The cart is for travellers. It will carry us up to the city.'

Xander's head was spinning with the strangeness of it all. The sickness seemed to be passing, but he felt terribly hot, and wished he could feel a sea breeze on his face. Sweat dripped into his eyes and he brushed it away with the sleeve of his tunic.

The donkeys plodded up the winding street through the lower town, moving ever upwards towards the city walls. The boy craned his neck to see the brightly painted houses, some awash with flowers, others decorated with carved wood. There were potters' homes with their goods piled high on wooden racks outside, metal workers plying their trade out in the open, protected from the heat of their furnaces by leather aprons, textile workshops with dyed cloth drying on racks outside. He could smell hot metal, baking bread and flowers, the rich scents of animal dung and perfumes, and a hundred smells he couldn't name. The noise all around was of laughter and complaint, the braying of donkeys, the creak of the cart's wheels and the leather traces, women's shrill voices and the calls of pedlars.

Xander could see the walls up close now. They rose from the rocky ground at an angle so gradual it seemed possible to climb them, but then straightened up suddenly and soared towards the sky.

The huge gate they were slowly approaching lay in the shadow of the tallest tower, almost twice as high as the walls, and as Xander craned his neck to see the top he felt as if the weight of it was falling towards him and he quickly looked away. In front of the tower was a line of stone pedestals on which stood six fearsome statues of ferocious warriors wearing crested helms and holding spears. Xander noticed the thin cartman cease to shout at his donkeys, and bow his head in brief silence, as the cart passed by the statues.

'This is the Scaean Gate, the first Great Gate of Troy,' said Odysseus. 'It is the main entrance to the city from the sea.'

'It is very big,' said Xander. 'I can see why it is called a great gate.'

'Troy has many gates, and towers now. The city is growing continually. But the four Great Gates guard the Upper City, where the rich and the mighty dwell.'

As the donkey cart reached the gate it was swallowed in sudden darkness. There was silence around them and the gateway felt cold out of the late day's sunshine. Now the boy could hear only the steady clop-clop of hooves and his own breathing.

Then they burst out into the sunshine again and he shaded his eyes, dazzled by the light and the glitter of gold and bronze. The road continued to stretch away from them, but inside the city gates it became a roadway of stone, made of the same great golden blocks that formed the walls. It was so wide Xander doubted he could throw a stone across it. The road wound ever upwards between huge buildings, the smallest of which was bigger even than Kygones' citadel at Blue Owl Bay. Xander felt the size of an ant beneath their walls, some of which were carved with mighty creatures of legend. The wide windows and the edges of roofs were decorated with shining metals and polished woods. High gates stood open and the boy saw glimpses of green courtyards and marble fountains.

He looked around him, open-mouthed. He glanced at Andromache, who had pulled up her veil and was wide-eyed too.

'Is this what all cities are like?' he asked at last.

'No, lad,' said Odysseus with amusement. 'Only Troy.'

The street was thronged with men and women, walking, or riding chariots or horses. Their clothing was rich and colourful and the glitter of jewellery shone at every neck and arm.

'They are all dressed like kings and queens,' the boy whispered to Andromache.

She didn't answer him but asked Odysseus, 'Do all these buildings belong to the king?'

'Everything in Troy belongs to Priam,' he told her. 'This poxy cart belongs to him, the road it travels on, that pile of apples over there, they are all Priam's. These buildings are the palaces of Troy's nobles.'

'Which one is the home of Hektor?' Andromache asked, looking around her.

Odysseus pointed up the roadway. 'Up there. It is beyond the crest of the hill and overlooks the plain to the north. But we are going to Priam's palace. After that Hektor's home will seem but a peasant's hovel.'

The cart trundled on and soon the palace came in sight. To Xander's eyes its walls were as high as those of the city itself, and he could see the golden roof gleam as the westering sun caught its edge. In front of the palace, once they had passed through the bronze-reinforced double gates, was a red-pillared portico, where the cart stopped and they descended. The portico was flanked by lines of tall soldiers garbed in bronze breastplates and high helms with cheek guards inlaid with silver, and white plumes which waved in the wind. Each had one hand on his sword hilt, the other grasping a spear, and each stared sternly over the boy's head, as still and silent as the statues at the Scaean Gate.

'Those are Priam's Eagles, boy,' said Odysseus, pointing at the soldiers. 'Finest fighting men you'll ever see. Look, Xander,' he went on. 'Is that not a sight to lift the spirits?' Xander turned to look back the way they had come, across the shining roofs of the palaces, the golden walls, and down over the lower town to the sea. The sky had turned rose pink and copper in the light of the dying sun, and the sea below it was a lake of molten gold. In the far distance Xander saw a glowing island of coral and gold on the horizon.

'What isle is that?' he asked, thinking it must be a magical place.

'Not one but two islands,' said Odysseus. 'The first you can see is Imbros, but the great peak beyond is Samothraki.'

Xander stood entranced. The sky darkened, blood-red streaks and clouds of gold and black forming before his eyes. 'And there?' he asked, pointing towards the north, and the dark hills over-looking a crimson sea.

'That is the Hellespont, lad, and the land beyond is Thraki.'

Andromache laid her hand on the boy's shoulder, gently turning him towards the south. Far away, across a shimmering river and a wide plain, Xander saw a mighty mountain. 'That is the holy mount of Ida,' whispered Andromache, 'where Zeus has his watch-tower. And beyond it is little Thebe, where I was born.'

It was now so hot that Xander could hardly catch his breath. He looked up at Andromache, but her face seemed to shimmer before his eyes. Then the ground shifted beneath his feet, and he fell. Embarrassed, he tried to rise, but his arms had no strength and he slumped down again, his face resting on the cold stone. Gentle hands turned him onto his back.

'He has a fever,' he heard Andromache say. 'We must get him inside.'

Then blissful darkness took away the heat, and he tumbled down and down into it.

XVI

The Gates of Horn and Ivory

i

THE MIST WAS GROWING THICKER, AND XANDER COULD SEE NO *buildings or trees, merely floating tendrils of white that wafted before his eyes, obscuring his vision. He couldn't recall why he was walking through the mist, but he could hear voices close by. He tried to move towards the sound, but could not make out the direction.*

'He is fading,' he heard a man say.

Then the voice of Odysseus cut in. 'Xander! Can you hear me?'

'Yes!' *shouted the boy.* 'Yes! Where are you?'

And then there was silence.

Xander was frightened now, and, in his panic, he began to run, his arms held out before him, in case he crashed into a wall or a tree.

'Do you have rings for his eyes?' he heard someone ask. Xander looked round, but the mist was thick and he could see no-one.

'Do not speak of death just yet,' *he heard Odysseus say.* 'The boy has heart. He is still fighting.'

Xander struggled to his feet. 'Odysseus!' *he called out.* 'Where are you? I am frightened.'

203

Then he heard voices, and the mist cleared. It was night and he was standing on a wide beach, the Xanthos drawn up on the sand. He could see Helikaon and the crew, standing around a large fire. The men were chanting, 'Hear our words, O Hades, Lord of the Deepest Dark.' Xander had heard this chant before. It was a funeral oration. He moved towards the men, desperately needing to be no longer alone.

He saw Oniacus at the outer edge of the circle, and could hear Helikaon speaking about the greatness of Zidantas. Then he remembered the awful sight of the head being drawn from the sack. Reaching the circle he called out to Oniacus. 'I don't know how I got here,' he said. The man ignored him. Xander crouched down in front of the seated man, but Oniacus' eyes did not register his presence. 'Oniacus! Please talk to me!' Stretching out his hand he tried to touch Oniacus on the arm. Strangely he could not feel anything under his fingers, and Oniacus did not notice his questing hand. So Xander sat quietly as Helikaon spoke on. Then Oniacus rose and began to tell stories about Zidantas and Epeus. Xander looked around.

Four men were standing outside the circle, quietly watching the orations.

One of them was Zidantas. Xander ran over to him. 'Please talk to me!' he said.

'Be calm, boy,' said Zidantas. 'Of course I will talk to you.' He dropped to one knee and put his arms round Xander.

'Oniacus wouldn't speak to me. Have I done something wrong?'

'You have done nothing wrong, son of Akamas. He cannot see you.'

'Why? You can see me.'

'Aye, I can.'

'I thought you were dead, Zidantas. We all thought you were dead.'

'What are you doing here, boy? Were you hurt in the fight?'

'No. I went to Troy with Odysseus. That's all I remember. I was sick. I am better now.'

'His heart is failing,' *said a voice.*

'Did you hear that?' Xander asked Zidantas.

'Yes. You must go back to Troy. And swiftly.'

'Can't I stay with you? I don't want to be alone.'

'We are walking a dark road. It is not for you. Not yet. Listen to me. I want you to close your eyes and think of Troy, and where you were. You understand? You are in a bed somewhere, or lying on a beach. There are people with you.'

'I keep hearing the voice of Odysseus,' said Xander.

'Then close your eyes and think of him. Think of Odysseus, Xander. Do it now! Think of life! Think of a blue sky and a fresh wind off the sea.'

Xander closed his eyes. He could still feel Zidantas' arms round him, and a great warmth settled over him. Then Zidantas spoke again. 'If you see my little Thea tell her she brought great joy to my heart. Tell her that, boy.'

'I will, Zidantas. I promise.'

'Can you hear my voice, lad?' he heard Odysseus ask. 'Listen to my voice, and come back to us.'

Xander groaned, and felt a weight upon his chest. His limbs were leaden and his mouth dry. He opened his eyes, and saw the ugly face of Odysseus leaning over him.

'Ha!' shouted the Ithakan king. 'Did I not tell you? The boy has heart.' He looked down at Xander and ruffled his hair. 'You had us all fearful for a while.'

Odysseus helped him to sit, then lifted a cup of water to his lips. Xander drank gratefully. He looked around, and saw sunlight streaming through a window, down onto the bed in which he lay. Beyond Odysseus was a tall, thin man, in an ankle-length chiton of white. His hair was dark, and thinning at the temples, and he looked very tired. He approached Xander and laid a cool hand on the boy's brow. 'The fever is breaking,' he said. 'He needs to eat and rest. I shall have one of the helpers bring him a little food.'

'How soon can he travel?' Odysseus asked the man.

'Not for a week at least. The fever could return, and he is very weak.'

After the man had gone Xander looked around the small room. 'Where is this place?' he asked.

'It is a House of Serpents – a healing house,' Odysseus explained. 'You have been here five days. You remember any of it?'

'No. All I remember is seeing Zidantas. He told me to come back to Troy. It seemed so real, but it was just a dream.'

'Did you see any gates?' asked Odysseus.

'Gates?'

'My Penelope tells me there are two kinds of dreams. Some come through a Gate of Ivory, and their meanings are deceitful. Others come through a Gate of Horn, and these are heavy with fate.'

'I saw no gates,' said Xander.

'Then perhaps it was just a dream,' said Odysseus. 'I am going to have to leave you here, Xander. The season is almost gone, and I need to get back to my Penelope before winter.'

'No!' said Xander fearfully. 'I don't want to be alone again. Please don't go!'

'You won't be alone, lad. The *Xanthos* is in the bay, and Helikaon is here. I shall get word to him about you. For now, though, you must rest, and do everything the healer tells you. Your strength needs to return.'

As he spoke, Xander realized how weak he felt. 'What was wrong with me?'

Odysseus shrugged. 'You had a fever. The healer said you might have eaten something bad, or breathed foul air. You are better now, though, lad. And you will be strong again. I can read the hearts of men, you know. I know the difference between heroes and cowards. You are a hero. You believe me?'

'I don't feel like a hero,' Xander admitted.

Odysseus tapped the cheekbone under his right eye. 'This eye is magical, Xander. It is never wrong. Now, I ask again, do you believe me?'

'Yes. Yes, of course.'

'Then tell me what you are.'

'I am a hero.'

'Good. When doubt comes, as it always does, remember those words. Say them to yourself. And I will see you again in the spring, if the gods will it.'

ii

Argurios of Mykene was not a man given to introspection. His life had been one of service to his king and his people. He did not question the decisions of the ruler, or wonder about the rights and wrongs of war and conquest. For Argurios life was stark and uncomplicated. Powerful men ruled, weaker men became servants or slaves. It was the same with nations.

Yet within this simple philosophy he had also absorbed the code of Atreus King, Agamemnon's father. Power with conscience, strength without cruelty, love of homeland without hatred for one's enemies.

Hence Argurios had never tortured a foe, raped a woman, nor killed a child. He had burned no homes, nor sought to terrorize those he had defeated.

The events leading to the horror of Bad Luck Bay continued to haunt him. The murder of Zidantas was brutal and sadistic. He wanted to believe that Kolanos was merely a savage; a monster who stood apart from the fine men of the Mykene race.

But was he?

He had pondered this on the voyage with Odysseus, but had still not found an answer. Now, as he walked up the long hill towards the Scaean Gate, he did not marvel at the beauty of the city, or notice the glittering gold of the palace roofs. He was thinking of other generals who had gained favour with Agamemnon King, cruel and ruthless men whose atrocities were a stain upon the honour of the Mykene. He had heard stories during the past months that had chilled his blood.

A village had been massacred, the men tied to trees, their ribs cut open, their entrails held in place by sticks. The women had been raped and murdered. The Mykene general in charge of the attack had been Kolanos.

Argurios had gone to Agamemnon with the tale. The king had listened intently.

'If all is as you said, Argurios, then the guilty men will be harshly dealt with.'

But they had not been. After that Argurios had rarely been invited into the king's presence. Indeed, when Agamemnon last visited the Cave of Wings Argurios was not one of the twelve, though Kolanos was.

Pushing aside such thoughts Argurios entered the lower town of Troy, seeking the Street of Ambassadors. He soon became lost, and was loth to ask directions. He paused by a well and sat down in the shade of a wall on which the figure of Artemis the Huntress had been incised. It was a fine work. Her image had been captured in full run, her bow bent, as if chasing a quarry.

'I want you to go to Troy,' Agamemnon King had said, on their final meeting.

'I am at your command, my king. What would you have me do there?'

'Study their defences. You may explain your findings to Erekos the ambassador. He will send me your reports.'

'With respect, my king, he can already describe the fortifications. What purpose is served by my travelling there?'

'*My* purpose,' said Agamemnon. 'And you know as well as I that fortifications alone are not the key to strength. *Men* win or lose wars. Study the soldiers. Look to their disciplines and their weaknesses. Troy is the richest city on the Great Green. It has enormous wealth, and even greater influence. No venture across the sea can succeed if Troy is against it. Therefore Troy must fall to the Mykene.'

'We are to attack Troy?'

'Not immediately. It may not even be necessary. We now have friends within the royal family. One of those friends may soon be king. Then there will be no need to storm the city. However, as my father taught me, it is always wise to have more than one plan. You will travel with Glaukos. He is related to Erekos the ambassador. He can also read and write – a skill I believe you have not mastered.'

'No, lord.'

'He may be useful to you.'

'The boy lacks heart. I would not trust him in a hard fight.'

'You will not be in hard fights, Argurios.'

'Might I ask the result of your investigations into the massacre?'

Agamemnon had waved his hand. 'Exaggerated stories. A few people were killed to emphasize the futility of opposing Mykene rule. There is a ship leaving later today. The captain will be expecting you.'

The memory of that last conversation hung on him like a shroud. Agamemnon had been more than cool towards him. There was an underlying feeling of hostility emanating from the king.

Rising from his seat, Argurios continued to walk through the city, becoming ever more lost in the maze of streets. Finally he was forced to seek help from a street seller.

Following the man's directions, he found himself in front of a large but anonymous house in the lower town, tucked under the west wall of the city. There was an armed man outside the gate. He wore no armour – Argurios was later to discover that the wearing of a breastplate and helmet was a privilege given in the city only to soldiers of Troy – but his demeanour told Argurios that he was a Mykene warrior. Tall, grim, with grey eyes, the soldier looked at the visitor but said nothing.

'I am Argurios, Follower to Agamemnon. I seek audience with Erekos.'

'He is in Miletos, sir,' the guard told him. 'He is due back in the next few days. He has gone to meet the king.'

'Agamemnon is in Miletos?' The news surprised Argurios. Miletos was a large port city, between Lykia and Troy. The *Penelope* had sailed that coastline. It was infuriating to have been so close to his king without knowing it. He could have informed him of the events at Bad Luck Bay.

The guard gave him directions to a house where visitors could find a bed and food. Argurios took his few belongings with him, and was offered a small room, with a tiny window overlooking distant hills. The bed was rickety, the room musty. Argurios did not care. It would be used only for sleep.

Every morning for the next six days he walked to the ambassador's house to seek news of his arrival. On discovering that Erekos had still not returned he would patrol the city, examining its defences as Agamemnon had ordered.

He soon discovered that Troy was not a single city. Its burgeoning wealth meant it was growing fast, spreading out over the hills and plain. At the highest point was the walled palace of the king. This had been the original citadel, and contained many ancient buildings, now used as treasuries, or offices for the king's counsellors. There were two gates, one leading through to the women's quarters, the second opening onto the courtyard before the huge double doors of the king's *megaron*.

Extending out in a wide circle round the palace was the Upper City, containing the homes of the rich: merchants, princes and noblemen. Here there were great palaces and houses boasting statues and flowering trees, and gardens of extraordinary beauty. There were several large areas where craftsmen and artisans produced goods for the wealthy: jewellers, clothes makers, armourers, potters and bronzesmiths. There were dining halls and meeting places, a gymnasium and a theatre. The Upper City was defended by huge walls, and cunningly placed towers.

Outside these walls was the continuously growing Lower Town. This was largely indefensible. There were no walls, merely a series of wide ditches, some still under construction. Any large force could march unopposed through the streets, but there would be little plunder. Here there were few palaces. Mostly the area contained the homes of the poorer inhabitants: servants and lesser craftspeople, workers in the dye trade, or the fishing industry. The air was, in places, noxious with the stench of lime ash and cattle urine, used by cloth dyers, and fermented fish guts, processed for soups and broths.

But here was not where any battle for the city would be won or lost.

The sack of Troy, Argurios knew, would come only when an enemy breached the Great Gates, or scaled the mighty walls.

The East Gate would be a nightmare to storm. The walls doubled back on themselves in a dog-leg, ensuring that invaders would be crammed together and assaulted by archers, peltasts, and spear throwers. Even heavy rocks thrown from such a height would crush an armoured man. And the gates themselves were thick, and reinforced with bronze. They would not burn easily.

However, the physical defences were not Argurios' main concern. His skills, as Agamemnon knew, lay in the study of soldiers and their qualities and weaknesses. Wars were won and lost on four vital elements: morale, discipline, organization, and courage. Flaws in any one and defeat was assured. So he had studied the soldiers on the walls, their alertness and their demeanour. Were they careless or slack? Were their officers decisive and disciplined? Were they confident of their strength, or merely arrogant? These were the questions Agamemnon sought answers to. So Argurios sat in taverns and eating houses, listening to the conversations of soldiers, and watched them as they marched, or patrolled the walls. He chatted to traders at their stalls, and to old men sitting round wells talking of their days in the army.

The Trojan troops, he discovered, were highly disciplined and well trained. In conversations he found out that Priam regularly sent troops in support of the Hittites in their wars, and even hired out horsemen, foot soldiers and charioteers to neighbouring kingdoms, in order that the men would gain combat experience. While Troy itself had suffered no wars in more than two generations, its soldiers were battle-hardened men. It had been difficult to gauge the exact number of fighting men Troy could call upon, but Argurios believed it to be no fewer than 10,000, including the 1,000 warriors of the Trojan Horse riding with Hektor against the Egypteians.

On first analysis it seemed Troy was unassailable, but Argurios knew that no fortress was ever unconquerable. How then to breach its defences? How many men would be needed?

For overwhelming force to destroy a besieged enemy the normal calculation was a factor of five. The Trojans had 10,000 men, therefore the minimum force to gather would be 50,000 warriors. That in itself precluded any Mykene invasion, for Agamemnon could not muster more than 15,000 fighting men if he conscripted every warrior in Mykene. And even if 50,000 could be gathered, a second logistical problem would arise. How to feed such an army? They would need to raid surrounding territories, and this would inflame the populations, causing uprisings and disaffection. The problem was a thorny one, but Argurios was determined to return to his king with a positive plan.

Then on the seventh day he learned that Erekos the ambassador had returned from Miletos.

iii

The screams echoed through his head, and Argurios felt his skull starting to pound. He looked up at the high roof of the circular tomb, trying to ignore the thick smell of blood and fear, and the sounds of the thrashing, dying horses. The sacrifice of noble horses to Zeus was an appropriate ritual at the funeral of a great king, and his heart lifted at the thought that Atreus King would ride such fine steeds on his journey to the Elysian Fields.

The two horses, dead at last, were being hauled into place at the sides of the king's bier in the centre of the tomb. Atreus lay in his gold and silver armour, his favourite sword at his right side, three jewelled daggers and a bow to his left. At his head was a great golden cup embossed with the Lion of Mykene, and flagons of wine and oil for his journey. Three of the king's beloved hounds lay slaughtered at his feet.

The dark, musty tomb was filled with the king's Followers, his grieving family, counsellors, and mourners. Agamemnon stood dressed in a simple woollen robe, tears pouring down his cheeks. His brother Menelaus was dry-eyed but looked stricken, his face ashen and empty.

There was a cacophony of noise from the musicians and singers milling around in the darkness. Then the sounds of lute and lyre started to fade away.

Argurios stepped forward to take his last look at his king. He frowned. The bearded face resting peacefully on the bier was not that of Atreus. The beard was wrong, and the face too broad. Was this an impostor?

Confusion and fear in his heart, he moved forward reluctantly and saw that the face on the bier was his own.

He looked around to see if anyone else had noticed. But there was no-one there. The mourners and musicians, sons and counsellors had all vanished, and the great circular tomb was dark and cold, the air heavy with damp and rot.

He was alone. No-one mourned Argurios. No-one marked his passing, and he would go to the earth unnoticed. No-one would know his name.

His head was splitting now. A terrible pain erupted in his stomach as well. He had just noticed it, but he knew it had been there all the time. He cried out . . .

He was lying in a stone doorway in the cool night air. The moon was high, and, by its light, Argurios could see that his tunic was drenched in blood. Three bodies lay close by, and he saw a blood-smeared sword by the doorway. He tried to rise, but fell again, a stabbing pain searing through his back and chest. Gritting his teeth, he rolled to his knees. His vision swam and he fell against the door frame.

After a while the pain ebbed a little and he gazed around him. In the moonlight he could see a small street of modest houses looking over a silver sea. Then he remembered. He was in Troy.

A fresh wave of pain surged over him. His head began to pound and he vomited on the ground. There was blood in the vomit. Once again he tried to rise, but there was no strength in his legs. He stared at the bodies of the men he had killed. One was facing him. He recognized him as the guard who had been on duty on the seventh day of his visit to the house of Erekos.

The man had informed him that Erekos had returned, and had gestured Argurios into the courtyard.

'Wait here, sir,' he said.

The courtyard was shadeless and without greenery. Argurios paced back and forth a few times then sat stiffly on a stone bench facing the westering sun.

From an inner door three men came out. The leader was tall and lean, with thin red hair. His beardless face was grey and his eyes red-rimmed as if from the cold. He wore a long dark cape over tunic and leggings, and was unarmed. The two others, one dark, one fair, both wore swords. Argurios noted their expressions and felt uneasy. They were staring at him unblinkingly. He rose from the bench.

'I returned last night,' said the red-haired man, without any form of greeting. This display of ill manners annoyed Argurios, but he held his anger in check. 'I was with the king when the lord Kolanos spoke of the cowardly slaughter by the killer Helikaon. He also named you as a traitor, in the pay of Helikaon.'

'Ah,' said Argurios, coldly. 'A coward and a liar as well.' The ambassador's eyes narrowed, and he reddened.

'The lord Kolanos claimed you killed one of his crew, and saved the life of Helikaon.'

'That is true.'

'Perhaps you would care to explain yourself.'

Argurios glanced at the armed men with Erekos. 'I am Argurios, Follower of Agamemnon and a Mykene noble. I answer only to my king, and not to some over-promoted peasant sent to a foreign land.'

The men with the ambassador reached for their swords, but Erekos waved them back. He smiled. 'I have heard in full of the events in Lykia. Many good Mykene men died – including my nephew Glaukos. You did nothing to save them, indeed you aided the killer Helikaon. You are not welcome here, Argurios. The rules of hospitality dictate that no blood will be shed in my house. But know that Agamemnon has spoken the words of banishment against you. You are no longer Mykene. Your lands are forfeit and you are named as an enemy of the Lion's Hall.'

Argurios strode from the house, back straight, head reeling. He was not a diplomat and this journey to Troy had not been one he had sought. Yet he was proud to serve his king, both to gather information on Priam's political and military situation, and to deliver messages to his brother Mykene abroad. Delving into his leather bag he snatched out the sealed papyrus letters he carried for Erekos. Anger tempted him to throw them to the winds, but he hesitated, then put them away again. They had been given to him by Agamemnon's chief scribe as he had left the palace on that last day. The man had come running out into the street. 'I hear you are sailing for Troy,' he said. 'These messages were meant to have been sent three days ago, but a fool of a servant forgot to give them to the captain. Will you take them, Lord Argurios?'

Each bore the seal of Agamemnon and he had carried them with reverence. He could not throw the king's words into the mud of the street.

Banishment!

He could scarcely believe such a sentence, but it hurt him more that Agamemnon, whom he had served with total loyalty, could have acted in such a fashion. Surely, he thought, the king, of all men, should have known he would never have sold out to Helikaon, or any other enemy of his people. Did the works of his life count for nothing, he wondered? In the twenty years since he reached manhood he had never sought riches, nor succumbed to any temptations that would hinder his service. He had not lied, nor taken part in the palace intrigues that saw men plotting against one another to rise in Agamemnon's favour. He had even remained unwed, so that his life could be entirely dedicated to the king and to the people.

And now he had been named a traitor, stripped of his lands, and his citizenship.

As he walked from the house of Erekos he decided to take ship back to Mykene, and to appeal to the king directly. Surely, he thought, he will realize he has been misled. His spirits rose. Once back in Mykene he would expose Kolanos for the liar and villain that he was, and all would be well.

He was close to his lodgings when he realized he was being followed.

And he knew then there would be no easy return to his homeland. The killers had been unleashed. As an enemy of the people his life was worth only what price Agamemnon or Kolanos had placed upon it.

Cold anger rose and he swung to await the assassins. He had carried no sword or dagger with him to the ambassador's house, and stood there unarmed as the five men approached.

The leader was swathed in a dark, hooded cloak. He stepped forward and spoke. 'Renegade, you know what dark deeds have brought you to this judgement.'

Argurios stood calmly and looked the man in the eye. 'There are no dark deeds to my name. I am Argurios, and the victim of a coward's lies. I intend to sail home and appeal to my king.'

The man laughed harshly. 'Your life ends here, traitor. There are no appeals.' A knife flashed into his hands and he leapt forward. Argurios stepped in to meet him, grabbing the knife wrist and thundering a fierce blow into the man's face. As the man fell back Argurios gripped his wrist with both hands, spun him round, then twisted the arm savagely, dislocating his shoulder. The assassin screamed and dropped his knife. The other four men surged forward. Lifting his foot Argurios propelled the crippled assassin into his comrades, then swept up the dagger.

'I am Argurios!' he thundered. 'To come at me is to die.'

They hesitated then, but all were armed with swords. The injured leader was on his knees. 'Kill him!' he screamed.

They rushed in. Argurios charged to meet them. A sword plunged into his side, a second cleaving into his left shoulder. Ignoring the pain he stabbed one man through the heart, kicked a second man in the right knee, causing him to fall, then grappled with the third. The fourth man stabbed at him, the blade glancing from his ribs. Argurios could feel his strength failing. Smashing a blow to one attacker's face he followed up with a head butt that broke another's nose. Half blinded, the assassin staggered. Argurios twisted to one side, then hammered his foot against an attacker's knee. There was a sickening crack as the joint snapped, followed by a piercing shriek of agony. The third attacker was on his feet again. Argurios dived to the ground, grabbing a fallen sword, then rolled just in time to block a downward cut. Surging up, he shoulder-charged the attacker, hurling him back. Before the man could recover Argurios drove his sword through the assassin's chest. Tearing the blade clear he swung in time to parry a ferocious lunge that would have disembowelled him. His sword lanced up, skewering the man through the chin and up into his brain. Argurios wrenched the blade loose and let him fall.

The man with the shattered knee was groaning loudly. Argurios glanced to his left where the leader now stood, his knife held in his left hand, his right arm hanging uselessly at his side.

'Your comrade cannot walk,' said Argurios. 'He will need you to help him to a house of healing.'

'There will be another day,' said the man.

'Maybe, but not for you, puppy dog. It'll take real hounds to hunt down this old wolf. Now get you gone.'

He stood tall and apparently strong as the leader hauled the groaning man upright. Then the two of them made their slow way back into the darkness.

Argurios managed to stay upright for a few moments more.

He had no idea how much time had passed since. The pain in his stomach had ceased, and he felt cold, though he could still feel warm blood flowing under his hand. He tried to lift himself up with one arm and the pain ripped through him again. Then he heard footsteps. So, they had come back to finish their work. Anger gave him strength and he levered himself upright, determined to die on his feet.

Several soldiers in crested helmets moved into sight. Argurios sagged back against the door frame. 'What happened here?' asked the first soldier, stepping in close. The world spun, and Argurios fell. The soldier dropped his spear and caught him, lowering him to the ground.

A second soldier called out: 'One of the dead men is Philometor the Mykene. He was said to be a fine warrior.'

An elderly man came out of the house and spoke to the soldier. 'I saw it from my balcony. Five men attacked him. He had no weapon and he defeated them all.'

'Well,' said the soldier, 'we must get him to the temple. Any man the Mykene want dead must be worthy of life.'

XVII

The Golden King

i

THE LAST TIME HELIKAON HAD STOOD ON THE BEACH BELOW TROY Zidantas had been alongside him. They had been on their way to Kypros, to take the *Xanthos* on her maiden voyage. It seemed a lifetime ago now.

The ship had been unloaded, the cargo carried to warehouses. With the season over there were few merchants on the beaches, and the *Xanthos* would continue north to Dardania with a much lighter load. The crew had been paid, and twenty-eight rowers had declared their intent to leave the ship. Oniacus had been scouring the taverns, seeking fresh men to crew the *Xanthos* on its journey home.

Helikaon glanced along the bay, and saw Odysseus and his crew preparing the *Penelope* for launch. The slender old ship slid gracefully into the water, the men hauling themselves aboard. Odysseus was shouting orders now. For a moment Helikaon wished the years could be swept away, and that he too was back aboard the *Penelope*, sailing off across the Great Green to winter in Ithaka. Life had seemed so uncomplicated then, his concerns small and focused on easily remedied problems: the tear in the sail that could be stitched, the blistered hands that could be bandaged.

Earlier that morning he had sat on the beach with his friend. It was their first meeting since the battle outside Blue Owl Bay. Odysseus had told him about the boy, Xander, and they had sat in comfortable silence for a while.

'You have not spoken of Zidantas,' said Odysseus, at last.

'He is dead. What else is there to say?'

Odysseus looked at him closely. 'You remember me talking about the lost hero, and your need to find him?'

'Of course. I was a weak and frightened boy. But he is long gone now.'

'He was frightened, yes, but not weak. Intelligent and thought-ful. Aye, and caring and gentle. And sometimes you need to seek him too.'

Helikaon forced a laugh. The sound was harsh. 'He could not survive in *my* world.'

Odysseus shook his head. 'Your world is full of violent men, heroic with sword and shield, ready to butcher their way to what-ever plunder they desire. Can you not see it is the boy you were who stops you from being like them? Do not lose sight of him, Helikaon.'

'Would he have destroyed the galleys of Kolanos? Would he have defeated Alektruon, or survived the treachery at Blue Owl Bay?'

'No, he would not,' snapped Odysseus. 'Nor would he have burned to death fifty or more unarmed and hobbled men. You want to defeat Kolanos – or become him?'

Helikaon felt a rush of anger at this outburst from his friend. 'How could you say that to me? You do not know what is in my heart.'

'Who does?' countered Odysseus. 'You have it sheathed in armour. You always did.'

'I do not need to hear this,' said Helikaon, pushing himself to his feet.

Odysseus rose alongside him. 'How many friends do you have, Helikaon? I love you like my own son, and you are wrong. I *do* see into your heart. I see you are suffering, and I know what Ox meant to you. You are grieving and you feel as if something is ripping out your guts from the inside. Your dreams are tortured, your waking hours tormented. You look for him always, just at the edge of your vision. You expect to wake one morning and find him standing there, big as life. And a part of you dies every time you wake and realize he isn't.'

Helikaon's shoulders sagged as his anger seeped away. 'How can you know all this?'

'I watched my son die.' Odysseus sat down and stared out to sea. Helikaon remained where he was for a moment, then seated himself alongside his friend.

'I am sorry, Odysseus. I had forgotten.'

'You didn't know him.' The ugly king sighed. 'Now, do you want to talk about Ox?'

'I can't.'

Odysseus looked disappointed, but he nodded. 'I understand. But one day, my friend, I hope you will learn to open your heart. Otherwise you will always be alone. We will not dwell on it, though. Let us return to Kolanos. He is likely to go to ground now. He'll either return to Mykene or seek shelter on the pirate isle southwest of Samothraki. The waters there are treacherous, and few ships will risk the winter storms. Even if they did there is a stockade there, and several hundred pirates to man it.'

'I know the island,' said Helikaon. 'The *Penelope* beached there on my first voyage. The pirates gathered round you, and you told them a story that had them laughing, crying and cheering. They showered you with gifts. I still think of it sometimes. A hundred cruel and barbaric men, weeping over a story of love and honour and courage.'

'Aye, it was a good night,' said Odysseus. 'If Kolanos is there he will be safe for the winter. But he will sail again in spring.'

'And I will find him, Odysseus.'

'I expect you will. More important, however, you need to watch yourself *now*. There are some canny killers out there. With that in mind, I have a small gift for you.'

Delving into the pack he was carrying he pulled forth a tunic of dark brown leather and passed it to Helikaon. It was heavier than

221

Helikaon expected, and he could feel something hard beneath the soft leather. 'Picked it up a few years back in Kretos,' said Odysseus. Helikaon hoisted the garment. It was a knee-length tunic, with a lining of silk. 'It is a cunning piece,' said Odysseus. 'Between the silk and the leather are thin, overlapping discs of ivory. It'll turn a dagger blade, though I doubt it would withstand a powerful sword thrust, a strike from an axe, or a well-aimed arrow from a bow of horn.'

'It is a fine gift, my friend. Thank you.'

'Pshaw! Too small for me anyway. Wear it when ashore – and try not to travel alone in the city.'

'I will be careful,' promised Helikaon. 'I shall be sailing for Dardania soon. Once home I will be surrounded by loyal soldiers.'

'As your father was,' pointed out Odysseus. 'Do not assume anywhere is safe. Equally, do not assume loyalty is made of stone.'

'I know.'

'Of course you do,' muttered Odysseus apologetically. 'Did you hear about Argurios?'

'No.'

'Word is he's been banished and declared outlaw. It is said you bought him.'

Helikaon shook his head in disbelief. 'You don't *buy* a man like Argurios. Who could think such a thing?'

'Men who *can* be bought,' answered Odysseus. 'I doubt he'll last a month. How long are you planning to stay in Troy?'

'A few days more. I must pay my respects to Priam, and there are still merchants I need to see. Why do you ask?'

'Something in the air,' said the older man, touching his nose. 'There is a feeling of unease in the city. I suspect there is another palace revolution brewing.'

Helikaon laughed. 'There is *always* a palace revolution brewing. My guess is that Priam enjoys them. It gives his devious mind something to gnaw at.'

'You are right,' admitted Odysseus, 'he likes risks. I knew a man once who placed wagers on almost anything. He would sit beneath a tree and wager on which pigeon would fly away first, or which dolphin would swim beneath the prow. His wagers grew larger and larger. One day he wagered his lands, his horses, his cattle and his ship on a single throw of the dice. He lost it all.'

'You believe Priam to be such a fool?'

Odysseus shrugged. 'A man who loves risks is a man seeking to test himself. Each time he wins he needs to increase the peril. Priam has many acknowledged sons, and only a few positions of power to award. Not all of his sons can succeed him.'

'He has Hektor,' Helikaon pointed out. 'He would never betray his father.'

'Hektor is the key in all this,' Odysseus replied. 'He is both loved and feared. Any who rose against Priam would have to face the wrath of Hektor. That alone is what prevents a civil war. Priam has alienated at least half his generals, and the gods alone know how many of his counsellors. He strips them of their titles on a whim, appointing others in their place. He revels in humiliating the men around him. His sons too are often chided publicly. Foolish man. If Hektor were to fall in battle this kingdom would rip apart like an old sail in a storm.'

Helikaon laughed. 'Hektor will not fall in battle. He is invincible. If his ship were to sink he'd emerge riding one of Poseidon's dolphins.'

Odysseus grinned. 'Aye, he does radiate a godlike quality.' The smile faded. 'But he is not a god, Helikaon. He is a man, albeit a great one. And men die. I wouldn't want to be in Troy if that were to happen.'

'It won't happen. The gods have always loved Hektor.'

'May Father Zeus hear those words and make them true.' Odysseus rose. 'I must be making ready to sail. Take care, my boy,' he said. The two men embraced.

'Fair winds and calm seas, Odysseus.'

'That would make a pleasant change. Tell me, will you be seeing Andromache?'

'Perhaps.'

'Fine woman. I like her enormously.' Odysseus laughed. 'I would love to have been present when she met Priam.'

Helikaon thought of the Trojan king. Powerful and dominant, he sought to intimidate all who came before him. Then he recalled Andromache's challenging gaze. 'Yes,' he agreed. 'I would like to have seen that too.'

ii

'My lady, wake up, my lady! Oh, please wake up!'

Andromache returned to consciousness slowly. She had been dreaming of a great storm, the sea rising like a mountain into the sky. Ever since she had seen the seer, Aklides, she had been haunted by dreams: visions of men with one sandal, or colossal storms. Once she had even dreamed she was married to a pig farmer, whose face had slowly become that of a boar, white tusks sprouting from his bearded cheeks.

Her bed was a tangle of white linen and she felt the slickness of sweat on her body. The dreams had been full of fear, leaving a lingering sense of dread behind them. Sitting up she regarded her handmaid, the young and heavily pregnant Axa.

Normally smiling and complacent, Axa was wringing her hands in worry, her plump, plain face a mask of anxiety.

'Thank the gods, my lady. I thought I would never wake you. You've been sent for,' she said, lowering her voice and looking around her as if Andromache's chambers were filled with spies. Which they might well be, thought Andromache. The entire palace was a sea of suspicious eyes. Servants appeared and hovered whenever people gathered together, and conversations were spoken in whispers.

Andromache shook her head to clear it and swung her long legs out of bed. Outside her high square window she could just see the paleness of dawn in the night sky. 'Who has sent for me at this hour?'

'The king, my lady.' Axa immediately started to pull Andromache's nightgown over her head. 'You must wash and dress quickly, my lady, and attend the king with haste. It would not do to delay.'

Andromache could sense the panic in the woman and realized Axa would be held responsible if Priam were kept waiting. As her maid thrust a wet sponge in her face, Andromache grabbed it from her.

'I'll do that. Find my saffron gown, and the calf sandals Laodike gave me yesterday.'

As she washed she wondered about the significance of being made to wait seven days to see Priam. Perhaps she should be honoured. Perhaps other young brides had to wait months before they met the king. She had asked Laodike but the king's eldest daughter had just shrugged. There were so many things Andromache did not know about Troy. What she did know, however, was that the palace of Priam was not a happy place. Stunningly beautiful, and filled with treasures, many of them of solid gold, it was a monument to ostentation, which contrasted mightily with the furtive manner in which people moved through it. Laodike had been assigned to guide Andromache through the customs of the palace: the areas in which the women could wander, and the rooms and corridors closed to them. But Andromache had learned far more than this. Laodike's conversation was always of warnings. What not to do. What not to say. Whom to smile at, and be civil to. Whom to avoid.

Laodike had listed names, but most of them had flown by Andromache with the speed of hunting hawks. Some had registered, but only after meeting the men they applied to: watery-eyed Polites, the king's chancellor, fat Antiphones, his Master of Horse. It would have amazed Andromache if the wheezing man could actually mount a horse. Then there was Deiphobos, the Prince of the Harbour. More commonly called Dios, he looked a little like Helikaon, though without the inherent power. In fact, he had frightened eyes, she thought.

She realized Axa was regarding her with a worried frown. 'The pretty sandals, my lady . . .' she faltered.

'Do you have them, Axa?'

'Yes, my lady, but . . . they are not appropriate.'

'Do not argue with me,' she said. 'You fear the king's anger. I understand that. But you should fear my anger too.' She kept her voice pleasant, but she looked hard into Axa's face and the young woman dropped her eyes.

'I'm sorry, my lady, but you do not understand. You *cannot* wear sandals. You are to meet the king on the Great Tower. The steps are treacherous, and his orders were for you to wear suitable shoes.'

Later, striding through the stone streets in the growing dawn light, Axa hurrying behind her, two royal Eagles, in armour of bronze and silver, by her side, Andromache wondered what game Priam was playing. She wished she had had a chance to speak to Laodike about the king's strange choice of meeting place.

She had heard a great deal of gossip about Priam in her seven days in Troy – most of it admiring, all of it meaningless. He was said to have fifty sons, Axa had confided to her, although the queen had borne him just four. He was known to be a great bull in his youth, and many of those sons, recognized by him or not, had made their home in Troy, close to the glory of their father. The king, now on his throne for over forty years, still had an eye for a pretty young girl, said another maid, giggling. Andromache had felt repulsed. Just another old man who couldn't accept that his rutting days were decently over, she had thought. But then rich men were also powerful men, and power was an aphrodisiac. And Priam was said to be the richest man in all the world.

She had been astonished by the treasures she had seen in the king's *megaron*, in the queen's apartments, and the gold and jewels that Laodike thought quite normal daily wear. Laodike was always festooned with gold, her wrists and throat sporting an assortment of bracelets, bangles and necklets, her corn-coloured hair inter-twined with gold wire, her gowns weighed down with brooches. None of which made her more pretty, thought Andromache. The jewels only served to draw attention to her small, hazel eyes, her long nose and a slightly receding chin. What she had, though, to compensate, was a smile of dazzling beauty, and a sweet nature that made her lovable.

'Poor Andromache,' Laodike had said, putting her arm through her new sister's. 'You have no jewellery, no gold at all, only a few cheap beads and a little silver. I shall make my father give you gold, amber and carnelian necklets and earrings to match your eyes, and gold chains to adorn your dainty ankles . . . and,' she laughed glee-fully, 'your big feet.'

'Big feet are said to be very beautiful,' Andromache had replied gravely. 'The bigger the better.'

She smiled to herself now, looking down at those feet encased in the clumsy rope-soled sandals Axa had borrowed for her. Then she looked up. The Great Tower of Ilion, standing proud of the south wall of Troy, was almost twice as high as the main city walls, and by far the tallest building she had ever seen. As she walked towards it she could see the ever-present guards on each corner of its roof. They looked like tiny insects, the rising sun glinting off their helmets and spear tips.

When she had asked Axa about her summons to the Great Tower, the maid had been strangely reticent. 'It must be a great honour,' she had said doubtfully. 'King Priam sometimes goes there to look over his city and to scan the sea and land for invaders. He is watchful for his people.'

'Does he usually greet visitors on the Great Tower of Ilion?'

Axa blushed and refused to meet her eyes. 'I don't know. I don't know what the king does. It is the highest point in the city. It must be a great honour,' she repeated.

Andromache had caught a look of dismay on her maid's face and she put her arms round her and hugged her close.

'I have a head for heights,' she reassured the woman. 'Don't worry.'

They entered the huge square tower at its base, just inside the Scaean Gate. The stone wall was very thick and inside the tower was cold and damp. Andromache saw a narrow flight of stone stairs spiralling up into the darkness. She looked up and saw the tower was merely a dank square shaft of empty air illuminated at intervals by holes punched through the thickness of the walls. The stairs hugged the inside walls in a series of sharp inclines, followed by horizontal walkways to the next rise, until they reached a tiny square of light high above. There was no hand rail. Torches flickered in wall brackets and one of the soldiers lit a brand to carry up the steps.

'Do you wish me to come with you, my lady?' Andromache saw Axa's eyes were huge and frightened in the torchlight, her hands straying unconsciously to her swollen belly.

'No. Stay here. Wait for me,' Andromache replied.

'Do you want the water?'

Axa started to unsling the water skin she held on her hip. Andromache thought for moment, then told her, 'No, keep it. I might want it later.'

She realized the two soldiers were preparing to escort her up. She held out her hand. 'Give me the torch,' she demanded.

The torch carrier, unsure, casting an eye at his fellow, passed the brand to her.

'Stay here,' she told them curtly, and before they could move she set off swiftly up the stairs, stepping lightly on the shiny stone.

On and up she climbed, her legs, strengthened by her many hours of walking or running on Thera, pushing her up the steep flights. The steps were each nearly knee-high, and she felt her body enjoying the exercise, her thighs and calves thrilling to be worked so hard. She had never suffered from the sickness sparked by heights, but she was not tempted to look down to see how far she had climbed. She looked up instead, towards the small square of light.

She felt she had the measure of the old king now. He had asked her to the tower to daunt her, perhaps to humiliate her, hoping she would collapse in tears at the foot of the tower and have to be carried up like a child. She was amazed that a king with such power, such riches, should feel the need to prove his superiority over a young woman. Petty bullies I can deal with, she thought.

The steps became narrower as she neared the top, and they seemed much more worn here and slick with damp. She became conscious of the dark abyss to her right and she placed her feet more carefully as she climbed. She wondered why the stairs would be most worn at the *top* of the tower. Then she realized and laughed. She stopped and held her torch high. Thirty or so steps below her, on the other side of the tower, was a dark recess. In it there was a narrow door. She had not seen it as she passed. It must be a door leading to the battlements of the south wall. The old man would have come that way, leaving her to climb the full height of the tower. Priam, she thought, already I do not like you.

When she emerged at the top it was with a sense of relief. The brightness of the low sun hurt her eyes and the wind buffeted her hair, and for a moment she was disorientated. She looked around slowly, steadying her breathing.

The wooden roof was half the size of the king's *megaron*, yet empty bar four guards, one at each corner of the tower, motionless, staring outward. A tall, wide-shouldered man was standing on the battlements of the southwest wall, the wind blowing through his long silver-gold hair.

He was powerfully built and deeply tanned. He wore a blue full-length tunic and, despite the coolness of the dawn, his tanned, muscular arms were bare. He was in profile to her and she saw a high, beaked nose and strong jaw. He didn't appear to have seen her and she stood uncertain.

'Well, are you going to stand there all day, girl?' he said, not turning.

Andromache walked over to him and stood, head bowed. 'I am Andromache of Thebe . . .'

The king turned suddenly. She was surprised at how young and vital he was. His height and the width of his shoulders dominated her, and his physical presence was colossal.

'Have you not been taught how to address your king, girl? On your knees.' He loomed over her and she was almost forced to her knees by his presence alone.

Instead she straightened her back. 'In Thebe Under Plakos we do not bow the knee to anyone, not even the gods.'

Priam leaned in close so she could see the yellowish whites of his eyes and smell the morning wine on his breath. He said quietly, 'You are not in little Thebe now. I will not tell you again.'

At that moment there was a clattering on the staircase and a Royal Eagle climbed onto the roof. His helmet bore the black and white crest of a captain. He strode quickly to the king.

'Lord.' He glanced at Andromache and hesitated. Priam gestured impatiently for him to go on. 'Lord, we have him! Someone must have warned him, for he had almost made it to the Egypteian ship. He is being questioned now.'

'Excellent! I shall attend the questioning later.' The king was once more looking down at the bay. 'Is that monstrosity Helikaon's new ship?'

'Yes, sir, the *Xanthos*. It arrived late last night.'

Andromache's interest quickened. She watched Priam closely but could not see from his expression whether he considered it good news or bad. After a moment he dismissed the captain and turned to regard Andromache again. 'Let me show you my city,' he said, then sprang lightly up onto the high battlement wall, before turning and holding out his hand to Andromache.

She did not hesitate, and he took hold of her wrist, drawing her up to stand alongside him. The wind buffeted her, and she glanced down at the awesome drop.

'So, you will not kneel to me?' he said.

'I will kneel to no man,' she answered, preparing herself for the push that would send her toppling to her death, and ready to haul him with her.

'You interest me, girl. There is no fear in you.'

'Nor in you, apparently, King Priam.'

He looked surprised. 'Fear is for weaklings. Look around you. This is Troy. *My* Troy. The richest and most powerful city in the world. It was not built by fearful men, but by men with imagination and courage. Its wealth grows daily, and with it the influence that wealth brings.'

Suddenly, to Andromache's surprise, the king reached out and weighed her left breast in his hand. She did not flinch.

'You will do,' Priam said, taking his hand away and waving his dismissal. 'You will breed strong children for me.'

An icy worm of fear slithered into her heart. 'For your son

Hektor, I think you mean, my king,' she corrected, her voice harder than was wise.

More quickly than she could have expected he stepped towards her, looming over her again. 'I am your king,' he whispered in her ear, his breath hot and wet. 'And Hektor is not here. He may well not return until the spring.'

The prospect of being confined to Priam's palace through the long weeks of winter filled Andromache with dismay.

'You may go now,' said Priam, turning away from her and staring out over the bay.

Andromache leapt lightly down to the ramparts and walked to the stairway. Then Priam called out to her. She turned towards him.

'You are still a virgin, I take it?'

'I am who I am, King Priam,' she replied, unable to keep the anger from her voice.

'Then remember who you are, and what you are,' he advised. 'You are the property of Priam, until he decides you should become the property of another.'

XVIII

The House of Serpents

i

THE HOUSE OF SERPENTS WAS LARGER THAN XANDER HAD FIRST imagined. There were four immense buildings, set in a square with an open garden area at the centre, in which an altar had been erected to the god Asklepios.

There were people everywhere, women in long green gowns, men dressed in white tunics, priests in flowing robes of blue and gold. Then there were crowds of supplicants, queuing before three tables set close to the altar. Everyone in the queues carried an offering, some holding caged white doves, others bearing perfumes, or gifts of copper or silver. Xander saw that each supplicant was given a small square of papyrus, which he or she held to their lips before dropping it into a large copper container beside the priest at the table.

Mystified, Xander moved on through the crowd, wandered around the garden, then decided to return to his room.

Except that he had no idea where it was. All four of the buildings looked exactly the same. He entered one, followed a corridor, and found himself in a huge, round chamber. There were statues of the gods set into alcoves. At the foot of each statue was a deep cup of silver, and a small brazier, filled with glowing coals. He recognized the statue of Demeter, Goddess of Fertility, for she carried a basket of corn in one hand, and the babe Persephone held against her breast. Others he could not identify. The air was full of incense, and he saw two priests moving to each of the statues. The first poured libations of wine into the silver cups, and the second sprinkled papyrus squares onto the fires in the braziers.

Then Xander understood. The suppliants' squares were being offered to the gods. He wondered how Demeter would know from the ashes exactly what each worshipper had asked for.

Moving out of the temple area he saw Machaon, the healer priest who had tended him. Xander called out and Machaon turned his head. He was tall and stoop-shouldered, with short dark hair thinning at the temples. His eyes looked tired.

'I see you are feeling stronger, Xander,' he said.

'Yes.'

'Do not over-exert yourself. You are still recovering.'

'Yes, sir. Can you tell me where my room is?'

Machaon smiled. 'The house is like a labyrinth. It takes time to find your way around. Do you read symbols?'

'No, sir.'

'You are in Fire Seven. Each building here is marked by a different symbol, and each room has a number.' He pointed to the closest door. 'The first symbol on the door represents the element after which the area was named.' Xander peered at the symbol carved into the wood. 'What does it look like to you?'

'Like a bow,' he answered.

'I suppose it does,' agreed Machaon. 'In fact the upturned half-circle is a cup. So this building is Water. The mark below it is the number of the room. To the north is Earth, and the symbol there is a full circle, for all things come from the earth and return to the earth. Fire is directly across the garden from here, and on each door you will see another half-circle, resting downwards on a straight line. This represents the rising sun. Air is the building to your left. On its walls you will see another half-circle standing upright, like a sail in the breeze.'

'Thank you, sir. How do the gods know who kissed the papyrus?'

Machaon smiled. 'The gods see all, Xander. They know what is in our hearts and in our minds.'

'Why then do they need the papyrus at all?'

'It is a ritual of worship; an indication of respect and adoration. We will talk about that tomorrow when I visit you. And now I must continue my work.' Machaon rose. 'You may walk around for a while. But try not to get in anyone's way.'

Xander crossed the now deserted gardens and found his room. He was feeling dreadfully tired and weak. On trembling legs he made it to his bed and lay down. The room seemed to be moving, as if it was on a ship. As he lay there he heard his door open and a figure came into sight.

It was Helikaon. Xander struggled to rise.

'Stay where you are, boy,' said the Golden One, sitting down on the bed.

'Thank you, lord.'

'The *Xanthos* is sailing for Dardania soon. Machaon believes you should stay here for the winter. He says it will take time for your strength to return.'

Xander did not reply. He was both relieved and disappointed. He had loved being part of the crew, but he dreaded another battle, and still had nightmares about burning men.

Helikaon seemed to read his thoughts. 'I am truly sorry that your first voyage should have seen such tragedy. Odysseus tells me you saw Zidantas while you were in your fever.'

'Yes, lord. Everyone was on the beach, and he was standing with some other men close by. One of them was Epeus.'

'Epeus died in the battle,' said Helikaon. 'Did Zidantas speak to you?'

'Yes. He told me to think of life and to come back to Troy. I wanted to go with him, but he said he was walking a dark road. He asked me to tell his daughter Thea that she gave him great joy.'

Helikaon sat silently for a few moments. 'I think it was not a dream, Xander,' he said at last. 'I think it was a true vision. I will leave gold with the temple to pay for your keep. In the spring I will still have a place for you among my crew. There is something you can do for me, in return.'

'Anything, lord.'

'Argurios is here. He was stabbed, and I am told he is dying. I want you to visit him, see to his needs. I have hired other men to watch over him, to prevent the killers returning. Will you do this for me?'

'Yes, lord, but Argurios does not like me.'

'It would surprise me to find that Argurios *liked* anyone.'

'What can I do?'

'He is refusing to eat or drink. So, bring him food and water.'

'Why doesn't he want to eat?'

'Evil men have taken away all that he has. I think a part of him does not want to live.'

'I can't make him eat, lord.'

'Tell him you spoke to me and I laughed when I heard of his plight. Tell him I said that one less Mykene warrior in the world was a matter to be celebrated.'

'He will hate you for that, won't he?'

Helikaon sighed. 'Yes, I expect he will. Go and find him when you are rested. He is in Air, and his room is close to the portico entrance.'

ii

Karpophorus the assassin followed Helikaon up the hill towards the palace. It had been almost twenty years since he had killed anyone in Troy. The city had changed greatly since then, expanding in almost every direction. His last assassination here had seen him escape across a pasture into a small wood. The pasture now boasted scores of small houses lining narrow streets, and the wood had been chopped down to make way for a barracks. The imposing house of the merchant he had slain was also gone. That was a shame, he thought, for it had been well constructed, with pleasing lines.

A little way ahead Helikaon paused beside a clothing stall, and chatted to the owner. Karpophorus hung back, watching the exchange. The sun was bright over the golden city, and there were many people gathered in the market place.

How curious, he thought, that Helikaon should seem so relaxed here. He knew there were Mykene in the city, and at any time a killer could attack him. Karpophorus scanned the crowd with suspicious eyes, seeking out any possible attacker, looking for signs of tension in the faces. He was determined that no other assassin should claim his prize.

Then Helikaon moved on.

Karpophorus followed him up another hill towards the golden-roofed palace of Priam.

It was then that he spotted a young man emerging from between two buildings. He was dark-haired, and slim, wearing a green tunic and sandals. There was a knife at his belt. Karpophorus had seen him in the crowd at the market. Increasing his pace Karpophorus closed the distance between them. As Helikaon turned another corner the newcomer slowly drew his dagger and stepped after him.

His own blade flashing into his hand Karpophorus broke into a run.

When he rounded the corner he saw the young man spread-eagled on the street, Helikaon standing above him.

'My apologies,' said Karpophorus. 'I was a little slow.'

'Nonsense, Attalus. It was my fault for ordering you to hang back.' Helikaon grinned at him. 'Let us hope that this fool is the best they have.'

'Indeed,' agreed Karpophorus.

The young man was still alive and conscious, though his knife was now in Helikaon's hand. He glared up at the Golden One with a look of pure hatred. Helikaon tossed the knife to the street and walked on. Karpophorus followed.

They walked in silence to the palace citadel, and Helikaon approached the guards at the double gates, then they passed under the shadow of the walls above and emerged onto a wide paved courtyard. 'I shall be some time in the palace,' Helikaon told him, 'so go and get yourself some food. I will meet you at the entrance at dusk.'

Helikaon strolled towards the red columns of the palace entrance and Karpophorus found a place in the shade. He sat on a stone bench alongside a sweet-smelling climbing plant with purple flowers. It was pleasant here and he relaxed. It had been a relief to see the *Penelope* sail that morning. Ever since Bad Luck Bay Karpophorus had been forced to plan his every step. Odysseus knew his face, and would no doubt have guessed that he was stalking Helikaon.

As a passenger on the *Penelope* some nine years ago Karpophorus had been surprised when the Ithakan king approached him after they had beached one night. As was his style, Karpophorus had found a place to sleep away from the men, and was sitting looking at the stars when Odysseus walked up. The ugly king had sat down on a rock close by. 'I know you,' he had said.

The shock had been great. Karpophorus' main talent lay in his anonymity. He had the kind of face no-one remembered, and merely by tying back his dark hair, or growing a chin beard, could change his appearance dramatically. And he had not met Odysseus before this trip to Dardania.

He had hedged. 'How so?'

The king had laughed. 'A friend of mine hired you. I saw you leaving his house one day. It is said you are the finest assassin in all the world, Karpophorus. You never fail.'

'You mistake me for someone else.'

'I don't make that kind of mistake,' said Odysseus. 'And I would like to hire you.'

'It is said you are a man without enemies. Who would you possibly want killed?'

Odysseus had shrugged. 'I don't care. I just want to be able to say I once hired the great Karpophorus.'

'You don't care who dies?'

'Not a jot.'

'You are suggesting I just kill anyone and then seek payment from you?'

'Hmm,' mused the ugly king. 'I can see how that would be a little too random.' He sat silently for a moment. 'All right, how about this: I will hire you to kill the next person who seeks to hire you.'

'I already know who seeks to hire me, and he is a powerful man and well protected. The cost of my services is in direct proportion to the risk I take.'

'Name a fee.'

'You don't want to know who it is?'

'No.'

Now it was Karpophorus who fell silent. He glanced back along the beach, to where the men were sitting round the fire. His gaze fell on the dark-haired young prince who travelled with Odysseus. And here was the difficulty. He had seen on the voyage so far that Odysseus was fond of the youth. Had the ugly king guessed that Karpophorus was being hired to kill him? If he had, and Karpophorus refused to accept his offer, then Odysseus would have him killed here on this beach. He looked up at Odysseus, meeting his gaze. The man was clever. He was seeking to save the young man by murdering his father, and yet, if Karpophorus was captured, there would be no blood feud. For the Ithakan king was, after all, only hiring Karpophorus on a whim, to kill someone anonymous.

'How will you know the deed is done?' asked Karpophorus, continuing the charade.

'Cut off the man's ear and send it to me. I will take that as proof of completion.'

'It will cost a sheep's weight in silver.'

'I agree – but then we have very thin sheep on Ithaka. One other thing. The man we are talking of may already have named the person he wants dead. Or he may name him before you fulfil your promise to me.'

'That is a possibility.'

Odysseus' eyes grew cold. In that moment Karpophorus had seen the briefest glimpse of the man legend spoke of, the young reaver who had terrorized settlements all across the Great Green. In the days of his youth Odysseus had built a formidable reputation as a fighting man and a killer. Karpophorus had stayed very calm. His life, at that moment, was flickering like a candle in a storm. One wrong word now and it would be extinguished.

'I think,' said Odysseus, 'it would be unwise to accept an offer from a man you are going to kill. You agree?'

'Of course.'

'Excellent.'

They had then agreed the manner of the payment. In the background the men of the *Penelope* were laughing. Karpophorus looked over to see the dark-haired young prince engaged in a mock wrestling bout with Odysseus' first mate, Bias.

'A fine lad,' said Odysseus. 'Reminds me of a young sailor who once served with me. He was murdered. It took me five seasons to find the killer. I left his head on a spear. My Penelope always tells me I am an unforgiving man, and I should learn how to put aside grudges. I wish I could.' He shrugged. 'But we are what we are, Karpophorus.' Then he had clapped his meaty hand on Karpophorus' shoulder. 'I am glad we had this little talk.'

It had irked Karpophorus to have been outmanoeuvred by the ugly king, and now, with the promise of Agamemnon's gold, it seemed fitting that the original wishes of Anchises the king would be honoured.

Helikaon would – at last – fall to the blade of Karpophorus.

He had originally planned to kill him in Kypros, and had followed him in the darkness to a high cliff top. The storm had come then, and Helikaon had walked to the cliff edge, and stood, arms raised, as if preparing to dive to the rocks below. Karpophorus had moved silently between the great stones of the shrine. No need for a blade. Just a swift push and the man would plummet into eternity.

Then the child had appeared. Karpophorus had faded back into the shadows, and listened as the terrified little girl spoke of her mother. With Helikaon kneeling by the girl it would have been a simple matter to step forward and bury a knife blade between his shoulders. Yet he could not take a life in front of a child.

Karpophorus thought back to the night in Kypros. He had learned a lot, both about Helikaon and about himself. Arrogance had crept in. It was almost a deadly lesson. Helikaon had known he was followed, and had set men outside the walls. And the Golden One had almost trapped him in the garden. He shivered with pleasure at the remembered excitement.

A sudden burst of moonlight had shone on Helikaon as he raced to intercept him. Karpophorus had made it to the wall, and into the darkness beyond. Then he had glimpsed Zidantas. The big man did not see him in the shadows. Then other men had appeared. Karpophorus had needed all his skills to evade them.

He sat in the shade, remembering, and began to doze. A shadow fell across him and he woke instantly, his dagger in his hand. The elderly servant standing before him almost let slip the tray of food and drink he held. Karpophorus sheathed his blade. 'Your master bade me bring you refreshment,' said the servant, sternly, laying the tray on the bench. There was a flagon of cool water and a goblet, alongside a loaf of bread and slices of salt-dried fish.

The servant left him without a word and Karpophorus ate and drank. His liking for Helikaon swelled. Here was a nobleman who considered the welfare of the men who served him. He must have glanced down from one of the upper windows and seen Karpophorus waiting. Such a man would be made most welcome by the All Father when Karpophorus delivered his spirit to Him. In a way, Karpophorus decided, the killing of Helikaon was a gift to the man.

Pleased with the thought, he settled back to doze once more, and remembered the first man he had killed. It had been an accident. Karpophorus had been working in the stone quarry. His chisel blade had snapped, and flown up. It caught the man working alongside him in the throat, opening the jugular. He had died writhing on the dust of the quarry. Karpophorus had been horrified, but a priest later put his mind at rest. His words remained with the assassin still. 'Hades, the Lord of the Dead, knows the moment of our birth, and the day and the moment of our death. It is written thus, that each man has a certain span allocated to him by Hades. And when that span is done his body returns to the earth.'

'So no-one dies except at their allotted time?'

'Exactly.'

'Then the Lord of the Dead used me to take his life?'

'Yes, indeed, my boy. So you should feel no guilt.'

Guilt was the last thing he felt. The young Karpophorus was invigorated. He had been touched by the gods, and, in that moment, had become a servant of Hades. It was the single greatest moment of his life, and it changed his destiny.

He thought again of Helikaon. He couldn't kill him today, for Oniacus had ordered him to be the Golden One's bodyguard. In order to remain close to Helikaon Karpophorus had joined the crew in Kypros, and – as a crew member – had sworn an oath of loyalty. Such matters were not to be taken lightly, which was why he had fought ferociously alongside the Golden One at the Battle of Blue Owl Bay.

But the deed could not be put off for much longer. The feast of Demeter was tomorrow night. He would quit the ship later today, and then kill Helikaon tomorrow.

Satisfied with his decision, he stretched out on the bench and fell into a dreamless sleep.

iii

Helikaon passed through the doorway into the king's *megaron*, a massive hall where petitioners waited in the hope of bringing their disputes before the king. There were merchants there, and commoners. It was packed and noisy, and Helikaon moved across it swiftly. A Royal Eagle in bright armour, with a white-crested helmet, opened the side door to the palace gardens, and Helikaon stepped out into the sunlight. There were stone walkways here, flowing around areas of brightly coloured flowers, and several sets of stone seats, shaded by an intricate series of climbing plants, growing between thick wooden roof slats.

There were people waiting here also, but these were of the royal line. Helikaon saw two of Priam's sons there, the king's chancellor Polites, and fat Antiphones. Polites was sitting in the shade, a mass of papyrus scrolls on his lap. Both men wore the ankle-length white robes and belts of gold that marked their rank as ministers of the king. It had been almost a year since Helikaon had last seen them. Polites looked tired, almost ill. His pale hair was thinning, and his eyes were red-rimmed. Antiphones was even larger than Helikaon had remembered, his belly bulging over his wide golden belt, his face flushed and bloated, his eyes heavily pouched. Hard to believe, thought Helikaon, that both were still in their twenties.

Antiphones saw him first and grinned broadly. 'Ho, Aeneas!' he called out. 'Welcome back!' Stepping forward swiftly for such a large man, he embraced Helikaon, kissing his cheeks. The man's strength was prodigious and Helikaon thought his ribs might snap. Then Antiphones released him. Polites did not rise, but smiled shyly. 'Your adventures are the talk of Troy,' continued Antiphones. 'Sea battles and burning pirate ships. You live a life that is not dull, my friend.'

'It is good to be back.'

Helikaon noted the use of the word *pirate*, and added no comment. Troy was still allied to Mykene, and no-one was going to risk causing offence to Agamemnon. He chatted to them for a while, learning that Priam was 'at rest', which meant he was rutting with some servant girl, or the wife of one of his sons. Polites seemed nervous and ill at ease. Perhaps it is your wife, thought Helikaon.

'What news of the city?' he asked them. He watched their expressions change, as if masks had fallen into place.

'Oh,' said Antiphones, 'it is much the same. Have you seen Hektor's bride?'

'We met.'

'Hard woman. Eyes like green flint. A Thera priestess, no less! Thin as a stick. Nothing to get hold of there!'

Helikaon had no wish to discuss Andromache with them. Ignoring the comment he said, 'Any news of Hektor?'

'Only rumour,' said Polites, dabbing at his watery eyes with the white sleeve of his gown. 'A trader reported that a huge battle was being waged. No-one knows who won.'

'Hektor won,' insisted Antiphones. 'Hektor *always* wins. He may be dull in conversation, and unable to tell a fine wine from a cup of cow piss, but he never loses a fight. Don't you find it baffling?'

'In what way?'

'Ever the diplomat, Polites!' said Antiphones scornfully. 'You know full well what I mean. We both grew up with Hektor. He never liked to fight, not even childish scraps. Always reasonable, good-natured, grinning like an oaf. How in the name of Hades did he turn out to be such a warrior?'

Helikaon forced a smile. 'Come, come, Antiphones! I remember when you were the fastest runner in Troy. Might not a similar question be asked? How did such a beautiful athlete become so fat?'

Antiphones also smiled, but his eyes were hard. 'You have a point, Aeneas. Hektor is what Hektor is. The beloved heir. Good for him, I suppose. But there is more to running a city than a warrior might suppose. When crops fail, or disease strikes, it will matter not a jot if the king can steer a chariot through a mêlée, or lop the head from an enemy.'

'Which is why Hektor is lucky to have brothers like you.'

A servant appeared and halted before Helikaon. 'The king is ready to see you, lord Aeneas,' he said. Helikaon thanked the man, and followed him back into the palace through a side door, and towards a wide flight of stairs leading to the queen's apartments at the top of the building.

'Is the queen in residence?' he asked the servant.

'No, lord, she is still at the summer palace. But King Priam has taken to . . . resting in her apartments during the day.'

Two Royal Eagles were standing before a doorway at the top of the stairs. Helikaon recognized one of them, a powerfully built warrior named Cheon. The soldier nodded a greeting and smiled as he opened the door to the queen's apartments, but he did not speak.

Helikaon entered the room and Cheon pulled the door shut behind him. Long curtains of gauze were fluttering in the mild breeze from the wide window, and the room smelt of heavy perfume. Through an open doorway Helikaon could see an unmade bed. Then a young woman emerged, her face flushed, her eyes downcast. Easing past Helikaon she opened the door and left.

Then Priam appeared, a large golden goblet in his hand, a golden flagon in the other. Moving to a wide couch he sat down, drained the goblet and refilled it. 'Well, come and sit down,' he said, gesturing to a chair on the other side of a low table. 'Unless, of course, you have plans to rush through my city burning Mykene pirates.' Helikaon sat and looked at the king. There seemed to be more silver in the gold of his hair, but he was still a powerful figure.

'Have you heard that Agamemnon was in Miletos?' asked Priam.

'No. He's a long way from home.'

'He's been travelling greatly these last two years. Thraki, Phrygia, Karia, Lykia. Offering gifts to kings, declaring friendship and making alliances.'

'Why would he need alliances on this side of the Great Green?'

'Why indeed?' The king fell silent. He leaned back. 'You saw the girl?'

'Yes.'

'Pretty – but dull. Was a time when all women seemed to be creatures of fire and passion. You could spend a glorious day rutting. Now it's all: "Yes, Great King, whatever pleases you, Great King. Would you like me to bark like a dog, Great King?" Why is that, do you think?'

'You already know the answer,' Helikaon told him.

'Then humour me.'

'No. I did not come here to argue with you. Why is it you always desire conflict when we meet?'

'It is not about desire,' said Priam. 'It is merely that we don't like

244

each other. Shall I tell you what you were thinking when I asked the question?'

'If it pleases you.'

'In past days the girls made love to Priam, the beautiful young man. Now they just seek to serve Priam the randy old king. Am I right?'

'Of course. In your own mind are you not always right?'

Priam's laughter boomed out. 'You know why you don't like me, boy. I am all you do not have the nerve to be. I became a king. You backed away from it, and allowed little Diomedes to bear the burden.'

'Moments like this remind me why I spend so little time in Troy,' said Helikaon, pushing himself to his feet.

'Oh, sit down!' said Priam. 'We need to talk, so we'll stop baiting one another for a little while. You want wine?'

'No.'

'Let us return to Agamemnon,' continued Priam, as Helikaon resumed his seat. 'Have you met him?'

'No.'

'Nor I, though I knew his father, Atreus. He was a fighting man – but then he had to be. The western peoples were constantly warring with each other in those days. But Agamemnon . . . ? He is a mystery. Most of his father's loyal men have been either replaced or killed. Those around him now are savages – like Kolanos. Did you know Agamemnon has reintroduced human sacrifice before battles?'

'No, I had not heard that. It is hardly surprising. The Mykene are a blood-hungry race.'

'Indeed so, Aeneas. Yet they have, since the time of Atreus and his father, maintained the heroic code laid down by Herakles. Glory and service to the gods. Courage and love of homeland. Strength without cruelty. All that is changing under Agamemnon. His generals are now brutal men, who encourage excesses among their soldiers. My spies tell me stories of horror from the lands they have plundered. Women and babes butchered, men tortured and maimed.'

'So why is Agamemnon mysterious?' asked Helikaon. 'Surely he is just another savage from a race of savages.'

'He is not so easy to analyse, Aeneas. His generals are blood-thirsty, and yet he takes no part in their excesses. At feasts he does not down wine, and laugh and sing. He sits quietly, watching others do these things. My ambassadors tell me he has a sharp mind, and he talks well about alliances with Troy, and the need for peaceful trade. Yet he also equips the pirate fleets which raid our coastlines. Now he seeks alliances with the kings of the east. His ambassadors have been offering gifts of gold in Maeonia, Karia, Lykia – even up as far as Phrygia. Kings require alliances with neighbours, to prevent unnecessary warfare. An alliance with Troy is understandable. We are the greatest trading city upon the Great Green. But Lykia and Phrygia? What point is there in such gift-giving? What does he hope to gain?'

Helikaon shrugged. 'With the Mykene it is always war, or plunder.'

'That is in my mind also,' said Priam. 'And there is the mystery. My spies tell me Agamemnon has fierce intelligence, and yet a war in the east would be foolhardy and doomed. The Hittites may not be the power they were, but their armies would dwarf those of the Mykene. The Gypptos too could be drawn in. Also, if Agamemnon attacked our allies then the Trojan Horse would be despatched – and there is not a force alive to match my Hektor.'

'All this is true. And still you are worried,' Helikaon pointed out.

'The shepherd is always concerned when the wolves are out,' quoted Priam. 'However, there is the added concern that Agamemnon has ordered the building of great numbers of ships. The question is, how will he use them? And where will he take them?' Priam rose from his seat and walked into the bedroom, returning with a length of cured hide, on which was etched a map of the Great Green. He spread it on the table. 'In my grandfather's time the Mykene attacked Kypros, and there is still a large Mykene settlement on the island. If they invaded in force they could seize the copper mines. But Kypros is allied with both Egypte and the Hittite empire, and both have armies ten times larger than that of

Agamemnon. Fleets would blockade the island. Massive armies would land and the Mykene would be defeated.' The king moved his finger to the coast of Lykia. 'Let us suppose they invaded the Fat King's realm. They already have colonies on Rhodos and Kos, and in Miletos. They could be supplied from there. But Kygones is an old soldier, and a good fighting man. More important, he is allied with me. I would send the Trojan Horse to his aid, and the Mykene would have no way to call reinforcements. The same can be said of Miletos and Maeonia. Wherever one looks there is no hope of victory for Agamemnon. And you know what that means, Aeneas?'

'Either Agamemnon is not as intelligent as your ambassadors report – or you are missing something.'

'Exactly! And I have no doubt as to his intelligence. In the spring will you ask your captains to gather information as they sail the west?'

'Of course.'

'Good. In the meantime my spies and ambassadors will continue to report. At some point Agamemnon's plans will become clear. When are you heading for home?'

'In a day or two. After I have paid my respects to the queen.'

A look of pain crossed Priam's features. 'She is dying,' said the king. He shivered. 'Hard to believe. I thought she would outlive us all.'

'That saddens me,' said Helikaon. 'I had heard she was ill. Can nothing be done?'

Priam shook his head. 'She has opiates for the pain. But the priests tell me she will not survive the winter. You know she is not yet fifty? By the gods, she was once the most beautiful woman in all the world. She filled my soul with fire and made my days golden. I miss her, Aeneas. She was always my best counsellor.'

'You speak as if she was dead already.'

'I have not seen her in weeks. Not since the priests told me. I cannot look at her. It is too painful. You will find her at the summer palace across the Scamander. She is there with Kassandra and young Paris.'

Helikaon rose. 'You are looking weary. I shall leave you to rest.'

'Rest would be good,' Priam admitted. 'I am not sleeping too well at the moment. However, there is something else you should be aware of,' he added. 'Agamemnon has hired Karpophorus to kill you.'

'I have heard the name.'

'Of course. We all have. What you may not have heard is that he is the man who murdered your father.'

It was as if the air had suddenly chilled. Helikaon stood very still, and felt his heart thudding against his chest. 'How do you know this?' he managed to say.

'Soldiers of mine captured a man yesterday. They took him away for questioning, where, naturally, he died. During the interrogation, however, a great deal was learned. The man we captured negotiates and arranges the missions undertaken by the assassin. One of my sons tried to hire Karpophorus to kill me. However, Karpophorus had already been hired by Agamemnon's agents to kill you.'

'Which of your sons wanted you dead?'

'Probably all of them, truth be told. They are – with the exception of Hektor – a sorry crew. However, the agent died without naming the traitor. In truth I do not believe he knew which of the princes he had been summoned to meet. A messenger took gold to him in Miletos, and invited him to Troy. He was to have been met and taken to the unknown prince. Unfortunately we captured him too soon. However, we have the messenger, but he is proving to be a man of considerable courage. I am not at all sure we will break him.'

'Do we know what Karpophorus looks like?' asked Helikaon.

'About forty years of age, of average height and slim. Sometimes he is bearded, sometimes not. Hardly a help, is it?' said Priam.

'No. Did you learn who hired him to kill my father?'

'No. Apparently it was not arranged through the intermediary. Someone went to Karpophorus directly. You need to be wary, Aeneas. And be careful whom you trust.'

'I have only loyal men around me.'

'Loyalty is a commodity,' sneered Priam. 'And Agamemnon is not short of gold.'

Helikaon felt his anger rise. 'Your curse is to believe that everything has a price,' he said.

Priam smiled. 'And your weakness is to believe that it doesn't.'

XIX

Wings over Olympos

i

THE DAYS WERE BECOMING INCREASINGLY STRANGE FOR HEKABE THE
queen. The statues that lined the garden path often smiled at her,
and, yesterday, in the sky above she had seen the white winged
horse, Pegasus, flying off to the west. It was an effort of will to
rationalize these images. The opiates were strong, and the statues
did not smile. Pegasus had taken a little more thought. In the end
she decided it was probably no more than a flock of gulls. On the
other hand, it was more pleasant to think that dying gave her
greater sight, and maybe, after all, she had seen the white horse flying back to Olympos.

Her back was aching now but she did not have the energy to
move the down-filled cushion to a more comfortable position. A
cool breeze blew off the sea and Hekabe sighed. She had always
loved the sea – especially at the Bay of Herakles. From the high,
cliff top garden she could look down on the Great Green, and
merely by turning her head to the right cast her gaze across the
shining Scamander river to the high golden walls of Troy in the
distance.

The summer palace of King's Joy had always been her favourite place, and it seemed entirely right that she should die here. Priam had built it for her when they were both young, when life seemed everlasting, and love eternal. Pain flared in her belly, but it was dull and thudding, not sharp and jagged as it had been only a few weeks before.

Some twenty paces ahead of her the young prince Paris was sitting in the shade, poring over Egypteian scrolls. Hekabe smiled as she watched him, his stern expression, his total concentration. Not yet twenty-five, he was already losing his hair, like his brother Polites. Slim and studious, Paris had never been suited to the manly pursuits his father so loved. He did not care for riding, save to journey from one place to another. He had no skill with sword or bow. His enthusiasms were focused entirely on study. He loved to draw plants and flowers, and, as a youngster, had spent many happy afternoons dissecting plant stems and examining leaves. Priam soon tired of the boy. But then Priam tired of everyone sooner or later, she thought.

Sadness touched her.

At that moment Paris looked up. Concern showed on his face and he put aside the scroll and rose. 'Let me move that pillow, mother,' he said, helping her to lean forward, then adjusting the cushion. Hekabe sank back gratefully.

'Thank you, my son.'

'I shall fetch you some water.'

She watched him walk away. His movements were not graceful like Hektor's, and his shoulders were already rounded from too many hours spent sitting and reading. There was a time when she too had been disappointed by Paris, but now she was grateful for the kindness of his spirit, and the compassion he showed her. 'I raised good sons,' she told herself. The pain began to worsen and she took a phial from a pouch at her belt and broke the wax seal. Lifting it to her lips with a trembling hand she drained the contents. The taste was bitter, but within moments the pain ebbed away, and she began to doze.

She dreamt of little Kassandra, reliving the dread day when the three-year-old had been consumed by brain fire. The priests all said she would die, and yet she did not. Most young children did not survive the illness, but Kassandra was strong, and clung to life for ten days, the fever raging through her tiny body.

When the fever passed Hekabe's joy was short-lived. The happy, laughing girl Kassandra had been was replaced by a quiet, fey child, who claimed to hear voices in her head, and would sometimes speak in gibberish that none could understand. Now, at eleven years old, she was withdrawn and secretive, avoiding people and shying away from intimacy, even with her mother.

A hand gently pressed on her shoulder. Hekabe opened her eyes. The sun was so bright, the face above her in silhouette. 'Ah, Priam, you *did* come to see me,' she said, her spirits lifting. 'I knew you would.'

'No, mother. It is Paris. I have your water.'

'My water. Yes. Of course.' Hekabe sipped the liquid, then rested her head on the back of the wicker chair. 'Where is your sister?'

'Swimming in the bay with the dolphins. She shouldn't do that. They are large creatures and could hurt her.'

'The dolphins won't harm her, Paris. And she loves to swim. I think her only happiness comes when she is in the water.'

Hekabe glanced back towards the Scamander river. A centaur was rising across the plain. The queen blinked and tried to focus. Centaurs were said to be lucky creatures. Half man, half horse, they always brought gifts. Perhaps he has come to cure me, she thought.

'Rider coming, mother,' said Paris.

'Rider? Yes. Do you recognize him?'

'No. He has long dark hair. Could be Dios.'

She shook her head. 'He is like his father and has no time for dying old women.' Hekabe shielded her eyes with her hand. 'He rides well,' she said, still seeing the centaur.

As the horseman came closer Paris said: 'It is Aeneas, mother. I did not know he was in Troy.'

'That is because you spend all your time with your scrolls and parchments. Go and greet him. And remember he does not like the name Aeneas. He likes to be called Helikaon.'

'Yes, I will remember. And you should remember that you have other guests awaiting an audience. Laodike is here, with Hektor's bride-to-be. They have been waiting all morning.'

'I told you earlier that I am not in the mood to talk to young girls,' said the queen.

Paris laughed. 'I think you will like Andromache, mother. She is just the woman you would have chosen for Hektor.'

'How so?'

'No, no! You must see her yourself. And it would be most rude to receive Helikaon and ignore your own daughter and Hektor's betrothed.'

'I am dying and do not concern myself with petty rules of behaviour.'

His face fell, and she saw him struggling to hold back tears. 'Oh, Paris,' she said, reaching up and stroking his cheek. 'Do not be so soft.'

'I don't like to think of you . . . you know? . . . not being here with me.'

'You are a sweet boy. I will see my guests. Have servants fetch chairs for them, and some refreshments.'

Lifting her hand to his lips he kissed the palm. 'When you are tired,' he said, 'and want them to go, just give me a sign. Say . . . ask for a honeyed fig, something like that.'

Hekabe chuckled. 'I do not need to give signs, Paris. When I am tired I shall tell them all to go. Now go and tell Kassandra to join us.'

'Oh, mother, you know she does nothing I ask of her. She delights in refusing me everything. I think she hates me.'

'She can be wayward,' agreed Hekabe. 'Very well. Ask Helikaon to go down to her. He has a way with her.'

ii

The cliff path was treacherous and steep, the path scree-covered, shifting beneath his sandalled feet. Moving with care Helikaon descended to the beach below, then gazed out across the waves, seeing Kassandra's dark head bobbing alongside the sleek grey forms of two dolphins. The sun was high and hot in a brilliant blue sky. The girl saw him and waved. Helikaon returned the wave, then walked to a shelf of rock and sat.

The meeting with Priam had unsettled him. The king was arrogant and Helikaon had never liked him. Yet he was also canny. He believed the Mykene were preparing to raid the east in force somewhere, and his arguments were persuasive. A people who lived for war would always be seeking fresh areas of conquest and plunder. And the east was ripe for such a venture. The Hittites were engaged in several wars. Battles with the Ashurians, the Elamites and the Kassites had sapped their strength, and now an Egypteian invasion into Phoenicia had further stretched their waning resources.

A fresh breeze blew off the sea and Helikaon drew in a deep breath, tasting the salt in the air. Kassandra was still swimming, but he did not call out to her. In the happy days when he had lived with Hektor, and Kassandra had come to stay with them, he had learned she was not a child who took well to commands.

He sat quietly in the sunshine and waited. After a little while he saw Kassandra swim smoothly back to the shore and wade from the water. Lifting a white knee-length tunic from the rock over which she had draped it she clothed herself and ran over the sand to where Helikaon waited. Slim and small, her face delicate and fine-boned, Kassandra would one day be a beautiful woman. Her long dark hair was thick and lustrous, her eyes a soft blend of grey and blue.

'The dolphins are worried,' she said. 'The sea is changing.'

'Changing?'

'It is getting warmer. They don't like it.'

He had almost forgotten how fey the child was, and how she could not tell fantasy from reality. Sometimes at night she used to wander the gardens chatting as if to old friends, though there was no-one with her.

'It is good to see you again, Kassandra,' he told her.

'Why?' Her eyes were wide, the question asked with great innocence.

'Because you are my friend, and it is always good to see friends.'

She sat down on the rock beside him, drawing up her knees and resting her arms on them, and stared out to sea. 'The big one is Cavala,' she said, pointing to the dolphins. 'That is his wife, Vora. They have been together for five migrations. I don't know how long that is. Do you think it is a long time?'

'I don't know,' he said. 'Your mother has guests. She was wondering if you would like to meet them.'

'I don't like guests,' said the girl, shaking back her long black hair. Droplets of water sprayed out.

'*I* am a guest,' he pointed out.

She nodded, her expression, as always, serious. 'Yes, I suppose that you are. Then I am wrong, Helikaon, for I like you. Who are the others?'

'Laodike, and Hektor's betrothed, the lady Andromache.'

'She shoots a bow,' said Kassandra. 'She is very skilled.'

'Andromache?'

'Yes.'

'I did not know that.'

'Mother will be dead soon.' The words were spoken without feeling, cold and detached.

He kept his voice calm. With anyone else he would have grown angry, but Kassandra could not be judged against any normal standards of behaviour. 'Does it not make you sad?'

'Why would it make me sad?'

'Do you not love her?'

'Of course I love her. She is my greatest friend. Mother, you and Hektor. I love you all.'

'But when she is dead you will not be able to see her, or hug her.'

'Of course I will, silly! When I am dead too.'

Helikaon fell silent. The sea was calm and beautiful, and sitting here in the quiet of the Bay of Herakles it seemed that all the world was at peace. 'I used to dream that you would marry me,' said Kassandra. 'When I was little. Before I knew better. I thought it would be wonderful to live with you in a palace.'

He laughed. 'As I recall you also wanted to marry Hektor.'

'Yes,' she said. 'That would have been wonderful too. Egypteian brothers and sisters marry, you know.'

'But you changed your mind about me,' he said, with a smile. 'Was it because you heard me snore?'

'You don't snore, Helikaon. You sleep on your back, with your arms spread out. I used to sit and watch you sleep. And I listened to your dreams. They were always frightening.'

'How do you listen to dreams?'

'I don't know. I just do. I love this bay,' she said. 'It is very peaceful.'

'So, are you going to tell me why you decided not to marry me?'

'I will never marry. It is not in my destiny.'

'In a few years you may change your mind. When you are grown. You are only eleven. I would wager that by the time you are my age the world will look very different to you.'

'It will look different to everyone,' she said. 'But I will be dead before then, and I will be with mother.'

Helikaon shivered. 'Don't say that! Children should not talk of death so lightly.'

Her grey eyes met his own, and he saw the sadness there. 'I will be on a rock,' she said, 'high in the sky, and three kings will be with me. And I will see you far below. The rock will carry me to the stars. It will be a great journey.'

Helikaon pushed himself to his feet. 'I must attend your mother. She would be happy if you came with me.'

'Then I shall make her happy,' said Kassandra.

Swinging back she gazed at the bay. 'This is where they will come,' she whispered. 'Just like Herakles did. Only this time their ships will fill the bay. As far as can be seen, all the way to the horizon. And there will be blood and death upon the beach.'

iii

For Laodike the afternoon was one of unremitting sadness. And it had started so well. She had been laughing and joking with Andromache in her high apartments overlooking the northern plains. Andromache had been trying on various hats and clothes presented to Laodike by foreign ambassadors. Most of them were ludicrous, and showed how stupid and primitive were the peoples of other nations: a wooden hat from Phrygia, with an integral veil so heavy that any woman wearing it would be half blind; a tall, conical Babylonian hat, made up of beaten rings of silver, that perched precariously on top of the head, held in place only by chin straps. She and Andromache had cavorted around the apartments, shrieking with laughter. At one point Andromache had donned a Kretan dress of heavy linen, embroidered with gold thread. It was designed so that the breasts could stand free, and a corset of bone drew in the waist, emphasising the curves of the wearer.

'It is the most uncomfortable clothing I've ever worn,' said Andromache, pulling back her shoulders, her breasts jutting proud and high. Laodike's good humour had begun to evaporate at that moment. Standing there, in a stupid dress, the flame-haired Andromache looked like a goddess, and Laodike had felt un-utterably plain.

Her mood had lifted as they were travelling to mother's summer palace, but not by much. Mother had never liked her. Laodike's childhood had been one of constant scolding. She could never remember the names of all the countries of the Great Green, and even when she did recall them, she found that she got the cities mixed up. So many of them were similar – Maeonia, Mysia, Mykene, Kios and Kos. In the end they all blurred in her mind. In mother's lessons she would panic, and the gates of her mind would close, denying all access – even to things she knew. Kreusa and Paris would always know the answers, just as – she had been told – Hektor did before them. She didn't doubt that strange little Kassandra also pleased mother.

Perhaps now that she is ill she will be less harsh, she had

thought, as the two-wheeled carriage crossed the Scamander bridge.

'What is she like, your mother?' Andromache asked.

'Very nice,' answered Laodike.

'No, I mean, what does she look like?'

'Oh, she's tall and her hair is dark. Father says she was the most beautiful woman in the world. She is still very attractive. Her eyes are grey-blue.'

'She is revered on Thera,' said Andromache. 'Part of her dowry built the Temple of the Horse.'

'Yes. Mother spoke of it. Very big.'

Andromache laughed. 'Very big? It is colossal, Laodike. You can see it from the sea, miles from Thera. The head is so large that inside it there is a great hall, in which fifty of the senior priestesses meet and offer prayers and sacrifices to Poseidon. The eyes are massive windows. If you lean out you can pretend to be a bird, so high are you in the sky.'

'It sounds . . . wonderful,' said Laodike dully.

'Are you ill?' asked Andromache, leaning in to her, and placing an arm round her shoulder.

'No, I am well. Truly,' answered Laodike. She looked into Andromache's green eyes, seeing the concern there. 'It is just . . .'

'Hera's curse?'

'Yes,' she said, happy that it was not a complete lie. 'Don't you find it strange that it was a goddess who cursed women with periods of bleeding? Ought to have been a capricious god, really.'

Andromache laughed. 'If all the tales are to be believed the male gods would surely prefer women to rut all the time. Perhaps Hera was just allowing us a little respite.'

Laodike saw the shoulders of the carriage driver hunch forward, as if he was trying to move himself further from the conversation. Suddenly her mood lifted, and she began to giggle. 'Oh, Andromache, you really do have a wonderful way of seeing things.' Settling back in her seat she glanced ahead at the walls of King's Joy, her fears melting away.

Laodike had not seen her mother for several months, and, when

Paris led them into the garden, she did not recognize her. Sitting in a wicker chair was a white-haired ancient, frail and bony, her face a mask of yellowed parchment, drawn so tightly across her skull it seemed that at any moment the skin would tear. Laodike stood very still, not knowing how to react. At first she thought the crone was also visiting mother, but then the ancient spoke. 'Are you just going to stand there, stupid girl, or are you going to kiss your mother?'

Laodike felt giddy. Her mouth was dry, her mind reeling, just as it had during those awful lessons. 'This is Andromache,' she managed to say.

The dying queen's gaze moved on. Laodike felt a surge of relief. Then Andromache stepped forward and kissed Hekabe's cheek. 'I am sorry to find you in such poor health,' she said.

'My son tells me I will like you,' said the queen coldly. 'I have always loathed that phrase. It instantly makes me feel I am destined to dislike the person. So *you* tell me why I should like you.'

Andromache shook her head. 'I think not, Queen Hekabe. It seems to me that in Troy everyone plays games. I do not play games. Like me if you will, dislike me if you must. Either way the sun will still shine.'

'A good answer,' said the queen. Then her bright eyes fixed Andromache with a piercing look. 'I hear you stood on the high parapet with Priam, and that you refused to kneel.'

'Did you kneel for Priam?'

'Not for Priam, or any man!' snapped the queen.

Andromache laughed. 'There you are then, Queen Hekabe. We have something in common already. We don't know how to kneel.'

The queen's smile faded. 'Yes, we have something in common. Has my husband tried to bed you yet?'

'No. Nor will he succeed if he tries.'

'Oh, he will try, my dear. Not just because you are tall and comely, but because you are very like me. Or rather as I once was. I too was once a priestess of Thera. I too was strong once. I ran through the hills, and bent the bow, and danced in the revels. I too had a sweet lover, full-lipped and heavy-breasted. How did Kalliope take your parting?'

Laodike was shocked at this news, and glanced at Andromache. She thought her friend would be crestfallen and shamed. Instead Andromache smiled broadly. 'What a city this is,' she said. 'Everywhere there are spies and whispers, and no secrets are safe. I had not thought the royal court would know so much of the happenings on Thera.'

'The royal court does not,' said the queen. 'I do. So, did Kalliope weep? Did she beg you to run away with her?'

'Was that how you parted from your lover?'

'Yes. It tore my heart to leave her. She killed herself.'

'She must have loved you greatly.'

'I am sure that she did. But she killed herself twenty years later, after a vileness grew in her throat, draining the flesh from her bones, and robbing her of speech and breath. She threw herself from the Eye of the Horse, her life dashed out on the rocks far below. Now I have a vileness in my belly. Do you think the gods punished us both for our lustful ways?'

'Do you?'

Hekabe shrugged. 'Sometimes I wonder.'

'I do not,' said Andromache. 'Angry men stalk the lands with sword and fire, burning, killing, and raping. Yet the gods are said to admire them. If this is true, then I cannot see how they would punish women for loving one another. However, if I am wrong, and the gods do hate us for our pleasures, then they do not deserve my worship.'

Hekabe suddenly laughed. 'Oh, you are so like me! And you are far more suited to my Hektor than your insipid sister. However, we were talking about Priam. He will not rape you. He will seek to seduce you, or he will find some other means to force your acquiescence. He is a subtle man. I think he will wait until I am dead, though. So you have a little time of freedom yet.'

'How could anyone love such a man?' said Andromache.

Hekabe sighed. 'He is wilful, and sometimes cruel. But there is greatness in him too.' She smiled. 'When you have known him a little longer you will see it.' Her eyes turned back to Laodike. 'Well, girl, are you going to kiss mother?'

'Yes,' replied Laodike meekly, stepping forward and stooping down. She closed her eyes and planted a swift peck on her mother's cheek, then moved back hurriedly. The queen smelt of cloves, the scent sickly and cloying.

Servants brought chairs and cool drinks and they sat together. Paris had wandered off, and was reading a scroll. Laodike did not know what to say. She knew now that mother was dying, and her heart ached with the knowledge of it. She felt like a child again, miserable, alone and unloved. Even on the verge of death mother did not have a kind word for her. Her stomach was knotted, and the conversation between Andromache and Hekabe seemed like the intermittent buzzing of bees. Mother summoned more servants to raise a set of painted sun screens around them, and, though the shade was welcome, it did nothing to raise Laodike's spirits.

And then Helikaon came, and once more Laodike's spirits lifted. She rose from her chair and waved as the young prince came striding across the pale grass of the cliff top, young Kassandra beside him. He smiled when he saw Laodike.

'You are more lovely than ever, cousin,' he said, taking her into his arms and hugging her close. Laodike wanted the hug never to end, and she clung to him, and kissed his cheek.

'By the gods, Laodike, must you act the harlot?' demanded mother.

The harshness of the tone cut through her. She had committed the most awful breach of protocol. A guest must first greet the queen. Helikaon leaned in and kissed her brow. Then he winked and mouthed the words: 'Don't worry!' Stepping forward he knelt beside the queen's chair. 'I brought Kassandra as you requested.'

'No-one brought me,' said Kassandra. 'I came to make you happy, mother.'

'You always make me happy, my dear,' said Hekabe. 'Now sit with us, Helikaon. I am told you have been battling pirates, and setting them ablaze, no less.'

'It is too beautiful a day,' he said, 'to be spoiled by tales of blood-shed and savagery. And the lady Andromache already knows of the battle and its aftermath. She was there on the beach.'

'I envy you,' said Hekabe. 'I would like to have watched those Mykene burn. Heartless dogs every one of them. I never met a Mykene I liked – nor one I trusted.'

'Tell mother about the disguise,' said Laodike. 'One of my servants heard it from a crewman.'

'Disguise?' echoed Hekabe, her brows furrowing.

'To escape assassins on the cliff,' said Laodike. 'It was very clever. Tell her, Helikaon.'

'It was a small matter. I knew the killers were waiting for me, so I bribed one of Kygones' guards and borrowed his armour. Nothing dramatic, I fear. I merely walked past the Mykene.' He suddenly chuckled. 'One of them even called me over to ask if I had seen Helikaon.'

'You were dressed as a guard?' said Andromache. 'Did you perchance lose your sandal on the beach?'

'Yes. The strap broke. How odd you should know that.'

'Not at all. I saw you.'

Laodike looked at her young friend. Her face seemed very pale, and for the first time since she had known her Andromache seemed tense and ill at ease. 'It was a cheap sandal,' said Helikaon.

'Tell me of the ship,' demanded Hekabe. 'I have always loved tales of ships.'

Laodike sat quietly as Helikaon spoke of the *Xanthos*, and the Madman from Miletos who designed and built her. He talked of her seaworthiness, and how she danced upon the waters like a queen of the sea. He told them of the storm, and how the ship weathered it. Laodike was lost in the wonder of it all. She dreamed of sailing far away from Troy, to live on a green island, where no-one would ever call her a stupid girl, or demand that she recite the names of lands she would never visit.

Towards dusk Hekabe complained of tiredness, and two servants were summoned to carry her back into the house. Helikaon left soon after. He had intended to sail today for

Dardania, but now would have to wait for the dawn. He kissed Laodike, and hugged her again. 'She does not mean to be cruel,' he said.

Oh yes, she does, thought Laodike, but said: 'I am sure you are right, Helikaon.'

Kneeling beside Kassandra he said: 'Do I get a hug from you, little friend?'

'No.'

'Very well,' he told her, and began to rise.

'I have changed my mind,' she said haughtily. 'I will allow you a hug because it will make you happy.'

'That is gracious of you,' he said. Kassandra threw her thin arms round his neck, and hugged him tightly. He kissed her cheek. 'Friends should always hug,' he added. Then he stood and turned towards Andromache.

'It was good to see you again, lady,' he said. Laodike expected him to step in and take her in his arms also, but he did not. The two of them looked at one another. Andromache's normally stern face had softened, and there was colour in her cheeks.

'Will you come back for the wedding?'

'I think not. I wish you every happiness. I have always known Hektor was lucky, but now I know the gods have blessed him.'

'But have they blessed me?' she asked softly.

'I hope so – with all my heart.'

'Are you going to hug her?' asked Kassandra. 'You should.'

Helikaon looked uncertain, but Andromache stepped in. 'I think we should be friends,' she said.

'We always will be, Andromache. You have my oath on that.' His arms swept round her, drawing her close.

Laodike felt a sudden chill in her belly as she watched them. She saw Helikaon's eyes close, and she heard him sigh. Sadness flowed through her. For several years now she had entertained the fantasy that father might arrange a marriage between her and Helikaon. She knew he did not love her, but she believed that if such a match was completed she could make him happy. When she heard he had refused to be wedded to the beautiful Kreusa she had been jubilant.

He had told Priam he would only marry for love. Laodike had held to the faintest hope that he might come to love *her*. That hope had shone like a spark in the lonely nights. Now it was extinguished. He had never held her like that.

And she knew in that moment he never would.

You will never know love, whispered the dark fear of her heart.

Andromache broke the embrace. She was flushed and seemed unsteady on her feet. Swiftly she stepped back from Helikaon, then knelt by the slim Kassandra. 'Can we be friends too?' she asked.

'Not yet,' said Kassandra. 'I am going to swim again. The dolphins are waiting for me.'

XX

The Temple of Hermes

i

KARPOPHORUS WAS UNEASY AS HE SAT ON THE ROOFTOP, STARING across the Scamander river at the distant cliff-top palace. Tonight, as the sun set, the feast of Demeter, the Corn Goddess, would begin. People would give thanks for the harvests of the summer. There would be strong drink, fine wines, platters of food and huge roasting pits. People would dance and sing, and throw off their cares and worries for a day. In nine months there would be hundreds of new babes born into the world, screaming and crying. Karpophorus loathed feast days.

However, this one was special.

When he had first been called to his ministry of death he had travelled to the island of Samothraki, to seek the wisdom of a seer who dwelt there. The man was famous across the Great Green. He lived in a cave, eschewing wealth in the search for spiritual perfection. There were always scores of people thronging the hillside below the cave, offering gifts and entreaties. The seer would sit silently in the sunshine, and occasionally call someone forward. Then he would speak in low tones, and the supplicant would listen before walking away quietly through the crowd. People would call out to the supplicant, 'What did he say?' But always there was no answer.

Karpophorus had waited for nineteen days. On the morning of the twentieth, as he stared at the old man, he saw that the seer's eyes were upon him. Then he was summoned. He could scarcely believe it, and glanced round to see if anyone was standing behind him. Finally he rose and walked up the hillside.

The seer was less old than he had thought. Though his beard was white his face was unlined.

Karpophorus sat cross-legged before him. 'What wisdom do you seek?' asked the seer.

'I have been called to serve the Great Father,' Karpophorus told him. 'But I need guidance.'

'How did this call come upon you?'

Karpophorus told him of the death of his co-worker, and of his realization that he was to serve the great god by sending souls on the long journey.

'You think Hades requires you to kill people?'

'Yes,' answered Karpophorus proudly.

The man looked at him, his face expressionless, his large blue eyes holding Karpophorus' dark gaze. 'How many have you killed now?'

'Nine.'

'Wait, while I commune with the spirits,' said the seer, then closed his eyes.

So much time passed that Karpophorus began to think the man had fallen asleep. Then his eyes opened.

'All men choose to follow one path or another, Karpophorus. If I were to tell you that you were deluded, and that the Lord of the Dead did not call upon you, would you believe me? Answer honestly.'

'No. The Great God has made me his servant.'

The man nodded. 'Tell me, do you believe he would want you to kill children?'

'No.'

'Or women?'

266

'I do not know. Does he want women slain?'

'There will be no children or women. And you will kill no-one between the Feast of Demeter and the Feast of Persephone. When the land sleeps between the seasons you also will rest. And for each mission you undertake successfully you will offer half of your fee to benefit the poor and the needy.' He pointed to the knife at Karpophorus' side. 'Give me the blade.' Karpophorus pulled it clear and offered it to the seer. It was a fine dagger, the hilt embossed with silver thread, the pommel shaped like a lion's head. 'You will use only this dagger for your missions. Never poison, nor sword, nor rope. Not your hands, not a spear, not a bow. And when this dagger breaks, or is lost, you will serve the Great God no more with death. If any of these instructions be broken then your life will end within seven days.'

'It will be as you say, holy one.'

Over the years Karpophorus had followed each instruction without complaint. In three cities there were houses of care for the poor and the destitute, funded by Karpophorus. Not one woman or child had fallen to his dagger, and the weapon was lovingly tended, and used only for his missions, lest the blade be damaged. He carried two other knives for general use, and these he had used in the Battle of Blue Owl Bay.

Tonight was the Feast of Demeter, and today the Lion-pommelled dagger would end Helikaon's life on this earth.

He had watched the lord ride across the Scamander bridge that morning, on a horse borrowed from the king's stable. The chances were that he would return it around dusk and then walk down through the town to the beach. He would pass through the square of the Hermes Temple. There would be crowds there.

It should not be difficult, Karpophorus thought, to kill him there. I will merely walk up, the dagger hidden in my sleeve. Helikaon will greet me with a smile. Then, swiftly and surely, I will let slip the dagger and slice it across his throat. Then I will merge with the crowds and be gone. Helikaon will be free to find the Elysian Fields and enjoy eternity in the company of gods and heroes.

Karpophorus sighed.

It should not be difficult to kill him there.

The slaying of Helikaon had proved far more difficult than any of his recent killings. The Golden One was a wary man, and sharp-witted; a thinker and a planner. Worse than this, though, Karpophorus realized, he was, in fact, reluctant to go through with the contract. Odd thoughts had been occurring to him lately, doubts and concerns. It had never happened before. Karpophorus loved his work, and felt immense pride that Hades had chosen him. But joining the crew of the *Xanthos* had unsettled him.

All his life Karpophorus had been a solitary man, comfortable in his own company. More than this, he positively disliked being surrounded by crowds. He had thought the journey on the *Xanthos* would be tense and unpleasant. Instead he had found a kind of solace. Oniacus had even hugged him on the beach yesterday, after Karpophorus told him he was quitting the crew. The sensation had been strange. Afterwards he tried to think of the last time he had been embraced. He couldn't remember. He supposed his mother must have cuddled him at some point, but try as he might, he could not recall a single touch from her. 'You'll be missed, Attalus,' Oniacus had told him. 'I know the Golden One sets great store by you. He will be sorely disappointed when he hears you are no longer with us.'

This kind of parting was alien territory to the assassin. It amazed him that he had found himself close to tears. Not knowing what to say he had trudged off, his copper wages in his pouch.

He had spent the night dozing in a doorway overlooking the palace entrance, and was awake with the dawn, watching for Helikaon.

Below the rooftop he heard children laughing and playing. Easing himself up, he glanced down at them. There were five boys, playing catch with a knotted ball of old rope. Then he saw another child, sitting apart from the others. He was thin and scrawny, and his face bore a sad look.

Don't just sit there, thought Karpophorus. *Go and join in. Do not set yourself apart. Make friends.*

But the boy just sat and watched. Karpophorus felt a sinking of the spirits, and toyed with the idea of walking down and speaking to him. Yet he could not. What would I say, he asked himself? And why should he listen?

Then one of the other boys, a tall, slim lad with long auburn hair, left the group and sat beside the smaller child. He put his arm round his shoulder. Then the child smiled. The taller boy pulled him to his feet, and drew him to where the others were playing.

Karpophorus felt a great sense of gratitude. He sat watching them playing until they wandered off to their homes. The little boy was laughing. 'Who knows now what you may become?' whispered Karpophorus.

And the sadness returned.

In the failing light he saw a horseman heading back across the Scamander bridge. It was too dark to make out his features, but he recognized Helikaon's riding style, one hand holding the reins, the other resting lightly on his thigh.

Karpophorus watched him return the horse, talk for a while with the groom, and then enter the palace. A short while later, now wearing a tunic of dark leather, two bronze swords scabbarded at his side, he strode out towards the streets leading to the beach.

Slipping his dagger into his sleeve, Karpophorus climbed down from the rooftop and moved out to intercept him.

ii

As he walked towards the harbour Helikaon thought of Andromache. He could still feel the warmth of her body pressed against him in that hug, and the remembered scent of her hair filled him with longing. He wished now that he had sailed from Troy earlier, and had not visited the dying Hekabe.

He glanced at the sky, and the lowering clouds in the west, and wondered if he had committed some sin against Aphrodite, the love goddess. Perhaps he had sacrificed less to her than to the other gods. The irony of the situation was not lost on him. He had refused to marry, save for love, and now, having met the woman of his heart and his dreams, she was to wed another. Worse, she was to be married to his closest friend.

Now is not the time to dwell on it, he warned himself, as the shadows lengthened on the streets of Troy.

He passed through milling crowds of brightly dressed Trojans thronging the marketplaces, seeking the best deals from traders anxious to pack up their wares for the night. A whore smiled at him, cupping her heavy breasts, and licking her painted lips. He shook his head and her interest waned, her bright smile fading.

With the crowds behind him he moved more warily down the hillside towards the beach. Mykene spies would be well aware that this was his last day in Troy. They knew he would be sailing with the dawn. If another attack was planned, then it would be now, as he returned to the *Xanthos*.

A cool westerly breeze was blowing, and several drops of rain began to fall. Helikaon gazed at the buildings ahead. He was approaching a narrow street, leading to the wide square fronting the Temple of Hermes, God of Travellers. There would be many people there, sailors offering gifts for safe passage, and others about to take journeys who would be seeking the blessing of the god.

A perfect place to ambush a single man in sight of his ship.

He felt the tension rise in him as he entered the street before the temple. Ahead he saw a man, hooded and cloaked. The man turned away sharply and walked back towards the square.

A cold anger settled on Helikaon. This was the scout, then. His appearance in the square would tell the others that Helikaon was approaching. How many would be waiting? His heart began to beat faster. They would want to be sure this time. Eight or ten killers would rush him. Certainly no more. A larger group would get in each others' way. Ten, he decided, would be the maximum. At least two would run behind, to block a retreat back along the street he now walked. The others would circle him, then rush in.

Helikaon paused and whispered a prayer to the war god. 'I know these Mykene worship you above all gods, mighty Ares, but the men in this square are cowards. I ask your blessing upon my blades today.'

Then he walked on.

At the entrance to the square he glanced left and right. As he walked on he saw two hooded men angling around behind him, blocking his retreat.

He saw Attalus moving through the crowd towards him.

At that moment four men threw off their cloaks, drew swords and rushed at him. They were wearing leather breastplates and round leather helmets. Helikaon drew his two swords and leapt to meet them. All around, the crowd scattered. Other Mykene rushed in. Helikaon blocked a savage thrust, plunging his blade through an attacker's throat. A sword blade hammered against his side. The pain was intense – but the hidden ivory discs within the leather tunic prevented his ribs being smashed. Helikaon swung his sword against the Mykene's leather helmet. The blade sliced down through the flesh of the man's face, snapping the jaw bone. Helikaon kept moving, cutting and parrying. Despite concentrating on the men coming against him he was aware of Oniacus and the hand-picked fighting men of the crew rushing from their hiding places and attacking the Mykene. The ringing clash of sword upon sword echoed in the square. The crowd had drawn back, leaving the central area to the combatants. Flipping his right-hand blade, and holding the short sword now as a dagger, Helikaon parried a thrust with his left-hand sword, then plunged the right down through the attacker's collar bone. The blade sank deep, and a ghastly scream tore from the Mykene's throat.

Helikaon spun and saw Attalus ram a dagger through the eye of a Mykene. There was blood on Attalus' tunic.

Now it was the Mykene who sought to flee. Helikaon saw a tall warrior cut down a crewman and run towards the narrow street.

Gershom cut off his retreat, the club of Zidantas thundering into the man's face. The Mykene was hurled from his feet, his skull smashed.

Two other attackers threw down their weapons, but they were ruthlessly slain.

Helikaon saw Attalus tottering towards him, his dagger dripping blood. The man staggered. Dropping his swords Helikaon stepped in to meet him. The injured man fell into his arms. Helikaon laid him down on the stone. Attalus' hand flapped, the dagger blade scraping across Helikaon's tunic. 'It is all right, Attalus,' said Helikaon, taking the blade from the man's hand. 'The fighting is over. Let me see your wound.'

There was a deep puncture just above the right hip, and blood was pouring from it. Then Helikaon saw a second wound in the chest. It was bleeding profusely. Oniacus crouched down alongside Helikaon. 'Eight dead Mykene, but we lost five, with three more carrying wounds.'

'You have a healer waiting at the *Xanthos*?'

'Aye, Golden One, just as you ordered.'

'Then let us get the wounded aboard.'

'Give me . . . my dagger,' whispered Attalus.

Helikaon laid his hand on the man's shoulder. 'You must rest, Attalus. Do not exert yourself. Your dagger is safe. I will look after it for you.'

'Looks like you are staying with us after all, Attalus, my friend,' said Oniacus. 'Don't worry. We'll have those scratches dealt with in no time.'

Helikaon stood and gazed around the temple square. People were gathering now, staring at the bodies. A troop of Trojan soldiers came running into sight, spreading out, swords drawn. Helikaon strode towards them. The officer approached him. Helikaon did not know the man.

'What happened here?' demanded the officer.

'Mykene assassins tried to kill me.'

'And why would they do that?'

'I am Aeneas of Dardania, known as Helikaon.'

Instantly the officer's attitude changed. 'My apologies, lord. I did not recognize you. I am new to the city.' He glanced at the corpses, and the wounded crewmen. 'Did any of the assassins escape?'

'None that I saw.'

'I will need to make a report to my watch commander.'

'Of course,' said Helikaon, and outlined the attack. As he concluded the officer thanked him and began to turn away. 'Wait,' called Helikaon. 'You have not asked me why the Mykene should want me dead.'

The officer gave a tight smile. 'Oh, I have been in the city long enough to understand why,' he answered. 'You stain the Great Green with their blood.'

Helikaon returned to his men. Stretcher bearers carried three badly wounded crewmen away to the House of Serpents, while others were helped down to the beach where the physician Machaon waited. The five corpses were also carried to the beach and laid out on the sand close to the *Xanthos*. Helikaon knelt alongside each of the bodies, placing silver rings in their mouths.

'Why do you do that?' asked Gershom.

Helikaon rose. 'Gifts for Charon the Ferryman. All spirits must cross the Black River to reach the Fields of Elysia. He ferries them.'

'You believe that?'

Helikaon shrugged. 'I don't know. But the gifts also honour the dead, and are tributes to their bravery.'

A tall, silver-haired man, wearing a long white cloak bearing the horse insignia of the House of Priam, approached them and bowed.

'My lord Aeneas, I come from the king with grim news.'

'Is Priam ill?'

'No, lord. The news is from Dardania.'

'Then speak, man.'

The messenger hesitated, then took a long, deep breath. He did not meet Helikaon's gaze. 'Word has reached us that a force of Mykene pirates, under cover of darkness, broke into the citadel at Dardanos.' He hesitated. 'It was not a plunder raid. It was a mission of murder.'

Helikaon stood very quietly. 'They were seeking me?'

'No, lord. They were hunting the boy king.'

A cold fear settled on Helikaon's heart. 'Tell me they did not find him.'

'I am sorry, lord. They killed Diomedes and raped and stabbed his mother. She still lives, but it is feared not for long.'

Several men, Oniacus among them, had gathered round. No-one spoke. Helikaon fought for control. He closed his eyes, but all he could see was the bright, smiling face of Diomedes, sunlight glinting on his golden hair. The silence grew.

'The pirates were beaten back, lord. But most of them made it to the beach and their waiting ships.'

'How did the boy die?'

'They soaked his clothing in oil, set fire to him, and hurled him from the cliffs. The queen's clothing was also drenched in oil, but General Pausanius and his men fought their way to her. The Mykene had no time to burn her, which, I suppose, is why they stabbed her. No-one knows who led the raid, save that it was a young warrior with white hair.'

Helikaon walked away from the messenger and the silent crew and stood staring out to sea. Oniacus joined him.

'What are your orders, my king?' he asked.

'We sail tonight. We are going home to Dardanos,' Helikaon told him.

Part Three

THE STORMS OF WINTER

XXI

The Man at the Gate

HABUSAS THE ASSYRIAN SAT ON THE CLIFF TOP, GAZING OUT OVER THE
sea. To the northeast the high mountained isle of Samothraki was
bathed in sunshine, but here, above the small island of Pithros,
heavy clouds cast dark shadows over the cliffs and the rugged land
behind them. The sea below was rough and churning, fierce winds
buffeting the waves. Habusas lifted the wine jug to his lips and
drank. It was cheap wine, and coarse, but none the less satisfying.
Behind him he could hear the laughter of his children, the three
boys chasing each other, long sticks in their hands – pretend swords
for pretend warriors. One day, he thought proudly, they will sail
with me, and the swords will be real.

It had been a good season, with fine raiding. Kolanos had led
them to many victories, and Habusas had returned to the winter
isle with a huge sack of plunder. There were golden torques and
wristbands, brooches of silver and lapis lazuli, rings set with
carnelian and emerald. Yes, a fine season – save for the horror of
Blue Owl Bay. A lot of good men had died that day, their bodies
burnt and blackened.

Still, they had revenged themselves in the attack on Dardanos.
Habusas recalled with pleasure watching the young king, his
clothes ablaze, fall screaming from the cliff. More pleasurable still,

277

though, was the memory of the queen. Sex was always good, but the pleasure was heightened immeasurably when the woman was unwilling. Indeed, when she begged and pleaded to be spared.

And how she had pleaded!

Habusas had been surprised when he had heard she had survived. Normally deadly with a dagger, he could only suppose that the necessity for speed had caused his blade to miss her heart. The queen's soldiers had fought their way through more swiftly than anticipated. It was a shame, for he and the others had drenched her clothes with oil, and it would have been fitting to watch her plummet in flames to join her son.

He thought of Helikaon. It warmed his heart to imagine the anguish he was suffering.

The last ship to arrive at Pithros, some three weeks back, brought news from the mainland. Helikaon had arrived back in Dardanos. Everywhere there was uproar and unrest. The murder of the boy king had unsettled the people – exactly as Kolanos had forecast.

And how galling it would be for Helikaon to know that the men who attacked the fortress were now wintering in the safety of Pithros, protected by both the angry sea and the fact that the island was Mykene. Even if he could convince his warriors to brave the wrath of Poseidon, Helikaon could not attack the island without bringing upon himself a war he could not win.

Kolanos had promised his men they would raid Dardanos again come the spring – this time with fifty ships and more than a thousand warriors. Habusas was glad the queen was still alive. He could picture her terror as she saw the warriors coming towards her again, and almost hear her cries for mercy as they ripped the clothes from her back. He felt a quickening of the blood. He had never raped a queen before. Though the pounding of royal flesh was exactly like his other conquests, the knowledge of her status had excited him greatly.

Habusas swung round to watch the sun begin to set in the west. His three sons gathered round him, and he hugged them. They were good boys, and he loved them dearly.

'Well, you rascals,' he said, 'time to get you home for your supper.'

The oldest boy, Balios, pointed out to sea. 'Look, father, ships!'

Habusas narrowed his eyes. In the far distance, towards the east, he saw four vessels, their oars beating powerfully. Well they might, he thought, for darkness was falling and they would not want to be at sea come nightfall. Why they were at sea at all at this dangerous time was a mystery. Their season must have been lean, and the captains desperate for plunder.

Habusas hoped they had been lucky, for some of their riches would flow to him. Habusas owned all the whores on Pithros. A feeling of great satisfaction swept over him. He had three fine sons, a loving wife, and burgeoning wealth. In truth these foreign gods had blessed him. And so they should, he thought. Before every voyage he offered sacrifices to all of them, bullocks for Zeus, Hera, Poseidon and Ares, lambs for Demeter, Athene, Artemis and Aphrodite, goats for Hephaistos, Hermes and Hades. Even the lesser deities received libations from him, for he wanted no ill will from the Fates, or the mischievous Discord. Habusas was a deeply religious man, and the gods had rewarded his piety.

His youngest son, six-year-old Kletis, was running along the edge of the cliff path. Habusas called out to him to be careful, then urged Balios to take his hand.

'Why must I always look after him?' argued Balios. He was thirteen, almost a man, and beginning to tear at the bonds of childhood. 'Why not Palikles? He never has to do any work.'

'Yes, I do!' retorted Palikles. 'I helped mother gather the goats while you hid in the haystacks with Fersia.'

'Enough arguing,' snapped Habusas. 'Do as you are told, Balios.'

The thirteen-year-old ran forward and snatched at little Kletis, who wailed miserably. Balios made to cuff him.

'Do not touch your brother!' shouted Habusas.

'He is so irritating.'

'He is a child. They are meant to be irritating. Have I ever struck you?'

'No, father.'

'Then follow my lead.'

Balios stalked off, dragging the unwilling Kletis behind him. 'So,' whispered Habusas to ten-year-old Palikles, 'your brother is chasing the lovely Fersia.'

'Won't have to chase much,' muttered Palikles. 'She's worse than her mother.'

Habusas laughed. 'Let us hope so. The mother is one of my best whores.'

Palikles stopped walking and stared out to sea. 'More ships, father,' he said.

Habusas saw that the original four galleys were now close to the beach, but behind them were seven more.

Thunder clouds were gathering, and the sea was growing increasingly angry.

From a little way ahead Balios shouted out. 'Five more, father!' He was pointing towards the north, past the jutting headland.

Fear struck Habusas like a spear of ice. And he knew in that moment that Helikaon was coming on a mission of vengeance. Sixteen ships! At the very least eight hundred enemy warriors were about to invade. He stood very still, almost unable to accept what his eyes were seeing. Only a madman would bring a fleet across the Great Green in the storm season. And how could he hope to escape the wrath of the Mykene? Habusas was no fool. Putting himself in Helikaon's place he swiftly thought it through. The Dardanian's only hope of avoiding a war lay in leaving no-one alive to name him as the attacker.

He will have to kill us all! Helikaon's men will sweep across the island, butchering everyone.

Habusas began to run down towards the town and the stockade, the boys trailing after him.

As he reached the first of the houses he yelled out to the closest men. 'Gather your weapons! We are under attack!' Racing on, he headed for his own house, continuing to call out to any he saw. Men emerged from the white-walled buildings, hastily buckling on breastplates, and strapping swordbelts to their hips.

At his own house his wife, Voria, had heard the commotion and was standing in the doorway. 'Fetch my helmet and axe,' he cried. 'Then get the boys into the hills and the deep caves. Do it now! ' The panic in his voice galvanized her, and she disappeared into the house. He followed her and dragged his breastplate from a chest. Lifting it over his head he began to buckle the straps. Little Kletis stood in the doorway, crying, Balios and Palikles behind him, looking frightened.

His wife returned, and handed him his helmet. Habusas donned it, swiftly tying the chin straps. 'Go with your mother, boys,' he said, hefting his double-headed axe.

'I'll fight alongside you, father,' offered Balios.

'Not today, lad. Stay with your mother and brothers. Go to the hills.'

He wanted to hug them all, and tell them he loved them, but there was no time. Pushing past the boys he ran towards the stockade. There were over two hundred fighting men on Pithros, and the walled wooden fort was well equipped with bows and spears. They could hold off an army from there! But then his heart sank. Even the fort could not stop eight hundred well-armed men.

Glancing back down towards the beach he could see soldiers gathering, the last of the sunlight glinting on shields, helms, breastplates and the points of spears. They were forming up into disciplined phalanxes. Transferring his gaze to the hillside above the settlement, he saw the women and children heading towards the relative safety of the caves.

'Let the bastards come,' he called out to the gathering pirates. 'We'll feed them their own entrails.'

He knew it wasn't true, and he could see in their faces that they knew it too. When it came to fighting on the seas they were second to none. In raids the lightly armoured pirates could move fast, striking hard, then departing with their plunder. Against a disciplined army on land they had no chance. Habusas was going to die. He took a deep breath. At least his sons would live, for the caves were deep, and Balios knew hiding places beneath the earth that no armoured soldier would dare to crawl into.

'Look!' cried one of the men, pointing up at the fleeing women and children. Beyond them armed soldiers had appeared from behind the hill, marching slowly in formation, spears levelled. The women and children began to stream back towards the town, seeking to escape the line of spears.

Despair flowed over Habusas. More ships must have landed on the west of the island. The massacre would be complete.

'To the stockade,' he shouted to the gathering warriors.

They set off at a run, angling through a narrow street and out onto the flat ground before the wooden fort. A little way behind them enemy soldiers were marching now, shields locked, spears at the ready. There would be little time to get all the men inside, and no time at all for the women.

Habusas reached the fort, and saw men milling there, beating at the barred gates.

'What in Hades is going on?' he shouted to the men standing on the ramparts. 'Open the gates! Swiftly now!'

'And why would we do that?' said a cold voice.

Habusas stared up – into the face of Helikaon. He wore no armour, and was dressed like a simple sailor, in an old, worn chiton tunic. The men with him were dressed similarly – though in their hands they held bows, arrows notched to the strings.

Habusas felt bile rise in his throat. Apart from feasts and gatherings the stockade was always empty. Helikaon must have landed with these men earlier in the day, and merely walked up to the deserted fort.

'This is Mykene territory,' he said, knowing even as he spoke that his words were a waste of breath.

The soldiers marching up from the beach were approaching now, forming a battle line, shields high, spears extended. Women and children began to arrive from the hillside, clustering close to their husbands and lovers. Balios moved alongside his father, holding an old dagger with a chipped blade. Habusas gazed down at his son, his heart breaking. How could the gods have been so cruel, he wondered?

'Throw down your weapons,' ordered Helikaon.

Anger surged through Habusas. 'So you can burn us, you bastard? I think not! Come on, lads! Kill them all!' Habusas hurled himself at the advancing line, his men pushing after him, screaming defiant battle cries. Arrows tore into them from the stockade, and the soldiers surged to meet them. The battle was short and brutal. The lightly armed Mykene were no match for the fully armoured soldiers. Habusas killed two Dardanians before being stabbed through the thigh. A thrusting shield crashed into his head as he fell.

When he regained consciousness he found his hands had been bound behind him, and he was lying against the stockade wall. The wound in his leg burned like fire, and blood had drenched his leggings. All around him in the bright moonlight lay the comrades he had fought beside for so many years. Not a man was left alive. Struggling to his knees and pushing himself upright he staggered around, seeking his sons. He cried out when he saw the body of Balios. The boy had been speared through the throat, and was lying on his back. 'Oh, my son!' he said, tears in his eyes.

Just ahead of him he saw Helikaon talking to an old soldier. He remembered him from the attack on Dardanos. He was a general . . . Pausanius, that was it. The old man saw him, and gestured to Helikaon. Then the Burner turned towards him, his gaze malevolent.

'I remember you from Blue Owl Bay. You stood with Kolanos on the cliff. You were beside him in the sea battle. You are Habusas.'

'You murdered my son. He was just a boy.'

Helikaon stood silently for a moment, and Habusas saw the hatred in his eyes. Yet when he spoke his voice was cold, almost emotionless – which made what he said infinitely more terrifying. 'I did not have time to soak him in oil, and throw him burning from a cliff top. But perhaps you have other sons. I shall find out.' The words ripped into Habusas like whips of fire.

'Do not hurt them, Helikaon! I beg you!'

'Did she beg?' Helikaon asked, his voice unnaturally calm. 'Did the queen plead for the life of *her* son?'

'Please! I will do anything! My sons are my life!' Habusas

dropped to his knees. 'My life for theirs, Helikaon. They did nothing to you or yours.'

'Your life is already mine.' Helikaon drew his sword and held it to Habusas' throat. 'But tell me where I can find Kolanos and I might offer mercy for your children.'

'He left here three days ago. He is due back in the spring with fifty ships. I do not know where he is now. I swear. I would tell you if I did. Ask me anything else. Anything!'

'Very well. Did Kolanos burn my brother and throw him from the cliff?'

'No. He gave the order.'

'Who set my brother ablaze?'

Habusas climbed to his feet. 'I tell you this and you promise not to kill my family?'

'If I believe what you tell me.'

Habusas drew himself up to his full height. 'I set the fire on the boy. Yes, and I raped the queen too. I enjoyed the screams of both, and I wish I could live long enough to piss on your ashes!'

Helikaon stood very still, and Habusas saw a muscle twitch in his jaw. Habusas hoped the man might be angry enough to just kill him, a single sword-thust through the throat. It was not to be. Helikaon stepped back, sheathing his blade.

'And now you burn me, you bastard?'

'No. You will not burn.' Helikaon swung round, and beckoned two soldiers forward. Habusas was hauled back to the stockade gates. His bonds were cut. Immediately he lashed out, knocking one soldier from his feet. The second hammered the butt of his spear into Habusas' temple. Weakened by loss of blood Habusas fell back. Another blow sent him reeling unconscious to the ground.

Pain woke him, radiating from his wrists and feet, and flowing along his arms and up his shins. His eyes opened and he cried out. His arms had been splayed out and nailed to the wood of the gates. Blood was dripping from the puncture wounds, and he felt the bronze spikes grating on the bones of his wrists. He tried to straighten his legs, to take the strain from his mutilated arms. Agonizing pain roared through him, and he screamed. His legs were bent unnaturally, and he realized his feet too had been nailed to the gates.

He saw that Helikaon was standing before him. All the other soldiers had gone.

'Can you see the ships?' asked Helikaon.

Habusas stared at the man, and saw that he was pointing down towards the beach. The galleys of the invaders were drawn up there. Helikaon repeated the question.

'I . . . see . . . them.'

'Tomorrow at dawn all the women and children of this settlement will be on those ships. They are slaves now. But I will not single out your family, nor seek any vengeance upon them. They will live.'

With that he walked away. The wind picked up, catching the open gate and swinging it gently. Habusas groaned as the nails tore at his flesh. As the gate continued to move he saw that the bodies of his men had been moved. They had been dragged to houses nearby, their corpses nailed to doors or fences. Some had been spiked to walls, others hung by their necks from ropes strung from upper windows.

Then he saw the body of his son, lying on the ground, his arms laid across his belly. His head had lolled to one side. In the bright moonlight Habusas saw a glint of shining metal in the boy's mouth. Someone had placed a ring of silver there, to pay the Ferryman.

Even through his pain Habusas felt grateful for that.

Fresh waves of agony ripped through him as cramp struck his twisted legs causing them to spasm. The weight of his body then sagged against his pierced wrists. Habusas cried out. He tried to close his mind against the pain. How long, he wondered, will it take me to die?

Sometime tonight? Tomorrow? Would days pass? Would carrion birds feed on him while he writhed? Would he be forced to watch wild dogs feast on the flesh of his son?

Then he saw movement to his right. Helikaon was walking back across the open ground, a sword in his hand.

'I am not Kolanos,' he said. The sword lanced forward, spearing through Habusas' chest and cleaving his heart.

And all pain faded away.

XXII

The Phrygian Bow

i

THE AUTUMN MONTHS DRIFTED BY WITH APPALLING LACK OF SPEED. Gloomy skies of unremitting grey, punctuated by ferocious storms and driving rain, dampened even Andromache's fiery spirit. She endeavoured to fill her time with pleasurable activities, but there were few opportunities for the women of the palace to enjoy themselves. They were not allowed to ride horses, or attend evening entertainments in the town. There were no revels, no gatherings to dance and sing. Day by day she missed the isle of Thera more and more, and dreamt of the wild freedom she had enjoyed.

For a little while her boredom had been allayed by the arrival of a new, temporary night servant, a Thrakian girl, Alesia. She had been willing and compliant, but the closeness of her body in the wide bed had only served to remind Andromache of how much she missed Kalliope. When Alesia returned to her regular duties Andromache did not miss her, and made no attempt to seduce her replacement.

Just before year's end Andromache acquired a Phrygian bow from the Lower Market. It was a fine weapon, with a heavy pull that even Andromache found difficult at first to master. It was cunningly contrived from layers of flexible horn and wood, and with it she had bought a heavy wrist guard of polished black leather.

She took it out on the practice fields to the north of the city, where many of the Trojan archers honed their skills. It was a day of rare sunshine, and Andromache, dressed in a thigh-length white tunic and sandals, had enjoyed herself for most of the morning. The Trojan men had at first been polite, but patronizing. When they saw her skill they gathered round her, discussing the attributes of the bow.

The following day Andromache had been summoned before Priam, in his apartments. The king was angry, and berated her for appearing before men of low class.

'No highborn Trojan woman would walk semi-naked among peasants,' he said.

'I am not yet a Trojan,' she pointed out, trying in vain to keep her anger in check.

'And you might not ever be! I could send you home in disgrace and demand the return of your bride price.'

'What a tragedy that would be,' she retorted.

She had expected an explosion of rage. Instead the king suddenly burst into laughter. 'By the gods, woman, you remind me of Hekabe, all spit and fire. Aye, you are very like her.' She saw his gaze move to her breasts, and flow down over her body. The thin blue gown she was wearing suddenly seemed flimsy and transparent. He drew in a deep breath and let it out slowly. 'You cannot flout the customs of Troy,' he continued, his face flushed, but his tone more conciliatory. 'Palace women wear full gowns when in public. They do not shoot bows. You, however, *may* shoot your bow. The men were impressed by you, which is no bad thing. The families of ruling houses should always be impressive.'

'It was easy to impress them,' she said. 'The bows you supply them with are inferior weapons. They do not have range or power.'

'They have served us well in the past.'

'It would surprise me if a shaft from a Trojan bow could pierce even a leather breastplate. More and more warriors these days are better armoured.'

The king sat quietly for a moment. 'Very well, Andromache. This afternoon you will attend me in the palace gardens, and we will see how well the Trojan bows perform.'

Back in her own apartments, overlooking the northern hills, she found Laodike waiting. She had been less effusively friendly of late, ever since, in fact, the meeting with Hekabe. Andromache put it down to the shock of seeing her mother so weak and ill. But today she seemed even more sad. Usually bedecked in jewellery she was dressed in a simple, unadorned, ankle-length chiton of pale green. Her fair hair, normally braided with gold or silver wire, hung free to her shoulders. In a curious way, thought Andromache, the lack of extravagant gems actually made Laodike look more attractive, as if the glittering beauty of the gems served only to emphasize her plainness. Greeting her friend with a kiss on the cheek, she told her of Priam's challenge.

'He is seeking to shame you, you know,' said Laodike quietly.

'What do you mean?'

The young woman shrugged. 'He does that. He likes to make people look foolish. Mother is the same. That is why they were so well suited.'

Andromache sat by her, putting her arms round her friend. 'What is wrong, Laodike?'

'I am all right.' Laodike forced a smile. 'Have you heard from Helikaon?'

Andromache was surprised by the question. 'Why would I hear from Helikaon?'

'Oh, I don't know. I wondered if he had sent a message and I hadn't heard about it. Nobody tells me anything.'

'No. As far as I know there have been no messages from Dardania.'

Laodike seemed a little happier. 'They say he killed twenty Mykene at the temple square. He was like a young god. That's what I heard. He had two swords and he killed all the assassins.'

Andromache too had heard the obviously tall stories about

Helikaon's prowess, and she had watched the *Xanthos* sail into the dawn with a heavy sense of loss. She looked at Laodike, and understood then that the young woman was infatuated with Helikaon. Sadness touched her. She had seen Helikaon greeting Laodike at Hekabe's palace, and there was no sign that he found her attractive. Yes, he had paid her a compliment, but there was no hint of passion in the comment. Then she realized why Laodike had thought he might have been in contact. He had made no secret of his desire for Andromache. 'What did you mean about your father shaming me?' she asked, seeking to change the subject.

'He plays games with people all the time. I don't know why. He doesn't do it with Kreusa or Hektor, but everyone else suffers at some time.'

Andromache laughed. 'He cannot shame me with a bow, Laodike. I can assure you of that.'

'It will be a contest,' said Laodike. 'You'll see. It will be Dios, or perhaps Agathon. They are superb bowmen. And father will fill the gardens with people to watch you beaten by one of his sons. You'll see,' she said again.

'They will need to be very, very good,' Andromache told her. 'And I am not cowed by crowds.'

'I wish I was like you,' said Laodike, with a sigh. 'If I was . . .' She hesitated and gave a soft smile. 'Ah well, I am not, so it doesn't matter.'

Andromache took Laodike's hands in hers. 'Listen to me,' she whispered. 'Whatever it is that you see in me, is in you also. You are a fine woman, and I am proud to have you as a friend.'

'I am a fine woman,' repeated Laodike. 'But I am twenty-three, with no husband. All my pretty sisters – save Kreusa – have wed.'

'Oh, Laodike! You have no idea how alike we are, really. I was the plainest of my family. No-one would have me. So father sent me to Thera. It was only when my little sister died that Priam accepted me for Hektor. And you are not plain. Your eyes are beautiful, and your smile is enchanting.'

Laodike blushed. Then she looked Andromache in the eye. 'I remember when Paleste came to Troy. I liked her, but she was very shy. Father took to her, but mother didn't like her at all. She said she was unworthy to marry Hektor. I remember mother saying that the wrong sister had been chosen. She knew of you even then, you know.'

'I didn't know. Poor Paleste. She was a sweet girl.'

'Do you like Helikaon?' asked Laodike.

Andromache didn't want to talk about it, and feared her friendship with Laodike might be damaged by the truth. But she could not lie. 'Yes, I do,' she said.

'And he is smitten with you. I could see that.'

'Men always adore what they cannot have. I am to marry Hektor, so let us not allow thoughts of men to come between us. You are my friend, Laodike. I love you like a sister. Now, will you come with me to the gardens later? It would help to have a friend close by.'

'Of course I will. Then I must go to the Temple of Asklepios. Mother needs more opiates.'

'I shall come with you. I have a little friend who helps there. His name is Xander.'

It was mid-afternoon when the two women emerged into the largest of the palace gardens. As Laodike had predicted, there were at least a hundred people present. Andromache had met many of them, but even now there were many names she could not recall. Priam was seated on an ornate gilded chair set on a stone dais. Beside him was his daughter Kreusa, a dark-haired beauty, slim and regal. Her eyes were cold, and she looked at Andromache with undisguised disdain. The soft-looking, round-shouldered chancellor, Polites, was also with the king, as was fat Antiphones, and the slender Dios. Once again Andromache was struck by his resemblance to Helikaon. There was another man with them, tall and wide-shouldered, his hair red-gold. Andromache had not seen him before. 'That is my half-brother, Agathon,' whispered Laodike. 'I told you it would be a contest.'

At the far end of the gardens, some sixty paces distant, Andromache saw a small cart with large wheels. On a tall spike at the centre a leather breastplate had been fastened. There were long ropes attached to the front and rear of the cart. 'Have you ever shot at a moving target?' asked Laodike.

'No.'

'You will today. Servants haul on the ropes, dragging the cart back and forth.'

Priam rose from his seat, and all conversation among the crowd ebbed away. Agathon and the slender Dios both took up bows and walked out to stand alongside Andromache. Laodike faded back a few steps.

'Today we are to witness a contest,' said Priam, his voice booming out. 'Andromache, of Thebe Under Plakos, believes Trojan bows are inferior weapons, and is going to entertain us with her redoubtable skills. My generals, Agathon and Deiphobos, stand for the pride of Trojan craftsmanship. And there is a fine prize to be won.' He held out his hand, and Kreusa stepped forward, offering him a wondrously crafted battle helmet, embossed with silver, and bearing a motif on the brow of the god Apollo drawing back his bow.

Priam lifted it high, and the afternoon sunshine glinted on the burnished metal. 'May the Lord of the Silver Bow bring victory to the most worthy,' cried the king. Andromache felt her anger swell. It was a warrior's prize, a *man's* prize, and the offering of it was a less than subtle insult to a female archer.

'Will you honour us by shooting first, Andromache?' asked Priam.

'It would hardly be fitting, King Priam,' replied Andromache sweetly. 'It is – I am assured – a woman's place to follow in a man's world.'

'Then it shall be Agathon,' said Priam, settling back into his seat. The wide-shouldered prince stepped forward, notching an arrow to his bow. At his command servants at the far end of the garden took up ropes and slowly drew the cart across to the left. Then the men on the right began to haul the cart swiftly across the paved stone.

Agathon let fly – the shaft striking and piercing the leather breastplate. The crowd cheered. Then Dios stepped forward. He too sent a shaft into the leather. Both arrows drooped after they struck, showing they had not penetrated far.

Andromache notched a black-feathered shaft and curled her fingers around the string. As she had watched the two men she had gauged the time it took for the arrows to fly to their target, and the speed of the cart. Even so, it would have been pleasant to be allowed a few practice shots. Calming herself, she drew back on the bow. The cart lumbered across her line of sight. Adjusting her aim, she loosed her shaft. The black-feathered arrow slammed into the breastplate, burying itself deep.

Each archer loosed six more shafts. Not one missed, and the breastplate began to resemble a porcupine. The crowd were less attentive now, and there was a short break while servants removed the ruined breastplate, and recovered the arrows.

Andromache glanced at the two princes. Both seemed tense and expectant. She saw Priam speaking to a soldier, who then ran off through the crowd. 'What is happening?' she asked Prince Agathon.

'The competition is about to begin in earnest,' he said, a touch of anger in his voice. He drew in a deep breath. 'It might be as well, Lady Andromache, for you to withdraw now.'

'Why would I?'

'Because we will not be shooting at targets. My father has other plans, I fear.'

As he spoke, soldiers emerged from buildings to the rear of the gardens. They were leading three bound men, each wearing a leather breastplate. The prisoners were taken to stand before the target cart. Then the soldiers, their spears levelled towards the prisoners, formed two lines in front of the crowd. The king rose. 'These wretches,' he said, 'are plotters. They were arrested yesterday. Stubborn, rebellious men, who have refused to name their confederates.'

Andromache stared at the prisoners. They were in a sorry state, their faces smeared with blood, their eyes swollen. Knowing now what was to come she walked away from the princes. Priam saw her. 'Not to your liking, girl? Ah well, this is *man's* work.' He turned back to the crowd. 'These traitors deserve death, but I am a merciful man. Their bonds will be cut.' Taking a spear from a Royal Eagle standing close by he hurled it out onto the grass, some sixty running steps from the prisoners. 'If any of them can reach that spear then they will suffer merely banishment. Loose the first! And let Deiphobos represent my honour.'

A soldier drew a dagger from his belt and walked to the first prisoner, a slim, middle-aged man. The soldier slashed his blade through the ropes binding the prisoner's wrists. The man stood very still, staring malevolently down the gardens at the king. Then he took a deep breath, and broke into a swerving run. Dios raised his bow. The running man increased his pace. The arrow took him through the throat, punching through to the back of his neck. He staggered on, then pitched to the right. He began to choke, his face growing purple. Andromache looked away, but could not shut her ears to the grotesque sounds as the dying man fought for breath. Finally there was silence.

'Now the second!' roared Priam.

This prisoner was a powerful man, with a heavy beard. He also glared at the king. When they cut him loose he did not run, but strode down the garden. Prince Agathon took aim. Suddenly the man darted to his right, then raced for the spear. Agathon loosed his shaft. It took the man in the chest, but did not fully pierce the breastplate. Without pausing in his run the prisoner sprinted for the spear. Dios let fly. His arrow also thudded home, but the prisoner reached the spear and swept it up. Then he swung towards Priam and charged. The move surprised everyone. A Royal Eagle leapt to bar his way, but the prisoner shoulder-barged him, knocking him from his feet.

Just as he reached the king a black-feathered shaft hammered through his back, burying itself deep, and cleaving his heart. The prisoner stood for a moment, then toppled sideways, the spear clattering to the ground.

Andromache lowered the Phrygian bow, and stared at the man she had killed. Agathon moved alongside her. 'A very fine shot. You saved the king.'

Priam stepped over the body. 'And now,' he roared, 'all can see why this woman was chosen as the bride for my Hektor! Let your voices sound for Andromache!' Obediently a cheer went up from the crowd. Then the king signalled to the soldiers at the far end of the gardens, and the last prisoner was led away.

The following month Andromache learned that Priam had ordered a thousand Phrygian bows for his archers.

ii

It was late in the afternoon before Andromache could slip away from the garden. Her status suddenly enhanced by the events of the day, she had been surrounded by well-wishers and sycophants. When at last she feigned tiredness she found Laodike waiting in her apartments.

Her friend ran to her, hugging her close. 'You were wonderful, Andromache!' she said. 'I am so proud of you. Your name is on everyone's lips.'

Andromache kissed her on the cheek, then slipped out of her embrace. 'Who was the man I killed?'

'A captain of the Eagles. Everyone thought him to be a hero. What makes a man become a traitor, do you think?'

'I do not know. But he was brave. He could have merely picked up the spear and taken banishment. Instead he accepted certain death, for even had he killed Priam the guards would have over-powered and slain him. Let us talk no more of it. A walk to the temple is just what I need.'

The sunshine continued, though there were rain clouds in the distance as the two women set out arm in arm. 'I think Agathon was impressed,' said Laodike. 'He couldn't take his eyes off you.'

Andromache laughed. 'He is an impressive man. Why have I not seen him before?'

'He spends much of his time east of the city. He leads the Thrakian mercenaries, and is almost as fine a general as Hektor. They are very close.'

'Do they look alike?'

Laodike giggled. 'Are you asking whether Hektor is handsome?'

'Yes.'

'Like a young god. His hair is golden, his eyes are blue, and he has a smile to win any heart.'

'And he is the oldest of Priam's sons?'

Laodike laughed again. 'Yes and no. He is the oldest of *mother's* children, and therefore the legitimate heir. But father was twenty-four when he and mother wed. And there were other children born to his lovers. The oldest was Troilus. He would have been almost forty now.'

'He died?'

'Father had him banished last year. He died in Miletos. Some think he was poisoned. I expect he was.'

'That makes no sense to me,' said Andromache. 'If Priam wanted him dead, why not kill him in Troy?'

Laodike paused in her walk and turned towards her. 'You should understand that before mother was ill Troy had two rulers. Mother hated Troilus. I think she hates all the sons she did not bear. When Troilus plotted to overthrow father she thought he should be killed instantly. Father refused.' Laodike shrugged. 'And he died anyway.'

'Hekabe had him poisoned?'

'I do not know, Andromache. Perhaps he just died. But you would be amazed at the number of people who have died young, following disagreements with mother.'

'Then I am glad she liked me. So how old is Hektor?'

'Almost thirty.'

'Why has he never wed?'

Laodike looked away. 'Oh, probably because of wars and battles. You should ask him when he comes home. There will be great parades and celebrations for his victories.'

Andromache knew something was being kept from her, but she decided not to press the point. Instead she said: 'He must be a great warrior indeed, if his victories can be anticipated before the battles are fought.'

'Oh, Hektor never loses,' said Laodike. 'The Trojan Horse is supreme in battle.'

It seemed to Andromache that such conviction was naïve. A stray arrow, a hurled spear, an unlucky blow, could all end the life of any fighting man. However, she let the moment pass, and the two women wandered down through the marketplaces, stopping to examine the wares on display. Finally they reached the healing houses.

They sat in a rear garden, Laodike having sent a servant to seek out the healer Machaon. Another servant, an elderly man, brought them goblets of juice squeezed from various fruits. Andromache had never tasted anything so deliciously sweet. The mixture was the colour of the sunset. 'What is in this?' she asked.

'Tree fruits from Egypt and Palestine. They come in various shapes and colours. Some are gold, some yellow, some green. Some are good on their own, and others are so sharp they make the eyes water. But the priests here mix them with honey. Very refreshing.'

'There is so much that is new in Troy,' said Andromache. 'I have never seen such colour. The women's gowns, the decorations on the walls.' She laughed. 'Even the drinks have many colours.'

'Father says that trade is what makes civilizations grow. Nations and peoples learn from one another, and improve on one another's skills. We have Egypteian cloth makers in Troy. They have begun experimenting with the dyes from Phrygia and Babylon. There are some wonderful colours being produced. But it is not just the clothes. Hektor brought back horses from Thessaly. Big beasts. Sixteen hands. He's bred them with our mares. They make superb war mounts. Men of skill and enterprise all come to Troy. Father says that one day we will be the centre of a great civilization.'

Andromache listened as Laodike spoke on about Priam and his dreams. It was obvious that she adored her father, and equally obvious that he had little time for her.

Laodike's voice faded away. 'I think I am boring you,' she said. 'I am sorry.'

'Nonsense. It is fascinating.'

'Really? You are not just saying that?'

'Why would I?' Andromache threw her arm round Laodike's shoulder and kissed her cheek.

The physican-priest Machaon entered the garden. He looked dreadfully weary, thought Andromache. His face was pale, and there was sweat upon his brow. Although a young man, he was already losing his hair, and his shoulders were rounded. 'Greetings to you, king's daughter,' he said. 'It is always a pleasure to see you. And you, Andromache of Thebe.'

'How is Xander faring?' Andromache asked. The young physician smiled.

'He is a fine lad, with great sensitivity. I have him working with the dying. He has a talent for lifting their spirits. I am glad he stayed with us.' He turned to Laodike, and handed her a small, cloth-wrapped package. 'These should last for another week or so. Be advised, though, that soon even these powerful opiates will not keep the pain at bay.'

'Mother says she is feeling a little better,' said Laodike. 'Perhaps her body is healing.'

He shook his head. 'She is past healing. Only her strength of mind and the courage of her spirit keeps her in these lands of the living. There is a small phial in the package. It is stoppered with green wax. When the pain becomes unbearable – and it will – break open the phial and mix it with wine. Then get your mother to drink it.'

'And that will take away the pain?'

His brows furrowed. 'Yes, Laodike. It will take away the pain. Permanently.'

'Then why can she not have it now? Her pain is very great.'

'I am sorry, I am not making myself clear. The phial is to be used to help your mother at the end. Once she has drunk it she will fall into a deep sleep, and pass peacefully to the world beyond.'

'Are you saying it is poison?'

'That is exactly what I am saying. During the last days your mother will be in dreadful agony. The pain will be excruciating, and beyond her ability to cope with. You understand me? At this point she will have only hours left to live. Better, I think,

298

if you rescue her from that suffering. It is, however, your choice.'

'I couldn't poison mother,' said Laodike.

'Of course you couldn't,' said Andromache. 'However, you can tell her exactly what the gentle Machaon has told you. And you can give her the phial. Let her make the choice.'

'Thank you, Lady Andromache,' said Machaon. 'Yes, that is of course the correct course.' He looked at her and seemed about to speak.

'Was there something else?' she asked.

'I understand you travelled with the Mykene warrior Argurios.'

'Yes,' she said. 'A hard man and unpleasant.'

'Ah! Then I shall not trouble you with my problem concerning him. I thought, perhaps, you might be . . . friends.'

'How is it,' she asked, 'that a physician is having trouble with a travelling warrior?'

'Did you not hear? He was attacked by other Mykene. His wounds were grievous. He is still likely to die of them. But I cannot make him rest, my lady. He insists on working for his bread and for the right to sleep here. I have explained that all costs have been met by the lord Helikaon, but this only seems to anger him. He has been sawing wood, carrying water. All kinds of menial duties, for which we have servants. He has torn open his stitches many times through such – and other – ill-advised exercise. I have tried to explain to him that his body was savagely damaged. He cannot breathe well, and becomes dizzy with any exertion. Yet he will not listen. I fear he is going to collapse and die, and then the lord Helikaon will view me with displeasure.'

'We will speak to him, Laodike and I,' said Andromache. 'Where is he?'

'I saw him a little while ago, beyond the House of Earth. He is trying to repair an old wall. There is no need. The wall no longer serves any real purpose. Yet he carries large stones, and exhausts himself.'

Machaon gave them directions and the two women walked off. Laodike was not happy.

'I do not like Mykene,' she said. 'I don't care if he dies.'

'He helped Helikaon at the Bay of Blue Owls,' said Andromache. 'He killed a Mykene assassin. Perhaps that is why he was attacked.'

'I expect he had unpleasant reasons for doing what he did,' said Laodike. 'Mykene always do.'

XXIII

The Wounded Lion

i

ARGURIOS COULD HARDLY BREATHE. IT WAS AS IF THE GODS HAD placed a gate in his chest, and no air was reaching his lungs. White lights danced before his eyes and dizziness threatened to bring him down. He staggered on for several paces, his arms burning with the weight of the rock. Even his legs were trembling and painful, especially the calves. Grimly he struggled on, lowering the rock to the breach in the ancient wall. His vision began to swim, forcing him to sit down. He gazed down at his trembling hands.

Nothing in his life had prepared him for the horror of such weakness. He had seen friends die in battle, and others struck down by wasting fevers. But always he had remained strong. He could run for miles, in full armour, and then fight a battle. His stamina was legendary. Yet now he struggled to lift a few pitiful rocks onto a ruined wall.

Sweat dripped into his eyes and he was too weary even to wipe it away.

He glanced across the old paddock, and saw the two men sitting in the shade. Both were armed with swords and daggers. Over the weeks he had tried to approach them, but they faded back from him, and he did not have the stamina to give chase. At first he had thought them to be more killers, ready to strike him down and claim the bounty from Erekos. The boy, Xander, had told him not to concern himself.

'Who are they, then?'

Xander became ill at ease. 'I am not supposed to say.'

'But you have. So tell me.'

'They are here to protect you.'

Argurios had learned then that they were men hired by Helikaon. It was a sickening discovery. 'You told me . . . he was glad I was dying,' said Argurios.

The boy looked crestfallen. 'He *told* me to say that. He thought it would make you fight for life.'

Argurios swore softly. The world had gone mad. Friends and countrymen wanted him dead. Enemies hired men to keep him alive. Somewhere on Olympos the gods were laughing at this grotesque jest.

As the weeks passed, and his condition did not improve, Argurios found himself wishing they *were* Mykene assassins. At least then he could end his life in battle.

A shadow fell across him, and he looked up. Two women were standing there, the sun behind them.

'What . . . do you want?' he asked gruffly, thinking them to be priestesses coming to chide him.

'A courteous greeting would be pleasant,' replied Andromache. With an effort Argurios pushed himself to his feet.

'The sun was . . . in my eyes,' he said, between shallow breaths. 'I did not . . . recognize you.'

He saw the shock of his condition register on her face. Argurios had lost weight, and his eyes were sunken and dark-rimmed, his arms and legs thin and wasted. 'Let us all sit,' said Andromache. 'This is my friend, the king's daughter, Laodike.'

Argurios blinked away sweat and looked at Laodike. She was tall, with long fair hair, and in her eyes he saw disdain. Swinging back to Andromache he asked: 'Why are . . . you here?'

'Mykene are always rude,' said Laodike. 'They are bred without manners. Let us go, Andromache. It is too hot to be standing here.'

'Yes, you go back inside,' Andromache told her. 'I will sit for a little while with this warrior.'

Laodike nodded. 'I will wait for you beneath the arbour trees.' Without a word to Argurios she walked away.

'You should . . . go with her,' said Argurios. 'We have . . . nothing to . . . talk about.'

'Sit down before you fall down,' ordered Andromache, seating herself on the stone wall. Argurios slumped down beside her, surprised at himself for obeying a woman. Shame touched him. Even in this small matter he was no longer a man. 'I know what you need,' she said.

'What I need?'

'To make you strong again. When I was younger my father was in a battle. A horse fell, and rolled on him. After that he – like you – could scarcely breathe. He tottered around like an old man. It went on for months. Then one day we heard of a travelling physician. He was healing people in local villages, while on his way to Egypt. He was an Assyrian. We brought him to my father.'

'He . . . cured him?'

'No. He showed my father how to cure himself.'

Argurios wiped the sweat from his eyes and looked at the young woman. His vision was hazy, his breathing ragged. Yet hope flared in his heart. 'Tell me,' he said.

'I will *show* you, Argurios. Tomorrow morning, whatever the weather, I will send a cart for you. It will bring you to cliffs above a beach. Bring Xander with you, for I would like to see the boy again. And now I will leave you to finish your work.' She rose.

'Wait!' said Argurios, painfully heaving himself to his feet. 'Take me . . . to the . . . king's daughter.'

She walked slowly alongside him. He staggered twice, and felt her arm link through his. He wanted to shrug it away, but her strength kept him upright. It was not a long walk, and yet Argurios felt exhausted by the time they reached the shaded arbour. Laodike was sitting on a bench. Argurios struggled for breath. 'Not . . . all . . . Mykene . . . are ill mannered. I apolo . . . gize for my lack . . .

303

of courtesy. I have . . . always been uncomfortable around . . . women. Especially . . . beautiful women.'

He expected a harsh response, but instead her expression softened. Leaving the bench she stood before him. 'Your apology is accepted,' she said, 'and I, too, am sorry for the curtness I showed you. You have been badly wounded and I should have realized you were suffering.'

Argurios could think of nothing else to say, and, as the silence grew, the moment became awkward. Andromache spoke then. 'I have invited Argurios to join us tomorrow. It will aid his healing.'

Laodike laughed. 'Do you sit awake at night planning events that will annoy father?' she asked.

ii

Xander enjoyed working in the House of Serpents. He felt useful and needed. People always seemed pleased to see him, and, as the weeks passed, he learned more about herbs and medicines, treatments and diagnosis. The application of warm, wet towels reduced fevers, the shredded and powdered barks of certain trees could take away pain. Festering sores could be healed by the application of wine and honey. Eager to learn more, he followed Machaon around, watching as he splinted broken bones, or lanced cysts and boils.

Yet despite his enthusiasm for all matters medical he was pleased today to be out in the open air, travelling in the wide cart with Argurios. The sky was cloudy with the promise of rain, but the sun was shining through, and the air was fresh with the smells of the sea.

He glanced at Argurios. The Mykene looked so ill. His face was drawn, and so thin it made him look like an old, frail man. Xander had helped him shave this morning, cutting away the stubble on his cheeks, and trimming the chin beard. He had combed his long dark hair, noting the increase of grey along the temples. The youngster struggled to remember the iron-hard warrior who had saved him on the *Xanthos*.

In the weeks since the attack Argurios' recovery had been painfully slow. Machaon told Xander that one of the wounds had pierced Argurios' lung, and come perilously close to the heart. And there had been much bleeding internally.

'He will recover, though?' Xander had asked.

'He may never regain his former strength. Often deep wounds turn bad, and vilenesses can form.'

Xander looked round. The cart was crossing the wide, wooden Scamander bridge. He wondered if they were heading for the white palace he could see on the cliff top to the southwest. It was said that the queen lived in King's Joy, with some of her daughters.

The cart hit a broken stone on the road and jolted. Argurios winced. 'Are you all right?' asked Xander.

Argurios nodded. He very rarely spoke, but each evening when Xander visited him he would sit quietly as the boy told him of the day's work among the sick, listening as Xander talked of herbs and discoveries. At first Xander had thought him bored. 'Am I babbling, Argurios?' he had asked, one evening. 'Grandfather says I chatter too much. Shall I leave you?'

Argurios had given a rare smile. 'You chatter on, boy. When I am . . . bored . . . I'll tell you.'

The cart left the road and angled out along a narrower road leading to the cliffs. There were two Eagles there, sitting beneath the branches of a gnarled tree, sunlight glinting on their armour of bronze and silver. They rose as the cart approached.

The driver, a crook-backed man with a thick white beard, said: 'Guests of the lady Andromache.'

One of the soldiers, a tall young man, wide-shouldered, and wearing a helmet with a white horsehair crest, walked up to the cart. 'You'd be Xander,' he said.

'Yes.'

The young soldier moved past the boy and stared hard at Argurios. His brows furrowed. 'By the gods, man, you look all in. Will you need help to get to the beach?'

'No.' Argurios hauled himself upright, then climbed down from the cart.

'I meant no offence, warrior,' said the soldier. 'I was wounded myself two years ago, and had to be carried by my comrades.'

Argurios looked at the man. 'Where was . . . the battle?'

'In Thraki. Took a lance-thrust in the chest. Smashed my breast-plate, broke several ribs.'

'Tough fighters . . .Thrakians.'

'True. No give in them. We have a regiment of them here now.' The man chuckled. 'Sooner have them with me than against me.'

Argurios walked away. Xander followed. The cliff path was steep, but fairly wide. Even so, if Argurios were to stumble he would pitch over the edge and plummet to the rocks far below. The young soldier came alongside.

'I would consider it an honour, Argurios, if you would allow me to walk with you to the beach.'

Argurios straightened at the sound of his name. 'You . . . know of me?'

'All soldiers know of you, man. I was told the story of the Bridge of Partha when I was a boy. They say you held the bridge all morning.'

'Not that . . . long,' said Argurios. 'But . . . by the gods . . . it felt . . . like it.' He gathered himself, then looked at the warrior. 'Let us . . . walk, then.'

Xander followed as the two men made their slow way down to the beach. He could see there were already people on the sand, and several men were swimming. Xander wondered what they were looking for. Perhaps they were hunting for shellfish, he thought. Yet they seemed to be swimming aimlessly. They neither dived deep, nor headed for the shore. Others waded into the sea, and Xander could hear the sound of laughter.

There were five yellow canopies set up below the cliffs and close by were tables laden with food and drink. The canopies were very bright – almost as gold as the sun. Xander remembered his mother dying cloth yellow, using the skins of onions, or crocus pollen. But the cloth never had the lustre of these canopies. And it faded so quickly.

Ahead Argurios stumbled. The Trojan soldier took him by the

arm, supporting him. Argurios did not – as Xander expected – pull away. When they reached the beach the Trojan thanked Argurios for the honour of his company. The Mykene remained grave.

'What is . . . your name . . . soldier?'

'Polydorus,' he answered.

'I shall . . . remember it.'

Xander looked around. He saw Andromache move away from a small group of women and walk across the sand towards them. She was wearing a thigh-length tunic of pale green, and her red hair was hanging loose to her shoulders. Xander thought her very beautiful. She smiled at him, and he blushed.

'Welcome to the royal beach, Xander.'

'What are those men looking for?' he asked, pointing to the swimmers.

'Nothing. They are swimming for the pleasure of it. Do you swim?'

'Grandfather taught me. He said a sailor needed to be able to float.'

'Well, today you will swim.' She turned to Argurios. 'And you, warrior.'

'Why would . . . I swim?' he asked. 'There is . . . no purpose to it.'

'A better purpose, perhaps, than repairing a paddock wall where there is no longer a paddock,' she observed. 'Come and sit for a while, and I will tell you of the Assyrian physician.'

She led them to a spot beneath a canopy. Argurios' breathing was ragged, and he seemed grateful to be sitting down. 'My father could not take deep breaths,' said Andromache. 'The physician told him to swim every day. He also taught him to breathe differently.'

'How many . . . ways . . . can a man . . . breathe?'

'I will show you. But first you will swim for a while with Xander. Gently and slowly. Do not over-exert yourself.'

'This is . . . foolish. I should not . . . have come.'

'But you did, warrior,' said Andromache. 'And if you want to be strong again you will do as I say.'

Xander expected Argurios to react angrily. But he did not. He looked into her green eyes. 'I need . . . my strength,' he said, at last. Rising wearily to his feet he struggled to remove his threadbare tunic. Xander helped him, and also untied his sandals. Argurios' naked body was pale and skinny, and Xander saw many old, white scars on his shoulders, arms, chest and legs. The angry red wounds of his recent fight were hideous to look upon. Pus and blood were leaking from the gash in his side, and there were deep scabs on three other wounds. But as he turned to walk to the shoreline Xander noted there were no scars on his back.

'Go with him, Xander,' said Andromache. 'He may need your help.'

Xander stripped off his tunic and sandals and caught up with Argurios as he waded into the blue water.

They swam together silently. Argurios struggled and gasped for breath. After a little while Andromache swam out to join them. She was still wearing the pale green tunic, but it clung so close to her body that she might as well have been naked, thought Xander, trying not to look at her breasts, and the raised nipples. She came alongside Argurios. 'Lie back in the water,' she said, 'and I will support you.' He obeyed her instantly. 'And now I want you to close your eyes and relax your body. Then I want you to breathe very slowly. I want you to breathe in for the count of four and hold the breath for the count of six. Then let it out very slowly for the count of ten. Four, six and ten.'

Xander watched for a while, and then, growing hungry, he swam back to the beach, waded ashore and clothed himself. Then he walked to the food tables. There were dishes of figs, barley bread and salted octopus, cuts of meats, cheeses and various breads. There were jugs full of water, and others filled with wine. A tall, stoop-shouldered servant stood staring at him. 'Are we allowed to eat?' he asked the man.

'What would you like, little fellow?'

Xander pointed to the bread, and asked for some cheese and figs. The man tore off a hunk of dark bread, then cut a section of cheese and placed it on a wooden platter with a handful of figs. 'You might need something to wash that down,' said the servant, with a smile. Lifting a jug he filled a clay cup with a golden liquid. 'Try it,' he said.

Xander sipped the drink. It was thick and deliciously sweet. He thanked the man and wandered back to the canopy to sit and eat. Andromache was still in the water with Argurios. Other people were moving on the beach now. A dark-haired man emerged from the water. For a moment Xander thought it was Helikaon, but it was not. Then a fair-haired young woman in a red gown came and sat beside him.

'You must be Xander,' she said. 'Andromache told me of you.'

'Yes, I am. Who are you?'

'I am Laodike. Are you a friend of the Mykene?'

'I don't think he has any friends.'

'But you like him.'

'Yes. He saved my life.'

'I would like to hear about that,' she said.

So Xander told her the story of the storm. She listened intently, then glanced back at the water, watching Andromache and the warrior. 'Why do you think he risked himself to save you?' she asked, at last.

'I don't know. Odysseus says that is what heroes do. And Argurios is a hero. Everyone knows that.'

'*I* did not know it,' she admitted. 'But then Troy is full of heroes. No-one can be expected to know all their names.'

Andromache and Argurios emerged from the water. Rising, Xander gathered up Argurios' tunic and ran down to the shoreline. 'How are you feeling?' he asked.

'Tired,' answered the warrior, taking the tunic and slipping it over his head. He turned towards Andromache. 'I am grateful to you,' he told her.

'It sounds as if you are already breathing a little more easily,' she observed.

'I think I am.'

Several men approached them. Xander saw the man who looked like Helikaon. He seemed angry.

He halted before Andromache. 'How dare you dishonour the house of Priam?' he said.

iii

For Xander the moment was shocking, and frightening. He looked around and saw the anger on the faces of the men. Andromache also looked startled – even uncertain. Then her expression hardened.

'I do not understand you, Dios,' she said.

'I am Prince *Deiphobos*. Only those of equal rank, or those I count my friends, can call me Dios. You are neither. And this beach is reserved for the use of the royal family. You are here as a guest, and had no right to bring a stranger to it. But that discourtesy pales beside the whorish display we have been forced to observe. We all know what disgusting excesses are practised by the priestesses of Thera. To bring them here is an affront that will not be tolerated.'

'I invited Argurios,' said Laodike, easing her way through the gathering crowd. Xander heard the nervousness in her voice, and her eyes were downcast.

'No more than one would expect, sister. You never were the sharpest arrow in the quiver.'

Laodike seemed to shrink beneath his contempt. Then Argurios stepped forward, and when he spoke Xander saw the shock register on the faces of everyone close by.

'Have you finished, puppy dog?' said Argurios. His tone was harsh and cold, and Dios took a sudden backward step. His face reddened. Argurios moved forward. 'Prince, is it? It seems . . . to me . . . that Troy is thick with princes. You must be . . . the runt of the litter.'

Xander gasped. Young as he was he knew that the situation had suddenly become far worse. Dios stood for a moment, too shocked to speak. Then his eyes narrowed.

'Have I offended you, puppy dog?' snarled Argurios. 'Then fetch swords and I'll cut your . . . damned Trojan heart out!'

'This has gone far enough,' came a voice from the back of the crowd. A tall, broad-shouldered young man with red-gold hair pushed his way clear. 'There will be no swords called for.' He stared hard at Argurios. 'I know of you, Mykene. You are a fighting man, but your heart demands what your strength cannot supply.' He turned to Andromache. 'I do not know the ways of your land, sister-to-be. Here in Troy noble women do not swim alongside men. It is considered . . . immoral. However, if no-one explained this to you, then you cannot be held at fault.' Then he swung back to the angry Dios. 'My brother, I don't doubt that our father will hear of this and make his own judgements. For now, however, let us put aside thoughts of combat.'

'This wretch insulted me!' stormed Dios.

'Yes, he did,' agreed the young man amiably. 'As you can see, though, he is recovering from severe wounds and in no condition to fight. So store your grievance for now. If you still feel the need to avenge the affront when Argurios is strong again, then so be it.'

'And I will!' insisted Dios. He glared at Argurios. 'We will meet again.'

The Mykene merely nodded. Dios stalked away, followed by a group of young men. The crowd thinned. 'What is . . . your name?' Argurios asked the newcomer.

'I am Agathon. Now, let us sit in the shade and talk of less violent matters. Dios is a hothead, but he is not malicious. I would not wish to see him killed – even by a great hero.'

It seemed to Xander that Agathon was the most noble man he had ever seen. He looked like a god. His eyes were the deepest blue, and he seemed to dwarf Argurios.

Andromache laid her hand on the prince's arm. 'That was well done, Agathon,' she said.

They walked back to the canopy, Xander following unnoticed. Laodike moved forward to kiss Agathon on both cheeks. 'You are so like Hektor,' she said.

'We are not so alike, sister. Believe me.'

Argurios stretched himself out on a rug placed on the sand, and seemed to fall asleep. Laodike sat alongside Agathon, and Xander moved to sit beside Andromache. Still no-one spoke to him.

'News of Hektor came in this morning,' said Agathon. 'There was a great battle at a place called Kadesh. The reports are sketchy, but it seems the Egypteians almost had the day. Only a charge from the Trojan Horse held them back.'

'See! I told you,' Laodike said to Andromache. 'Hektor always wins.'

'Is the fighting over?' asked Andromache.

'No. The battle was undecided. There were great losses, however, on both sides. We have no details as yet.'

'A pox on the details,' muttered Laodike. 'Hektor will have the victory, and he will come home to a great parade.'

'I hope that you are right, sister. However, according to one report the Trojan Horse were cut off, and had not rejoined the main Hittite army by dark. We must pray to the gods of war that Hektor is not among the fallen.'

'Do not say things like that!' Laodike admonished him. 'I don't want to hear such talk.'

Xander saw the prince glance at Andromache. 'Will you walk with me on the sand? There are some matters I would dearly like to discuss with you.'

'As long as it is not considered immoral,' said Andromache, rising smoothly to her feet.

Xander watched them walk away. Laodike seemed downcast. 'Shall I fetch you something to drink?' Xander asked her.

'No. I am not thirsty.' She glanced down at Argurios. 'He is very thin, and his colour is not good. Perhaps you should fetch him some fruit nectar. Mother says it is good for the blood. He is a very rash man, isn't he?' she added. 'He took a dreadful risk by angering Dios. Dios is a good swordsman, you know, and very quick.'

'He is . . . a puppy,' said Argurios, heaving himself to a sitting position. 'And you are correct. I am too thin.'

'I did not mean to offend you, sir,' said Laodike, embarrassed. 'I thought you were asleep.'

'You did not offend me. And these . . . days . . . I cannot sleep lying . . . down. It seems easier to breathe while upright.' Argurios looked at Xander. 'That nectar sounds good,' he said.

Xander ran to the food tables and brought back a goblet of thick golden juices and handed it to the warrior, who drank deeply. 'You are a good lad,' he said, as he laid the empty goblet on the sand. 'Makes me . . . wonder . . . why I never had personal . . . slaves . . . before.'

'I am not your slave,' said Xander.

Argurios thought for a moment. 'That was ill-spoken . . . by me, lad. Of course you are . . . not. You are a friend. That means . . . much to me.'

'Why have you never had a personal servant?' asked Laodike. 'Are you not a famous hero in your own land?'

'Never . . . desired them. I have always . . . been . . . a soldier. I had a shield carrier once. Fine young man. Died in Thessaly.'

'What about your home?'

He shook his head. 'My father had no wealth. I have . . . in my life . . . acquired farmlands, and there are . . . slaves who . . . toil upon them. I leave them to themselves mostly.' His expression darkened. 'But they are my lands no longer. I am a banished man. Outside the law.' He glanced out at the sea. 'I think I will . . . swim again.' Struggling to his feet he walked down to the shoreline and removed his faded tunic.

'A strange man,' Laodike observed.

'He called me his friend,' said Xander happily.

'And you should be honoured. Such a man does not give his friendship lightly.'

XXIV

Warnings of War

i

ANDROMACHE WAS ENJOYING THE WALK WITH AGATHON. IN SOME ways he reminded her of Odysseus. She smiled at the thought. Odysseus was an ugly old charmer, and would have been delighted to be compared to the Trojan prince. It was not the good looks, however, more the easy manner which encouraged familiarity. She listened as he spoke of his love for the city, and sensed a genuine warmth in him. They paused by a rocky outcrop. The clouds above were thickening, and the sky was growing gloomy. At last he fell silent, and stared out to sea.

'Are we now going to speak of the matter that is closest to your heart?' she asked him.

He gave a wry grin. 'Yes. You are sharp as a sword.'

'I am intelligent. Why do so many people find that intimidating?'

'I cannot answer that – though I know it to be true.' He paused, then met her gaze. 'I wanted to talk about Hektor. The news is less good than I implied to Laodike. She is a sweet girl, but she adores our brother and I did not want to alarm her. According to our reports, Hektor led a reckless charge to turn the Egypteian flank. He succeeded, but the last anyone saw of him he was cleaving his way into the centre of the enemy ranks. The Hittites were forced to withdraw. Hektor did not return to their camp, though some riders did. They said Hektor and around fifty men were cut off in a blind ravine, with thousands of soldiers bearing down upon them.'

'You think he is dead?'

'I hope not. I *pray* not! Hektor is my greatest friend, as well as my half-brother. But it is more than that. Hektor is the heart of Troy. If he falls there will be chaos. Can you imagine it? Brother princes vying for supremacy? We would be racked by civil war.'

'I do not see why,' said Andromache. 'Priam is a strong king.'

'Oh, he is strong,' agreed Agathon, 'but he is hated. There are few of his sons he has not slighted, or publicly shamed. However, there is also discord among the brothers. Deep divisions and even hatreds. Hektor alone holds us all together. First, because we all love him.' Agathon gave a wide smile. 'Second, he would kill anyone who went against father.'

'This is all fascinating to a foreigner,' said Andromache, 'but how does it concern Hektor's bride-to-be? If he is dead I will return to Thera, and be with my friends.'

'I hope you might consider a different path,' he said.

'Why would I?'

'I am also unwed, Andromache. And in all my twenty-eight summers I have never seen a woman who fires me as you do. Therefore – unless there is another who holds a place in your heart – I would ask that you consider me as a suitor.'

Andromache smiled. 'What a strange city this is, Agathon. It is immoral for a woman to swim with a man, but acceptable for a man to woo his brother's bride? In truth it will take me a while to master the rules here.'

He sighed. 'That was neatly parried, Andromache. But think on what I have said. If news reaches us that Hektor is gone I will petition my father for your hand.'

Before she could answer him a young soldier came running across the beach. 'The king calls for you, lord,' he told Agathon.

'I must go. Think on what I have said.'

'Oh, I shall think on it,' she assured him, and watched as he walked away. He carried himself well, but as she looked at him her mind pictured another young prince, his hair dark, his eyes gleaming with suppressed passion.

. . . unless there is another who holds a place in your heart . . .

She thought again of the night at the Bay of the Blue Owls, and of the young man from the golden ship who had stepped away from the crowd. And then again, the following morning, when he had stood, heartbroken, holding the severed head of his friend in his hands. More than this, though, she remembered his arms enfolding her at the palace of Hekabe.

'Oh,' she whispered, gazing out over the wide, blue bay, 'if Hektor is dead let the golden ship come for me.'

ii

For Helikaon the first few weeks after the raid on Pithros had been arduous and draining. The camaraderie he had enjoyed among the soldiers and officials of Dardania had been replaced by a cautious coolness that reeked of fear.

He was no longer the Prince of the Sea, a merchant and a man of the people. He was Helikaon the Burner, the avenger, the ruthless killer. Servants averted their eyes when he passed. Even men he had known for years – like Oniacus, and the old general Pausanius – measured their words, anxious to avoid causing offence. The atmosphere within the citadel was fraught and tense. Outside the fortress the storms of winter raged, lightning forking the sky, thunder rolling across the land.

Everywhere there was disorder. The murder of the young king had created a feeling of unease and fear among the general populace in the countryside.

The people of Dardania were from many diverse cultures: migrants from Thraki had settled the northern coasts; Phrygians, Mysians, and Lydians had formed scores of small farming communities in the once empty heartland east of the capital. Merchants – Egypteians, Amorites and Assyrians – had built trading centres to the south, linking with Troy. Even at the best of times, when harvests were good, and trade thriving, tempers flared and violent incidents erupted between the various ethnic groups.

Since the death of Diomedes tensions had been running high. A small settlement of Mykene exiles had been attacked, and five men hacked to death by an angry mob. A riot had developed in a Phrygian community, following the theft of a sheep. Two women from a Mysian settlement claimed to have been raped by travelling Hittite traders. A revenge party had set out and seven men were killed in the skirmish.

Dardanian troops were spread thin across the hills and valleys, and along the bleak coastlines, seeking to restore order. Into this chaos had come outlaw bands, and roving groups of unemployed mercenaries, attacking isolated villages, and raiding merchant caravans.

The problem was compounded by the laws imposed by Helikaon's father, Anchises. All Dardanian land belonged to the king, and those who built houses, farms or trading posts here were merely tenants. The rents were exorbitant – half of all crops, produce, or trading profit. For this relationship to work, Helikaon knew, the people needed to hold to two truths. First, that the king and his soldiers would protect them from bandits and raiders, and second, that failure to obey the king's laws would result in a swift and terrible punishment.

The people's trust was tarnished by the assault on the fortress. If the soldiers could not protect Diomedes and Queen Halysia, how could they ensure the safety of the populace? And the fear instilled in the people by Anchises had been eroded by the more conciliatory government of Queen Halysia, and her general, Pausanius.

Helikaon called a meeting of settlement leaders, inviting them to the fortress. They were worried and uneasy as they gathered in the great columned throne room, surrounded by cold statues of the warrior kings of Dardania.

Before the meeting Pausanius had urged conciliation. 'They are good people, my king,' he told Helikaon. 'They are frightened, that is all.' Helikaon liked the ageing general. The man was fearless in battle, and he had served Queen Halysia loyally.

'What you say is true, Pausanius,' he said, as they stood on the broad balcony of the royal apartments, looking out over the sea. 'Answer me this, though. When you are about to go into battle do you pause and consider your enemy, whether his soldiers have children at home? Whether they are good men? Whether their cause is as just as yours?'

'No, of course not. But these people are not our enemy.'

'And what is?'

The general looked confused. He scratched at his red beard. 'I . . . don't know what you mean, my king.'

'We are close to anarchy, and what happens here today will either begin the process of unifying the people – or see the realm splintered by scores of small uprisings, and then a rebellion. Understand this, Pausanius: all kingdoms survive on the shield and the sword. The people need to believe the king's shield will protect them. They also need to be certain that if they disobey, then the king's sword will cut them down. Belief in the shield was fractured by the assault on the fortress. Fear of the sword has also been lost. What is the enemy? We have an army of fifteen hundred men. If the multitude no longer trusts and fears us, then we will be overthrown. Some bandit chief will raise an army. Some foreign power will sail ships into our bays. The enemy, Pausanius, is gathering in the throne room.'

The old general sighed. 'What would you have me do, lord?'

Later, after the haggard old soldier left his apartments, Helikaon sent a messenger to the queen, requesting that she admit him to her presence.

Halysia had survived the stabbing, but was still so weak that she did not leave her apartments. According to her handmaidens she would sit silently all day, staring out over the sea. Then the women would help her to her bed, where she would lie awake, staring up at the moonshadows on the ceiling. Three times Helikaon had visited her. She had sat silently as he talked, her gaze distant. Helikaon did not even know if she truly heard him.

The servant returned. 'The handmaiden awaits you, lord,' he said.

Helikaon dismissed the man and made his way along the open walkway to the queen's apartments. Two guards were stationed outside the doors. They stepped aside as he entered.

The handmaiden, a young, plump, flaxen-haired woman, came out from the rear rooms to greet him. 'She seems a little better today,' she said. 'There is colour in her cheeks.'

'Has she spoken?'

'No, lord.'

Looking around he found himself remembering the first time he had entered these rooms as a young man. He had returned home after two years on the *Penelope*. That same night – as Helikaon enjoyed a farewell feast with the crew on the beach – his father had been murdered. Everything changed that day. The queen, fearing for her life and that of her child, had sent soldiers to kill him. Pausanius and other loyal men had rushed to protect him. In the standoff that followed Helikaon had taken a great risk. The leader of the men sent to kill him was a powerful soldier named Garus. Helikaon approached him. 'You and I will go alone to see the queen,' he said.

'No, lord, they will kill you,' argued Pausanius.

'There will be no killing today,' Helikaon had assured him, though he was less confident than he sounded.

Helikaon had gestured for Garus to precede him, and followed him up the long cliff path to the fortress. He saw Garus finger the hilt of his sword. Then the warrior stopped and slowly turned. He was a big man, wide-shouldered and thick-necked. His eyes were piercingly blue, his face broad and honest. 'The queen is a good and fine woman, and little Diomedes is a joy,' he said. 'Do you plan to kill them?'

'No,' said Helikaon.

'I have your oath on that?'

'You do.'

'Very well, my lord. Follow me.'

They walked further along the open balcony to the queen's apartments. Two guards were there. Both wore shields and carried long spears. Garus signalled to them to stand aside, then rapped his knuckles against the door frame. 'It is I, Garus,' he said. 'May I enter?'

'You may enter,' came a woman's voice.

Garus opened the door, stepped inside, then made way for Helikaon. Several soldiers inside surged to their feet. 'Be calm!' said Helikaon. 'There are no warriors with me.' He had looked at the young queen, seeing both fear and pride in her pale eyes. Beside her was a small boy with golden hair. He was staring up at Helikaon, head cocked to one side.

'I am your brother, Helikaon,' he told the child. 'And you are Diomedes.'

'I am Dio,' the boy corrected him. 'Papa won't get up. So we can't have breakfast. We can't, can we, mama?'

'We'll have breakfast soon,' said Helikaon. He looked at the queen. When Anchises had married this slender, fair-haired Zeleian girl Helikaon had not been invited to the ceremony. In the year before he sailed on the *Penelope* he had spoken to her on but a handful of occasions, and then merely to exchange short pleasantries.

'We do not know each other, Halysia,' he said. 'My father was a hard, cold man. He should have let us talk more. Perhaps then we could have grown to understand one another. Had we done so you would have known that I would never order my father's death, nor kill his wife and son. You have nothing to fear from me.'

'I wish that I could believe you,' she whispered.

'You can, my queen,' said Garus. Helikaon was surprised but kept his expression even.

'And now,' he said, 'you should think of your son's breakfast. Then we will discuss my father's funeral arrangements.'

He shivered now at the memory, then walked through to the rear apartments. Halysia was sitting hunched in a chair, a blanket over her thin frame. She had lost a great deal of weight, and her eyes were dark-rimmed. Helikaon drew up a chair alongside her. The hand-maiden was wrong. She did not look better. Helikaon took her hand in his. The skin was cold. She did not seem to notice his touch.

The sun broke through the clouds, bathing the sea in gold. Helikaon glanced down and saw an untouched bowl of broth and some bread on a table beside Halysia. 'You must eat,' he said, gently. 'You must regain your strength.'

Leaning forward, he lifted the bowl and dipped the spoon into it, raising it to her mouth. 'Just a little, Halysia,' he prompted. She did not move.

Helikaon replaced the bowl on the table and sat quietly, watching the sunlight dancing on the waves. 'I wish I had taken him with me when I sailed,' he said. 'The boy loved you. He would be filled with sorrow if he could see you now.' He looked at the queen as he spoke, but there was no change of expression. 'I don't know where you are, Halysia,' he whispered. 'I don't know where your spirit wanders. I don't know how to reach you and bring you home.'

He sat quietly with her, holding her hand. In the silence he felt his own grief welling up like a swollen river beating against a dam. Ashamed of his weakness, he struggled to concentrate on the problems he faced. His body began to tremble. He saw young Diomedes laughing in the sunshine, and Zidantas chuckling with him, after the fall from the golden horse. He saw Ox lift the boy and hurl him high in the air, before catching him and spinning round. And the dam burst.

He covered his face with his hands and wept for the dead. For Zidantas, who had loved him like a son. For Diomedes, the golden child who would never become a man. For the son of Habusas the Assyrian, who had fallen alongside his father. And for the woman dressed in blue and gold, who had hurled herself from these cliffs so many years ago.

He felt a hand on his shoulder and then someone was kneeling beside him, cradling his head. He leaned in to her, and she kissed his cheek.

Then she spoke. 'They took my little boy,' she said. 'They killed my Dio.'

'I know, Halysia. I am so sorry.'

She felt so frail, and her flesh was cold despite the sunshine.

Helikaon put his arms round her, drawing her close, and they sat together silently as the sun sank into the Great Green.

iii

Andromache had never been so angry. The rage had been building since her arrival in this cesspit of a city, with its army of liars, eavesdroppers, spies and sycophants. Kreusa was the worst of them, she thought, with her hard, metallic eyes, her vicious tongue, and the sweet honeyed smile for her father.

A week ago she had invited Andromache to her own apartments. Kreusa had been friendly, and had greeted her sister-to-be with a hug and a kiss on her cheek. The rooms were everything Andromache would have expected for the king's favourite daughter, beautifully furnished with items of glistening gold, painted vases, elaborately carved furniture, rich drapes, and two wide balconies. There were thick rugs upon the floor and the walls had been painted with colourful scenes. Kreusa had been wearing a gown of pale blue. A long and delicately braided length of silver was looped around her neck, crossing under her breasts and then around her slender waist. Her face was flushed, and Andromache realized she had been drinking. She filled a golden cup with wine, added a little water, and passed it to her. Andromache sipped it. It was strong, but underlying the taste she recognized the bitter tang of meas root. It was used on Thera during revels and feasts to heighten awareness and release inhibition. Andromache had never taken to it, though Kalliope used it regularly. Kreusa had sat close to her on the wide couch, and as she talked she reached out and took Andromache's hand. 'We should be friends,' she said, her smile bright, her eyes gleaming, the pupils wide and distended. 'We share so many . . . interests.'

'We do?'

'Oh, do not be coy, Andromache,' whispered Kreusa, moving closer. 'There are few secrets in the king's palace that I am not privy to. How was slender Alesia? Did she please you? I chose her for you myself.'

'And why would you do that?' asked Andromache, thinking back to the young Thrakian servant, and recalling how simple had been the seduction.

'I wanted to know if our . . . interests . . . were truly shared.' Kreusa leaned in closer, her arm sliding over Andromache's shoulder. Andromache's hand closed over Kreusa's wrist, lifting the arm clear, and she eased herself to her feet. Kreusa rose alongside her, her expression puzzled. 'What is wrong?' she asked.

'Nothing is wrong, Kreusa.'

'You spurn my friendship?' Kreusa's eyes were angry.

'Not your friendship,' replied Andromache, trying to be conciliatory.

'Then be with me,' she said, moving in closer. Andromache realized then that there was no diplomatic way to end this meeting.

'We will not become lovers,' she told Kreusa. 'You are very beautiful, but I do not desire you.'

'*You* do not desire *me*? You arrogant bitch! Get out of my sight!'

Andromache had returned to her rooms, her spirits low. She had not desired to make an enemy of Kreusa, and had known that trouble would follow.

She had not, however, anticipated the depth of Kreusa's malice.

It was Axa who bore the brunt of Kreusa's revenge. The little maid had been suffering in miserable silence since word had come that Hektor's men were lost. Her husband, Mestares, was shield bearer to Hektor and one of the men who was missing with him. As if the uncertainty and fear for her husband were not enough, Axa had birthed her baby son ten days ago. Seeking the reassurance of her palace duties, she had left him with a female relative in the lower town to return to Andromache's side during the day.

Yesterday had started like most days. With the help of another serving girl Axa had laboured to carry bucket after bucket of hot water for Andromache's bath, and sprinkled into it perfumes and rose petals. But when Andromache wandered half naked into the bathroom, she found her maid slumped on the floor.

She crouched down beside her. 'Axa! What's wrong?'

323

'I'm sorry, lady.' Axa struggled to sit up. 'I have had a weakness since the birth of my son. He is a big boy. It has passed. I'll carry on now.'

'No you won't.' Andromache looked into her face and saw the greyness of exhaustion. 'Sit there for a while and tell me about your baby. Has he a name?'

'No, lady. It is for my husband to decide. When he returns.' Her face crumpled then, and a moan born of tiredness, pain and grief arose from her.

'Come.' Andromache started to unwrap the woollen shawl round Axa's waist. 'You need a rest. Get up.' She put an arm round her and raised her to her feet. She undid the straps of the apron Axa wore and it fell to the ground.

'Now, out of that tunic,' she said. 'You're going to have a bath. It will make you feel better.'

'Oh no, lady,' Axa cried, fear in her voice. 'I mustn't. I'll get into trouble. Please don't make me.'

'Nonsense,' Andromache said, laughing a little. 'If you're modest get into the bath like that, in your shift.'

Axa cast an agonized look at Andromache's face, recognized the determination there, and stepped reluctantly into the warm bath. She sat bolt upright in the water, her face a picture of misery.

'Relax, lie back,' said Andromache, hands on her shoulders. 'See, isn't that good?'

Axa gave a weak smile and said, 'It feels very strange, lady. It doesn't feel natural to be wet all over.' Growing in confidence, she splashed the water a little and watched the rose petals float on the ripples.

Andromache laughed and stroked her maid's thick brown hair. 'We'll have to wash this, too, you know.'

Just then there was a rattle of curtains and they both looked round. In the doorway stood Kreusa. She said nothing, but gave a radiant smile before turning and leaving the room.

Axa had climbed clumsily out of the bath, water sluicing from her linen shift onto the floor.

'She saw me. I'll be in trouble now,' she wailed.

'Nonsense,' Andromache repeated. 'I won't let anyone hurt you.'

Her words had been hollow. When she had awoken today it was to find a new servant by her bedside, a round-faced girl, who told her, after much shilly-shallying, that Axa had been flogged and dismissed from the palace that morning, on the orders of the king.

Andromache went immediately to the *megaron*, where she found Priam seated among his advisers. Barely reining in her anger, she demanded, 'What have you done with my servant?'

The king sat back on his throne, waving away his counsellors. They moved back a few steps but remained within earshot. Priam gazed at her for a moment. She thought she could see satisfaction on his face, though he spoke mildly.

'*Your* servant, Andromache? Every servant in this palace is mine. These greybeards in their bright clothes and gaudy jewellery are mine. *You* are mine.'

'I was told . . .' Andromache forced herself to think coolly. 'I was told she was flogged and thrown from the palace. I wish to know why. She was a good servant and deserved better.'

Priam leaned forward and she smelled wine on his breath. 'A good servant,' he hissed, 'does not frolic naked with the daughter of a king. She does not cavort in a bath with rose petals on her breasts.'

There was amused whispering among the counsellors.

'You have been misinformed about *cavorting*,' Andromache replied. 'Axa was exhausted and in pain. I ordered her to rest and take the bath.'

Priam's face darkened. 'And you thought you would take it with her? What is done is done. Be more careful of your behaviour in the future.'

'Either that, or ensure I am not spied upon by people with minds like shit buckets,' said Andromache, her anger flaring dangerously out of control. 'The person who should have been flogged is the vile bitch . . .'

'Enough!' roared Priam, surging to his feet. 'If you want to plead for your servant, then get on your knees!'

Andromache stood very still. All her pride urged her to turn away from this harsh and arrogant man, and to walk from the room, back straight, spirit defiant. And yet it was because of her that poor Axa had been flogged and humiliated. Axa herself had warned her, but proud Andromache had not listened. Yes, she could retain her pride and walk from the room, but what would that pride be worth thereafter?

Her mouth was dry as she closed her eyes and dropped to her knees before the king. 'I would ask . . .' she began.

'Silence! I have matters here to attend to. Remain where you are until I bid you to speak.'

Now the humiliation was complete. Priam gathered his courtiers around him, and they discussed their matters of state. Time passed, and her knees began to ache against the cold stone of the floor. But she did not move, nor open her eyes.

After a while she did not even listen to their conversation. At one point she felt the warmth of sunlight on her back, and realized the afternoon was wearing on.

When Priam spoke to her, and she opened her eyes, she saw that the courtiers and scribes had gone.

'Well?' he said. 'Make your plea.' She looked at him. He seemed more weary now, and his eyes had lost their gleam.

'Does guilt or innocence not matter to you, King Priam?' she asked him, her voice soft. 'Are you not the First Magistrate of Troy? Does justice not flow from this throne? Had I been *cavorting*, as you call it, with a young servant, I would not hide it. I am who I am. I do not lie. Axa is the wife of Hektor's shield bearer. Only days ago she gave birth to a son. In your long experience do you know of many women who desire to *cavort* so soon after childbirth, with their bodies torn and bruised, their breasts swollen with milk?'

Priam's expression changed. He sat back on his throne, and rubbed his hand across his grey-gold beard. 'I was not aware it was the wife of Mestares. Stand up. You have knelt long enough.'

She was surprised by this sudden change in him, and, pushing herself to her feet, remained silent. 'There has been a misunderstanding,' he said. 'I shall have a gift sent to her. You want her back?'

'Indeed I do.'

He looked long at her. 'You would not kneel to me when your life might have depended on it. Yet you abase yourself for a servant.'

'It was my foolishness that caused her suffering. I ordered her into that bath. I thought it would ease her pain.'

He nodded. 'As you thought it would be good to swim naked with a Mykene warrior on my beach? Or to shoot arrows with my soldiers? You are a strange woman, Andromache.' He rubbed his eyes, then reached for a cup of wine, which he drained. 'You seem to arouse great passion in those who know you,' he continued. 'Deiphobos wants you expelled from Troy. Kreusa wanted you flogged and shamed. Agathon wants to marry you. Even dull little Laodike has blossomed in your company. Answer me this, Andromache of Thebe: had I told you that the only way to rescue Axa was to have you come to my bed, would you have done so?'

'Yes, I would,' she said, without hesitation. 'Why did you not?'

He shook his head. 'A good question, Andromache, and one which you need to answer for yourself.'

'How can I? I do not know your thoughts.'

Rising from his throne he beckoned her to follow him, then strode the length of the *megaron*, and up the stairway towards the queen's apartments. Andromache was nervous, but not for fear that he might ravish her. In their conversation he had not once stared at her breasts or her legs, and his eyes had not possessed their normal hungry look. The King reached the top of the stairs and turned right, walking along the gallery to a balcony high above the royal gardens. Andromache joined him there.

People were milling in the gardens below, talking in low voices. Andromache saw Agathon and fat Antiphones talking together, and, beyond them, Laodike sitting with Kreusa. Laodike's head was bowed, and Kreusa was gesticulating with her hands. Around them were counsellors, in their white robes, and Trojan nobles, some with their wives or daughters.

'Everyone you see,' said Priam softly, 'requires something from the king. Yet each gift to one will be seen as an insult to another.

Among them will be those who are loyal to the king. Among them will be traitors. Some are loyal now, but will become traitors. Some *could* become traitors, but a gift from me will keep them loyal. How does the king know whom to trust and whom to kill, whom to reward and whom to punish?'

Andromache felt tense and uneasy. 'I do not know,' she said.

'Then learn, Andromache,' he told her. 'For, if the gods will it, one day you will be queen of Troy. On that day you will look out from this balcony and all those below will be coming to you or your husband. You will need to know their thoughts, their dreams, their ambitions. For when they are before you the loyal and the treacherous will both sound the same. They will all laugh when you make a jest, they will weep when you are sad. They will pledge undying love for you. Their words, therefore, will be meaningless. Unless you know the thoughts behind the words.'

'And you know all their thoughts, King Priam?'

'I know *enough* of their thoughts and their ambitions to keep me alive.' He chuckled. 'One day, though, one of them will surprise me. He will plunge a dagger through my heart, or slip poison into my cup, or raise a rebellion to overthrow me.'

'Why do you smile at the thought?'

'Why not? Whoever succeeds me as king will be strong and cunning, and therefore well equipped for the role.'

Now it was Andromache who smiled. 'Or he might be stupid and lucky.'

Priam nodded. 'If that proves true he won't last long. Another of my cunning sons will overthrow him. However, let us return to your question. Why did I not demand your body in payment? Think on it, and we will talk again.' He gazed down at the milling crowds below. 'And now I must allow my subjects, both loyal and treacherous, to present their petitions to their king.'

Returning to her own rooms, Andromache wrapped herself in a hooded green cloak and left the palace, heading for the lower town and the poorer quarter where the soldiers' wives were billeted. Asking directions from several women gathered round a well, she located the dwelling occupied by Axa and three other wives. It was small and cramped, with dirt floors. Axa was sitting at the back of the building, in the shade, her babe in her arms. She saw Andromache and struggled to rise.

'Oh, sit, please,' said Andromache, kneeling beside her. 'I am so sorry, Axa. It was my fault.'

'Mestares will be so angry with me when he gets home,' said Axa. 'I have shamed him.'

'You shamed no-one. I have seen the king. He knows it was a mistake. He is sending a gift to you. And I want you back. Oh, Axa! Please say you will come!'

'Of course I will,' replied Axa dully. 'How else could I feed myself and my son? I will be there tomorrow.'

'Can you forgive me?'

The babe in Axa's arms began to make soft little mewing sounds. Axa opened her shift, exposing a heavy breast, and lifted the child to it. The babe nuzzled at the teat ineffectually, and then with more confidence. Axa sighed. She looked at Andromache.

'What difference does it make whether I forgive or don't forgive?' she asked. 'We are called servants, but we are slaves really. We live or die at the whim of others. I was flogged for being seen in a bath. Were you flogged for being with me?'

'No, I wasn't flogged. But believe me when I say I would rather it had been me. Can we be friends, Axa?'

'I am your servant. I must be whatever you want me to be.'

Andromache fell silent, watching as Axa finished feeding her babe and lifted the mite to her shoulder, gently rubbing his back. 'Did they hurt you badly?' she asked at last.

'Yes, they hurt me,' replied Axa, tears in her eyes. 'But not with the blows from that knotted rope. I am the wife of Mestares the shield bearer. Ten battles he has fought for the king and for Troy. Now he might be dead, and I live every day fearing the news. And what do they do to ease my suffering? They flog me and throw me from the palace. I will never forgive that.'

'No,' said Andromache, rising to her feet. 'Neither would I. I will see you tomorrow, Axa.'

The little woman looked up at her, and her expression softened.

'You went to the king for me,' she said. '*You* I will forgive. But no more baths.'

Andromache smiled. 'No more baths,' she agreed.

Returning to the palace Andromache walked through the private royal gardens. There were still some twenty people there, enjoying the shade and the scent of the blooms. By the far wall, beneath a latticed bower, Kreusa was talking to Agathon. She was wearing a white gown edged with gold, and had thrown back her head in a parody of careless laughter, her raven hair rippling in the breeze.

As she approached them Agathon saw her, and gave a tight smile. He is embarrassed, thought Andromache. Kreusa, by contrast, looked at her with an expression of smug satisfaction.

'How are you, beautiful lady?' asked Agathon.

'I am well, Prince Agathon. I saw the king this morning. You heard of the misunderstanding concerning my servant?'

'Yes,' he said. 'I was sorry to hear of it.'

'As was I. However, the king has reinstated her, and is sending her a gift in apology.' She swung towards Kreusa. 'I think he understands now that poor Axa was merely the victim of malice. Some poor, demented creature, driven by envy and spite.'

Kreusa's hand slashed out, slapping Andromache hard on the cheek. Stepping in, Andromache punched her full on the jaw. Kreusa spun and hit the ground hard. She struggled to rise, then slumped down.

Agathon knelt by the half-stunned young woman, helping her to stand. There was blood trickling from a split in her lip, and her white gown was smeared with dirt.

Andromache took a deep breath, and turned away. All conversation among the crowd had ceased and she felt all eyes on her as she walked back into the palace.

XXV

The Silent Head

i

CTHOSIS THE EUNUCH HAD WORN HIS LATEST CREATION TO THE meeting, and no-one had noticed. It was most galling. The ankle-length gown was jet black, and edged with silver thread. It was a magnificent piece, which he had been convinced would be the envy of every man present. No-one had ever produced a black dye that would remain fast to the cloth. Two problems always occurred. First, if rained upon the dye would seep out, staining the skin for days. Second, the dyes were so powerful that they would stink until the garment had been washed several times and faded to a dull and lifeless grey.

Cthosis had spent years refining the process, eliminating these problems. Oak bark from the gnarled trees in the lands of the Sombre Sea had provided the source of a finer dye, but obtaining it had consumed much of his wealth. So treacherous and powerful were the currents that it was almost impossible to sail a ship up the Hellespont and into the Sombre Sea. All trade goods had to be carried overland.

Now here he was, with sixty of the most influential men in Dardania, and not one had mentioned the gown. He wondered if, as an Egypteian, he had failed to realize that there was some antipathy for the colour black among these peoples of the Northern Sea. Ah well, he thought, come the spring I will ship the cloth to Memphis and Luxor. Egypteian men will pay heavily in gold for such finery. Even so, the lack of appreciation here was dispiriting.

Raised voices cut through his meditations. The Phrygian cattle trader – whose name Cthosis could never recall – was shouting at a Hittite merchant, and waving his powerful fist in the man's face. Before long there would be blows struck, and the entire conference would degenerate into an unseemly brawl. With this in mind Cthosis eased his way to the left-hand wall, to stand beneath a fearsome statue of a helmeted warrior carrying a spear. Cthosis was not a fighting man, and had no wish to be drawn into an unseemly scrap – especially in his new garment.

Indeed, had it not been for the chance to display it, Cthosis would have avoided the meeting altogether.

People were not hard to read. When times were good they moved about their business smiling at neighbours. But add a touch of fear, or uncertainty, and the smiles would disappear. Rows and feuds would erupt. If a storm washed away crops the cry was: 'Who is to blame?' Not the vagaries of the weather, obviously. No, it had to be a mischievous spell cast by a jealous neighbour. Probably a witch. If everyone's crops were washed away – well, then it was the fault of the king, who had angered the gods in some inexplicable way.

It was not dissimilar back in Egypt. Fear and blame, leading to idiots gathering in mobs, followed by riots, and unnecessary deaths.

A long time ago, when Cthosis was still a small boy, he had seen lightning strike a tree around which a herd of cattle had been quietly feeding. The cattle bunched together and took off in a stampede that carried half of them over a cliff.

People and cattle. Not a great deal of difference, he thought.

Life had been harsh in Egypt for the mutilated child he had been. Yet at least at the palace the people had enjoyed a love of poetry and painting, and men would sit in the evenings discussing the beauty of the sunsets. The wall paintings depicted gentle scenes, of ships sailing mighty rivers, or pharaohs receiving tributes from vassal kings.

Oh, do not fool yourself, stupid man, he chided himself. They were not so different. Here in Dardania they do not clip the balls from a ten-year-old boy so that he can wander among the palace women, carrying their goblets of wine, fetching their cloaks and their hats. The pain had been excruciating, but nothing compared to the knowledge that his father had sold him for just that purpose.

Cthosis sighed. The betrayal still hurt, even after fifteen years.

Dust from the statue had rubbed off onto the shoulder of his tunic. Idly he brushed it away. As he did so the stump of his little finger caught on a loose stitch in the cloth. He shivered as he remembered the day, three years ago, when it had been cut away. Cthosis had been running to collect some bauble a princess had left in the royal gardens. As he turned a corner he had collided with Prince Rameses, knocking the young man sideways. The prince had reacted with customary savagery, hurling Cthosis against a painted pillar. He was prepared for a beating, but Rameses had dragged his sword from its sheath and lashed out. Cthosis had thrown up his hand. The blade sliced through one finger and cut into the next. Cthosis had stood there, staring at the severed digit. Then he realized that it was not over. Rameses stepped in, pressed the sword point against his chest, and tensed for the killing thrust.

Death was a heartbeat away when a powerful hand grabbed Rameses' cloak and dragged him back. 'Get you gone, eunuch,' said Prince Ahmose. Cthosis had needed no further instruction, and had run back to the women's quarters, where the servant girls had fussed over him, and called for the royal physician.

As he sat there, blood seeping from the ruin of his hand, the aftershock of the violence had hit him. He had begun to tremble. Then he had wept. When he told the women what had happened they went suddenly quiet, and began to cast nervous glances towards the doors.

He knew then that Rameses would send for him, and finish what he had begun. Cthosis had struck a prince. It would not matter that it was accidental. The punishment would be the same.

He had sat miserably while the Nubian physician prepared pitch for the stump. The other injured finger, he was told, was broken, and would need a splint. Then the women suddenly scattered. Cthosis felt tears beginning again. Death was once more upon him.

But it was not the terrifying Rameses who entered the room, but the powerful figure of Prince Ahmose. The big man spoke quietly to the Nubian, and then turned to Cthosis, who kept his head down. No slave could ever look into the eyes of a prince. 'You are released from service, eunuch,' said the prince, in his deep voice.

Inadvertently Cthosis looked up. 'Released, lord?' Ahmose was not a handsome man. His face was too rugged, the nose too prominent, the chin too broad. And it had a cleft in it that looked like a scar. But his eyes were dark and magnificent.

'Best you leave tonight,' said the prince softly. 'I would suggest travelling to a far place.' He placed a pouch in Cthosis' good hand. 'There is gold there, and a few baubles, rings and such like. I am told they have some value.' Then he had left.

The pouch contained fourteen small gold ingots, and several rings set with precious stones. There was also an emerald the size of a dove's egg. With this fortune Cthosis had travelled to Dardania.

The shouting began again in the great throne room, jerking Cthosis back to the present. He glanced around the crowd. Many nationalities were represented here. He saw Hittites, in their curious woollen leggings, Phrygians, tall and red-headed, Samothrakians, Mykene, Lydians. All wore the clothes of their races. Three Babylonians were standing on the far side of the throne room, their beards curled with hot irons. How foolish was that in this wet, autumn climate? There were Trojans – horse traders and chariot makers – who had fallen foul of Priam and made their home in Dardania. They also stood apart, staring disdainfully at the noisy throng.

'You miserable son of an ugly pig!' someone shouted.

An odd insult, Cthosis thought. Would it be a compliment to be called the son of a *beautiful* pig? The two men flew at one another. Blows were struck and they fell, struggling, to the stone floor.

Cthosis considered leaving. No-one would notice the absence of a single merchant among so many angry men. But he did not. He was interested to see this new king. He had heard much of Helikaon the trader, and a little of Helikaon the fighter. But all he knew of the man's nature was contained in the story of how he had put aside his rights to the throne in favour of the child, Diomedes, his half-brother. Such an action did not speak highly of his ambition, or indeed of his ruthlessness.

And ruthlessness was what was required now. Helikaon needed to enter this throne room dressed in armour, and carrying a sword of fire, to quell this mob.

The two fighting men were dragged apart, still yelling abuse at one another.

Then the great doors opened, and soldiers marched into the throne room. Garbed in bronze breastplates and helmets, and carrying long spears and deep shields, they formed two lines and stood silently with their backs to the walls. The crowd fell silent and glanced back towards the doors. Cthosis saw a slim young man enter. His long dark hair was tied back from his face by a single strip of leather. His tunic was a pale, listless green, with a blue tinge. Probably privet berries, thought Cthosis, and not enough salt in the boil.

The young man stepped up to the dais at the far end of the throne room, and halted beside a long table. Then he turned and surveyed the crowd. Men were still talking to one another, and another argument broke out. The young man raised his hand. Immediately all the soldiers began to hammer their spears against their bronze shields. The sudden noise was startling.

Silence fell on the hall.

'I thank you all for coming. I am Helikaon the king,' said the young man.

'I hope it's worth our while,' shouted someone from the back.

'Let us be clear about something,' said Helikaon, his voice

displaying no anger. 'There will be no interruptions when I speak. The next man whose voice cuts across mine will rue it. I will call upon each of you to voice his thoughts, and – equally – no-one will interrupt *you* as you speak. That is the only way we will achieve unity.'

'Who says we need unity?' called out the same man.

Helikaon raised his hand. Two soldiers moved forward, grabbing the speaker – a red-headed Phrygian – and hauling him from the throne room. 'Now all of you here,' continued Helikaon, 'have grievances. There are enmities, hatreds, discords. We are here to put an end to them. And we will achieve this by discussing our grievances and solving them. Almost all of you men come from lands far away. But when you die your bodies will go into the earth of Dardania, and become part of it. And your spirits will reach out and touch your children, and they too will become the land. They will be Dardanians. Not Phrygians, Maeonians, Trojans, Lydians, but Dardanians.'

Helikaon fell silent as a soldier, carrying a small sack, moved through the crowd. He advanced to the dais and waited. Helikaon gestured him forward. The man stepped up to the dais, opened the sack, and lifted out a severed head. Cthosis blinked when he saw it. Then the soldier laid the head on the table, where the dead eyes stared out at the crowd. Blood oozed from the mutilated neck, and dripped to the stone floor. It was the head of the red-headed man who only moments before had been hauled from the throne room.

'Now what I intend to do,' said Helikaon, his voice still calm and agreeable, 'is to call each of you forward to speak your minds. I do not do this in any order of preference, and you should not consider yourself slighted if you are not called until later. Are there any questions?'

The men stood in shocked silence, staring at the head upon the table.

'Good,' said Helikaon. 'Then let us begin. I will speak first. Every man here lives or dies upon *my* sufferance. Every man here dwells upon *my* land, and is subject to *my* laws. Obey those laws and you will prosper. You will be protected by my soldiers, and your wealth will grow. You will be able to come to me, or my generals, and seek help when you need it. Disobey my laws and you will come to rue it. Now what are these laws? They are simple. You will render to me the king's due from your profits, or your crops, or your herds. You will not take up arms against me, or against any other man under my protection. And that is *all* men who obey my laws. There will be no blood feuds. Grievances will be brought before me, or those appointed by me. That is where judgements will be sought. Those judgements will be final. Should a man commit murder, I will see him dead, and his entire family sold into slavery. His lands, his goods and his chattels will revert to me.'

Ghosis listened as the young man continued to speak. Not a sound came from anyone else in the throne room. Helikaon did not refer to the dead man, or even so much as glance at the severed head. The contrast between his measured words and the ghastly image was chilling. When at last he finished speaking he called out for a scribe to be sent for. A middle-aged man with a twisted back entered the room and nervously made his way forward. He was carrying a wicker basket full of soft clay tablets. A soldier brought him a chair and he sat quietly at the end of the table, as far from the severed head as he could.

'This man,' said the king, 'will write down your grievances, and I will examine them later, and give judgement.' He pointed to a tall, bearded Phrygian. 'Now we shall begin the discussion. First say your name, then speak your grievance.'

The man cleared his throat. 'If I speak, lord, and you do not like what you hear, will my head also grace your table, like my poor brother's?'

'You may speak freely. There will be no recrimination. Begin with your name.'

'I am Pholus of Phrygia, and I breed horses for sale in Troy. My people have a settlement a day's ride from the fortress, and we have water rights, granted by Queen Halysia. Some months back a cattle trader drove his herds onto our lands. When my brother remonstrated with him he was beaten with cudgels. The cattle muddied the water, and collapsed the stream banks. How can I breed horses without water?'

And so it went on.

Cthosis stood quietly as one man after another spoke of problems, fears, and the reasons for discord with neighbours. The king listened to them for several hours, then called a halt, telling them they would meet again tomorrow. Then he invited them to join him at a feast later in the main courtyard, and with that he strode from the dais towards the far doors.

As he came abreast of Cthosis he paused. 'That is a very fine gown, my friend,' he said. 'I have never seen the like.' He stepped forward and sniffed. 'There is no smell from the dye. It has already been washed?'

'Indeed, lord. Three times.'

'Extraordinary. Where did you acquire it?'

'It is from my own cloth, and my own dye, lord.'

'Even better. We shall find time to talk. A cloth of jet will earn gold in every country around the Great Green.'

He smiled at Cthosis, and walked away.

The soldiers filed out after him, and the doors closed. For a moment no-one said anything. Then the Phrygian horse breeder walked to the dais, dropped to his knees, and laid his hand on the severed head. 'You never learned how to listen, little brother,' he said. 'But you were a good lad always. I shall miss you greatly.'

He picked up the sack, then stood by, uncertain. Cthosis approached him.

'I do not believe the king would object if you removed your brother's head,' he said.

'You think so?'

'I am sure of it.'

The man sighed. 'He paid a heavy price for a few ill-spoken words.'

'Indeed he did.'

Cthosis left the hall and strolled out to the courtyard. Many of the leaders were now gathered together and talking quietly. Cthosis eased his way through the group, heading out towards an open area overlooking the cliff path leading up to the fortress gates.

A line of men was moving through the gates, carrying baskets of food, ready for the feast.

Idly he watched them. Then his interest quickened. A big man was coming through the gate, carrying a sheep upon his shoulders.

Cthosis walked swiftly down towards him, fully expecting to be wrong in his identification. As he came closer his heart began to beat rapidly. He was heavily bearded now, but there was no mistaking those magnificent eyes. It was Prince Ahmose.

What wonder was this? The second in line to the Great Pharaoh was working as a servant in the fortress of Dardanos.

The big man saw him and smiled. 'It seems you have done well for yourself, eunuch,' he said.

Cthosis lowered his head and bowed. 'Oh, no need for that,' said Ahmose. 'As you can see, I am no longer the pharaoh's grandson. I am, like you, a man with a price on his head.'

'I am sorry, lord. You were kind to me.'

'No need for pity. I am content. Do you serve here?'

'No, lord. I am a merchant. I make and sell cloth. It would be an honour to fashion you a tunic.'

'You may stop calling me lord – Cthosis, isn't it?'

'Yes, lord. Oh . . . I am sorry.'

Ahmose laughed. 'I am known now as Gershom.'

'How strange,' said Cthosis. 'A long time since I heard that word. My people use it to describe foreigners.'

'That is why I chose it. You are one of the desert folk?'

'Yes . . . well, I was once. Before my father sold me to the palace.'

'A curious race,' said Gershom. 'However, I cannot stand here talking of old times. There is work to be done for your feast.' He clapped Cthosis on the shoulder. 'Rameses was furious when he found out I'd freed you. It cost me two hundred talents of silver and my best war horse.'

'I will always be grateful, lord. If ever you need anything . . .'

'Don't make promises, my friend. Those who are discovered to have aided me will face a harsh reckoning.'

'Even so. Should you ever need anything you have only to ask. All that I have is at your disposal.'

ii

Helikaon left the assembly and strode through the palace. The old general Pausanius tried to intercept him, but he shook his head and waved the man away. Climbing the worn steps to the battlements he tilted his head to the sky, drawing in deep, calming breaths. His stomach began to settle.

Noticing a sentry watching him, he moved back inside, making his way through to the old royal apartments, and his childhood rooms. Dust lay over the floor, and there were cobwebs across the balcony entrance. Brushing them aside, he stepped out. The ancient, rickety chair was still there, the wood paled and cracked by the sun. Kneeling down, he traced his fingers over the carved horse in the backrest.

This was the throne he had sat upon as a child, king of a pretend world, in which all men were contented, and there were no wars. He had never, in those days, dreamed of battle and glory. Moving back from the chair he slumped down to the cold stone, and rested his head on the low balcony rail. Closing his eyes he saw again the severed head on the table. It merged with that of Zidantas.

He could almost hear Ox speak. *You think that boy in the hall deserved to die, so that you could make a point? Could you not have won them over with the conviction of your words, the power of your mind? Does it always have to be death, with you?*

Helikaon stared at the chair, picturing the little boy who had sat there. 'Sometimes,' he told him, 'such deeds are necessary. I once saw Odysseus cut open a crewman's chest, in order to pull out an arrow head that had lodged there. Sometimes the evil needs to be cut free.'

Do not seek to fool yourself, said the voice of Ox. *Do not rationalize your evil, and seek to make it something good. Yes, the men will follow you now. Yes, the realm is safe from discord. Yes, you are a king. Your father would be so proud of you!*

Helikaon's anger rose. It is not Ox talking to you, he told himself. It is your own weakness. The man was warned and chose to ignore it. His death achieved more in one blood-drenched moment than a torrent of words could have. And that is the truth of it!

The truth is a many-costumed whore, came Odysseus' voice in his mind. *Seems to me she will offer a man valid reasons for any deed, no matter how ghastly.*

A rumble of thunder came from the distance, and a cold wind began to blow.

Helikaon pushed himself to his feet and took a last look around the home of his childhood, then walked out, and down to the lower apartments, where the wounded men of his crew were being cared for. He stopped and spoke to each man, then went in search of Attalus.

He found him in a side garden, his chest and side bandaged. Sitting alone in the shadows of a late-flowering tree, he was whittling a length of wood. Helikaon approached him.

'The surgeon says you were lucky, my friend. The knife missed your heart by a whisker.'

Attalus nodded. 'Lucky day for you too,' he said.

'It always helps when good friends are close by. It surprised me to see you there. Oniacus tells me you had decided to quit the crew.'

'Surprised me too,' admitted Attalus. Helikaon sat alongside him. The man continued to whittle.

'If you want to leave for Troy when you are well, I will see you are given a good horse and a pouch of gold. You are welcome, though, to stay in Dardanos, and enjoy my hospitality for the winter.'

Attalus put down his knife, and his shoulders sagged. 'You owe me nothing.'

'I owe any man who chooses to fight alongside me – most especially when he is no longer a member of my crew.'

'I just got drawn in, that's all. Had my own reasons for being there.' Attalus sat silently for a moment. Then he looked at Helikaon. 'It is not over, you know.'

'I know that. The assassin Karpophorus has been paid to end my life. They say he is the finest killer on the Great Green. He was also the man who murdered my father. Here in this very fortress.'

'Oniacus told me no-one knew who killed Anchises.'

Helikaon sat down opposite Attalus. 'I only found out recently.' He gazed around the garden. 'This is a peaceful place. I used to play here as a child.'

Attalus did not respond, and returned to his whittling.

'Rest and regain your strength, Attalus. And if you need anything, ask and it will be supplied for you.' Helikaon stood up, ready to leave.

'I am not a good man,' said Attalus suddenly, his face reddening. 'Everyone treats me like a good man. I don't like it!'

The outburst surprised Helikaon. Attalus had always seemed so calm and in control. Resuming his seat, he looked at the crewman. He was tense now, and his eyes looked angry. 'We are none of us good men,' said Helikaon softly. 'Today I had a man killed merely to make a point. He may well have been a good man. We are all flawed, Attalus. We all carry the weight of our deeds. And we will all answer for them, I think. All I know of you is that you have proved a loyal crewman, and a brave companion. I also know you were hired by Zidantas. The Ox was a fine judge of fighting men. Your past means nothing here. Only the deeds of the present and the future.'

'Past, present and future, it is all the same,' said Attalus, his shoulders slumping. 'They are what they are. We are what we are. Nothing changes.'

'I don't know if that is true. My life has changed now three times. Once when I was a small child and my mother died. Once when Odysseus came and took me aboard the *Penelope*. And then when my father was murdered. That still haunts me. I left here as a frightened boy. My father told me he loathed me. I came back as a man, hoping that he would be proud.' Helikaon fell silent, surprised at himself for sharing his thoughts with a relative stranger. He saw that Attalus was looking at him. 'I don't usually talk like this,' he said, suddenly embarrassed.

342

'A man who tells his child he loathes him,' said Attalus, his voice trembling, 'isn't worth rat's piss. So why care whether he would have been proud or not?' Sheathing his dagger he threw aside the whittled wood and rose to his feet. 'I'm tired. I'll rest now.'

Helikaon remained where he was as the slim sailor returned to the fortress.

Not worth rat's piss.

The simple truth of the words cut through years of hidden anguish. The weight of regret suddenly lifted. Anchises had never been a father to him, had cared nothing for him. He was cold-hearted, and manipulative, and had spent years tormenting a lost and lonely child. Attalus was right.

And the dark shadow of Anchises melted from his mind like mist in the sunlight.

XXVI

Aphrodite's Leap

i

THAT AUTUMN AND WINTER IN DARDANIA WERE THE WORST IN living memory. Fierce storms lashed the coastline. Swollen rivers burst their banks, bringing down bridges. Several low-lying villages were washed away in the floods. Into this chaos came bands of outlaws and rogue mercenary groups, preying on the populace.

Helikaon travelled the land leading troops to hunt them down. Three battles were fought before midwinter. Two were indecisive, the mercenaries escaping into the mountains. The third saw a mercenary force of some seven hundred men routed. Helikaon had the leaders executed, the hundred or so survivors sold into slavery.

Messengers from Troy brought no good news. Hektor was still missing, even though the brief war between the Hittite empire and Egypte was over. The last anyone had seen of the Trojan prince he had been facing impossible odds, with no escape route. Helikaon did not believe Hektor was dead. The man was vibrant with life. If a mountain fell on him he would burrow his way out. If the sea rose over him, he would emerge riding a dolphin.

Hektor was invincible.

Even so, as the weeks went by, a gnawing worry gripped him.

What if the inconceivable proved to be true?

Priam was hated by most of his sons, and many of his followers. If he was toppled civil war would follow. All alliances would be voided. The war would inevitably spread to encompass all the lands of the eastern coastline, as Priam's warring sons forged new alliances. Trade would suffer, the flow of wealth drying up. Merchants, farmers, traders, cattle breeders would see their profits tumble. Without markets for their goods they would release workers. More and more people would find themselves without the means to buy food. This in turn would lead to unrest, and the swelling of outlaw bands. Agamemnon and the Mykene would be jubilant. How much more simple their plans would become if the armies of the east tore into each other in a great bloodletting.

As the first cold winds of winter blew in from the north, Helikaon was back at the fortress of Dardanos. The queen, Halysia, had recovered from her physical wounds, but rarely ventured out into the public eye. Helikaon tried to draw her in to the running of the realm, but she refused. 'Everyone knows what was done to me,' she said. 'I see it in their eyes.'

'The people love you, Halysia. And so they should. You are a caring queen. The works of evil men have not changed that.'

'Everything has changed,' she said. 'The sun no longer shines for me.'

He had left her then, for he had no words to pierce the walls of her sorrow. That afternoon Pausanius came to him, telling him a Mykene ambassador had arrived from Troy.

'You want me to send him away?' The old general looked nervous.

'Why would I do that?'

'He may have learned of the attack on Pithros.'

'I am sure that he has.'

'You do not fear war with the Mykene?'

'Bring him to me, Pausanius, and then remain, but say nothing.'

The ambassador was a slender, red-headed man, who introduced himself as Erekos. He entered the *megaron* and offered no bow.

'Greetings, King Helikaon. I hope I find you well.'

'Indeed you do, Erekos. How may we assist you?'

'We have received disturbing news, king, from the island of Pithros. A ship beached there recently and found hundreds of corpses. All the houses were empty and plundered, and most of the women and children removed.'

'Consider it my gift to King Agamemnon.'

'Your gift? The island of Pithros is Mykene land.'

'Indeed it is, and so it remains,' said Helikaon. 'It had also become a pirate haven, and from its bays their galleys attacked merchant vessels, or raided coastal settlements. You will know that my own fortress was attacked, and my brother slain.' Helikaon paused and watched the man. Erekos looked away.

'Yes, the news of the . . . atrocity . . . reached us. Appalling. But you had no right to bring troops to a Mykene island, without first seeking the permission of Agamemnon King.'

'Not so, Erekos. My father, Anchises, forged a treaty with King Atreus. In it both nations pledged to support the other against pirates and raiders. What greater support could I offer the son of Atreus, than to expel pirates from a Mykene island, and to make the Great Green safer for Mykene trading ships?'

Erekos stood silently, his face pale. 'You wish me to convey to my king that you invaded Mykene lands as a gift to him?'

'What else could it be but a gift?' asked Helikaon. 'Two hundred dead pirates and an island returned to Mykene rule. And you can assure your king that come the spring my fleet will continue to hunt pirates and kill them *wherever* they find them.'

'You will not again invade Mykene lands, King Helikaon.'

'Mykene lands?' responded Helikaon, feigning surprise. 'By the gods, have pirates conquered even more Mykene territory? This is grim news.'

'No territory has been conquered,' replied Erekos, his voice becoming shrill. He took a deep, calming breath. 'What I am saying, King Helikaon, is that the Mykene will deal with any pirates who might seek to hide on Mykene lands.'

'Ah, I see,' said Helikaon, nodding. 'It is a question of martial pride. I understand that, and would wish to cause King

Agamemnon no embarrassment. He has suffered so much of late. It must be galling for him.'

'Galling? I do not understand.'

'Two of his Followers turning rogue. First Alektruon, who I understand was a favourite of the king. Then Kolanos becoming a pirate. Oh – and I almost forgot – then there is Argurios, who I understand has been declared a traitor and an outlaw. And now to discover that pirates had overrun a Mykene island . . .' Helikaon shook his head, adopting an expression of sympathy. 'It will make him wonder what disasters are yet to befall him. However, you can assure the king of my friendship. Now, will you stay and dine with us, Erekos?'

'No, King Helikaon – though I thank you for your courtesy. I must return to Troy. There are matters there that need my attention.'

After Erekos had left Pausanius stepped forward, a wide smile on his face. 'I enjoyed that, my king. It was all I could do not to laugh out loud.'

'Agamemnon will not laugh when he hears of it.'

'You think he will declare war on us?'

'I doubt it. How can he make war on a friend who has aided him?'

'But they were *his* pirates.'

'Indeed they were. We know it, he knows it, but other kings around the Great Green do not. If he makes war on Dardania, following an attack on pirates, it will be an admission that he is behind the pirate raids.'

'I hope you are right, my king.'

ii

On midwinter's night another messenger arrived from Troy. Nasiq was a young Phrygian scribe employed by one of Helikaon's merchant allies. He brought scrolls and messages concerning the needs of the coming trading season, and accountings of the previous trading year. More than this, though, he was a raconteur and an outrageous gossip. Helikaon always enjoyed his winter visits.

'What news, Nasiq, my friend?' he asked, as they sat down to eat in the king's apartments.

The slender Phrygian lifted a small delicacy from a silver plate. It was minced lamb, wrapped in a vine leaf. He sniffed at it, then took a bite. 'Oh, my dear, there is so much to tell. Who would you like to hear of first?'

'What of Hektor?'

'No word. Many of the Trojan Horse have now returned to the city. Others remained around Kadesh with Hittite soldiers, searching for him. It does not look as if there will be good news. The last time anyone saw him he and around fifty of his men were surrounded and outnumbered, and night was falling.'

'What is the mood in the city?'

'Fractious. Two of Priam's sons – Isos and Pammon – have fled the city. They were about to be arrested, I understand.'

'I know them both. Neither has the wit to organize a revolt, or the following to inspire insurrection.'

'I agree. They would be serving someone else. Fat Antiphones has been stripped of his titles and ordered not to leave his palace. He was seen meeting in secret with the Mykene ambassador, Erekos.'

'I met him,' said Helikaon. 'A cold and unpleasant man. It would surprise me, however, to learn that Antiphones was a traitor. He is more interested in food than power. Polites is a possibility. He is no warrior, but he has a sharp mind.'

'And Priam is said to enjoy riding his wife. Rumour has it that Polites' two sons share an interesting trait. Their father is also their grandfather.'

Helikaon chuckled and shook his head. 'You really are a dreadful gossip, Nasiq. It shames me that I am amused by it.' His smile faded. 'However, Polites is a possibility, as is Agathon.'

'Agathon has always been as loyal as Hektor,' Nasiq pointed out.

'Largely *because* of Hektor. They are great friends. But Priam does not favour Agathon. Never has. He judges him against Hektor. I remember once the king saying publicly that Agathon and Hektor were like two identical statues, save that one was cast in gold, the other copper.' Helikaon swore. 'Priam is an unpleasant man, and always finds exactly the right insult to wound the deepest.'

'Is there anyone in high position that Priam has not insulted?' queried Nasiq.

'Probably not. Let us talk of other news. What of Andromache?'

'Ah, wonderful stories!' Nasiq hesitated. 'Are you friends with the lady?'

'What difference would that make to the stories?'

'I'm not sure. She is the talk of Troy . . . for many reasons. Some high, some low.'

'I want no low tales concerning her,' said Helikaon sharply. The wind blew in from the open balcony, causing a lamp to gutter. He rose and pulled the doors closed, then relit the lamp. Nasiq sat silently for a few moments more. Then he gave a wry smile.

'Rather a large difference then.'

Helikaon relaxed. 'Begin your tale,' he said.

'Very well. You heard she saved the king's life?'

Helikaon was shocked, then he chuckled. 'Is there some fine and witty line that ends this Odyssean fable?'

'No, it is true,' insisted Nasiq. Helikaon listened as the Phrygian told the story of the archery tourney, and how Andromache had killed the assassin. 'The traitor had reached the king and was poised to strike him down when Andromache's arrow pierced his heart. The king praised her before the crowd, saying she was indeed a fit bride for his Hektor.'

'By the gods,' whispered Helikaon, 'she is a woman to treasure.'

'Prince Agathon obviously agrees with you. It is said he has asked Andromache to marry him, if Hektor does not return.'

'Has she . . . accepted Agathon's advances?'

'I have no knowledge that she has or she hasn't,' answered Nasiq. 'Of course she would be a fool not to. He is young, rich, and . . . depending on circumstances . . . could one day be king.'

'What else can you tell me of Andromache?'

Nasiq chuckled. 'She swam with a naked man, in front of the royal princes.'

'Is this gossip, or reality?' asked Helikaon, holding back his anger.

'Reality, my lord. A friend of mine was on the royal beach at the time. The king's daughter, Laodike, had invited a wounded Mykene warrior to the beach. All skin and bone he was, apparently. Hardly able to breathe. Andromache went swimming with him.'

'Argurios,' said Helikaon.

'Yes, that was the man. Famous, they say.'

'Go on.'

'When they emerged from the water Prince Deiphobos harangued her, and then the Mykene challenged him. It should have been amusing. A tottering skeleton demanding a sword. But he frightened Deiphobos. Agathon came to his rescue and calmed the situation. Who else would you like to hear of?'

'Was that what you meant by low tales?'

Nasiq leaned back. 'Now you are drawing me into dangerous territory, Golden One. You have already made it clear the lady is a friend of yours, and you want to hear no ill of her. So what would you have me say?'

Helikaon sat silently for a moment. 'Tell me all,' he said, at last.

'When I arrived here earlier the palace servants were talking of a man who offended you at a recent meeting. They said his head was put on display. I am rather fond of my head.'

'Your head is safe, Nasiq. You are too good a gossip to kill. My winter evenings would be dull indeed without you.'

'Very well – but remember you asked. Kreusa claimed to have discovered her frolicking naked with a female servant. This was reported to the king, who had the servant whipped, and then dismissed from the palace. Andromache was furious and accosted Kreusa publicly. Kreusa slapped her, and Andromache hit her with her fist. Said to have been a fine blow. An uppercut, according to one witness. Kreusa was knocked senseless and had to be carried to her bed. Everyone expected Andromache to be sent back in shame to her father. Priam chose to ignore the incident. Probably because he owed her his life. Now the palace is seething with rumours concerning the king and Andromache.'

'I have heard enough,' said Helikaon stiffly. 'How is Queen Hekabe?'

'She continues to cling to life. She is even entertaining guests. The youngest daughter of the king of Sparta is staying at the palace. Ostensibly she is here to find a suitable husband. The belief though is that her father sent her away to keep her safe. Mykene armies are massing on Sparta's borders. There is likely to be a war in the spring. And Sparta's small army cannot stand against Agamemnon's forces.'

Just then there was a soft knocking at the outer door. The old general Pausanius entered.

'My apologies for disturbing you, lord,' he said. 'I need to speak to you . . . privately.'

Nasiq rose. 'Matters of state must always take precedence,' he said, with a smile at Pausanius. Then he left the room.

'What is wrong?' asked Helikaon.

'The queen has left her apartments. Her handmaiden says she saw her walking towards Aphrodite's Leap.' The old general paled. 'I am sorry, my king. That was crass of me.'

'I will find her,' said Helikaon.

iii

As she walked the high rocky path in the faint light of dawn, Halysia could barely distinguish between the mist rising from the crumbling cliff edge under her bare feet and the dark fog lying across her mind. People talked of broken hearts, but they were wrong. Broken was somehow complete. Finished. Over. The real sensation was of continual breaking. An everlasting wound, sharp and jagged, like claws of bronze biting into the soft tissue of the heart. The mind became a cruel enemy, closing off reality for brief periods. Sometimes she would forget that Dio had been murdered. She would look at the sunlit sky and smile, and wonder – just for a moment – where he was. Then the truth would plunge home, and the bronze talons cleave once more into her wounded heart.

The dawn breeze was cool with the promise of rain. It was a long time since she had walked this path. Aphrodite's Leap they called it, though the words had been whispered behind the old king's back. His first wife had thrown herself from this cliff onto the unforgiving rocks hundreds of feet below. Halysia had heard the tale many times.

Wandering to the cliff edge she peered down. Mist was heavy upon the sea, and she wondered how it would feel to let go, to plummet down and end the agony of her life.

Thoughts of the past stirred in her. She remembered the bright days of her childhood in Zeleia when she and her brothers rode with the horse herds in summer, taking them from water pastures beside the dark river Aesipos to the cities of the coast. For days her feet would barely touch the ground as she travelled wrapped in a warm blanket on a gentle mare, listening to the night sounds across the plains.

Dio was already a fearless rider and she had planned to take him on a night journey, to camp out under the cold stars . . .

The sky was lightening, but the fog grew darker on her mind. She faltered to a halt and fell to her knees, her strength running out like water from a cup. She thought she heard a sound, running steps behind her, but she could not move to look round.

Her tortured mind returned again to the past, to comforting thoughts of her first arrival at Dardanos. True, she had not been happy then; she was just seventeen and homesick and frightened of the grey old man she was to marry. But now she always thought of it as a good time, because she was quickly pregnant with Dio. Anchises was not a bad husband, not unkind, and once Aeneas had been banished from his thoughts she was the mother of the son in whom he placed all his hopes. He gave Dio a toy horse, she recalled with a smile, that he had carved himself from pale wood. It was a crude thing, for he had little skill with his hands, but he had decorated it with gold leaf on mane and tail, and it had sky-blue chips of lapis lazuli for eyes.

She remembered the blue eyes of Garus, her personal bodyguard. He had soft blond eyelashes that lay gently on his cheek as he slept. She liked to wake him, to see the pale lashes open, to see his eyes rest on her in love and wonder.

He had fallen in the last desperate struggle, a spear through his chest, a sword in his belly, still trying to protect her and her son. He was dead before they all raped her. She was glad of that. He was dead before they flung Dio from the high walls.

She heard a thin keening sound. It was her own voice, but she knew of no way to stop it.

'Halysia!' Another voice in the fog. 'Halysia!'

She thought back to her childhood and her father holding her in his arms, smiling down at her. He smelled of horses, of their pungent hides he always wore. She reached up and pulled the greasy braids of his beard. He laughed and clutched her fiercely to his chest.

She felt his arms round her now, gentle and tender.

'Halysia. It is Aeneas. Come back to me.'

Aeneas. They called him Helikaon. There were many Aeneases, many Helikaons in her mind. There was the shy, frightened youth she had barely noticed, consumed as she was in her love for her baby. He disappeared one day on a foreign ship, and Anchises said he would not return. But he did, on a day of great terror. With Anchises dead she was sure Aeneas would have her killed, or kill her himself, and her son with her. But he didn't. He sailed away again after a few days, leaving Dio king and herself safe under the protection of Garus and old Pausanius. Those were the happiest years . . .

'Halysia, look at me. Look at me!'

She looked up, but it was not her father who held her. His eyes had been brown; these were blue. She remembered blue eyes . . .

'Halysia!' She felt strong hands shaking her. 'It is I, Aeneas. Say Aeneas.'

'Aeneas.' She frowned and looked around, at the treacherous cliff edge, and the grey sea far below their feet. 'What are you doing here?'

'Your maid saw you walking here. She feared for your life.'

'My life? I have no life.' He pulled her into his arms again and she rested her cheek on his shoulder. 'My son was my life, Aeneas,' she said calmly. 'I have no life without him.'

'He walks in the green fields of Elysium now,' he said. 'He has your bodyguard . . . was it Garus? . . . to hold his hand.'

'Do you believe that?' she asked, searching his face.

'Yes, I do.'

'Do you believe also in the power of dreams?'

'Dreams?'

'When I lay . . . as I thought . . . dying I had many dreams, Aeneas. And all but one of them were terrifying. I saw blood and fire, and a city burning. I saw the sea full of ships, carrying violent men. I saw war, Aeneas. I saw the fall of kings and the death of heroes. Oh . . . so much death.' She looked up at him. 'Do you believe in the power of dreams?'

He led her away from the cliff top and they sat on a green slope. 'Odysseus says there are two kinds of dreams. Some born of strong wine and rich food, and some sent by the gods. Of course you dreamt of blood and war. Evil men had attacked you. Your mind was full of visions of vileness.'

His words flowed over her, and she clung to the hope they were true. They sat in silence for a while. Then she sighed. 'Garus loved me. I was going to ask if you would object to our marriage. They took both my loves that night, Aeneas. My Dio, and strong-hearted Garus.'

'I did not know. And, no, I would have offered no objection. He was a good man. But you are young still, Halysia, and beautiful. If the gods will it you will find love again.'

'Love? I do so hope not, Aeneas. Yes, it was the only part of the dream that was bright and joyful. But if what I saw does come to pass, does it not mean that the other visions, of war and death, will also come?'

'I have no answers for such fears,' he said. 'What I do know is that you are the queen of Dardania, and the people love you. No-one will supplant you, and, while I live, no-one will ever threaten you again.'

'They love me now,' she said sadly. 'Will they love me still when the monster is born?'

'What monster?'

'The beast in my belly,' she whispered to him. 'It is evil, Aeneas. It is Mykene.'

He took her hand. 'I did not know you were pregnant. I am sorry, Halysia.' He sighed. 'But it is not a monster. It is merely a child, who will love you as Dio did.'

'It will be a boy, dark-haired and grey-eyed. I saw this too.'

'Then he will be a prince of Dardania. People are bred to evil, Halysia. I do not believe it is born in them. No matter how they are conceived.'

She relaxed in his arms. 'You are a good man, Aeneas.'

'My friends call me Helikaon. I would hope you are my friend.'

'I am your friend,' she said. 'I always will be.'

He smiled. 'Good. I will be leaving for Troy in a few days. I want you and Pausanius to continue meeting the leaders and resolving disputes. They trust you, Halysia. And now that they have witnessed my harshness they will be more amenable to your wisdom. Are you ready to be queen again?'

'I will do as you ask,' she said. 'For friendship.'

Then the vision came back to her, bright and shining. Helikaon standing before her in a white tunic edged with gold, and in his hand a bejewelled necklet.

Closing her eyes she prayed with all her strength that he would never bring her that golden gift.

iv

The young Hittite horseman rode at a gallop across the plain, bent low over the horse's neck, his imperial cloak of green and yellow stripes flowing behind him.

He glanced again at the dying sun and saw it was closing on the horizon. He could not ride after dark in this unknown country, and leaned forward on his horse to urge it on. He was determined to reach Troy before sunset.

He had been on the road for eight days, and had used five horses, at first changing them daily at imperial garrisons. But in this uncharted western end of the empire there were no troops stationed on a regular basis and this horse must last him until he reached Troy. Since leaving Sallapa, the last civilized city in the Hittite empire, he had followed the route he had memorized – keep the rising sun warm on your back, the setting sun between your horse's ears, and after four days you will see the great mountain called Ida. Skirt this to the north, and you will reach Troy and the sea.

The messenger, Huzziyas, had never seen the sea. He had lived all his nineteen years in and around the capital Hattusas, deep in the heart of Hittite lands. This was his first important commission as an imperial messenger and he was determined to fulfil it with speed and efficiency. But he was eager to gaze upon the sea when the emperor's task was done. His hand crept to his breast again and he nervously touched the papers hidden in his leather tunic.

He was riding now across a flat green plain. He could see a plateau in front of him, the sun falling directly towards it. The last sunlight was shining off something on the heights of the plateau. Troy is roofed with gold, they had told him, but he had scoffed at this. 'Do you think me a fool?' he asked. 'If it is roofed with gold why do bandits not come and steal the roofs?'

'You will see,' they replied.

It was almost dark by the time he rode up to the city. He could see nothing but great shadowed walls towering above him. Suddenly his confidence evaporated and he felt like a small boy again. He walked his tired horse round the south of the walls, as instructed, until he reached the high wooden gates. One gate had been opened a little, and six riders awaited him, silent men clad in high-crested helmets seated on tall horses.

He cleared his throat of the dust of travel, and called out to them in the foreign words he had been schooled in. 'I come from Hattusas. I have a message for King Priam!'

He was beckoned forward and rode slowly through the gate. Two horsemen rode in front of him, two at his sides, and two behind. They were all armed and armoured and they said nothing as they made their way through the darkened streets. Huzziyas looked curiously around him but in the torchlight he could see little. Steadily, they climbed towards the citadel.

They passed through the palace gates and halted at a great building lined with red pillars and lit with hundreds of torches. The riders sat their horses and waited until a man clad in long white robes hurried out. He was grey-faced and his eyes were red-rimmed and watery. He peered at Huzziyas.

'You are an imperial messenger?' he snapped.

Huzziyas was relieved he spoke the Hittite tongue.

'I am,' he answered with pride. 'I have travelled day and night to bring an important message to the Trojan king.'

'Give it to me.' The man held out his hand, gesturing impatiently. The Hittite took out the precious paper. It had been wrapped round a stick and sealed with the imperial seal, then placed in a hollow wooden tube and sealed again at each end. Huzziyas ceremoniously handed the tube to the wet-eyed man, who almost snatched it from him, merely glancing at the seals before breaking them and unrolling the paper.

He frowned and Huzziyas saw disappointment on his face.

'You know what this says?' he asked the young man.

'I do,' said Huzziyas importantly. 'It says the emperor is coming.'

XXVII

The Fallen Prince

i

IN THE DAYS FOLLOWING HER FIRST MEETING WITH ARGURIOS, LAODIKE had found herself thinking more and more of the Mykene warrior. It was most odd. He was not good-looking, like Helikaon or Agathon. His features were hard and angular. He was certainly not charming, and seemed possessed of no great wit. And yet he had begun to dominate her thoughts in a most disconcerting manner.

When he had been beside her on the beach she had experienced an almost maternal longing, a desire to help him regain his physical strength, to watch him become again the man he had been. At least, that was how it had begun. Now her thoughts were more obsessive, and she realized she was missing him.

Xander had told her of the soldier who had walked Argurios to the beach, saying that he had treated him with great respect. Laodike knew Polydorus and had called out to him one afternoon, when the blond-haired soldier was off duty and walking through the palace gardens.

'It is a fine day,' she began. 'For the time of year, I mean.'

'Indeed it is,' he answered. 'Is there something you need?'

'No, not at all. I wanted to . . . thank you for your courtesy

358

towards the wounded Mykene. The boy, Xander, spoke of it.'

Now he looked bemused and Laodike felt embarrassment swelling. 'I am sorry. I am obviously delaying you. Are you going into the lower town?'

'Yes, I am meeting the parents of my bride-to-be. But first I must find a gift for them.'

'There is a trader,' she said, 'on the Street of Thetis. He is a silversmith, and crafts the most beautiful small statues of the goddess Demeter, and the babe Persephone. It is said they are lucky pieces.'

'I have heard of him, but I fear I could not afford such a piece.'

Now Laodike felt foolish. Of course he couldn't. He was a soldier, not a nobleman with rich farms, or horse herds, or trading ships. Polydorus waited, and the moment became awkward. Finally she took a deep breath. 'What do you know of the Mykene?' she asked.

'He is a great warrior,' answered Polydorus, relaxing. 'I learned of him when I was still a child. He has fought in many battles, and under the old king was twice Mykene champion. You have heard of the bridge of Partha?'

'No.'

'The Mykene were in retreat. A rare thing! They had crossed the bridge, but the enemy were close behind. Argurios stood upon the bridge and defied the enemy to kill him. They came at him one at a time, but he defeated every champion they sent.'

'Why did they not all just rush at him in a charge? One man could not have stopped them all, surely?'

'I suppose that is true. Perhaps they valued his courage. Perhaps they wanted to test themselves against the best. I do not know.'

'Thank you, Polydorus,' she said. 'And now you must go and find that gift.' He bowed his head and turned away. On impulse she reached out and touched his arm. The young soldier was shocked. 'Go to the silversmith,' she said, with a smile. 'And tell him I sent you. Pick a fine statue and instruct him to come to me for payment.'

'Thank you. I . . . do not know what to say.'

'Then say nothing, Polydorus,' she told him.

That afternoon she had walked down to the House of Serpents, ostensibly to collect more medicines for Hekabe. In fact, though, she wandered the grounds until she caught sight of Argurios. He was chopping wood. She stood in the shadows of a stand of trees and watched him. He had put on weight, and his movements were smooth and graceful, the axe rising and falling, the wood splitting cleanly.

She stood for a while, trying to think of what she might say to him. She wished she had worn a more colourful dress, and perhaps the gold pendant with the large sapphire. Everyone said it was a beautiful piece. Then grim reality struck home, and her heart sank. You are a plain woman, she told herself. No amount of gold or pretty jewellery can disguise it. And you are about to make a fool of yourself.

Turning away she decided to return to the palace, but she had taken no more than a few steps before the healer Machaon came round the corner of a building and saw her. He bowed deeply. 'I did not know you were here, Laodike,' he said. 'Has your mother's condition worsened?'

'No. I was just . . . out walking,' she replied, reddening.

He glanced beyond her to where Argurios was still working. 'His recovery is amazing,' he said. 'His breathing is almost normal, and his strength is returning at a fine rate. Would that all those I treated showed such determination. How goes it, Argurios?' he called out.

The Mykene thunked the axe into a round of wood, and swung to face them. Then he walked across the grass towards them. Laodike tried to breathe normally, but felt panic rising.

'Greetings,' said Argurios.

'And to you, warrior,' she said. 'I see that you are almost well.'

'Aye, I feel power in me again.'

Silence fell. 'Ah well,' said Machaon, with a knowing smile, 'I have patients to see to.' Bowing once more, he went on his way.

Laodike stood very quietly, not knowing what to say. She looked at Argurios. His cheeks were shaved, the jutting chin beard trimmed, and sweat gleamed on his bare chest. 'It is a fine day,' she managed. 'For the time of year, I mean.' The blue sky was streaked with clouds, but at that moment the sun was shining brightly.

'I am glad you came,' he said suddenly. 'I have been thinking of you constantly,' he added, his tone awkward, his gaze intense.

In that moment Laodike's nervousness vanished, and she felt a sense of calm descend on her. In the silence that followed she saw Argurios becoming ill at ease. 'I never did know how to speak other than plainly,' he said.

'Perhaps you would like to walk for a while in the sunshine. Though, first, I suggest you put on your tunic.'

They walked through the gardens and out into the lower town. Argurios said little, but the silence was comfortable. Finally they sat on a stone bench beside a well. Glancing back, she saw that two men had followed them, and were now sitting on a wall some distance away. 'Do you know them?' she asked, pointing.

His expression darkened. 'They have been hired by Helikaon to protect me. There are others who come at night, and stand beneath the trees.'

'That was kind of him.'

'Kind!'

'Why does it make you angry?'

'Helikaon is my enemy. I have no wish to be beholden to the man.' He glanced at the two bodyguards. 'And any half-trained Mykene soldier could scatter those fools in a heartbeat.'

'You are proud of your people.'

'We are strong. We are unafraid. Yes, I am proud.' A group of women carrying empty buckets approached the well. Laodike and Argurios moved away, up the slope towards the Scaean Gate. Passing through it they climbed to the battlements of the great wall and strolled along the ramparts.

'Why were you banished?' asked Laodike.

He shrugged. 'Lies were told and believed. I can make little sense of it. There are men at the royal court with honeyed tongues. They fill the king's ear with flattery. The old king I could talk to. Atreus was a warrior – a fighting man. You could sit with him at a campfire, like any other soldier.'

Another silence grew. It did not bother Laodike, who was enjoying his company, but Argurios became increasingly uncomfortable. 'I have never known how to talk to women,' he said awkwardly. 'I do not know what interests them. At this moment I wish I did.'

She laughed. 'Life,' she told him. 'Birth and growth. Flowers that bloom and fade, seasons that bring sunshine or rain. Clothes that mirror the beauty that is all around us, the blue of the sky, the green of the grass, the gold of the sun. But mostly we are interested in people. In their lives and their dreams. Do you have a family back in Mykene?'

'No. My parents died years ago.'

'Not a wife at home?'

'No.'

Laodike let the silence grow once more. She gazed out over the bay. There were few ships now, save for some fishing boats. 'You were very rash with Dios,' she said.

'I did not like the way he spoke to you,' he told her, and she saw anger again in his eyes.

The sun was low in the sky and Laodike turned. 'I must be getting back,' she said.

'Will you visit me again?' His nervousness was obvious, and it filled her with a confidence she rarely experienced in the company of men.

'I might come tomorrow.'

He smiled. 'I hope you do,' he told her.

For the next ten days she came every day and they walked the great walls together. There was little conversation, but she enjoyed those times more than any she could remember. Especially the moment she slipped on a rampart step, and his arm swept round her before she could fall. Laodike leaned in to him then, her head upon his shoulder. It was exquisite, and she wished it could last for ever.

ii

Andromache thought she had never seen such a tall man as the Hittite emperor. Hattusilis was even taller than Priam, and of much the same age, but he stooped as he walked and Andromache was sure he had bad feet, for he shuffled a little as if anxious not to lift them far from the ground.

He was thin to the point of emaciation, his hair oiled black and partly covered by a close-fitting cap. He glanced around Priam's great, gold-filled *megaron*, looking strangely out of place in his simple, unadorned leather riding clothes. He had ridden into the city, but Andromache knew the Hittite force had been camped out on the plain of the Simoeis overnight while the emperor rested, and that he had travelled much of the way from his capital in a rich and comfortable carriage.

Hattusilis carried two curved swords, one at his waist, the other unsheathed in his hand, and Andromache wondered at the frenzied negotiations that had taken place between the two sides since dawn to agree to that. He was attended by a retinue of eunuchs and counsellors, all wearing colourfully patterned kilts clasped at the waist with belts of braided gold wire, some attired in bright shawls, others bare-chested. All were unarmed, of course.

One huge half-naked bodyguard, so muscle-bound that Andromache decided he was more ornament than use, stood close to the emperor's shoulder.

Hattusilis III, emperor of the Hittites, advanced halfway down the *megaron*, then stopped. Priam, standing in front of his carved and gilded throne, walked forward to meet him, flanked by Polites and Agathon. There was a pause while the two men locked eyes, then Priam bowed briefly. Had the Trojan king ever bowed to anyone before? Andromache doubted it. It was only his concern for Hektor that persuaded him to make this gesture, she guessed, even to his emperor.

'Greetings,' said Priam loudly, but without enthusiasm. 'We are honoured to welcome you to Troy.' Each courteous word seemed to cost him effort. He added flatly, 'Our people rejoice.'

A small bald-headed man wearing striped robes of yellow and green spoke quietly to the emperor. Andromache realized this was the translator.

The emperor smiled thinly and spoke. The little man said, 'Troy is a valued vassal kingdom to the great Hittite empire. The emperor takes a kindly interest in his subjects.'

Priam's face grew red with anger. He said, 'This *vassal* is honoured to fight the emperor's battles for him. We are told the Trojan Horse won a great victory at Kadesh for the emperor.'

Hattusilis replied, 'The greater Hittite army has crushed the ambitions of the pharaohs for generations to come. We are grateful to Troy for its brave cavalry.'

Priam could contain his impatience no longer. 'My son has not returned from Kadesh. Do you bring news of him?'

Hattusilis handed the unsheathed sword to the muscle-bound bodyguard, then placed both his hands upon his heart. The *megaron* fell silent. The bald translator said, 'We regret Hektor is dead. He died a valiant death in the cause of the Hittite empire.' The emperor spoke again. 'Hektor was a good friend to us. He fought many battles for the empire.' His dark gaze rested on Priam's stricken face, and Andromache saw genuine concern there. 'We grieve for him as if he were our own son.'

Andromache heard a soft sigh from beside her, and she put her arm round Laodike as the young woman sagged against her. Hektor dead, she thought. Hektor is really dead. Her mind buzzed with possibilities but she ruthlessly pushed them away to listen to Priam's words.

The king looked straight into the black eyes of the emperor. 'My son cannot be dead,' he said, but there was a tremor in his voice.

Hattusilis gestured and two unarmed Hittite soldiers struggled forward with a heavy wooden chest. At a nod from the emperor they unbarred it and flung back the lid, which clanged hollowly against the stone floor.

The emperor said, 'His body was discovered with those of his men. They had been trapped, surrounded and killed by the Egypteians. By the time he was found his body had decayed, so I have returned his armour to you as proof of his death.'

Priam stepped forward and reached into the chest. He took out a huge bronze breastplate decorated with silver and gold. From where Andromache stood she could see that the pattern represented a golden horse racing across silver waves. Laodike said in a small breathless voice, 'Hektor. It is Hektor's.'

Hattusilis stepped forward and took from the chest a heavily decorated gold urn. 'Following the custom of your people we burned the body and placed Hektor's bones in this vessel.'

He held it out. When Priam did not move Polites darted forward and took the golden urn from the emperor's hands.

Never in her life had Andromache felt such a confusion of emotions. She grieved for Laodike's pain at the death of her brother, for the loss on the faces of the people gathered around the *megaron*, the soldiers, counsellors and palace servants. She even grieved for Priam as he stood there holding the breastplate, a stunned look on his face, desolation in his eyes as he stared at the funeral urn.

Yet in her heart joy welled up irresistibly. Her hands flew to her throat for fear she would cry out for gladness. She was free!

Then Priam turned away from the emperor and walked with halting steps to his throne. Hugging the breastplate to his chest he slumped down. A gasp of shock came from the Hittite retinue. No-one sat in the presence of the emperor. Andromache glanced at Agathon, expecting the prince to step in and ease the situation, but he was standing, almost mesmerized, staring at his father, his expression torn between sadness and shock. Andromache felt for him. Then the dark-haired Dios moved smoothly forward, bowing deeply to Hattusilis.

'My apologies, great lord. My father is overcome with grief. He intends no disrespect. Priam, and the sons of Priam, remain, as always, your most loyal followers.'

The emperor spoke, and the translator's words echoed in the silent *megaron*. 'There is no slight. When a great hero falls it becomes men to show their feelings truly. Hektor's courage did indeed turn the battle in our favour. I would have expected no less from him. That is why I felt it right to come myself to this far city, so that all would know that Hektor was honoured by those he served most heroically.'

With that the emperor swung on his heel and walked from the *megaron*.

iii

Shortly before dark a hooded and cloaked figure slipped out through the Dardanian Gate into the lower town. One of the gate guards caught a glimpse of the man's face and turned to speak to his colleague, but the other soldier was part-way through a good joke about a Hittite, a horse and a donkey, so the first guard laughed and said nothing. There was no reason to question anyone leaving the citadel, after all.

The hooded man made his way through the eastern quarter to where the city engineers had been digging a wide fortification ditch, designed to stop the advance of horses and chariots. Houses all along the line of the trench had been emptied to permit the work. But the digging had revealed a horde of burial jars, dating from many generations ago, which were now being carefully dug up and moved to another site south-east of the city.

In the grey twilight the man identified a white house with a yellow mark like a paw-print on the door. Looking around him, he entered the abandoned house swiftly, and waited in the shadow of an inner doorway. A short while later two others entered. 'Are you here?' a man with thin reddish hair asked quietly.

The hooded man stepped from the shadows. 'I am here, Erekos,' he said.

The Mykene ambassador's voice betrayed his anxiety. 'No names, if you please, Prince.'

The hooded man snorted. 'This meeting-place is well chosen. No-one will come within a hundred paces of it. They fear the shades of the dead are lingering around the burial ground.'

'Perhaps they are right,' said the ambassador nervously.

'Let us not waste time on religious debate,' snapped the third man, a tall, white-haired warrior. 'The death of Hektor is a gift from the gods. We must seize the chance now.'

There was silence for a moment.

'And what of the Hittites, Kolanos?' the hooded man said coldly. 'You think we should spark a revolution while the emperor is in Troy? Do you have any idea of the numbers of troops his sons could bring? And they would cry out for joy at the opportunity. Troy's independence is based on three simple facts. We pay enormous taxes to fund the Hittite wars, we are far distant from the centre of their empire, and we send the finest warriors to aid them. But there are those who look upon Troy with great envy and greed. We must offer them no insult, no opportunity to seek our ruin.'

'This is all true, Prince,' put in Erekos, 'but even if we wait for the emperor's departure, will he not send men to the aid of Priam?'

'Not if Priam is dead,' said the hooded man. 'It is well known that Hattusilis has little liking for him. But then who does? The emperor has far more important worries than domestic problems in Troy. The Hittite army leaves at dawn. When Hattusilis hears Priam is dead I will send a rider to him, pledging my continued allegiance. He will, I believe, accept it. We must be patient and wait nine more days.'

'It is easy for you to be patient, sitting in your palace,' sneered Kolanos. 'But it is not so easy to conceal four galleys off the coast for so long.'

'Easy?' snapped the hooded man. 'Nothing about this venture will prove *easy*. I have troops loyal to me – but that loyalty will wear thin when the murders begin. Easy? You think it will be easy to defeat the Eagles? Every one of them is a veteran of many battles. They were promoted for their courage and for their fighting abilities. They were trained by Hektor.'

'And like Hektor they will die. They have not come against Mykene warriors before,' replied Kolanos. 'I have the best with me. Invincible. The Eagles will fall.'

'I hope you are right,' said the prince. 'We will also have the advantage of surprise. Even so it is vital that we do not deviate from the plan. Apart from the Eagles the only people to die will be the men inside the *megaron* when we attack: Priam, and those of his sons and counsellors who will be there. The deaths must be swift, and the palace taken by dawn.'

'Why wait nine days?' asked Erekos. 'Do you need so long?'

'The king has been rotating the troops who guard the Upper City,' answered the prince. 'I will need the time to ensure *both* regiments are loyal to me.'

'With two thousand troops against a hundred or so Eagles why do you need us at all?' Kolanos asked.

'I will not have two thousand troops. You need to understand the complexities here, Kolanos. *My* regiment will fight for me without question. Other Trojan units will serve me loyally once I am king. The regiment guarding the walls will be led by one of my men. He will ensure they keep the gates closed and remain at their posts. But not even he could command them to *attack* the palace and kill the king. Why do I need you and your men? Because Trojan troops should not be used in the slaughter of Priam and his sons. My regiment will take the two palace gates, hold the walls, and do battle with the Eagles. Then, when the King and his followers are safely contained in the palace itself, you and your Mykene will assault the *megaron* and kill all men within.'

'What of the royal daughters and the women of the palace?' asked Kolanos.

'Your men can take their pleasures with the servants. No royal daughters are to be harmed in any way. Enjoy the others as you will. There is one woman, however, named Andromache. She is tall, with long red hair, and cursed with too much pride. I am sure your men will find a way to humble her. It would please me to hear her beg.'

'And you will. I promise you,' said Kolanos. 'There is nothing quite so sweet after a battle as the squealing of captured women.'

Erekos spoke: 'Thoughts of rape should be left until the battle is over, Kolanos. Tell me, Prince, what of the other troops close to the city? The barracks in the Lower Town contain a full regiment, and there is a cavalry detachment based on the Plain of Simoeis.'

The prince smiled. 'As I said, the gates will be closed until dawn. I know well the generals commanding the other regiments. They will swear allegiance to me – if Priam is dead.'

'Might I ask one favour?' said Kolanos.

'Of course.'

'That the traitor Argurios be invited to the *megaron* that night.'

'Are you insane?' snapped Erekos. 'You want the greatest warrior of the Mykene facing us?'

Kolanos laughed. 'He will be unarmed. Is that not so, Prince?'

'Yes. All weapons will be left at the gate. The king allows no swords or daggers in his presence.'

But Erekos was not convinced. 'He was unarmed when he defeated five armed assassins. It seems to me an unnecessary risk. Many of the warriors with you hold him still in high regard. I urge you to withdraw this request, Kolanos.'

'Agamemnon King wants him dead,' said Kolanos. 'He wants him cut down by his former comrades. It will be a fitting punishment for his treachery. I will not withdraw my request. What say you, Prince?'

'I agree with Erekos. But if you wish it I shall see that he is there.'

'I do.'

'Then it will be done.'

XXVIII

Of Ancient Gods

i

GERSHOM HAD NEVER ENJOYED RIDING. IN EGYPTE THE HORSES HAD been small, their buttock-pounding gait bruisingly uncomfortable for a heavy man. He had also felt faintly ludicrous, his long legs hanging close to the ground. But the Thessalian-bred horse he now rode was a joy. Just under sixteen hands, golden-bodied, with white mane and tail, it all but flew across the terrain. At full run there was little upward movement of the beast's back and Gershom settled down to revel in the speed. Helikaon rode alongside him, on a mount the twin of Gershom's own. Together they thundered across the open ground under a pale, cloudy sky. At last Helikaon slowed his horse, then patted its sleek neck. Gershom drew alongside.

'Magnificent beasts,' he said.

'Good for speed,' said Helikaon, 'but poor for war. Too skittish and prone to panic when swords clash and arrows fly. I am breeding them with our own ponies. Perhaps their foals' temperament will be less nervous.'

Swinging their mounts, they rode back to where they had left the baggage pony. The beast was grazing on a hillside. Helikaon gathered the lead rope, and they set off again towards the southwest.

Gershom was happy to be on the move again. The fortress of Dardanos – despite being a rough dwelling place compared to the palaces back home – was still a reminder of a world he had lost, and he was glad of the chance to accompany the Golden One back to Troy.

'I do not think that merchant would have betrayed me,' he said, as they rode.

'Perhaps not knowingly,' said Helikaon, 'but people gossip. Troy is larger, and there is less chance of your being recognized.'

Gershom glanced around at the bleak landscape. The old general, Pausanius, had warned Helikaon that there were bandits abroad in these hills, and had urged him to take a company of soldiers, as a personal guard. Helikaon had refused.

'I have promised to make these lands safe,' he had said. 'The leaders know me now. When they see the king riding through their communities without armed escort it will give them confidence.'

Pausanius had been unconvinced. Gershom did not believe it either.

Once they were travelling together he became convinced that Helikaon had needed to get away from Dardanos, and all the trappings and duties of royalty. Yet with each mile they rode Helikaon grew more tense.

That night, as they camped in the foothills, beneath a stand of cypress trees, Gershom said, 'What is worrying you?'

Helikaon did not answer, merely added dry wood to the small campfire, then sat quietly by it. Gershom did not press the question further. After a while Helikaon spoke. 'Did you enjoy being a prince?'

'Aye, I did – but not as much as my half-brother, Rameses. He was desperate to become pharaoh, to lead Egypteian armies into battle, to build his own great pillars at the Temple of Luxor, to see his face carved on massive statues. Me, I just loved being fawned upon by beautiful women.'

'Did it not concern you that the women only fawned upon you because they were obliged to?'

'Why would that be a concern? The result is the same.'

'Only for you.'

Gershom chuckled. 'You Sea People think too much. The slave women at the palace were there for *my* pleasure. That was their purpose. What did it matter whether or not they *desired* to be slave women? When you are hungry and you decide to kill a sheep do you stop and wonder how the sheep feels about it?'

'An interesting point,' observed Helikaon. 'I will think on it.'

'It is not a point to *think* on,' argued Gershom. 'It was supposed to end the debate, not widen it.'

'The purpose of debate is to explore issues, not end them.'

'Very well. Then let us debate the reason for your original question. Why did you ask if I enjoyed being a prince?'

'Perhaps I was just making conversation,' said Helikaon.

'No. The first reason was to deflect me from questioning you about your concerns. The second was more complex, but still linked to the first.'

'Well, now you have me intrigued,' said Helikaon. 'Enlighten me.'

Gershom shook his head. 'You need enlightenment, Golden One? I think not. Back in Egypt there are statues of mythical beasts that used to fascinate me. Creatures with the heads of eagles, the bodies of lions, the tails of serpents. My grandfather told me they actually represented men. We are all of us hybrid beasts. There is the savage in us, who would tear out an enemy's heart and devour it raw. There is the lover, who composes songs to the woman who owns his soul. There is the father, who holds his child close, and would die to protect it from all harm. Three creatures in one man. And there are more. In every one of us is the total of all we have ever been, the sullen child, the arrogant youth, the suckling babe. Every fear endured in childhood is lodged somewhere in here.' He tapped his temple. 'And every act of heroism or cowardice, generosity or meanness of spirit.'

'This is fascinating,' said Helikaon, 'but I feel as if I have just sailed into a mist. What is the point you are making?'

'That *is* the point I am making. Our lives are spent sailing in the mist, hoping for a burst of sunlight that can make sense of who we are.'

'I know who I am, Gershom.'

'No, you don't. Are you the man who concerns himself about the secret desires of slave women, or the man who cuts the head from a farmer who speaks out of turn? Are you the god who rescued a child on Kypros, or the madman who burned to death fifty sailors?'

'This conversation has lost its appeal,' said Helikaon, his voice cold.

Gershom felt his anger swell. 'I see,' he said. 'So the issues that *can* be debated are only those that do not affect the actions of the Golden One. Now you are truly becoming a king, Helikaon. Next you will surround yourself with sycophants who whisper to you of your greatness, and offer no criticism.'

Gathering up his blanket he lay down, facing the fire, his heart hammering. The night was cold, and he could scent rain on the breeze. He was annoyed at himself for reacting with such anger. Truth was, he was fond of the young king, and admired him greatly. Helikaon was capable of great kindness and loyalty. He was also courageous and principled. These attributes were rare, in Gershom's experience. But he also knew the dangers Helikaon would face as his power grew. After a while he threw back his blanket and sat up. Helikaon was sitting with his back to a tree, a blanket round his shoulders. 'I am sorry, my friend,' said Gershom. 'It is not my place to harangue you.'

'No, it is not,' Helikaon replied. 'But I have been thinking of what you said, and there was truth in it. Your grandfather is a wise man.'

'He is. Do you know the story of Osiris and Set?'

'Egypteian gods at war with one another?'

'Yes. Osiris is the hero god, the Lord of Light. Set is his brother, a creature vile and depraved. They are in a constant war to the death. My grandfather told me of them when I was young. He said that we carry Osiris and Set struggling within us. All of us are capable of great compassion and love, or hatred and horror. Sadly we can take joy from both.'

'I know that is true,' said Helikaon. 'I felt it as those sailors burned. The memory of it is shameful.'

'Grandfather would say that when you burned those sailors Set was dominant in your soul. It is Osiris who feels the shame. That is why you dislike being king, Helikaon. Such power brings Set closer to total control. And you fear the man you would become if ever the Osiris in you was slain.'

Gershom fell silent. Helikaon added fuel to the fire, then walked to the pack pony and brought back some bread and dried meat. The silence grew as the two men ate. Then Helikaon stretched himself out by the fire, and covered himself with his cloak.

Gershom dozed for a while. The night grew colder, and a clap of thunder sounded. Lightning blazed across the heavens. Helikaon awoke and the two men ran to where the horses were tethered. The beasts were frightened, ears flat to their skulls. Helikaon and Gershom led them away from the trees and out onto open ground.

Rain began to fall, slowly at first, then in a torrent.

Lightning flashed, and by its light Gershom saw a cave high up on the hillside. He beckoned to Helikaon and they led the mounts up the slope. It was not easy. The golden horses – as Helikaon had warned – were skittish, rearing constantly and trying to break free. The little baggage pony was calmer, but even he dragged back on the lead rope when the thunder crashed. Both men were weary when they finally reached the cave.

Leading the horses inside, they tethered them. Then the two men sat at the cave mouth, watching the storm wash over the land.

'I used to enjoy storms,' said Gershom. 'But since the ship-wreck . . .' He shivered at the memories.

'It will pass swiftly,' said Helikaon. Then he looked at Gershom. 'I thank you for your honesty.'

Gershom chuckled. 'Always been my curse – to speak my mind. Hard to think of anyone I haven't insulted at some time or other. Are you planning to stay long in Troy?'

Helikaon shook his head. 'I will attend the funeral feast for Hektor.' He shivered suddenly. 'Just saying the words chills the soul.'

'You were friends?'

'More than friends. I still cannot accept that he is gone.' He smiled suddenly. 'Some five years ago I rode with Hektor. Priam had sent him and two hundred of the Trojan Horse to Thraki, to aid a local king against some raiders. We were pursuing an enemy force through woodland and they caught us in an ambush. Once we had fought our way clear we realized Hektor was not with us. Someone then recalled seeing him struck in the head by a hurled rock. Night was falling, but we rode swiftly back to the battle site. The bandits had removed the bodies of their fallen. Six of our dead were there, but Hektor was not among them. We knew then that he had been taken. The Thrakians were known to torture their captives, slicing off fingers, putting out eyes. I sent out scouts and we went in search of their camp. We found it just before dawn, and as we crept forward we could hear the sounds of merriment. And there, standing tall in the firelight, a huge cup of wine in his hand, was Hektor. He was regaling the drunken raiders with ribald stories, and they were shrieking with laughter.' Helikaon sighed. 'That is how I will remember him.'

'But you have a second reason for this journey,' said Gershom.

'Are you a seer, Gershom?'

'No. But I saw you talking to Hektor's betrothed, and I heard you call her goddess.'

Helikaon laughed. 'Yes, I did. I fell in love with her, Gershom. If she feels the same I mean to make her my wife, though I will probably have to offer Priam a mountain of gold for her.'

'If she feels the same?' echoed Gershom. 'What difference does it make? Buy her anyway.'

Helikaon shook his head. 'You can buy gold that is bright as the sun, and diamonds as pale as the moon. But you cannot buy the sun. You cannot own the moon.'

ii

As dawn approached Laodike wrapped herself in a shawl and walked out of the palace. The streets were silent and empty, save for a few stray dogs seeking scraps. She liked walking, particularly in the fresh air of the early morning, and thought she must know more about the city and its everyday life than any soldier or common worker. She knew which baker had the first loaves fresh and aromatic outside his bakery before dawn. She knew the prostitutes and their regular patrols as well as she knew those of the Trojan regiments. She knew when the first lamb was born on the hillside at the end of winter because Poimen the ancient shepherd, blessed with four generations of sons, would open his only jug of wine of the year and get rolling drunk, then sleep it off in the street in the dawn air, barred from his home by his tiny ferocious wife.

Laodike walked on out of the town, her sad steps taking her across the new defensive ditch by a bridge, then down towards the Scamander.

Mist lay heavy and grey in the river valley. Beyond it the hills were touched with pink still, though the sun was rising in the sky behind her. She could hear no sounds but the crowing of cocks and the bleating of sheep in the distance.

She walked on towards the tomb of Ilos, on a small hill between the city and the river. Ilos was her great-grandfather and a hero of Troy. Hektor would often come here and talk to his ancestor when he was troubled. So she came now, hoping to find comfort.

She plodded up to the small cairn of rocks and sat down on the short, sheep-cropped grass, facing the city. Her body no longer busy, her grief overwhelmed her again and tears welled in her eyes.

How could he be dead? How could the gods be so cruel?

Laodike could see him now, his infectious smile lifting her heart, the sun glinting on the gold of his hair. He was like the dawn, she thought. Whenever he entered a room spirits lifted. When she was young and frightened Hektor was always the rock she would run to. And he was the man who would have persuaded Priam to allow Argurios to marry her.

Shame touched her then, and with it the weight of guilt. Are you sad because he has passed to the Elysian Fields, or are you thinking of yourself, she wondered?

'I am so sorry, Hektor,' she whispered. Then the tears flowed once more.

A shadow fell across her and she looked up. The sun was behind the figure, bright and dazzling, and, just for a moment, as her tear-swollen eyes took in the glinting breastplate, she thought it was the ghost of her brother, come to comfort her. Then he knelt beside her, and she saw it was Argurios. She had not seen him for five days now, and she had sent him no message.

'Oh, Argurios, I cannot stop weeping.'

His arm curved round her shoulder. 'I have seen the same throughout the city. He must have been a great man, and I am sorry I did not know him.'

'How did you know I would be here?'

'You told me that when troubles were weighing heavy you liked to walk through the city in the dawn light. You talked of an old shepherd in these hills.'

'And how did you guess I would be here today?'

'I did not. I have been at the Scaean Gate every day at dawn for the last five days.'

'I am sorry, Argurios. It was thoughtless of me. I should have sent a messenger to you.'

There was a silence between them, and then Laodike asked, 'Where are your bodyguards?'

He smiled, a rare event. 'I am stronger now, and faster. I walked through the city a few days ago, then doubled back and came upon them. I told them I had no more need of their services, and they agreed to leave me be.'

'Just like that? So simply?'

'I spoke to them . . . firmly,' he said.

'You frightened them, didn't you?'

'Some men are easily frightened,' he replied.

His face was inches away from hers, and as she looked into his eyes Laodike felt the pain and sorrow of the last few days ease away. This was the face she had so often summoned to mind. His eyes were not just brown, as she'd remembered, but had flecks of hazel and gold in them, and his eyebrows were finely shaped. He watched her steadily and she lowered her gaze. There was a warm flowering in the pit of her belly and she became aware of the rub of cloth against her skin.

She felt a touch on her arm and saw his hand lightly graze her skin, barely stirring the fair hairs. The warmth in her belly flared.

Reaching up she began to untie the thongs holding Argurios' breastplate in place. His powerful hand closed over hers. 'You are a king's daughter,' he reminded her.

'You do not want me?'

His face was flushed. 'I never wanted anything so much in all my life.'

'The king will never allow us to wed, Argurios. He will order you from Troy. He will send me away. I cannot bear the thought. But we have this moment. This is our moment, Argurios!' His hand fell away. Even as a child she had helped Hektor don and remove his armour. I have few skills, she thought to herself, but taking off a cuirass is one of them. Her nimble hands untied the thongs and Argurios lifted the breastplate clear.

Unbuckling his sword and laying it by the breastplate, he led her into the circle of stones by the tomb of Ilos, and they lay together on the grass. He kissed her then, and for a long time made no other move. Taking his hand she lifted it to her breast. His touch was gentle – more gentle in that moment than she desired. Her lips pressed against his, her mouth hungry to taste him. His hands became less hesitant, pulling at her gown, lifting it high. Laodike raised her arms and he threw the gown clear. Within moments they were both naked. Laodike revelled in the feel of his warm skin against hers, the hard muscles under her fingers. Then came the swift pain of entry, and the exquisite sense of becoming one with the man she loved.

Afterwards she lay in a daze of joy and satisfaction, her body warm and fulfilled, her mind swimming with shame and exhilaration. Slowly she became aware of the grass under her and the uneven ground pressing into her back.

She lay with her head in the crook of Argurios' shoulder. She realized he had not spoken for a while. She twisted to look up at him, thinking him asleep, but he was staring up at the sky, his face, as always, grave.

Laodike was suddenly filled with foreboding. Was he regretting his actions? Would he leave her now? He turned to look down at her. Seeing the look on her face, he said, 'Are you hurt? Did I hurt you?'

'No. It was wonderful.' Feeling foolish, but unable to stop herself, she said, 'It was the most wonderful thing that's ever happened to me. The maidservants told me . . .' She hesitated.

'Told you what?'

'Told me . . . told me it was painful and unpleasant. It was a bit painful,' she conceded, 'but it wasn't unpleasant.'

'It wasn't unpleasant,' he repeated, smiling a little. Then he kissed her again, long and tenderly.

She lay back, all doubts in her mind vanished. The look in his eyes told her everything she needed to know. She had never been so happy. She knew this moment would live with her for the rest of her life.

Suddenly she sat up, her shawl falling from her naked breasts, and pointed to the east.

A great flock of swans were beating their way on silent white wings over the city towards the sea. Laodike had never seen more than one or two swans before and she was awestruck by the sight of hundreds of the great birds flying overhead, for a moment blotting out the sunlight like a living cloud.

They watched silently as the flock winged its way to the west, disappearing at last into the grey mist on the horizon.

Laodike felt a touch on her bare leg and looked down. A soft white feather lay curled on her skin, motionless as though it had always been there. She picked it up and showed it to her lover.

'Is it an omen?' she wondered.

'Birds are always omens,' he said softly.

'I wonder what it means.'

'When a swan mates it is for life,' he said, pulling her to him. 'It means we will never be parted. I will speak to your father tomorrow.'

'He will not see you, Argurios.'

'I think he will. I have been invited to the funeral gathering tomorrow night.'

Laodike was surprised. 'Why? As you said, you did not know Hektor.'

'I said the same to the messenger who came to the temple two days ago. He told me that Prince Agathon had requested my presence.'

'That was all he said?'

'No, there was abundant flattery,' he told her. Laodike laughed.

'About being a great warrior and a hero, and it being fitting that you should attend?'

'Something similar,' he grunted.

'It is a great honour to be invited. There is already discord in the family. My father has upset a number of his sons, who will not be present. Antiphones is out of favour, as is Paris. And there are others.' She sighed. 'Even at such a time he still plays games with people's feelings. Do you really think he will listen to you, Argurios?'

'I do not know. I have little to offer, save my sword. But the sword of Argurios has some value.'

She leaned in to him, her hand sliding down his flanks. 'The *sword* of Argurios has great value,' she told him.

XXIX

The Blood of Heroes

i

ANTIPHONES WATCHED FROM AN UPPER WINDOW AS HIS VISITOR LEFT, a feeling of dread in the pit of his stomach. He turned to the hearth where a platter of smoked fish and corn cakes lay cooling. He munched some fish and washed it down with a swig of undiluted wine, sweet and thick. His fears eased a little, but he knew they would return. He had caught himself in a net of his own making.

He had always liked and admired Agathon. Though they had different mothers, they were much of an age and had played together as children. They even looked similar then, with blond hair and blue eyes. Priam's three eldest sons – Hektor, Agathon and Antiphones – were often mistaken for one another by visitors to the king's *megaron*, and he winced as he recalled Priam saying to his guests, 'Alike in looks but not in character. Remember: Hektor the brave, Agathon the sly, and Antiphones the stupid!' His visitors would snigger politely, and the king would smile his cold smile and study the reactions of the three boys.

Antiphones knew he wasn't stupid. As the years passed he came to realize he was sharper than most people he knew. It was he who first understood it was better to ship wine from Lesbos than to grow vines on the land north of the city best used for horse paddocks. Breeding strong horses and sending them all round the Great Green raised more for Priam's treasury than trading in wine. It was he who suggested reorganizing the treasury and keeping an inventory of the king's wealth in the script learned from the Hittites and written on Gyppto papyrus.

As a result of all this, with typical cruel humour, Priam had made Polites his chancellor and fat Antiphones Master of the Horse. He knew people laughed when they heard his title; few bothered to hide it. It had been many years since he had been able to mount a horse.

He walked to the window again and looked down on the quiet street. Unlike most of the king's sons, he chose to live in the lower town, close to the bakers, wine merchants and cheese makers he loved. Each afternoon, after his nap, he would stroll down through the streets and wander among the food stalls, taking his choice from the ripest figs and the sweetest honey cakes. Sometimes he would walk slowly down to the far side of town to where a young woman called Thaleia offered spiced pomegranates and walnuts glazed with honey. It was an effort to get that far, but he could not ride and he feared being carried in a litter in case it broke. This had happened once two years ago. He still felt the shame of it and had not travelled in one since.

But that shame was as nothing to what he felt now.

When he had been made aware of the plot to kill the king he had joined in with zeal. Priam was a tyrant, and tyrannicide was an honourable mission. The king gathered wealth to himself at the expense of all else in the city. Antiphones, with his knowledge of the treasury, had best reason to know that. Children in the lower town starved in winter, slaves in the fields died of exhaustion in summer, yet Priam's treasure house was bursting with gold and precious gems, most of it covered with the dust of ages. Hektor, defending his father, would say, *Yes, the king can be harsh, but he never scrimps in his defence of the city*. Yet Antiphones knew this not to be true. The Thrakian mercenaries were grossly underpaid, and the city engineers had still not been instructed to rebuild the weak west wall.

With Hektor dead, all restraint on Priam's acquisitiveness would be gone.

Antiphones had been asked to join the rebellion because Agathon recognized in him the skills they would need to reorganize the administration of the city, renegotiate treaties with neighbouring kings, and rethink their defences. For the last few days he had made feverish plans, staying up into the depths of the night working on his dreams for the future of Troy once his father was dead. But today's meeting with Agathon had toppled his hopes and plunged him into despair.

'It is tonight, brother. You must stay clear of the palace.'

'You mean to kill him after the funeral feast?'

Agathon had shaken his head. 'During. My Thrakians have orders to kill all our enemies tonight.'

Antiphones felt a hollow opening up in his chest. 'All our enemies? What enemies? You told me Karpophorus was being hired to kill father.'

Agathon shrugged. 'That was my original thought, but he cannot be found. But think on it, brother. Merely killing father would only have been the beginning anyway. Dios and many of the others would start to plot our downfall. Don't you see? Civil war would follow. Some of the coastline kings would ally themselves with us, but others would follow Dios.' He lifted his hand and slowly made a fist. 'In this way we crush them all and Troy remains at peace with all its neighbours.'

'You said all our enemies. How many are we talking about?'

'Only those who might turn on us. Only those who have laughed when father mocked us. Only those who have sniggered behind our backs. A hundred or so. Oh, Antiphones, you have no idea how long I have waited for just this moment!'

He had looked into Agathon's eyes then, and seen for the first time the depth of his half-brother's malice.

'Wait!' he said desperately. 'You cannot allow the Thrakians loose in the palace. They are barbarians! What of the women?'

Agathon laughed. 'The women? Like Andromache? Cold and disdainful. You know what she said? I cannot marry you, Agathon, for I do not love you. By the gods I'll watch her ravished by my Thrakians. They'll pound the arrogance out of her. She'll not be so haughty after tonight.'

'You cannot allow it! Trojan troops must not be used to kill Trojan princes! How would they be regarded thereafter as they patrol the city? Will father's murderer be sitting in a local tavern talking of how he cut the throat of Troy's king?'

'Of course you are right, brother,' said Agathon. 'You think that has not occurred to me? Once the Thrakians have taken the palace walls our allies will arrive. It is they who will kill those inside the *megaron*.'

'Our allies? What are you talking about?'

'A Mykene force will be landing after dusk. *Their* soldiers will kill our enemies.'

Antiphones had sat very quietly, trying to absorb this new information. Father had talked of Agamemnon building great fleets of ships, and had questioned how they would be used. Now it was clear. Agathon had been duped by the Mykene. He would be king in name only. Agamemnon would be the true power, and he would use Troy as a base for Mykene expansion into the east.

He had looked at Agathon with new eyes. 'Oh, my brother,' he had whispered. 'What have you done?'

'Done? Merely what we have planned. I shall be king, and you will be my chancellor. And Troy will be stronger than ever.'

Antiphones had said nothing. Agathon sat quietly, watching him. 'You are still with me, brother?' he had asked.

'Of course,' answered Antiphones, but he had not been able to look him in the eye as he said it. The silence grew again. Then Agathon had risen.

'Well, there is much to do,' he said. 'I will see you tomorrow.' He had walked to the doorway, and then looked back, an odd expression on his face. 'Farewell, Antiphones,' he had said, softly.

Antiphones shivered as he recalled the moment.

The streets were quiet now as the shadows lengthened. Antiphones looked up towards the upper city walls, shining gold in the fading sunlight.

Despair swept over him. There was nothing he could do. If he got a message to Priam he would have to implicate himself in the plot, and that would mean death for treason. And even were he to accept this fate, how could he get through to the king? Agathon controlled all access to the palace, and who knew how many officers or soldiers he had suborned.

He thought of the people who were to die tonight. More than a hundred would be gathered at the funeral feast. Polites would be there, and Helikaon, and Dios. Face after face swam before his eyes. Yes, many of them had – as Agathon observed – sniggered at fat Antiphones. Many had laughed when Priam mocked Agathon. In the main, however, they were good men who served Troy loyally.

He looked up the hill towards Helikaon's palace with its stone horses at the gates. He could see no guards there, but the general bustle in and out of the gateway showed that Helikaon was in residence.

Antiphones took a deep breath. His own death would be a small matter, compared to the horror that awaited the innocents at the palace. He decided then to send a message to Helikaon. *He* would be able to reach the king.

He called out to his body servant, Thoas, and walked ponderously to the door. Outside, a blond-haired Thrakian soldier was crouched over Thoas's body, wiping a bloody knife on the old servant's tunic.

And two others were standing in the doorway, swords in their hands.

Antiphones knew he was going to die. In that moment, rather than the sickening onrush of terror, it was like sunshine bursting through dark clouds. All his life he had lived with fear – fear of disappointing his father, fear of failure, fear of rejection. There was no fear now.

His eyes met the pale blue gaze of the Thrakian assassin.

'He was my body servant,' said Antiphones softly, pointing at the dead Thoas. 'A simple man with a good heart.'

'Ah well,' said the Thrakian, with a wide smile. 'Maybe he will serve you, fat man, in the Underworld.' Rising smoothly he advanced on Antiphones. The soldier was young, and, like so many of the Thrakian mercenaries, hard-eyed and cruel. Antiphones did not move. The soldier paused.

'Well, carrying that amount of blubber you can't run,' he said. 'Do you want to beg for your life?'

'I would ask nothing from a Thrakian goat shagger,' said Antiphones coldly.

The man's eyes narrowed and, with a snarl of anger, he leapt at the prince. Antiphones stepped in to meet him, his huge left arm parrying the knife blow, his right fist hammering into the man's jaw. Lifted from his feet, the Thrakian hit the wall head first and slumped to the floor. The remaining two soldiers raised their swords and rushed at Antiphones. With a bellowing shout he surged forward to meet them. A sword cut into his side, blood drenching his voluminous blue gown. Grabbing the attacker, Antiphones dragged him into a savage head butt. The man sagged, semi-conscious, in his grip.

Pain lanced through him. The other Thrakian had darted behind and stabbed him in the back. Wrenching the sword clear the assassin pulled back his arm for another strike. Still holding on to the stunned man, Antiphones twisted round, hurling him at the swordsman. The Thrakian sidestepped. Antiphones lurched forward. The Thrakian's sword jabbed out, piercing Antiphones' belly. Antiphones' fist thundered against the man's chin, hurling him against the wall. Dropping to one knee Antiphones picked up a fallen sword. Heaving himself upright he blocked a wild cut then drove his blade towards the man's throat. It was a mistimed thrust, for he had never been skilled with the sword. The blade lanced through the man's cheek, slicing the skin and scraping along his teeth, before exiting through the jaw. With a gurgling cry he stabbed at Antiphones again. Stepping back Antiphones swung his sword against the man's temple, and the assassin staggered to his right and half fell. Antiphones struck him three more times, the last blow severing his jugular.

The second assassin was struggling to rise. Antiphones ran at him. Flipping the short sword into dagger position he plunged it past the man's collarbone, driving it down with all his considerable weight. The Thrakian let out a terrible scream, and fell back, the sword so deep inside him that only the hilt guard protruded from his body.

Blood was soaking through Antiphones' gown. He could feel it running down his belly and back. He felt light-headed and dizzy. Slowly he walked back to the first Thrakian. Scooping up the man's dagger he knelt by the unconscious assassin. Grabbing him by the collar of his breastplate he heaved him to his back. The man groaned and his pale eyes opened. Antiphones touched the dagger blade to his throat.

'This *fat man*,' he said, 'is a prince of Troy, and his blood is the blood of heroes and kings. When you get to Hades you can apologize to Thoas. You can tell him the *fat man* thought highly of him.'

The Thrakian's eyes widened and he started to speak. Antiphones plunged the blade through his throat, ripping it clear and watching the blood spray from the awful wound. Then he dropped the knife and sagged back against the door frame.

Farewell, brother, Agathon had said. Antiphones had known that some dread meaning lay behind that last chilling look. Agathon had gone from the house and sent his Thrakians to murder him. And why not? Most of the other brothers were marked for death.

Blood continued to flow. Antiphones closed his eyes. He felt no terror of the dark road. In fact he was surprised at the sense of calm that had settled on him. He thought of Hektor and smiled. Would he have been surprised to see me defeat three killers?

Then he thought again of the murder plot against Priam and his sons and counsellors.

With a mighty effort he made it to his feet. Staggering through to the back of the house he donned a full-length cloak of grey wool, drawing it about him to disguise the bloodstains. Then he moved slowly out into the rear gardens, and into a side street.

He could not see the stones of the street clearly. A haze seemed to be lying on them like the mist on the Scamander at daybreak.

They wavered and shimmered, and with every jarring footstep they threatened to vanish into darkness.

As he bent forward the pain in his side and back redoubled, but with a soft cry he pushed forward another step. Then another.

Blood was still flowing freely, but the cloak disguised his injuries, and the few people who passed him in the street merely glanced. They thought him drunk, or just too fat to walk properly, so they looked away, amused or embarrassed. They did not notice the bloody footprints he was leaving.

Reaching the gate of Helikaon's palace he stood for a moment in the shadow of the stone horses. He saw a servant crossing the courtyard towards the main entrance, and called out to him. The servant recognized him and ran to where Antiphones was now leaning against the base of one of the statues.

'Help me,' he said, unsure if he was speaking the words or just saying them in his head.

He sank into unconsciousness, then felt hands pulling at him, trying to lift him. They could not. The weight was too great.

Opening his eyes he looked up and saw a powerful, black-bearded man with wide shoulders looming over him. 'We have to get you inside,' said the man, his accent Egypteian.

'Helikaon . . . I must speak to . . . Helikaon.'

'He is not here. Give me your hand.' Antiphones raised his arm. Several servants moved behind him. Then the Egypteian heaved, drawing Antiphones up. On his feet again, Antiphones leaned heavily on the Egypteian as they made their slow way into Helikaon's palace. Once inside Antiphones' legs gave way, and the Egypteian lowered him to the floor.

The man knelt beside him, then drew a knife. 'Are you going to kill me?' asked Antiphones.

'Someone has already tried that, my friend. No. I have sent for a physician, but I need to see your wounds and staunch that bleeding.' The knife blade sliced through Antiphones' gown. 'Who did this to you?'

Antiphones felt as if he was falling from a great height. He tried to speak. The Egypteian's face swam before his eyes. 'Traitors,' he mumbled. 'Going to . . . kill everyone.'

Then darkness swallowed him.

ii

Argurios sat quietly in the temple gardens, burnishing his breastplate with an old cloth. The armour was old, and several of the overlapping bronze discs were cracked. Two on the left side were missing. The first had been shattered by an axe. Argurios still remembered the blow. A young Thessalian soldier had burst through the Mykene ranks and killed two warriors. The man was tall, wide-shouldered, and utterly fearless. Argurios had leapt at him, shield high, sword extended. The Thessalian had reacted brilliantly, dropping to one knee and hammering his axe under the shield. The blow had cracked two of Argurios' ribs, and would have disembowelled him had it not been for the quality of the old breastplate. Despite the searing pain Argurios had fought on, mortally wounding his opponent. When the battle was over he had found the dying man, and had sat with him. They had talked of life; of the coming harvest and the value of a good blade.

When the short war was concluded Argurios had travelled up into Thessaly, returning the man's axe and armour to his family, on a farm in a mountain valley.

Slowly, and with great care, Argurios polished each disc. Tonight he planned to approach Priam and he wanted to look his best. He had no great expectation of success in this venture, and the thought of being banished from Laodike's presence caused a rising feeling of panic in his breast.

What will you do, he wondered, if the king refuses you?

In truth he did not know, and pushed his fears away.

Finishing the breastplate he took up his helmet. It was a fine piece, crafted from a single sheet of bronze. A gift from Atreus the king. Lined with padded leather to absorb the impact of any blow, the helmet had served him well. As he stared at it he marvelled at

389

the skill of the bronzesmith. It would have taken weeks to shape this piece, crafting its high dome and curved cheek guards. He ran his fingers lightly down the raised ridges over the crown that would hold the white horsehair crest in place for ceremonial functions. He would not wear the crest tonight. It was weather-beaten and needed replacing. Carefully he burnished the helmet. Had he not been a warrior he would have enjoyed learning the craft of bronze making. Swords needed to hold an edge, and yet not be too brittle; helms and armour required softer bronze, that would give and bend and absorb blows. Greater or lesser amounts of tin were added to the copper to supply whatever was required.

Finally satisfied with the shine of the helmet, he placed it at his side and began to work on the greaves. These were not high quality. They were a gift from Agamemnon King, and should have indicated Argurios' steady fall from favour.

He was still working when he saw Laodike approaching through the trees. She was wearing a sunshine-yellow gown, with a wide belt embossed with gold. Her fair hair was hanging free, and her smile as she saw him lifted his heart. Putting aside the greaves he stood and she ran into his embrace.

'I have such a good feeling about today,' she said. 'I woke this morning and all my fears had vanished.'

Cupping her face in his hands he kissed her. They stood for a moment, unspeaking. Then she glanced down at his armour. 'You are going to look magnificent tonight,' she told him.

'I wish I could see myself through your eyes. The last time I saw my reflection it showed a man past his prime with a hard angular face and greying hair.'

Reaching up she stroked his cheek. 'I never saw a more handsome man. Not ever.' She smiled at him. 'It is very warm out here. Perhaps we should go to your room, where it is cooler.'

'If we go to my room you will not be cool for long,' he told her.

Laodike laughed and helped him gather his armour. Then they walked back through the gardens.

*

390

Later, as they lay naked together on the narrow bed, she talked of the coming feast. 'There will be no women there,' she said. 'The high priestess of Athene is holding a separate function in the women's quarters. She is very old, and very dull. I am not looking forward to it. Yours will be much more exciting. There will be bards singing tales of Hektor's glory, and storytellers.' Her face suddenly crumpled and she held her hand to her mouth. Tears fell. Argurios put his arms round her. 'I still can't believe he is dead,' she whispered.

'He was a hero. The gods will have welcomed him with a great feast.'

She sat up and wiped the tears from her eyes. 'Kassandra upset everyone by saying he was going to come back to life, rise from the dead. Hekabe was so angry she sent her away to father's palace, so she could listen to the priestess and learn to accept the truth. Do people ever rise from the dead, do you think?'

'I never knew anyone who did,' said Argurios. 'Orpheus was said to have entered the Underworld to ask for his wife to be returned to him. But she was not. I am sorry for your grief, Laodike. He was a warrior, though, and that is how warriors die. I expect he would have wanted it no other way.'

She smiled then. 'Oh, not Hektor! He hated being a warrior.'

Argurios sat up beside her. 'How is that possible? Every man around the Great Green has heard of the battles fought by Hektor.'

'I cannot explain the contradiction. Hektor is ... was ... unusual. He hated arguments and confrontations. When in Troy he would spend most of his time on his farm, breeding horses and pigs. There is a big house there, full of children, the sons of fallen Trojan soldiers. Hektor pays for their tutoring and their keep. He used to talk with loathing about war. He told me even victory left a bad taste in his mouth. He once said that all children should be forced to walk on a battlefield and see the broken, ruined bodies. Then, perhaps, they would not grow to manhood filled with thoughts of glory.'

'As you say, an unusual man.' Argurios rose from the bed and put on his tunic. Pushing open the window he looked out over the temple courtyard. Crowds had gathered before the offertory tables, and priests were collecting the petitions.

'An odd thing happened to me today,' he said. 'I went down into the lower town, seeking a bronzesmith who could repair my breastplate. I saw Thrakian troops there. Many had been drinking. They were loud and ill disciplined.'

'Yes, I saw some on my way here. Agathon will be angry when he hears.'

'One of them staggered into me. He said: "You are supposed to be in hiding." I am sure I didn't know the man. Then another one dragged him away, and told him he was a fool.'

'I don't know why they are back so soon,' Laodike told him. 'Father is very careful about rotating the regiments. Yet the Thrakians were here a week ago. They should not have been assigned city duties for some while yet.'

'You should get back to the palace,' said Argurios. 'I need to prepare myself.'

Laodike donned her gown, then walked to a chest by the far wall. On it was a sword and scabbard, a slim dagger, and two wax-sealed scrolls.

'Have you been writing letters?' she asked.

'No. I never mastered the skill. I was given them back in Mykene to deliver to Erekos the ambassador.'

Lifting the first Laodike broke the seal. 'What are you doing?' asked Argurios. 'Those are letters from the king.'

'Not your king any longer,' she said. 'He has banished you. I am curious to know what he writes about.'

'Probably trade tallies,' he said.

Laodike unrolled the scroll and scanned it. 'Yes,' she told him. 'He is talking about shipments of copper and tin, and telling Erekos to ensure supplies are increased.' She read on. 'And something about supplying gold to "our friends". It is all very boring.' She opened the second. 'More of the same. There is a name. Karpophorus. Gold has to be assigned to him for a mission. And Erekos is thanked for supplying details about troop rotations.' She laid the papyrus on the chest. 'Your king writes dull letters.' Moving back across the room, she kissed him. 'I will not see you tonight, but I will be here tomorrow to hear how your meeting with father went. Remember he is a very proud man.'

'So am I,' said Argurios.

'Well, try not to anger him. If he refuses, merely bow your head and walk away. Nothing he can do can keep us apart for long, my love. If he sends me away I will find a way to get word to you.'

'It is good to see your confidence growing.'

'I believe in the message of the swans,' she told him. Then, after another lingering kiss, she left the room.

Argurios walked back to the window. The sun was sliding towards sunset.

Turning back to his armour he finished burnishing the greaves, then the bronze discs on the old leather war kilt. Lastly he polished the curved forearm guards given to him by the soldier Kalliades two years before. Kalliades had stripped them from a dead Athenian and brought them to where Argurios was resting after the battle. 'Thank you for saving my life, Argurios,' he had said. Argurios could not recall the incident. 'I was wearing a helmet embossed with a snake,' persisted Kalliades. 'I was knocked from my feet and a spearman was about to thrust his blade through my throat. You leapt at him, turning away his spear with your shield.'

'Ah, yes,' said Argurios. 'I am glad you survived.'

'I brought you these,' he said, offering the arm guards. Some of Kalliades' friends were close by, keeping a respectful distance. Argurios recognized Banokles of the One Ear, and Eruthros, who was renowned for his practical jokes. There were others, new soldiers he did not know.

Accepting the gift he had said, 'They are very fine. You may leave me now.' The soldiers had backed away. As he remembered the moment Argurios found himself wishing he had spoken to the men, drawing them in and getting to know them.

He glanced at the sword belt and scabbard. These too needed polishing, but he was not intending to wear a sword to the palace.

On the chest lay the papyrus scrolls, covered with their

indecipherable symbols. Copper and tin for the making of more weapons and armour. Gold for 'our friends'. Those friends would be Trojan traitors. As to the troop rotations, that could only refer to the regiments guarding the city. Argurios could not read script, nor could he fashion his own armour. He knew nothing about the growing of crops, nor the weaving of linens and wools.

What he did know as well as any man alive was strategy and war.

If Agamemnon desired to know which troops were guarding the city at any time it could only mean that an advantage could be gained if a *specific* regiment was in control. Otherwise it would matter little which force patrolled the walls.

You are no longer the king's *strategos*, he chided himself. The ambitions of Agamemnon no longer concern you.

Unless, of course, Priam agreed to let him marry Laodike. Then he would, by law, become the king's son, and a Trojan. How inconceivable such an idea would have seemed as he set out with Helikaon on the *Xanthos*.

The shadows were lengthening outside. Argurios strapped on his greaves then donned his breastplate and kilt. Lastly he fastened the straps of the forearm guards and stood.

He walked to the door – and paused. Glancing back, his eyes rested on the sword and scabbard.

On impulse he swept them up and left for the palace.

Part Four

THE HERO'S SHIELD

XXX

Blood on the Walls

i

IT HAD BEEN A FRUSTRATING DAY FOR HELIKAON. HE HAD WALKED TO the palace in search of Andromache, only to find the gates closed. An Eagle on the walls above the gate had called down that no-one was to be allowed entry until dusk, on the orders of Agathon. So he had returned to the House of the Stone Horses, thrown a leopard-skin shabrack over the back of his horse, and ridden across the Scamander to Hekabe's palace, hoping to find Andromache there.

Instead he found the palace virtually deserted. Hekabe's youngest son, the studious Paris, was sitting in the shade of some trees overlooking the bay. Beside him, poring over some old parchments, was a thickset young woman with a plain, honest face and pale auburn hair.

'Mother is sleeping,' Paris told him, setting aside the parchment he held. 'She had a troubled night.'

'I am sorry to hear it. I was seeking Andromache.'

'She was here yesterday with Laodike. Today everyone is in the city, preparing for the feast.'

'But not you?'

Paris gave a shy smile. 'I was not invited. Agathon knows I am uncomfortable in crowds. I am much happier here.' His pale eyes flickered towards the young woman. 'Oh, I am sorry, cousin,' he said. 'This is Helen. She has been staying with us.'

'I am Helikaon,' he told her.

'I have heard of you,' she said softly, meeting his gaze. She swiftly looked away, her face reddening.

'Helen shares my interest in matters historical,' said Paris, gazing at her fondly.

'Do you read?' Helikaon asked her, in an effort to be polite.

'Paris is teaching me,' she told him.

'Then I shall disturb you no longer,' he said. 'I must go home and prepare for the feast.'

Paris rose from his chair and walked with Helikaon back through the silent palace. 'Isn't she a joy?' he said excitedly.

Helikaon smiled. 'It seems you are in love.'

'I think I am,' said the young man happily.

'When is the wedding?'

Paris sighed. 'It is all too complicated. Helen's father is at war with the Mykene. I do not understand the mysteries of battles and strategies, but Antiphones told me that Sparta will lose the war. So, either her father will be killed, or he will be forced to swear allegiance to Agamemnon. Either way Helen will be subject to Agamemnon's will.'

'She is Spartan? Paris, my friend, she is not for you.'

The young prince was defiant. 'Yes, she is,' he protested. 'She is everything to me!'

'That is not what I meant.' Helikaon took a deep breath, marshalling his thoughts. 'The Spartan king has no sons. If Sparta falls then Helen will be married off to one of Agamemnon's generals, in order to provide a claim to the throne. And even if by some miracle Sparta wins, then the king's daughter will be wed to a highborn Spartan, who would then be named as heir.'

Paris looked crestfallen. 'What if father intervened for us?'

Helikaon hesitated. He liked the quiet young prince. Of all Priam's sons he was the least like his father. Paris had no interest in war or combat, or political intrigue. He had never taken part in athletic tourneys, nor even attempted to become proficient with sword or spear or bow. 'Paris, my friend, you said yourself you do not understand strategies or battles. Whoever weds Helen will have a claim on the throne of Sparta. Can you imagine that Agamemnon would allow a Trojan prince to have such a claim? Even Priam, with all his power, could do nothing to alter that. Put it from your mind.'

'I cannot do that. We love each other.'

'Princes do not marry for love, Paris. I fear disappointment awaits you,' said Helikaon, taking hold of his horse's white mane, and vaulting to its back. Touching heels to his mount he rode back towards the Scamander bridge.

The conversation with Paris had unsettled him. He had ridden to Troy convinced that he could win Andromache, but was he also blinded by emotion? Why would Priam allow such a match? Why indeed would he not merely wed her to Agathon? Or bed her himself?

That last thought brought a wave of anger, and with it an image that sickened him. As he rode back towards the city his mind began to conceive plans of action that became increasingly absurd. As he rode through the Scaean Gate he was even considering abducting Andromache and fleeing back to Dardanos.

Are you an idiot, he asked himself?

His small, mostly militia army could never withstand the might of Troy. Such an action would bring disaster on the realm. Forcing himself to think coolly he considered all that he could offer Priam, in terms of wealth and trade. Lost in his calculations, he rode slowly through the city to the House of the Stone Horses.

He saw some twenty soldiers in the courtyard, and, as he approached, noticed blood smeared on the stones.

'What is going on?' he asked a young Thrakian officer. The man recognized him.

'Someone was attacked, Lord Aeneas,' he said. 'Your servant has refused us entry.'

Moving past the officer, Helikaon hammered his fist on the door. 'Who is it?' came the voice of Gershom.

'Helikaon. Open the door.'

He heard the bar being lifted and the door opened. The first thing he saw was a body on the floor, covered by two cloaks. Blood had drenched the rug on which it lay. Despite the fact that the face was covered, Helikaon knew the dead man was Antiphones. No-one else in Troy was that size. The Thrakian officer entered behind him and gazed down at the covered corpse.

'We did not know what to do, lord,' said Gershom, bowing low. 'This man staggered in here asking for you. Then he collapsed and died.'

Helikaon looked closely at Gershom. The man had never before been servile, and not once had he bowed. Meeting his gaze, he sensed there was more to this than Gershom could say. Helikaon turned to the Thrakian officer. 'The dead man is Antiphones, son of Priam. I suggest you send for a cart, and have the body taken to the palace.'

'I will indeed, sir,' said the Thrakian. He swung to Gershom. 'Did he say anything before he died?'

'He tried, lord,' said Gershom, head bowed. 'He kept asking for the lord Helikaon. I told him he wasn't here. I tried to stop the bleeding, but the wounds were too deep. Then he died. I couldn't save him.'

'Why did you not let us in?' asked the officer.

'I was frightened, lord. I am a stranger to the city. A man comes in and drops dead, and then other armed men are banging at the door. I did not know what to do.'

The answer seemed to satisfy the officer. 'I will have a cart sent,' he told Helikaon, and went out. As the door closed Gershom knelt by Antiphones and pulled the top cloak away from the man's face. Antiphones' eyes were open. Helikaon saw him blink. The physician Machaon emerged from a side room.

'What is happening here?' asked Helikaon, mystified.

Gershom looked up. 'He was attacked by Thrakian soldiers sent by his brother Agathon,' he said, all trace of servility vanished. Machaon also knelt by Antiphones, drawing back the cloak still further. Antiphones' upper body was covered in blood, and Helikaon could see jagged lines of stitches applied to many wounds.

Machaon examined the wounds, then placed his hand over Antiphones' heart.

'He is a strong man,' said the physician, 'and the depth of fat, I think, prevented the blades from causing mortal blows.'

'Why did Agathon do this to you?' Helikaon asked the wounded man.

'I have been such a fool. So much I did not see. I thought that, like me, Agathon wanted revenge on Priam for all the hurts and insults. But he is lost on a sea of hatred. Not just for Priam, but for everyone who has ever offered him what he considers a slight. Tonight will be a massacre. A thousand Thrakians and some two hundred Mykene will descend on the palace. Every man inside the *megaron* is to be killed. All the princes, the counsellors, the nobles. Everyone. I tried to convince him of the madness of it. He sent three men to kill me.' Antiphones gave a weary smile. 'I slew them. Hektor would have been proud of me, don't you think?'

'He would. What of the women?'

Antiphones' smile faded. 'Our sisters should be safe. All others will be spoils of war,' he said. 'I didn't see all that hatred in him. I was blinded by my own loathing of Priam. You must get out of the city. Once Priam is dead Agathon will send killers after you.'

'Priam is not dead yet,' Helikaon told him.

'You can do nothing. The Great Gates are guarded by a regiment controlled by one of Agathon's men. They have orders not to leave their posts, and to keep the gates shut until dawn. They will not come to Priam's aid. And there are only a hundred or so Eagles at the palace. They cannot win against such odds.'

'What of the Lady Andromache? Where is she?'

'Oh, she has joined his list of enemies. She refused him, Aeneas. He said he would enjoy watching her raped by his Thrakians.'

ii

It was the afternoon of the funeral feast, and Andromache stood on the balcony of her apartment, staring out over the green hills to the north of the city. There were sheep grazing there, and in the far distance she saw two riders cresting a rise. How good it would be, she thought, to be free of Troy. How wonderful to be riding on a hillside, without a care.

'You wanted a plain white garment today,' said Axa, moving onto the balcony and disturbing her reverie. The maid held out two identical robes. Andromache pointed to one. Axa examined the embroidery on the hem and then, tutting, rushed off to her sewing box. Armed with needle and silver thread she sat herself comfortably on a padded stool. She was now moving more easily and her bruises were fading, Andromache noticed.

'Kassandra is at the palace,' said Axa, peering short-sightedly at her sewing. 'She returned yesterday. The gossip is that the queen lost her temper with her. She kept saying that Hektor will come back from the dead. Must be difficult for a mother to have a child with a blighted soul.'

'Her soul is not blighted,' said Andromache. 'Paris told me that Kassandra almost died as a babe. She had the brain fire.'

'Poor mite,' said Axa. 'My boy will not suffer that. I have a charm. It carries the blessing of Persephone. Mestares bought it.' As she spoke her husband's name Axa ceased her sewing, her plain, plump face crumpling in sorrow. Andromache sat beside her. There was nothing she could say. The arrival of the emperor had put paid to all hopes that Hektor and his men would return.

Axa brushed away her tears with a callused hand. 'This won't do. Won't do at all,' she said. 'Must get you looking nice for the gathering.'

'Andromache!' A door slammed and there was a rattle of curtains, then Kassandra appeared in the doorway, her dark curls dishevelled and the hem of her long blue gown dragging on the floor. 'I want to go to the gardens. Laodike won't let me. She keeps telling me off.'

Laodike appeared behind her. 'Kassandra, don't bother Andromache. This is a time of sadness. We must be quiet and stay in the women's quarters.'

'You're not sad.' Kassandra's blue-grey eyes flashed at her sister. 'Your heart is singing like a bird. I can hear it.'

Laodike flushed, and Andromache gave her a quick smile. She had guessed there was someone in Laodike's life. Her confidence had increased over these last few weeks, and her happiness yesterday had been wonderful to see. She had hoped Laodike would confide in her, but she had seen little of her, and when they did speak the subject of love was not raised. Andromache guessed she might have formed an attachment for one of the soldiers, hence the need for secrecy.

'My heart is *not* singing, wicked child!' exclaimed Laodike. 'You really are irritating! And I have so much to do. I am to greet the priestess, and she is a daunting woman.'

'Leave Kassandra with me,' said Andromache. 'I enjoy her company.'

Laodike sighed. 'That's because you have not had to endure it for any length of time.' She gave a hard stare at Kassandra, but it softened as the child cocked her head and smiled back at her sister.

'I know you love me, Laodike,' she said.

'You don't know anything!' She turned to Andromache. 'Very well, I shall leave her with you. But be warned, by this evening you will have grey hairs and lines upon your face.'

After Laodike had gone Andromache said, 'I don't see why we can't take a stroll in the gardens. Come, Axa, give me the gown. A little fraying on the hem does not worry me. No-one will be looking at my feet.'

Axa was obviously unhappy with the decision, but passed the garment to Andromache, who stripped off the green robe she was wearing and donned the white. Axa brought her an ornate belt, decorated with silver chains.

Leaving the apartment the trio walked down the corridors of the women's quarters, through the high oak doors decorated with gold and ivory. Beyond these was a staircase leading up to the queen's apartments, followed by another set of stairs which descended into Priam's *megaron*. Servants were bustling about making ready for the night's great feast. Already guests were arriving, and Andromache spotted Polites and Dios, the latter giving her a scalding look. Dios still harboured resentment over the incident at the beach, and had not offered her a polite word since.

'Why do people eat lots of roast meat when someone dies?' Kassandra asked, watching the servants toiling with huge slabs of beef.

Andromache shrugged. 'It is tradition. When a hero like Hektor dies the men like to sit together and tell stories of his greatness. The gods are said to take part, and they are invited to eat and drink in tribute to the warrior.'

Andromache looked around the *megaron*. She had been here several times, but had never had the chance to truly study it. The walls were heavy with arms and armour. Axa, who searched now for every opportunity to please her, started explaining the pieces decorating the walls. 'Those,' she said, pointing to the far wall, 'are all weapons of Herakles. Those are his spears, and that is the great hammer he used to knock down the west wall.'

Andromache gazed up. Above their heads were five shields. Four were brightly polished, but the middle one was battered and untended, its style archaic. Wide at the top and tapering at the waist, it was intricately worked and plated with ten circles of bronze. Crowning the shield was a giant serpent with nine heads, and a warrior armed with sword and flaming brand. The shield strap was edged and circled with a silver snake.

'That is magnificent,' she said.

'That is the shield of Ilos, one of the great warriors of Troy,' Axa explained happily. 'There is a legend that says only the greatest hero can take it down from the wall. The king offered it to Hektor, but he refused. Prince Agathon asked for it last year, after winning a battle in the east. The king said that if Hektor did not consider himself worthy of it, then no man was.'

'That may change now,' said Andromache. 'I imagine Agathon will succeed Priam?'

'Priam will outlive all his sons,' Kassandra said suddenly, her high voice cold and detached. Andromache felt the hairs on her arms stand up and a shiver ran like sweat down her spine. The child's eyes suddenly became wide and frightened. 'There is blood on the walls,' she cried, then bolted away, back up the stairs towards the queen's apartments. They heard her sandals slapping on the stone steps as she ran. Leaving Axa where she was, Andromache set out after the fleeing girl.

But Kassandra was running fast, sidestepping the servants, twisting and weaving through the crowd. Andromache followed as swiftly as dignity allowed. She could hardly hitch up her ankle-length gown and give chase, so she walked on until she reached the women's quarters and her own apartment. The door opened, and Kassandra stepped out, carrying Andromache's bow and quiver of arrows.

'You will need these,' she said. 'They are coming.'

XXXI

The Siege Begins

i

A BRISK WIND HAD BEGUN TO BLOW AS ARGURIOS MADE HIS WAY UP towards the palace of Priam. In the marketplace traders were struggling to take down the linen or canvas covers on their stalls. The cloth billowed, and one tore itself loose and lifted into the air, like a sail. Several men ran after it, and there was much laughter from the many onlookers.

The sun was setting over the distant isles of Imbros and Samothraki, and rain clouds were scudding over the city.

Argurios walked on across the square before the Temple of Hermes, the wind buffeting him. He hoped he would make it to the palace before the rain came. He did not relish the thought of standing before King Priam with water dripping from his armour.

Truth to tell he did not relish the thought of standing before the man at all.

For as long as he could remember Argurios had found conversation awkward. Invariably he would say something that alienated a listener, or, at best, gave the wrong impression. He had been able to relax with very few people. One had been Atreus the king, and Argurios still missed him.

He recalled the night at the battlesite campfire. Argurios had been drawn into a furious row with one of Atreus' generals. Afterwards the amused king had sat him down, urging him to breathe deeply and find calm. Atreus had struggled not to laugh, which made Argurios all the more angry.

'I do not find this amusing,' he had snapped.

'Of course you don't,' agreed Atreus amiably. 'You are Argurios. Nothing amuses you. You are a serious man, and a compulsive truth teller.'

'The truth should be valued,' Argurios had argued.

'Indeed it should. However, the truth has many faces. You told Rostides that he was an idiot for leading an attack against a position he had not scouted. You said the losses suffered were inexcusable.'

'All true.'

'I agree. However, it was I who ordered Rostides to attack. He merely followed my orders as any loyal soldier should. Am I an idiot?'

'Yes,' answered Argurios, 'for the situation remains the same. There was no reconnaissance, and therefore our men were caught in a trap.'

'You are quite correct, my friend,' said Atreus, his smile fading. 'I acted rashly, and, in this instance, was less than wise. You acted no less rashly by insulting Rostides before you had scouted the situation. By your own terms of reference that makes you an idiot. Not so?'

'I shall apologize to him.'

'That would be wise. You know, Argurios, I have always valued your honesty. I always will. Kings tend to surround themselves with flatterers.' He laughed suddenly. 'Indeed, I have gathered quite a few myself. There should, however, always be one truth teller. But try to remember that not all men think as I do.'

'I cannot be anything but what I am, lord.'

'I know. So let us hope we both live long, eh?'

Atreus had died two years later. And now Argurios understood exactly what he meant. Agamemnon was not like his father. He wanted no truth tellers.

Would Priam?

Argurios doubted it.

He paused in his walk and looked up at the lowering sky. 'In all my life, Father Zeus, I have asked you for nothing,' he said. 'Be with me on this day, and guide me so that I will not lose Laodike.'

Thunder rumbled in the distance. Argurios glanced back down towards the sea. In the setting sun he saw four dark-sailed galleys slowly beating their way towards the beach far below. The last of the sunlight glistened on the bright helms and shields carried by the warriors on board.

Argurios walked on, composing in his mind his speech to Priam.

Reaching the open area before the gates he saw several finely clad Trojan nobles speaking to soldiers of Priam's Eagles. Voices were raised. 'This is outrageous!' he heard someone say. 'Not even a dagger? How are we to eat, or are they serving only soup at Hektor's feast?'

Inside the gateway two long tables had been set side by side. They were covered with swords, daggers and knives.

'I am sorry, my lord,' said a soldier. 'The orders were specific. No-one is to take a weapon into the *megaron*. They will be here for you when you leave.' Argurios recognized the speaker as Polydorus, the soldier who had walked with him to the beach on the day he had swum with Andromache. Still grumbling, the visitor slammed his dagger to the table top and stalked off. As the light faded servants came out of the king's palace, lighting torches and placing them in brackets on the walls of the gate tower. Lamps were also suspended from poles lining the walkway to the high palace doors.

Argurios waited until the last of the Trojan nobles had entered, then approached Polydorus. The young soldier looked harassed, but smiled when he saw the Mykene. 'I will take personal care of your weapon, sir,' he said. 'Is that the blade you wielded at Partha?'

'No. That broke long ago.'

Just then they heard the clatter of a horse's hooves upon the road. A golden horse galloped up to the gateway. Helikaon leapt from its back. He was wearing a fitted breastplate and helmet, and bearing two swords in scabbards over his shoulders.

'Where is the officer of the watch?' he demanded.

A tall soldier stepped forward from the shadows beyond the gateway. 'I am Aranes, my lord. You must leave your weapons here, on the orders of Prince Agathon.'

'You must close the palace gates, Aranes,' said Helikaon. 'Traitors are coming to kill the king. They are close behind me. And there is a Mykene force to aid them. Even now their ships are beaching.'

'What is this nonsense? Are you drunk?'

'Do I look drunk? The Prince Antiphones has been stabbed. Agathon is a traitor and his Thrakians are heading here, intent on murder. Now close the damned gates, or we are all dead.'

The soldier shook his head. 'I need to seek authorization. We are ordered to keep the gates open.'

Helikaon stood silently for a moment, then stepped in and slammed a sudden blow to the man's jaw. Aranes spun, then hit the ground face first. Several of the Eagles ran forward, drawing their swords.

'Listen to me!' shouted Helikaon. 'Death is coming. Gather all the men you can. And, for pity's sake, bar those gates!'

'Do as he says!' called out Polydorus, running to the first of the gates. Argurios went with him, and slowly they began to swing it shut. Soldiers moved to the other gate.

A hurled javelin slammed into the timber.

From the darkness beyond armed men surged forward, screaming war cries.

And the gates were still open.

ii

Helikaon swung round as the javelin thudded home. Thrakian soldiers were rushing towards the gates. Some held javelins or spears, others short swords. In that fraction of a heartbeat Helikaon registered that the warriors were wearing light leather breastplates and round leather helmets. They carried no shields.

Fury swept through him. They had not even returned to their barracks to change into battle armour, so confident were they in their mission of murder. All they expected to face were a few Eagles and a hundred unarmed men mourning a dead hero.

Drawing the two leaf-bladed swords from the scabbards at his back, Helikaon charged at the milling Thrakians. There was no thought in his mind of glory. No thought of death. No thought of anything, save a savage, reckless desire to visit vengeance on these treacherous men, to see their blood flow, and to hear their anguished cries.

Some of the Thrakians had hurled themselves against the gates, forcing them back. Some twenty Eagles were on the inner side, straining to close them. Helikaon darted between the yawning gap, slashing his right-hand blade through the throat of a blond warrior, then lancing the left-hand sword into the neck of a second. His assault was sudden, his swords slashing, cutting and cleaving. A few Thrakians tried to rush him, others sought to pull back from the fray, dismayed by the deadly speed of his strokes. Swords clattered against his breastplate, and a thrusting spear struck against his helm.

Now he was in their midst. Bodies lay at his feet, and his swords glittered as they rose and fell. Even in the midst of his battle fury he realized he had advanced too far. They were all around him now, and it would not be long before he was hamstrung, or dragged from his feet. Even as the thought came, a huge Thrakian leapt at him, his shoulder cannoning into Helikaon's breastplate. As Helikaon fell back he plunged a blade through the man's cheek. A hand grabbed him, steadying him. He saw Argurios alongside him. A Thrakian ran in, thrusting his spear at Argurios. The Mykene swayed aside from the thrust, killing the wielder with a ferocious cut that split his skull.

'Kill them all!' bellowed Argurios, his voice ringing with authority. A few of Priam's Eagles rushed into the fray, tall men, wide-shouldered and strong. Heavily armoured and bearing great shields of bronze, they clove into the Thrakian ranks. The enemy fell back to regroup.

Helikaon started to charge towards them. 'Not now!' shouted Argurios, grabbing him again. 'Back to the gates!'

The red battle fury seeped away, and Helikaon raced back with the others. The Thrakians, realizing too late what was happening, gave chase.

Helikaon was the last man through the closing gates. As they slammed shut Polydorus and another soldier tipped a long timber locking bar into place.

Men were streaming from the palace now. 'Arm yourselves with bows,' Helikaon yelled at the soldiers. 'Get to the walls. More will come.' Turning to Argurios he said: 'My thanks to you.'

'There were only around fifty or so out there,' said Argurios. 'Must have been an advance party. How many Thrakians are there in all?'

'A thousand.'

'And you say there are Mykene coming?'

'So I am informed.'

'I believe I saw them. Four galleys beached as I was walking here. At least two hundred warriors. Maybe more. I thought they were Trojans.'

Priam the king pushed through the crowd. 'What in Hades is happening here?' he asked Helikaon, his breath stinking of un-watered wine, his legs unsteady.

'Betrayal,' said Helikaon. 'Agathon's Thrakians have been ordered to kill every man in the palace. And there are two hundred Mykene warriors marching towards us as we speak.'

Priam rubbed at his eyes and sucked in a great breath. 'This is madness,' he said. 'One regiment of Thrakians? As soon as word reaches the other garrisons they will come in their thousands. And it is after dark. The Great Gates will be closed. No Mykene will be allowed to enter.'

'You are wrong, sire,' said Helikaon. 'The soldiers on the Scaean Gate have been ordered to let them in, and then close the gate behind them. No other troops will be allowed to enter. The Eagles here are the only loyal men left in the Upper City. We are on our own.'

Priam said nothing for a moment, then swung to a nearby Eagle. 'Fetch me my armour,' he ordered. Turning back to Helikaon he said, 'We'll hold them. By the gods we'll teach them the price to be paid for treachery.'

'You'll not hold these palace walls for long,' said Argurios. 'They are not high enough, and you don't have the men. Even now they will be searching for ladders, carts, timber . . . anything to allow them to scale the ramparts.'

'Do I know you?' retorted Priam, squinting in the lantern light.

'I am Argurios, Priam King.'

'*The* Argurios?'

'Even so.'

'And *you* are fighting for *me*?'

'It appears that I am.'

The drunken king suddenly laughed, but there was no humour in the sound. 'My Hektor has been taken from me. His brother wants me dead, and my city is under attack. Now a Mykene hero has come to aid me.' His face hardened. 'Oh, how the gods favour me!'

'I share your feelings,' said Argurios. 'It was no dream of mine to fight for Troy. However, we can talk of capricious gods at another time. *Now* we need to arm every one of your guests, with whatever weapons are inside the palace. We will need bowmen on the palace balcony covering this courtyard. Even so the odds will be long indeed.'

Priam gave a cold smile. 'Odds fit for a hero, Argurios. Where is that damned armour?' Priam turned away, and staggered off in search of his weapons.

On the walls above a few Eagles began loosing shafts down into the Thrakian ranks.

'We cannot hold the walls for long,' repeated Argurios, this time to Helikaon. 'They will come back with ladders and ropes and grappling hooks. They will swarm over like ants.'

'I know.' Helikaon swung to Polydorus. 'You go inside. Get all the older counsellors and servants up into the queen's apartments, away from the fighting. Then barricade all unnecessary entrances.

412

Make sure all windows are shuttered and barred. If you can find tools have them nailed shut.'

The officer he had struck earlier was now on his feet, but still groggy. Helikaon approached him. 'How many men are at the outside gate to the women's quarters?' he asked.

'No-one is stationed there,' said the officer, rubbing his jaw. 'The gates are locked. There is no way through.'

'Then the enemy will scale the walls unopposed!' stormed Helikaon. 'Argurios, you stay here and command the defence. You!' he said to Aranes. 'Gather twenty good swordsmen and follow me! '

iii

Outside her apartments, deep in the palace, Andromache looked into Kassandra's grey eyes, seeing the terror there. 'Who is coming?' she asked softly.

Kassandra blinked. 'Swords and daggers and spears.' She gazed around her, eyes wide. 'Blood on the walls. Blood . . . everywhere. Please take the bow.'

The child had begun to tremble. Andromache stepped forward, lifting the weapon from her hand. Kassandra offered her the quiver, with its twenty black-shafted arrows. Andromache swung it over her shoulder. 'There now! I have the bow. Be calm, little one. No-one is going to hurt you.'

'No,' agreed Kassandra, with a sigh. 'No-one is going to hurt *me*.'

Holding out her free arm Andromache took Kassandra by the hand. 'Let us go down and listen to the priestess. She is said to be very dull. Then later you and I will sit in the starlight and we will talk.'

'Helikaon is coming for you,' said Kassandra, as they walked hand in hand along the wide corridor towards the gathering hall of the women's quarters.

'Why would he be doing that?' asked Andromache.

413

'Because he loves you,' answered the child. 'You knew that, didn't you?'

Andromache sighed. 'Helikaon is in Dardania.'

Kassandra shook her head. 'He was on a golden horse, riding through the streets. He is frightened for you. He knows that blood is coming. The fat one told him.' Suddenly the child began to cry. Andromache laid the bow on a couch, set by the corridor wall, and sat down, drawing Kassandra to her. Hugging the girl and kissing her dark hair she tried to calm her. She had heard many stories of the fey child, and knew there was nothing she could say to pierce the veils of illusion. So she waited for the tears to pass, and held her close.

They sat there for some time. 'I don't want to see so much,' said Kassandra, drawing away, and sitting with her back to the wall. 'I hate it. I can't tell sometimes what is *now* and what was *then*.'

'This is now,' said Andromache. 'You and I sitting here.'

'You and I,' repeated Kassandra. She glanced across the corridor. 'Look there. What do you see?'

Andromache followed the line of her pointing finger. 'I see a tapestry hanging from the wall. Very pretty embroidery.'

'No! In front of the tapestry.'

'The corridor?'

Kassandra's shoulders sagged. Andromache saw her smile at nothing, and give a little wave. 'What is it that *you* see?' she asked.

'It doesn't matter. The dolphins told me the sea is changing. They are frightened. I am frightened too. Everything is changing, Andromache.'

'Why did you say that Helikaon loves me? Is it something he said?'

Kassandra gave a shy smile. 'I love Helikaon. I used to watch him sleeping. Helikaon is in the *now*. He is the Lord of the Silver Bow.'

'You think Helikaon is Apollo?'

'No, silly! Helikaon is Helikaon.'

Andromache smiled at the child. 'I don't understand.'

'No-one does. Well, no-one who feels the rain, or the sun's heat.'

'Isn't that everyone?'

'We must be going! Keep your bow ready. We must rescue Laodike. We must bring her to the shield bearer.'

Andromache could think of no more to say to this strange child, so they walked together in silence through to the Hall of Gathering.

A small crowd of some twenty women were already there, dressed in flowing gowns, and bedecked in jewellery of gold and silver. Servants moved among them, bearing trays of golden cups brimming with wine. Andromache saw Laodike and waved. By the great double doors stood a tall, silver-haired woman, carrying a small ceremonial helmet of bright gold. 'That is the priestess,' whispered Kassandra. 'I don't like her. She gives false prophecies.'

'If they were false,' said Andromache, 'then surely people would realize it, when they failed to come true.'

'No, she is very clever,' said Kassandra. 'Pandates the merchant went to her last year to ask if his wife would ever become pregnant. She told him the gods favoured him, but they required his patience. She said he would have a son, as long as he did nothing to offend the gods. Pandates was drowned when his ship sank. She said that he had offended Poseidon.'

'Perhaps he had,' offered Andromache.

'After tonight,' said Kassandra, 'she will speak the truth, and her prophecies will be real. But no-one will hear them.'

It seemed to Andromache that holding a conversation with Kassandra was not dissimilar to trying to catch a butterfly. Every time you thought you had it in your grasp it fluttered away. 'There are not many women here,' she ventured. 'Did Hektor have no female friends?'

'Everyone loved Hektor,' replied Kassandra. 'They will be so happy when he comes home. Keep your bow ready.'

Laodike moved across to join them. She was wearing a bright yellow gown, and her fair hair had been braided with gold wire.

'This is not the place for an archery display,' she said, frowning.

'I know. I will explain later. I see Kreusa isn't here.'

'She always arrives late,' said Laodike. 'Kreusa likes to make a dramatic entrance. She will be disappointed, I think. There are so few people here. The wives of father's closest counsellors, but none of Hektor's friends.' She leaned in close. 'Oh dear, the priestess is about to speak, and the drab part of the evening begins.'

'She will not speak for long,' whispered Kassandra, backing away, her face pale. Suddenly she turned and darted back along the corridor.

The silver-haired priestess held the ceremonial gold helmet above her head and began to chant: 'Athene, hear your children! Goddess of Wisdom, hear your followers. Let our words and our grief flow to you, and bring us peace and understanding in these days of sorrow.'

Just then the far doors burst open, and Thrakian soldiers surged into the room, swords and spears in their hands. The women stood shocked. No men were allowed into the women's quarters, and certainly no male could invade a sacred ceremony.

The priestess was outraged. She rushed at them, screaming for them to leave at once, or face the curse of Athene. What followed then stunned Andromache. A burly Thrakian lashed out at her, sending the priestess sprawling to the floor, the ceremonial helm clattering away to strike a table leg. For a moment there was shocked silence. Then the priestess pointed at the man. 'May the goddess strike you down, and curse your family for nine generations!' she shrieked.

The man laughed – and then his sword slashed down. The priestess threw up her arm, and the bronze blade hacked into it, spraying blood. A second cut tore open her throat. Women began to scream and run. Soldiers rushed at them, dragging them back.

Then Laodike ran towards the warrior who was still stabbing his sword into the squirming priestess. 'You cowardly dog!' she shouted.

'You want to bleed too, bitch?' he responded, charging towards her. Andromache swiftly notched an arrow to her bow and drew back on the string. As the soldier reached Laodike, his sword raised high, a black-feathered shaft plunged through his eye. He staggered back several steps, dropping his sword, then slumped to the floor.

'Laodike!' yelled Andromache. The young woman started to run towards her. A Thrakian soldier hurled a spear, which took her in the back. Laodike screamed and stumbled. Andromache shot the spearman through the throat. More Thrakians pushed through into the gathering hall. Laodike half fell against Andromache. A soldier charged at them. Andromache loosed a shaft that tore through the man's leather breastplate, spearing his chest. He faltered, then came on, sword raised. With no time to draw the string Andromache dropped the bow and stepped forward to meet him, the shaft held like a dagger in her hand. Weakened by the arrow in his chest the soldier gave a feeble thrust. Andromache parried the blow with her arm, then plunged the bronze-headed arrow into the man's neck. He fell back with a gargling cry.

Sweeping up her bow Andromache notched another shaft to the string. She glanced down at Laodike, who had fallen to the floor, and was trying to crawl towards the corridor, the long black spear still embedded in her back.

Other women ran past Andromache. All was pandemonium.

Then soldiers appeared from behind – Royal Eagles led by Helikaon. They surged into the Thrakians.

Andromache ran to where Laodike was crawling. Grabbing the spear she tore it loose. Laodike cried out, then slumped down. Hurling the spear aside, Andromache tugged at Laodike's arm, dragging her to her feet. 'Lean on me,' she urged her. 'We must get away from here.'

More Eagles ran into the fray. Andromache struggled on towards the double doors leading to the steps up to the queen's apartments. Several Eagles were already there. One of them left his post and swept Laodike into his arms.

'Get her to safety,' ordered Andromache.

'There is nowhere safe tonight,' he said grimly. 'But I'll carry her upstairs. We'll hold these doors as long as we can.'

iv

Helikaon and the Eagles battled their way into the gathering hall. The Trojans were all veterans and fought with ruthless efficiency. Well armoured, with shields and helms, they drove the Thrakians back towards the double doors leading to the outer gates. The twenty defenders were heavily outnumbered, but the Thrakians, without shields and in their light city armour of leather breast-plates and helmets, took terrible losses. Helikaon fought with cold fury, his two swords cutting and plunging with awesome speed.

The leading Thrakians fell back in disarray, then turned and ran into more of their comrades, still trying to force an entry. This led to a chaotic scene as panicking soldiers struggled to push their way through their own ranks. The Eagles rushed in, sinking their swords into unprotected backs and necks. The Thrakians broke, and streamed away from the double doors.

Helikaon yelled an order to the Eagles to pull back. Most obeyed him, but four men, battle lust having overtaken them, continued after the Thrakians. Back inside the gathering hall Helikaon ordered the double doors pushed shut. There were two wooden brackets for a locking bar, but the bar itself was nowhere in sight. It had not been needed for decades, and had obviously been removed. Helikaon sent two Eagles in search of it. The sounds of fighting in the corridor beyond had ceased now, and Helikaon guessed the Thrakians had turned on the four chasing Eagles. There was little time left to bar the doors. Soon the Thrakians would regroup.

'Gather up those spears,' he called out, pointing to the weapons of the dead Thrakians. The Eagles rushed to obey, and nine thick-shafted spears were wedged into the locking brackets.

'It will not hold for long,' said an Eagle. Helikaon gazed around the hall. More than forty Thrakians had died here, but there were also the bodies of eight Eagles and five women, two of them elderly. Four more of the Eagles carried wounds.

'There is nothing more we can do here,' said Helikaon, and led them back to the second set of double doors, leading to the queen's apartments and the king's *megaron*. Here the locking bar had been found and he ordered the heavy oak doors closed and barred.

Leaving two Eagles to watch the doors, he climbed the stairs to the queen's apartments. In the largest of the rooms he found the surviving women. Some were looking frightened, others shocked and uncertain. Laodike lay on a couch, flanked by Kassandra and Andromache. Blood had soaked the embroidered cloth beneath her. Sheathing his swords Helikaon moved towards them.

A middle-aged woman stepped into his path. 'What is happening?' she asked him, grabbing his arm. She was frightened and trembling, her face unnaturally pale.

'We are being attacked,' he told her, his voice calm. 'There are wounded men who need aid. There will be more. Can you search the apartments for needles and thread, and tear up linens for bandages?'

Her expression calmed. 'Yes, I can do that.'

'Good. Organize the other women, ready to tend those who will need it.'

'Who is behind this treachery?' she asked.

'Agathon.'

She frowned and shook her head. 'I always liked him,' she said.

'So did I.' Moving past her he knelt by the couch. There was a great deal of blood, and Laodike seemed to be sleeping. He glanced at Andromache.

'A spear,' she whispered. 'It took her low in the back. I have stopped the bleeding and her heartbeat is strong. I think she will recover. '

Helikaon reached out and gently brushed a wisp of hair back from Laodike's brow. Her eyes opened.

'Helikaon!' she cried, with a wide smile. 'Are the traitors slain?'

'Not yet.'

'They killed the priestess. It was dreadful. Were they drunk?'

'No, Laodike. There is a plot to kill your father.'

'Antiphones or Dios,' she said. 'Or both.'

'No. Agathon.'

'Oh, no,' she whispered. 'No, it cannot be true.'

'Sadly it is. He had Antiphones stabbed, and he has ordered the deaths of everyone inside the palace.'

'He and you were friends,' said Laodike. 'I don't understand. Is Argurios here?'

'Yes. He is down in the courtyard, organizing the defences.'

'Defences?' She seemed bemused.

'Agathon's Thrakians have surrounded the palace – and there is a Mykene force coming to aid them.'

'What about our troops?'

'The soldiers inside the city are loyal to Agathon. It will be a long night, I think.'

Laodike sighed, then winced. 'If feels as if I have been kicked by a horse,' she complained.

'Stab wounds are like that,' he told her. 'And now I must go. You rest now and gather your strength.'

'Yes, I will. I am very tired. Tell Argurios to be careful. I don't want anything to happen to him.'

'Argurios?' Helikaon glanced at her quizzically.

'We will be wed,' she said. 'It is our destiny.'

Helikaon smiled, then leaned forward and kissed Laodike's brow. 'I am happy for you,' he told her. Then he stood. Andromache rose alongside him. 'Walk with me a little way,' he said.

Moving through the apartment they emerged onto a gallery above a wide stairway leading down to the king's *megaron*. Below they could see men arming themselves with weapons and shields from the walls.

'I am glad you came,' said Andromache.

Helikaon looked into her green eyes. 'I came for you,' he said.

'Why?'

'I think you know.'

'Perhaps. But there may be little time left to hear the words.'

Taking her hand he lifted it to his lips. He had expected the words to come haltingly, but they did not. 'I love you, Andromache,' he said. 'I have loved you since that first moment on the beach at Blue Owl Bay. You have been in my heart and my mind constantly since that night. If we survive here, will you come back to Dardania with me?'

'Yes,' she said simply.

He kissed her. As their lips met all thoughts of peril vanished from his mind. Nothing else existed, and he knew that this exquisite moment would remain etched in his memory for the rest of his life.

As they finally drew back from one another cold reality rushed in.

The rest of his life. It was likely to be no more than a single night.

'What are you thinking?' she whispered.

He smiled. 'All my life I have been waiting for this moment, only I did not know it. I was thinking that I would rather be here now, standing with you, than anywhere else on the Great Green.'

XXXII

Spears in the Night

i

WITH THE GATES CLOSED, AND THE INITIAL BURST OF COMBAT BEHIND him, Argurios stood in the courtyard before the palace. On the walls above him some forty Eagles, armed with Phrygian bows, were waiting for the next attack. Behind him he could hear orders being shouted within the king's *megaron*. Argurios stood silently, heavy of heart.

He had come here, as a Mykene outlaw, determined to seek Priam's permission to wed his daughter. Now he was caught up in a civil war. The thought of battle did not disturb him. His whole adult life had been honed in combat. What troubled him, as he stood quietly in the calm before the onslaught, was that Mykene warriors were coming. If Agamemnon had agreed to support Agathon with a small force, it would be made up of the finest warriors of his army. Argurios would have fought beside most of them, celebrated victories with them, commiserated with them when mutual comrades fell. Faces swarmed before his mind's eye: Kalliades the Tall, Menides Spear Carrier, Banokles One Ear, Eruthros the Joker, Ajax the Skull Splitter . . .

Were they, even now, marching towards the citadel?

And if they were, how could he, as a Mykene warrior, take up arms against them?

Could he stab Tall Kalliades and watch him fall? Could he send Banokles into the Underworld?

Yet these same men were coming to kill the father of the woman he loved. And what would be her fate if they succeeded? This was, at least, a question he could answer. Though Argurios himself had never raped a woman he knew that such activity was common after a battle.

Anger built in him at the thought of such a fate for Laodike. No, I will not allow that, he decided. I would cut the heart from Agamemnon himself rather than see Laodike hurt.

Moving swiftly to the foot of the rampart, he climbed the twenty steps to where Polydorus was crouched down behind the crenellated wall. Argurios raised his head above the parapet, swiftly scanning the open ground beyond. There were no warriors in sight, though he could see men massing in the shadows of the narrow streets some eighty paces away.

'They will be seeking ladders,' said Argurios.

'They will find plenty of them,' replied Polydorus. 'There is always new building work in Troy.'

The walls themselves were no more than the height of two tall men. If the enemy set wagons against them, they would be able to leap from them and haul themselves over the battlements. Argurios glanced back at the palace. Above and to the left of the doors was a long balcony, with high windows. Once the enemy opened the gates they could bring their ladders to the palace walls and scale them, entering the building from above. With enough men Argurios could have held the outer walls for days. Similarly, with three hundred hardened warriors he could defend the palace against a horde. It was galling to have such a fortress, and too few soldiers to keep it secure.

'I am going inside,' he told Polydorus. 'I need to study the *megaron* and plan for its defence. If they attack before I return loose several volleys into them, and hold the first assault. That is vital.'

'We will hold, Argurios,' muttered Polydorus. 'All night if we have to.'

'It will not be all night. I will explain more when I return.'

Polydorus smiled. 'Something to tell my children when they grow, eh? I fought beside Argurios.'

'You have children?'

'Not yet. But a man must think ahead.'

Argurios ran down the steps and across the courtyard. Inside the *megaron* all but the main doors had been barricaded. He saw Priam sitting on his throne, dressed in elaborate armour, decorated with gold and silver, a high-crested helmet upon his lap. Everywhere there were armed men. They had almost stripped the walls of shields and spears. Alongside the king stood Prince Dios. He wore no armour, though a sword was belted by his side.

Argurios approached them. Priam looked up. 'Have the dogs fled?' he asked, sober now, though his eyes were bloodshot and weary.

'No, Priam King. They are gathering ladders. They will come soon. We need archers on the outer balcony above the doors. Thirty should suffice. I will order the men on the walls to pull back to the *megaron* once the attack begins in earnest.'

'Who are you to give orders?' snapped Dios, his eyes angry.

'He is Argurios,' said Priam calmly. 'He is fighting at my side.'

'We should put every man we have on the outer walls,' raged Dios. 'We can hold them.'

'What say you to that, Argurios?' asked Priam.

'With three hundred men I would agree with Prince Dios. However, with so few the risk is encirclement. If they get behind us we will be cut to pieces. We must keep a line of withdrawal secure for as long as possible. My plan is to hold the wall for the first attack, then quietly pull back. When they come again we will hit them with volley after volley of arrows from the balcony.'

'And then we bar the doors?' asked Priam.

'No, king. We leave them open.'

Priam was surprised. 'Explain that strategy,' he said.

'There are many ways for an enemy to come at us. There is the door to the palace gardens. They could bring their ladders and climb to the balcony. They can come through the rear. We want them attacking where we are strongest. The open doors will be an invitation they will not resist. They will be drawn to us like flies to horse shit, and we will hold them there. At least until the Mykene arrive.'

'By the fates, father,' said Dios, 'how can we trust this man? He too is Mykene.'

Argurios took a deep, calming breath. 'Indeed I am, prince. Believe me when I tell you I would rather be anywhere than here at this moment. If the Mykene succeed here I will be killed along with all of you. Now, we have little time to prepare, and no time at all to vent personal feuds.' He turned to the king. 'If you have a better man than I to command this defence appoint him, and I will stand and fight wherever called upon to do so.'

'I am the king,' said Priam coldly. 'I will command my own defence. You think I am a weakling, some ancient unable to wield a sword?'

'It is not a question of your strength or your abilities,' answered Argurios. 'If I were commanding the attackers I would pray to all the gods that you would do *exactly* that. They win when you die. Every man among them will be seeking to kill you. Your armour shines like the sun, and every attack will home in on you. Every arrow, every spear, every sword will seek you. Your men will fight valiantly – but only so long as there is a king to fight for.'

At that moment Helikaon came through to the *megaron* and stood alongside Dios. 'We have blocked the rear entrances,' he said, 'but they will not hold long. What are your orders?'

Priam sat quietly for a moment. 'Argurios advises that I withdraw myself from the fighting. What say you?'

'Sound advice. This fight will not just be about holding the palace, but about defending you.'

'Let me take command in your stead, father,' urged Dios.

Priam shook his head. 'You have too little experience, and, as Argurios says, there is no time for debate. The men will follow you, Aeneas. This I know. Equally, Argurios is known across the

Great Green as a *strategos* and a fighting man. What is your opinion?'

'I have little experience of siege warfare, and less of Mykene battle tactics,' said Helikaon. 'I would follow the lead of Argurios.'

'Then let it be so.' Priam suddenly laughed. 'A renegade Mykene in charge of the defence of my citadel? I like it. When we win, you can ask me anything. I will grant it. We are yours to command, Argurios.'

Argurios swung to Dios. 'You will command the defence of the upper balconies. Take thirty good archers, and also the men with the least armour. They will be protected from arrows by the balcony walls. The enemy will bring ladders. Hold them off as long as you can, then retreat to the *megaron* and we will pull back to the upper buildings at the rear.'

Dios, his face pale, his expression furious, was struggling to hold his temper.

'Do as he says,' snapped Priam.

'This is madness,' responded Dios. 'But I will obey you, father. As always.' With that he stalked away.

'Let us survey the battleground,' said Argurios, striding away through the *megaron*. Priam and Helikaon followed him. Argurios reached the foot of the stairs. They were wide enough for two warriors to fight side by side. Then he glanced up at the gallery above and to the right of the stairway. 'We will have archers placed there. They will have a good view of the *megaron* itself. We need as many shafts as possible placed there. Spears and javelins too, if we have enough. What is beyond the gallery?'

'The queen's apartments,' said Priam. 'They are large and spacious.'

Argurios strode up the stairs, Helikaon and Priam following him. In the queen's apartments he saw Laodike upon her blood-stained couch, Andromache sitting on the floor beside her. All thoughts of the defence fled his mind. Pulling off his helmet he moved to Laodike and took her hand. Her eyes opened, and she gave a wide smile. 'What happened?' he asked her.

'I was wounded,' Laodike told him. 'Do not concern yourself. It is nothing.' Reaching up she stroked his face. 'I am glad you are here. Have you spoken to father?'

'Not yet. I cannot stay with you. There is much to be done. I will come back when I can. You rest now.' Kissing her hand he rose and walked back to where the king and Helikaon waited. Only then did he see the shock on Priam's face. Argurios moved past them and walked through to the rear stairs. Then he turned back and strode through the many apartments. 'The balconies are largely inaccessible,' he said. 'Therefore the enemy will be forced to come at us through the *megaron*. I believe we can hold the Thrakians at the doors. The Mykene will be another matter.'

'We could retreat to the stairs,' said Helikaon.

'We will do that, but the timing is crucial,' answered Argurios, walking back to the gallery above the stairs. 'We must keep their blood up, forcing them to come at us. We must not allow them time to stop and think. For, if they do, they will realize that this gallery is the key to victory. Once inside the *megaron* all they need to do is bring in ladders and scale it. That way they would bypass the stairs and surround us.'

'And how do we keep their blood up?' demanded Priam.

'They will see me, and come at me. I will be their target, and the focus of their attack. We will pull back to the stairs. They will surge after us. Then their hearts will be full of pride and battle lust. Will you stand beside me, Helikaon?'

'I will.'

'Good, for however much they will desire to bring me down it is you they hate. Seeing us together will blind them to better strategies. And now I must return to the wall.'

'A moment more,' said Priam. 'How is it my daughter greets you with a kiss?'

Argurios could see the anger in the king's eyes. 'You said if we survived the night you would grant any wish I had. My wish is to marry Laodike. I love her. But is this truly the time to discuss it?'

Priam relaxed, then gave a cold smile. 'If I am still king tomorrow we will discuss it at length.'

Argurios stood quietly for a moment. Then he turned to

Helikaon. 'Organize the defenders within the *megaron*. Then watch the walls. We need to turn back the first attack with heavy losses. It will dismay the mercenaries. When the moment is right come to our aid.'

'Rely on it,' said Helikaon.

'Judge it finely, Golden One.'

And with that he moved off, striding towards the double doors and the courtyard beyond.

ii

Polydorus peered through the gap in the crenellations of the ramparts. The Thrakians were gathering in the shadows of the buildings. Anger touched him, but he quelled it. Yesterday Casilla's parents had finally agreed to the wedding – in part owing to the intervention of Laodike. She had visited the family home, and had spoken to Casilla's mother. She had also taken a gift for the father, a golden wine goblet encrusted with red gems. This powerful link to the nobility had finally won them over. Casilla had been overjoyed, and Polydorus considered himself the luckiest man alive.

Now he felt as if he were part of some grim jest being played out by the gods. Polydorus was no fool. There were not enough men to defend the palace against the Thrakians, let alone the Mykene. Once the Thrakians gathered enough ladders to storm the walls the battle would be all but over. The fighting would be fierce and bloody, and the Eagles would take a terrible toll on the enemy, but the end was certain. Casilla would mourn for him, of course, but she was young, and her father would find another suitor.

Argurios climbed to the ramparts alongside him. 'Any movement?'

'They are gathering. I have not seen any Mykene yet.'

'They will come once the gates are open.'

'What is the battle plan?' asked Polydorus.

'Hold here for a while, then back to the palace itself.'

'The palace doors are sturdy,' observed Polydorus, 'but they'll not hold for long.'

'They won't have to,' said Argurios. 'I don't intend to close them. I want the enemy funnelled towards those doors. We'll hit them from above, and hold them in the doorway.'

'Surely barring the palace doors would give us more time?'

'It would,' agreed Argurios. 'It would also leech away the spirit of those inside, listening to the hacking of axes upon the timber. Better to face your enemy eye to eye. My father used to say a wall of men was stronger than a wall of stone. I have seen it to be true in many battles.'

Polydorus raised his head, and peered through the darkness. An arrow struck the ramparts close to his head, then ricocheted past him.

'You are all going to die tonight!' came a shout from the shadows. It was immediately followed by the trilling battle cry of the Thrakians.

Then came another voice. 'Are you there, Argurios Traitor?'

'I am here, puppy dog!' Argurios shouted back.

'That gladdens my heart! I will see you soon.'

'Not while I have a sword in my hand, you gutless worm. I know you, Kolanos. You'll slink in the shadows while braver men die for you.' He leaned towards Polydorus. 'Get ready! They are coming!'

Polydorus hefted his Phrygian bow, notching a shaft to the string. All along the wall the Eagles followed his lead.

Suddenly there came the sound of pounding feet, and once more the Thrakian battle cry filled the air.

The Eagles stood and sent a volley into the charging men. Polydorus shot again, and saw a man dragging a ladder go tumbling to the ground. The ladder was swept up by the fallen man's comrades. Volley after volley slashed into the Thrakians, but there were too few archers to turn the charge. Scores of ladders clattered against the walls. An enemy shaft bounced from Polydorus' breastplate. Another hissed past his face.

Then the Thrakians began to storm the walls. Dropping his bow

Polydorus drew his leaf-shaped short sword, and took up his shield. Beside him Argurios waited, sword in hand. 'Move along a little,' he said calmly. 'Give me some fighting room.'

Polydorus edged to his right.

The first of the Thrakians appeared. Polydorus leapt forward, thrusting his sword into the man's face. Desperately the Thrakian tried to haul himself over the ramparts, but Polydorus struck him again and he fell. Now the night was full of the sounds of battle, men screaming in pain or fury, swords ringing, shields clashing. Several warriors clambered over the battlement wall to Polydorus' right. He rushed them, plunging his sword into the chest of the first. The blade went deep and lodged there. Unable to drag it clear Polydorus threw the man from the wall, down into the courtyard below, then hammered his shield into the face of the second. Argurios appeared alongside him, stabbing and cutting. Picking up a fallen sword Argurios tossed it to Polydorus, then swung to face a fresh attack.

All along the wall the Thrakians were gaining a foothold. The Eagles did not break, but fought on with relentless courage. Glancing along the line Polydorus saw that around a third of his men were down. Then he saw Helikaon and some thirty Eagles running across the courtyard. They surged up the battlement steps to join the fighting. The lightly armoured Thrakians fell back. Some even jumped from the walls to the street below. Others already on ladders leapt clear. Letting his shield fall Polydorus swept up his bow and shot into the fleeing men.

A feeling of exultation swept over him. He was alive, and he had conquered.

Argurios approached him. 'Get our wounded back into the *megaron*,' he said. 'And strip our dead of all weapons and armour. Also gather the swords and spears of the enemy. Do it swiftly, for we will not have long before the next attack.'

'We will beat them again,' said Polydorus. 'We are the Eagles and we are invincible.'

The older man looked at him closely. 'That was merely the first attack. They will come harder and faster now. Look around you.

We lost fourteen men, with six others wounded. Half of the fighting men on the wall. Next time we would be overrun. That is why we will not be here next time. Now do as I say.'

All the excitement drained out of the young soldier. He ran down the rampart steps, calling out orders. Other men raced from the *megaron* to assist in the collection of weapons. Argurios strode along the ramparts, occasional arrows flashing by him.

iii

Argurios moved among the defenders left on the rampart walls. Like Polydorus, they were exultant now, for they had met the enemy and vanquished him. Their spirits were high, and Argurios had no wish to douse them with cold reality. The first attack had been rushed and ill conceived, attempting to sweep over the ramparts in a wide front. Better to have come at both ends of the wall, drawing the defenders out of position, then assaulting the centre. The next charge would be better planned.

Even so, Argurios was content. This first action had lifted the hearts of the defenders, and dispirited the enemy. The confidence of the Thrakians was dented. The enemy leaders would know it was vital for them to score a swift victory, in order to repair the damage. Even now the officers would be gathered, with Agathon seeking to inspire them, building their confidence for the next assault. He would be assuring them of victory, promising them riches. Argurios called a soldier to him. 'Go to Prince Dios on the balcony. Tell him we will be pulling back from the wall before the next attack. Ask that he holds back his archers until the enemy reaches the courtyard. They will be massed there, and easy targets. Then go to the lord Helikaon. Fifty men with shields are to be ready to defend the palace doorway.'

Swinging his shield to his back the soldier ran down the rampart steps and across the stone courtyard.

Argurios raised his head above the ramparts. The moon was rising, silver light bathing the streets and houses. He could see the

Thrakians standing ready, officers moving among them. There was still no sign of the Mykene.

This was to be expected. They were an elite force, and would not be used early in the battle. They will come when we are weary, he thought, striking like a hammer at the heart of the defence. Arrows and spears would be largely useless against them. Well-armoured and carrying tall, curved tower shields of bronze-reinforced ox hide, and armed with both heavy spears and stabbing swords, they would advance in formation, forcing the defenders back. The spears would give them a reach advantage over the sword-wielding Eagles. The only hope of success against such a force would be to break their formation. This could be done on the open field of battle, but not inside the confines of a palace *megaron*. Argurios knew that the Eagles were well disciplined, and fine fighters. Could they hold, though, against the finest of the Mykene? He doubted it.

Time wore on, and still the Thrakians did not attack.

Polydorus returned to the battlements, and then Helikaon emerged from the palace and joined them. 'When will the Mykene come?' he asked.

'When the gates are open.' Argurios turned to Polydorus. 'Go back into the palace and gather the tallest and the strongest of the Eagles. No more than thirty of them. Hold them back from the initial fighting. When the Mykene come we will need the best we have. See if you can arm them with heavy spears, as well as their swords.'

'Yes, Argurios.'

After Polydorus had gone Argurios raised his head above the battlements. 'Not long now, I would think.'

'This must be hard for you,' said Helikaon, as Argurios sat back down.

Argurios felt his anger surge, but swallowed it down. He looked at the young man beside him. 'In a little while I will be slaying my comrades. I will be fighting alongside a man I have sworn to kill. *Hard* does not begin to describe this night.'

'There are times,' said Helikaon softly, 'when you can almost hear the gods laugh. I am truly sorry, Argurios. I wish I had never asked you to accompany me on that walk to Kygones' palace. Had I known the heartache it would bring you I never would have.'

Argurios' anger ebbed away. 'I do not regret my actions that day,' he said. 'As a result I met Laodike. I had not realized until then that my life had been lived in the darkness of a perpetual winter night. When I saw her it was as if the sun had risen.' He fell silent for a moment, embarrassed at this display of emotion. 'I sound like a doting fool, I expect.'

'No. You sound like a man in love. Did you feel as if some invisible fist had struck your chest? Did your tongue cleave to the roof of your mouth?'

'Exactly that! You have experienced it?'

'Every time I see Andromache.'

Just then an Eagle away to the left shouted, 'Here they come!'

Argurios pushed himself to his feet. 'Now it begins in earnest,' he said.

iv

Prince Agathon watched his Thrakians rushing towards the walls. There were no battle cries now, merely a grim determination to kill and conquer, and earn the riches Agathon had offered. He longed to be with them, scaling a ladder and cutting his way through to Priam. He wanted to be there when the king was dragged to his knees, begging for his life. Yet he could not be with them yet. With Priam's death success was his, but if *he* were to die in the assault all these years of planning and scheming would come to nothing. He would walk the dark road to Hades as a failure.

A failure.

In Priam's eyes he always had been. When Agathon defeated the rebel Hittites at Rhesos his father had railed at the losses he sustained. 'Hektor would have crushed them with half your men and a tenth of your dead.' No parade for Agathon. No wreath of laurels.

When had it ever been different? As a child of ten, frightened of the dark, and fearful of cramped, gloomy places, he had been taken by his father to the subterranean Caves of Cerberus. Priam had told him of demons and monsters who inhabited the caves, and that a wrong path would lead straight to the Underworld. Father had been carrying a torch. Agathon had stayed close, his panic growing. Deeper and deeper they travelled. Then they had come to an underground stream. Father had doused the torch and stepped away from him. Agathon had screamed, begging his father to take his hand.

The silence had grown. He had cowered in the darkness for what seemed an eternity, weeping and terrified.

Then he had seen a light. It was his eleven-year-old half-brother Hektor, carrying a flaming torch. 'Father is gone. Demons have taken him,' Agathon had wailed.

'No, he is outside, waiting for you.'

'Why did he leave me?'

'He thinks it will cure your fear of the dark.'

'Can we go now?'

'I cannot leave with you, Agathon. Father does not know I came here. I entered on the south side. We will douse the torch, and you will take my hand. I will lead you to where you can see the sunlight. Then you must walk out on your own.'

'Why does he hate me, Hektor?'

'He just wants you to be strong. I am going to douse the torch now. Are you ready?'

Hektor had led him slowly up through the tunnels, holding close to the walls. Agathon had not been afraid then, for he could feel the warmth of Hektor's hand, and knew his brother would not abandon him. The gloom had slowly lifted, and ahead Agathon had seen sunlight against the cave walls.

'I'll see you later, little brother,' said Hektor, ducking back into the darkness.

Agathon had walked out, to see father, mother, and twenty or more counsellors and advisers, all sitting in the sunshine. As Agathon emerged Priam looked over to him. 'Gods, boy, have you been weeping? You are a disgrace to me.'

Shaking himself free of the memory he watched his Thrakians scale the walls. Strangely there was no sound of fighting.

The white-haired Kolanos appeared alongside him. 'They have retreated to the citadel,' he said.

Then came the cries of wounded and dying men. Agathon knew what was happening. Archers were shooting down into the massed ranks of his Thrakians. Swinging round, he called out to one of the officers commanding the reserves. 'Send in bowmen!' he shouted. 'The enemy will be massed on the balcony above the doors. Pin them down!' The officer gathered his men and a hundred archers ran to the ladders.

This should have been so simple. Agathon's men were to march to the palace, overpower the few guards, and allow the Mykene in to complete the massacre. Instead the gates were barred, and a defence had been organized.

Who would have thought that Fat Antiphones could have fought off the assassins? There was no doubt in Agathon's mind that he had lived long enough to warn Helikaon. Agathon had heard that a rider on a golden horse had swept past his Thrakians as they marched to the citadel. Helikaon alone bred these mounts. Then had come the news that a warrior in Mykene armour had scattered his men when they were about to storm the gates.

Helikaon and Argurios. Two men who were never a part of his original plan. Two men who were only invited at the request of Kolanos.

Ultimately their actions could do nothing but delay the inevitable, yet it was still galling.

The gates to the courtyard swung open. 'Prepare your fighters,' he told Kolanos, then crossed the open ground to seize his destiny.

XXXIII

The Shield of Ilos

i

ARGURIOS ENTERED THE *MEGARON*, EASING HIS WAY PAST THE THREE ranks of Eagles preparing to defend the wide doorway. Helikaon, a curved shield slung across his back, approached him. 'Ensure the men know they must hold their position,' said Argurios. 'If the enemy fall back there must be no chase.'

'Already done,' said Helikaon. 'When do you expect the Mykene?'

'Soon.'

Argurios left him then and strode across the mosaic floor. He needed a shield, but the walls had been all but stripped of weapons and armour. Then he saw it. It was an ancient piece, beautifully wrought, decorated with tin and blue enamel. At its centre was a battle scene, featuring the great hero Herakles fighting the nine-headed Hydra. Borrowing a spear from a soldier, he hooked the point under the strap and lifted the shield from the wall.

Swinging it to his back he walked across to where Polydorus stood, with some thirty Eagles, tall men and wide-shouldered, their faces grim. He scanned them all, looking into their eyes. He was unsure of two of them, and sent them to join Helikaon at the doorway. The rest waited for his orders. 'When the Mykene come,' he told them, 'I want you to form three lines behind the defenders. At my order . . .' Just then came the sounds of screams and battle cries from outside, as the Thrakians surged towards the doorway. The Eagles tightened their grips on their weapons and adjusted their shields. 'Look at me and listen,' said Argurios calmly. 'Your turn will come soon enough. You are to face the Mykene. When they come they will be in tight formation. They will charge the doorway and seek to scatter the defenders with their weight and power. As they rush forward Helikaon will break his line to left and right. We will counter the Mykene charge with one of our own. Thus we will form three sides of a square. We will hold the Mykene while Helikaon's men attack them on the flanks. Is this clear?'

'It is clear, sir,' said Polydorus. 'But how long can thirty hold back two hundred?'

'I do not know,' said Argurios, 'but this is how legends are carved. We will be forced back. We will conduct a fighting retreat to the stairs below the queen's apartments. We will not break and scatter. Each man here will stand beside his comrades, as if we were all brothers of the blood.' As he spoke he swung the shield round, settling his left arm into the straps. He saw the Eagles staring at it, shock on their faces.

'Brothers of the Blood,' said Polydorus. 'We will not fail you, Argurios.'

'Then let us form up behind the defenders. Rank of Three.'

The Eagles moved into position, Argurios at the centre of the first line.

Ahead of them Helikaon and his warriors were battling the Thrakians.

Argurios took a deep breath, letting it out slowly. Torches flickered in brackets upon the walls, and the sounds of war echoed around the *megaron*. On the stairs leading to the balcony above the doorway Argurios saw wounded men being helped down. Thrakian archers were beginning to take their toll on Dios and his

---

men. Several of the Eagles with Helikaon had also fallen, the men behind dragging them clear.

And the long night wore on.

ii

Andromache rose from beside the sleeping Laodike and gazed around the queen's apartments. Injured men were being brought in all the time now, some with hideous wounds. Priam's chief physician, Zeotos, was tending them, his long white robes now bloodstained, his hands and arms crimson with gore. The elderly physician had arrived a little while ago, and moved straight to Laodike's side. 'She is all right,' Andromache assured him. 'The bleeding has all but stopped and she is resting well.'

'We will all be resting well after this night,' he said despondently.

Axa and several other servants were assisting the noblewomen, bandaging wounds and administering stitches. Even young Kassandra was busy cutting up linens. By the balcony wall there were six dead bodies, all stripped of armour and weapons. There was little space to lay them out, and they had been laid atop one another, arms entwined.

Andromache walked out of the apartments onto the gallery above the stairs. Quivers of arrows had been laid here, and a stack of throwing spears. Moving to the far left of the gallery she looked down into the *megaron*. Men were battling by the doors, and she saw Helikaon among them, his bright bronze armour gleaming like gold in the torchlight.

Behind the defenders stood another group of warriors, tall shields on their arms, heavy thrusting spears in their hands.

Off to the right she saw the king and around a dozen of his counsellors. Many of them were older men, but they were holding swords or spears, and a few bore shields. From her high vantage point Andromache could see past the fighting men, and out into the courtyard beyond. Hundreds of Thrakians were massing there. It seemed inconceivable that the few defenders could keep them out for long.

More wounded were dragged back from the front line. She saw Priam gesture to his counsellors, and several of them ran forward, heaving the injured to their feet and half carrying them back towards the stairs. One soldier – an older man, perhaps in his forties – was gouting blood from a neck wound. He sagged against the men assisting him, then slumped to the floor.

Andromache watched as the pumping blood slowed, and the man died. Almost immediately other men crowded round him, unbuckling his breastplate and untying his greaves. Within moments the dead Eagle was merely another body, hauled unceremoniously back and left against the wall, so as not to encumber the living. The dead man had been flung on his back, and his head lolled, his vacant eyes staring up at her. Andromache felt suddenly light-headed, a sense of unreality gripping her. The clashing sounds of battle receded, and she found herself staring into the eyes of the corpse below. The difference between life and death was a single heartbeat. All that man's dreams, his hopes and his ambitions, had been dashed in one bloody moment.

Her mouth was dry, and she felt the beginnings of terror clawing at the pit of her stomach.

Would she too be dead in a little while?

Would Helikaon fall, his throat slashed, his body stripped and discarded?

Her hands were trembling. Soon the enemy would sweep past the tiring defenders, and surge into the *megaron*. She pictured them running at her, their faces distorted with rage and lust. Strangely the image calmed her.

'I am not a victim waiting for the slaughter,' she said aloud. 'I am Andromache.'

Kassandra came running from the queen's apartments. 'We need more bandages,' she said.

Andromache reached out. 'Give me the scissors.' Kassandra did so, and Andromache hacked into her own full-length white gown just above the knees, cutting the material clear. Kassandra clapped her hands.

'Let me help!' she cried, as Andromache struggled to complete the circular cut. The child took the scissors, slicing swiftly through the cloth. The lower half of Andromache's gown fell away.

'Do mine! Do mine!' said Kassandra.

Andromache knelt by the child and swiftly snipped through the thin cloth. Kassandra swept up the material and darted away. Andromache followed her back into the main rooms, then took up her bow. Returning to the gallery she hefted a quiver of arrows, and settled it over her shoulder.

'Fear is an aid to the warrior,' her father had said. 'It is like a small fire burning. It heats the muscles, making us stronger. Panic comes when the fire is out of control, consuming all courage and pride.'

There was still fear in her, as she stared down at the battle in the doorway.

But the panic had gone.

iii

The two hundred and twelve warriors of the Mykene stood patiently before the Temple of Hermes, awaiting the call to battle. There was little tension among them, even with the distant sounds of battle, and the screams of dying men echoing over the city. Some joked, others chatted to old comrades. Kalliades the Tall, his tower shield swung to his back, walked along a line of statues outside the temple doors, marvelling at the workmanship. In the moonlight they could almost be real, he thought, gazing up into the face of Hermes, the winged god of travellers. The face was young, little more than a youth, the wings on the heels beautifully fashioned. Reaching out he stroked his thick fingers across the stone. Banokles One Ear joined him. 'It's said they brought in Gyppto sculptors,' said Banokles. 'I had an uncle once who went to Luxor. They got statues there tall as mountains, so he said.'

Kalliades glanced at his friend. Banokles was already wearing his full-faced helmet, and his deep voice was muffled. 'You must be sweating like a pig in that,' ventured Kalliades.

440

'Better to be ready,' answered Banokles.

'For what?'

'I don't trust the Trojans. They have a thousand men on the Great Walls.'

Kalliades chuckled. 'You never were a trusting man. They opened the gates for us, didn't they? They serve the new king. No problem for us.'

'No problem?' countered Banokles. 'Does it sound to you like no problem? There was to be no major battle. The Thrakians would take the citadel and we were to clean out a few guests at a funeral feast. It is not going well, Kalliades.'

'We'll put it right when they call us.' Kalliades pointed to the statue of a woman, holding a sheaf of corn in one hand and a sword in the other. 'I can recognize most of the gods, but who is that?'

Banokles shrugged. 'I don't know. Some Trojan deity maybe.'

A powerfully built warrior with a square-cut black beard emerged from an alleyway and made his way over to join them.

'What news, Eruthros?' Banokles asked him.

'Good and bad. The gates are open,' answered the man. 'Won't be long now.'

'And the bad?' enquired Banokles.

'I spoke to Kolanos. Argurios is with the Trojans.'

'By Hades, I wouldn't have thought it possible,' said Kalliades. 'When word came he'd turned traitor I didn't believe it for one heartbeat.'

'Nor me,' admitted Banokles.

'Well, I hope it's not me who cuts him down,' said Eruthros. 'The man is a legend.'

Kalliades wandered away from his friends. He had no fear of battle, and no qualms about fighting inside a foreign city. It seemed to him that the world was neatly divided into lions and sheep. The Mykene were lions. Any who could be conquered were sheep. It was a natural order, and one which Argurios understood. Indeed it had been Argurios who had first offered him this simple philosophy.

Now Argurios, the Mykene Lion, was standing with the sheep. It made no sense. Still worse was the fact that Kalliades and his friends were being led by Kolanos. They called him the Breaker of Spirits, but the Despicable was closer to the truth. For the first time since they landed Kalliades felt uneasy.

He had fought with Argurios at Partha, and in Thessaly, and on the Athenian plains. He had stormed towns and sacked cities alongside him, and stood shoulder to shoulder with him in a score of skirmishes and fights. Argurios had never been interested in plunder or riches. His entire life had been one of service to his king. There was not enough gold in all the world to buy a man like Argurios. So how was it possible that he had betrayed the Mykene and allied himself with the Trojan enemy?

Banokles approached him. 'The Eagles are holding the Thrakians at the palace doors. The butcher Helikaon is with them.'

This was better news. The thought that the vile Burner would pay for his hideous crimes lifted Kalliades' spirits. 'If the gods will it,' he said, 'I shall cut his head clear.'

'And put out his eyes?'

'Of course not! You think I am a heathen savage like him? No, his death will be enough.'

Banokles laughed. 'Well, *you* can hunt down the Burner. Once we've cleaned out the Eagles I'll be looking for some softer booty. Never shagged a king's daughter before. It is said that Priam's daughters are all beautiful. Big round tits and fat arses. You think they'll let me take one home?'

'Why would you want to?' countered Kalliades. 'With the gold we've been promised you can buy a hundred women.'

'True, but a king's daughter is special. Something to brag about.'

'It seems to me you've never needed anything *special* to brag about.'

Banokles laughed with genuine good humour. 'I used to think I was the greatest braggart on the Great Green. Then I met Odysseus. Now *that* man can brag. I swear he could weave a magical tale about taking a shit in a swamp.'

All around them the Mykene troops began to gather. Kalliades saw Kolanos moving among the men.

'Time to earn our plunder,' said black-bearded Eruthros, putting on his helmet.

Kalliades strode back to where he had left his helmet, shield and spear. Banokles went with him. As Kalliades garbed himself for battle, Banokles removed his helmet, and ran his fingers through his long yellow hair.

'Now that it is time to put on your helmet you are removing it,' Kalliades pointed out.

'Sweating like a pig,' responded Banokles, with a wide grin.

They lined up with their comrades and waited as Kolanos mustered the men.

'You know what is required of you, men of Mykene,' shouted Kolanos. 'The palace is held by a few royal guardsmen. This is a night of blood. This is a night of slaughter. Drench your spears. Kill them all. Leave not a man alive.'

iv

The bodies of dead Thrakians were piled high around the palace doors, and scores more corpses littered the courtyard, shot down by arrows from the balcony above. Helikaon lowered his sword as the surviving Thrakians pulled back towards the shelter of the gates.

Around him the Eagles relaxed, and there was silence at last. Helikaon turned to the warriors alongside him. 'Now the Mykene will come,' he said. 'When they charge take up positions left and right of the doors.'

'Not many of us left,' said a tall soldier, glancing round at the surviving defenders. No more than twenty Eagles manned the doorway. Argurios and his twenty-eight men stood a little way back, shields and spears at the ready.

'Might be a good time to shut the doors,' offered another warrior.

'No,' said Helikaon. 'They would not hold for more than a few moments. It would also give them time to move the bodies. As it is their charge will be slowed as they clamber over them.'

'Never fought Mykene,' said the first man. 'Said to be fine fighters.'

'They think they are the greatest warriors in all the world,' said Helikaon. 'They are going to learn a sad truth tonight.' He moved back to where Argurios waited. The men were standing in three ranks. Polydorus shuffled to his right, allowing Helikaon to stand alongside Argurios.

No-one spoke and the silence grew. Then Prince Dios came running down from the upper balcony, followed by his archers.

'No more shafts,' said Dios.

'Take your men to the far balcony,' said Argurios. 'There are quivers there.'

'You don't have enough men to hold them here,' said Dios. 'We'll stand with you.'

'No,' said Argurios. 'Your men have no armour. They will be cut to pieces. Defend the stairwell.'

Dios moved away without a word, and the warriors waited. From where he stood Helikaon could see out into the courtyard. It was deserted, save for the dead and dying. So many had died this night, and many more would walk the dark road before the dawn. Time drifted by. Helikaon's mouth was dry.

Then he heard the sound of marching feet. 'They are coming!' shouted a warrior in the doorway.

At that moment Prince Dios appeared, dressed in a breastplate of bronze and silver, and carrying a long shield. An Eagle's helmet was pushed back on his head. At his side was a stabbing sword, and in his hand a heavy spear.

He moved in alongside Argurios. 'Do you object to fighting alongside the runt of the litter?' he asked, with a tight smile.

'It will be an honour, Prince Deiphobos,' said Argurios softly.

'Call me Dios,' said the young man, with a smile. 'And try to forget I can be a pompous fool sometimes.'

'As can we all,' Argurios told him. Then he raised his voice to address the waiting warriors. 'Do not stab at the body,' he said. 'Their armour is well made and will turn any blade. Go for the throat, the lower thigh, or the arms.'

Helikaon gazed out into the courtyard. The Mykene had formed up in tight ranks of eight abreast. Then they began to march towards the palace. As they came closer they surged into a run.

The Eagles in the doorway faded left and right. The Mykene slowed as they reached the wall of Thrakian corpses.

Argurios hefted his spear. 'For the King and for Troy!' he bellowed.

And the Eagles charged.

XXXIV

The Lost Garden

i

ANDROMACHE FELT HER HEART GO OUT TO THESE VALIANT MEN. FROM
her vantage point on the rear gallery she could see how unequal
was the struggle. There seemed to be hundreds of heavily armed
Mykene warriors, powering forward with brute strength into a
mere three ranks of Eagles. Even so, the Mykene charge faltered,
as the Eagles from the doorway gathered on both sides of the
advancing phalanx, hacking and cutting at the Mykene flanks.

None of the archers on the gallery could afford to shoot yet, for
fear of hitting their own men. But slowly, as the phalanx inexorably entered the *megaron*, some bowmen began to send shafts
into the warriors still massing in the doorway. Few arrows pierced
the great shields, or the heavy helmets and breastplates of the
invaders. But they caused the fighting men at the centre to raise
their shields against this new attack, lessening the pressure on the
front of the line.

Argurios gave no ground, fighting with ruthless economy of
effort, his spear lancing into the enemy, his shield a wall they could
not pass. Beside him Helikaon was also holding, and Andromache
saw the first Mykene fall to his spear. Soon other bodies were

falling as the fighting became ever more brutal. At least two Mykene were going down to every Eagle.

It was not enough.

Notching an arrow to her bow she took careful aim – and sent a black shaft slashing through the air to bury itself through the eye socket of a glittering bronze helm. The victim vanished under the feet of his comrades.

The battle wore on, the Eagles now being pushed back, bent like a bow of human flesh. Andromache and the other archers continued to shoot down into the fighting, scoring less than one good hit in twenty.

The Eagles were engaged in a fighting retreat, the Mykene seeking to circle them, and cut them off from the stairs. At the centre of the Trojan line Argurios, Helikaon and Dios were fighting hard, but the flanks were giving way faster than the centre. At any moment the Mykene could sweep round and encircle the battling men.

Andromache saw the danger. 'Aim for the wings!' she cried to the bowmen around her. A greater concentration of shafts hammered into the Mykene on the left of the battle line, and they were forced to raise their shields and pull back, allowing the Trojan line to steady.

At the back of the mêlée Andromache saw the white-haired figure of Kolanos, urging his men on, but keeping back from the point of impact.

Just then Andromache felt the frayed hem of her chiton being tugged. She glanced down and saw little Kassandra standing there. 'You must come. Quickly,' said Kassandra. Andromache struggled to hear her above the clash of swords and shields, and the screams of wounded men. Kneeling down, she drew the girl to her.

'What is it?'

'Laodike! She is dying!'

'No, she is just resting,' she said. Kassandra shook her head.

'You must come,' she said.

Allowing the child to take her hand she followed her back into the queen's apartments. They were filled now with wounded men, and she saw Axa helping to carry a soldier to a wide table where the physician Zeotos, his robes now utterly drenched with gore, sought to save him.

Kassandra moved away and Andromache hurried to where Laodike lay. The young woman's face was unnaturally pale, and sheened with sweat. Her lips and eyelids had a bluish tinge. Andromache knelt beside her, taking her hand. The fingers seemed thick and swollen, and they too were bruised and discoloured.

'Zeotos!' she shouted. The sounds of fighting outside were closer now, and Andromache sensed the battle was all but over. In that moment she did not care. 'Zeotos!' she screamed again.

The old physician came to her side. His face showed his exhaustion. 'What is happening to her?' cried Andromache.

Zeotos hauled at Laodike, half turning her, and using a small knife to slice through her dress. Once the skin of her back was exposed Andromache saw a huge, black and swollen bruise extending from her shoulder to her hip.

'Why did you not tell me she had such a wound?' said Zeotos. 'I thought she was merely scratched.'

'I believed her to be healing,' answered Andromache.

'Well, she's not,' said the physician. 'She's dying. The sword or spear must have pierced a vital organ. She is bleeding to death from within.'

'There must be something you can do?'

Zeotos' shoulders sagged. 'Within a few heartbeats I will be able to do nothing for anyone. We are lost. As she is lost. We are going to die.' With that he returned to the wounded man on the table.

Priam approached. He had a sword in his hand. He looked down on his stricken daughter. 'Her death will be a merciful release,' he said. Then he looked at Andromache. 'When they come do not struggle. Do not fight. Women have been raped before and have survived. Live, Andromache.' Then he strode away towards the gallery. Little Kassandra appeared from a hiding place behind the couch.

'I didn't want father to see me,' she said. 'He is angry with me.'

'He is not angry, little one.'

Kassandra grabbed Andromache's hand. 'Yes, he is. Ever since I told him Hektor is coming home. He won't be angry when he sees him. He'll be here soon.'

'Oh, Kassandra.' Andromache reached out and hugged the girl. 'Hektor is dead.'

'No!' exclaimed Kassandra, pulling away. 'Listen to me. I thought he was dead too. But the voices told me. Then they showed me.'

'What did they show you?'

'Climbing high cliffs. Perils and adventures. Down long rivers . . .'

'Slow down!' said Andromache. 'Tell me calmly from the beginning. What cliffs?'

Kassandra took a deep breath. 'Hektor and his men were trapped. It was night. Hektor knew the enemy would come again at dawn to kill him, so he exchanged armour with a dead man. Then he and his men climbed the cliffs. Hektor is a good climber. We used to climb sometimes—'

'Stay with your story,' Andromache interrupted. 'What happened after they climbed the cliffs?'

'It took them a long time to reach a big river, and then to find a boat to bring them to the sea. A long time. That is why no word came. But he is here tonight. Please believe me, Andromache. Hektor will be here soon, with lots of soldiers. He will.'

Just then Laodike cried out, and opened her swollen eyes. She saw Andromache, who once more gripped her hand and kissed her cheek.

'Rest, sister,' she whispered.

'I think I'm dying. Oh, Andromache!' A tear fell and she blinked more away. 'I don't want to die!'

Andromache's vision misted and she bit her lip. 'I'm so sorry.'

Laodike sighed. 'It was all to be so perfect. Argurios and I would . . . live in a palace overlooking the Scamander. I went there only yesterday. It is so . . . beautiful . . . I . . . sat in the garden . . . in the garden . . .' Her voice tailed away. Then she spoke again. 'Where is Argurios?'

'He is fighting. For you. For all of us.'

'He will win. Like my Hektor. Always wins. I am very thirsty.'

Kassandra ran away to find some water. There was little to be had, and she came back with a small goblet, containing barely a mouthful.

Andromache held it to Laodike's lips. She drank a little, then sagged back. 'Will you find him for me, Andromache?' she asked. 'Bring him to me. I . . . don't want to be alone when . . . I die.'

'I will find him.'

Laodike closed her eyes and smiled. 'Find . . . my . . . Argurios,' she whispered.

ii

Argurios was exultant. Everything had worked precisely to plan, and now was the moment he had waited for. Once he was on the stairs, Helikaon beside him, Polydorus and Dios behind, the enemy advance had been halted. Now the Mykene were forced to attack in twos, driving up towards the warriors above them, while the mass of enemy soldiers milled below, helpless against arrows shot at them from above, or spears hurled from the gallery. In essence it was the Bridge of Partha yet again, the entire battle being fought on a narrow line between consistently equal fighting men. It no longer mattered that the Mykene outnumbered them, for at the point of impact there could only be two enemy facing them on the stairs.

Argurios hammered his shield against his next opponent, forcing an opening. His spear plunged forward, lancing up between helmet and flesh. The warrior stumbled and fell. Argurios slammed his foot against the man's shoulder, sending him rolling into his comrades. Another Mykene leapt to the fray. He stumbled over the fallen man and Helikaon killed him.

Again and again fresh warriors surged against the men on the stairs, but there was no give in them, and the death toll continued to rise.

As Argurios had hoped, the Mykene were no longer thinking clearly about their objective. Instead they were focused only on the need to kill the men facing them. This blinded them to alternatives. Argurios knew what they were thinking. One last push and the citadel would be theirs. All they had to do was brush aside the few fighting men on the stairs and victory was within their grasp.

Now all forward momentum had ceased. Argurios and Helikaon, their legs braced against the rising steps, their shields held firmly, their deadly lances cleaving into the enemy, were blocking the way like a wall of death.

At first it would have seemed to the Mykene that they were winning. Now they had been baulked, and were losing men without reply. One after another strong warriors were being cut down, their bodies dragged back to make way for the men behind. Now, Argurios knew, the worms of doubt would start to burrow into the hearts of the Mykene. This was not like an ordinary battle. There was no retreat for them here, no safe camp to return to at the end of a day's fighting. They were no less trapped than the Trojans. If they could not clear this citadel and kill the king before the dawn, then other troops would come to Priam's rescue, thousands of them, from the forts on the Scamander plain, or from the barracks in the lower town.

Argurios fought on, no longer tired, every sense alert. He was fighting for more than life now, more than honour. He was fighting for love, and determined that nothing would destroy his chance at happiness with Laodike. He held her face in his mind's eye, the sweetness of her smile, the radiance of her company. Not one Mykene warrior would be allowed to mount these stairs.

A spear scraped along his cuirass, ripping clear two more of the bronze discs. Argurios twisted to the right, his own weapon lunging home. It was a poor hit, thudding into the armoured shoulder and spinning the man. Helikaon kicked the man in front of him, spilling him to the stairs, then spun and drove his lance through the throat of Argurios' opponent. Then both heroes brought their shields to bear against the next attackers.

Moments later it was Helikaon who was thrown back, losing his footing. Argurios blocked a downward lunge that would have ripped out Helikaon's throat, then hammered his shield against the Mykene, forcing him back. Helikaon made it to his feet, and fought on.

The stairs were slippery with blood now, but there was no let up in the fighting. There were no more arrows to shoot from the gallery, and men and women stood there helplessly, staring down at the combatants.

At the top of the stairs Priam waited, sword in hand, staring down at the two men who stood between triumph and disaster.

It was hard to believe these were men of flesh, for they fought like gods, untiring and unbending. The king had already come to believe the battle was lost. Now he was not so sure. Hope flickered. The king glanced around him. On every face there was grim determination, and a sense of awe and pride at what they were witnessing.

For the first time in many years Priam gazed with pride on his son Deiphobos, standing behind Argurios, and ready to take his place in the battle on the stairs.

Transferring his gaze to the Mykene he saw there was no give in them either. They were not frightened, nor dismayed. They waited patiently for their chance at the fighters on the stairs, their expressions hard and unyielding.

The fragile hope faded in the king's breast. No matter how valiant the heroes on the stairs, nothing would hold back these blood-hungry barbarians. Soon either Helikaon or Argurios would be cut down, and the murderous assault on the upper levels begin.

Well, he thought, I shall show these savages how a king dies.

Hefting his sword he strode forward to stand beside the last defenders.

iii

Kalliades spat blood from his mouth, and wedged a lump of cloth into his cheek. Argurios' spear had sliced up under his helmet, ripping through the flesh of his face. He had been lucky. The point had missed his eye by a hair's breadth. He had then been ignominiously kicked back down the stairs, and was now sheltering by a rear doorway, Banokles beside him, his tall shield swung to his back.

'At least there are no more arrows,' said Banokles, passing Kalliades a fresh cloth. Blood was flowing freely now. 'Thought he had you,' he added.

'Too damn close,' answered Kalliades, spitting more blood.

'He killed Eruthros. Opened his throat.'

'I saw.'

Kalliades gazed back at the stairs. 'We should pull back,' he said. 'Gather ladders from the walls. Then we could hit them from several sides.'

'They can't hold much longer,' said Banokles.

'That is Argurios,' Kalliades pointed out. 'He could hold all night.'

'Ah well,' answered Banokles, with a wide grin, 'when the king makes you a general I'll be your ladder man. Until then I think I'll keep my head down.'

'I need stitches, otherwise I'll bleed to death,' grumbled Kalliades. Together the two men moved out into the *megaron*. There were some forty wounded Mykene warriors already there, being attended by comrades. Kalliades pulled off his helm and sat down on Priam's throne. Banokles doffed his own helmet, then reached into the small pouch at his sword belt, drawing out a curved needle and a length of thread. With a cloth he tried to wipe away the blood, but it was flowing too freely.

'Made a real mess of your face,' he offered. 'Luckily you always were an ugly whoreson.'

'Just stitch it,' snapped Kalliades.

Leaning his head back he gritted his teeth against the stinging of the needle, and the tightening of the raw flesh. Banokles' fingers kept slipping as fresh blood pumped over them, but eventually the flow slowed.

'Are you going to try Argurios again?' asked Banokles, as he tied the last knot.

Kalliades shook his head. 'I did my duty once. I don't want to be the man who killed Argurios. Let someone else send his shade on the dark road. He may be the enemy now, but I'll be sad when he falls.'

'Well, I'm going back,' said Banokles. 'If someone doesn't clear the path I'll never get to ride one of Priam's daughters.'

'May Ares guide your spear,' said Kalliades.

'He always does,' replied Banokles, donning his helm. Gathering up his spear, the big man walked back to the fighting.

Kalliades felt a heaviness descend on his spirit. This entire venture was turning to goat shit. Argurios had fooled them, drawn them in to where he wanted to fight. Kolanos was an idiot not to have seen his strategy. They would not break Argurios. Instead the night would slowly drift by, and by morning the entire city would turn on them.

Some of the wounded men were gathering up their weapons again. Others were stretched out, leaking blood to the floor.

A short and a simple battle, with plenty of plunder. That was what Kolanos had promised.

Even as he thought of the man he saw him, moving across the *megaron*, a bow in his hand. Kolanos was wearing no helmet, his white hair flowing free to his shoulders.

Kalliades' view of him sunk to a new depth. Heroes did not use bows. They fought with sword and lance, facing their enemies, eye to eye, hand to hand.

Then, in the distance, he heard a horn blow. It echoed mournfully through the night. Then the sound was repeated, over and over.

Kolanos paused and swung back to where the Trojan prince, Agathon, was standing. Kalliades could not hear their conversation, but he saw that Agathon was concerned by the blowing of the horn. His face looked tight and tense, and he kept casting nervous glances towards the door.

Then Kolanos ran back to the scene of the fighting. Agathon headed in the opposite direction, and Kalliades saw him pass out into the night.

Kalliades remained where he was, lost in thought. Had he known Argurios was an enemy here he would never have accepted the mission. Not through fear of the man, for Kalliades feared nothing. Simply because Argurios had an uncanny knack of never losing.

The damned horn continued to blow. It sounded closer now. Kalliades heaved himself to his feet and walked out into the night. There were Thrakians milling in the courtyard, talking in urgent voices.

'What is happening?' asked Kalliades.

'The Great Gates are open,' a man told him. 'More Trojans are coming.'

Then another Thrakian came sprinting through the gates, shouting, 'Hektor has returned! The prince is back! Fly for your lives!'

The Thrakians stood still for only a moment. Then they began to stream away through the palace gates.

Kalliades swore, and ran back into the *megaron*.

XXXV

The Swan's Promise

i

ARGURIOS BATTLED ON, HELIKAON BESIDE HIM. THE OLDER WARRIOR was beginning to tire now, and knew that soon he would have to step back, allowing either Dios or Polydorus to take his place for a while. He had still not fully recovered from the assassination attempt back in the autumn, and his arms were beginning to feel heavy, his breath coming in harsh rasps.

Blocking a spear-thrust, he slammed his shield into the warrior facing him, then drove his spear high and hard at the man's helmet. It hammered into the brow, snapping the warrior's head back and throwing him off balance. Argurios hurled himself against the man, knocking him back into the warrior behind him. Both fell clumsily. For a moment only there was a gap in the fighting, as the Mykene struggled to rise.

In the distance Argurios could hear a horn blowing. He glanced at Helikaon.

'It is the Call to Arms,' shouted Helikaon. 'Reinforcements are coming!'

A cheer went up from the people on the gallery, and many of them began to shout down jeers and threats to the Mykene.

'You are finished now!' bellowed one man. 'Like rats in a trap!'

But the Mykene did not run. Instead they launched a fresh attack on the stairs. Argurios fought on. His spear point snapped against a shield. Hurling the weapon aside he drew his sword. His opponent, a huge warrior, threw himself at him, knocking him from his feet. The enemy's lance stabbed towards Argurios' face. Twisting away from the blade Argurios lashed out with his foot, catching the man in the ankle. He stumbled. Argurios surged up, his sword plunging through the man's spear arm at the biceps. The Mykene jerked back, but the sword was stuck fast. Forced to release his hold on the weapon Argurios leaned back and hammered his foot against the man's hip. The Mykene fell heavily. Other warriors clambered over him.

'Argurios!' shouted Polydorus, thrusting his own spear into Argurios' hand. Even as he took it Argurios twisted his body and surged forward, the point of the spear piercing a warrior's throat, and snapping the neck.

The Mykene warriors at the foot of the stairs were streaming back through the *megaron* to face the fresh troops arriving there. Argurios could not see them, but he could hear the sounds of battle.

Then he saw Kolanos, by the far wall, a bow in his hand.

In that instant a Mykene soldier leapt at Helikaon, knocking him from his feet. Half stunned, Helikaon tried to roll. The Mykene standing over him raised his spear for a death lunge. Argurios spun and blocked the blow with his shield.

Something sharp and hot tore into his side, ripping through his ribs and driving up into his chest. He staggered, righted himself, and thrust his spear into the warrior threatening Helikaon. As the man fell the others below him turned away from the stairs.

Argurios wanted to follow them but his legs were suddenly weak and he sank to the stairs. The Shield of Ilos fell from his arm, and he gazed down at the arrow buried deep in his side. It had struck exactly the point on his cuirass where the bronze discs were missing.

Helikaon and Polydorus carried Argurios to the gallery, laying him gently down. Fire was running through him now, and he gritted his teeth against the insistent agony. Helikaon pulled Argurios' helmet clear and knelt alongside him. Then Polydorus placed his hand over the shaft, ready to pull it clear.

'No!' said Argurios. 'This arrow and I are brothers now. It has killed me. It is also keeping me alive for a little while. Draw it out and my life blood will flow with it.'

'No!' insisted Polydorus. 'I will fetch the physician. He will find a way to cut it clear. You will live, Argurios. You *must* live.' He rushed away.

Argurios sighed, then looked at Helikaon. 'The boy doesn't know wounds,' he said. 'We do, though, Golden One.'

'Yes,' agreed Helikaon, lifting clear his own helmet. 'I am sorry, Argurios.'

Priam the king came then, and knelt on Argurios' left. For a moment he said nothing, then he reached out and gripped Argurios' hand. 'I said you could ask anything of me,' he said.

'Nothing left to ask for, Priam King.' He smiled, grimly. 'If I had the power I would go down there and rescue my friends, and carry them back to Mykene. I recognized many.'

'Is there anything I can do for you? Or your family?'

'I have no family. I need nothing.'

Priam sighed, then stood. 'I thank you, Mykene. The Shield of Ilos will return to its place of glory on the walls of my palace. It will be known from now on as the Shield of Argurios. No-one will ever forget what you did here.'

With that the king, flanked by Royal Eagles, strode down to the *megaron*.

Polydorus returned with the physician Zeotos, who only confirmed what Argurios already knew. The arrow was too deep. Polydorus knelt beside the dying warrior, and there were tears in his eyes.

'I cannot tell you how proud I am to have stood with you in battle, Argurios,' he said.

'Spare some pride for yourself, boy. You did well. Now go and join your comrades, and let me sit quietly for a while.'

Polydorus leaned forward and kissed Argurios on the brow. Then he gathered his sword and followed his king down the stairs.

Andromache came then. 'Am I to get no peace?' asked Argurios. Her face was tight and tense, and he could see the marks of tears upon her cheeks.

'Laodike needs you,' she said.

'I don't want her to see me like this.'

'No, you must come. She . . . she is dying too, Argurios.'

'No!' Argurios groaned. 'It cannot be!'

'Her wound was deeper than we thought. You must come to her.'

Argurios looked up at Helikaon. 'Help me rise,' he said. Helikaon took his arm and drew him upright. Argurios groaned again as the arrow point shifted, firing fresh agony through him. He staggered back against the wall, but Helikaon held him. Slowly they made their way to the queen's apartments. The wounded were everywhere, and Argurios saw Laodike lying on her couch, her eyes closed. Steadying himself, he told Helikaon to let him go, then walked to the couch and knelt beside it. Reaching out, he took her hand. Laodike's eyes opened. Her face was pale, her eyes heavy-lidded. Argurios felt in that moment he had never seen such beauty. Laodike smiled, her face instantly radiant with happiness. 'Oh, Argurios,' she said. 'I was dreaming of you.'

'Was it a good dream?' he asked her.

'Yes. All my dreams of you are wonderful.'

'And what did you dream?'

'It was our house. I have been to see it. You will . . . love it. It has a deep garden and a fountain. There are flowering trees against the western wall. We can sit there in the evenings, when the sun sets.'

'I will look forward to that, my love.'

'Did you see father?'

'Yes. Everything is well, Laodike.'

'We will not be parted then?'

Argurios opened the small pouch at his sword belt and lifted out the crumpled swan feather.

'You kept it!' she whispered.

'Yes. I kept it. We will never be parted. Not even in death.'

Placing the feather in her hand, he closed his own fingers around hers. With the last of his strength he eased himself down to the floor, laying his head upon her breast.

'I am so happy, Argurios,' she said. 'I think I'll sleep a little now.'

'We'll both sleep. And when we awake you can show me the garden.'

ii

Kalliades ran back into the *megaron*, his mind racing. With enemy troops coming in behind them, and an undefeated force still holding the upper levels, the insurrection was now doomed. Casting his veteran's eye around the palace he knew it could not be defended for long. The *megaron* was almost a hundred paces long, and some fifty wide. Too large to resist a superior force – as the Trojans had discovered only a few hours before. Now the roles were about to be reversed – save that the Mykene would not be able to retreat to the upper levels. They would be assailed on two fronts, through the great doors, and from the gallery above. He scanned the columned walls. Their only hope – albeit a transient one – would be to form a shield wall.

All around him lay Mykene casualties, having their wounds stitched or plugged with cloth. He called out to the men closest by, 'Get the wounded together! More Trojans are coming!'

Instantly warriors began helping their comrades to their feet, or carrying them back to the shelter of the wall. Then they began to gather shields and helmets. Kalliades ran the length of the *megaron* to the rear of the hall, where the battle of the stairs was still raging. Argurios was still fighting there, but Kalliades did not look up at him. Instead he sought out Kolanos. He saw the general standing in the shelter of a great column, his bow bent. An arrow flashed towards the stairs. Kalliades flicked his glance to the left, seeing the shaft punch home in Argurios' side.

'I have you, you bastard!' said Kolanos gleefully.

Kalliades came alongside him. 'Trojan reinforcements are upon us,' he said. 'The city gates are open and the Thrakians have fled.'

He saw fear in Kolanos' eyes. 'Where is Prince Agathon?'

Kalliades shrugged. 'Gone. I don't know where. We need to make a stand. I have started a shield wall.'

'A stand? I'll not die here!' Kolanos threw away the bow and headed down the *megaron*, racing towards the open doors. Kalliades followed him, awaiting orders.

But there were none. The general ran out into the courtyard. Kalliades paused in the doorway, wondering what the man was doing. Then he realized. Kolanos was trying to flee the palace before the enemy arrived. He was almost at the gates when Trojan soldiers appeared. Kolanos spun round and fled back to where Kalliades waited, pushing past him and into the palace. There he stood, eyes wide and staring, his face a mask of panic.

Kalliades' loathing for the man swelled still further. Pulling away from the general he sprinted back to the mass of fighting men below the stairs. 'Back! Back!' he yelled. 'We are betrayed! Form a shield wall! Now!'

The first man he saw was Banokles. He had lost his helmet and his face was grey with pain. A sword blade had cut through his arm, and was jutting from his biceps.

'Pull this damn thing out!' he urged Kalliades.

Kalliades wrenched the blade clear. Banokles swore loudly. 'Shield wall!' shouted Kalliades once more, his voice carrying over the fighting. Years of harsh discipline cut through the battle lust and the Mykene began to stream back from the stairs.

Swinging his shield to his forearm, Kalliades moved with them. Trojan soldiers were pouring through the doors now, armed with spear and sword. Kolanos had retreated behind some twenty men with shields and spears, while other Mykene ran to join them, forming a tight wall round their wounded.

A group of seven warriors made a charge at the doors, seeking to block the entrance. Kalliades saw a huge, golden-haired Trojan enter, carrying two swords. He was helmetless and wearing an ordinary breastplate. On either side of him were shield bearers, protecting his flanks. Kalliades expected to see the man swept aside

461

by the Mykene charge. Instead he tore into the seven warriors, killing two and punching a third from his feet. There had been many shocks that night, but this stunned Kalliades. The Trojan did not fight like a man, but advanced like a tempest, invincible and unstoppable.

A great cheer went up from the people on the gallery, a sound rich and joyous. Then they began to chant.

'Hektor! Hektor! Hektor!'

Kalliades felt suddenly cold. He shivered as he watched the great Trojan hero charge into the warriors facing him.

A Mykene stabbed at Hektor with a spear, but he sidestepped the thrust and drove his sword through the attacker's skull. The blade stuck fast. Two more Mykene rushed at him. A shield bearer blocked the charge of the first, but the Trojan met the second head on. As the Mykene opened his shield to stab out with his spear Hektor stepped inside and delivered a punch to the man's helm. It rang like a bell, and the warrior was hurled from his feet. The remaining Mykene fell back to join the shield wall, as more and more Trojans swarmed into the *megaron*.

Kalliades killed a soldier, knocked another to the floor, then took up his place alongside Banokles.

The shield wall at last in place and bristling with spears, the Trojans fell back momentarily, pinning down the Mykene, but making no attack.

'So that's Hektor,' said Banokles. 'Always wondered if he was as good as the legends say. Big bastard, isn't he?'

Kalliades did not reply. The Mykene were finished now. Fewer than fifty warriors were left. True they would take a few score more Trojans with them, but they could not fight their way out of this mess.

'You think this could get any worse?' asked Banokles.

Kalliades saw King Priam walk out into the *megaron*, flanked by Royal Eagles. The vile Helikaon was also with him. The king cried out Hektor's name, and the giant walked over to him, embracing the older man. The moment was almost dream-like. The Mykene were waiting to die, surrounded by a furious enemy. And yet two men were embracing and laughing. The Trojans continued to shout Hektor's name.

The golden-haired warrior raised his arms, acknowledging their tribute, then swung back to stare with cold eyes at the surviving Mykene.

'I don't see Argurios,' said Banokles. 'That's a small blessing. Wouldn't want both him and the Man Killer against me.'

'Kolanos shot him with an arrow.'

'Damn! No way for a great man to go down.'

'May Zeus hear that and curse Kolanos for it,' replied Kalliades, in a low voice. 'Maybe Argurios will wait for us on the dark road, and we'll journey together.'

'I'd like that,' said Banokles.

The voice of Kolanos called out, 'Priam King, may we speak under a truce?'

The king stepped back from his son, and stared hard at the general. Then he gestured him to come forward. Kolanos eased himself through the front rank and walked through the Trojan line.

'If he can talk us out of this I'll kiss the man,' said Banokles.

'Your lips would turn black,' muttered Kalliades.

XXXVI

The King's Wisdom

HELIKAON WATCHED THE HATED MYKENE WALK FROM THE SHIELD wall. His hand gripped his sword hilt more tightly, and he fought to control the rage swelling within him. This man had tortured Zidantas, murdered young Diomedes, and had now killed Argurios. Every instinct in Helikaon urged him to step out and slash his head from his shoulders.

Yet he had asked for a truce, and it had been granted. Honour demanded he should be allowed to speak. After that I will kill you, thought Helikaon.

Kolanos approached the king, and offered a bow. 'Your men have fought well, Priam King,' he said.

'You have no time for idle chatter,' replied the king. 'Speak – and then return to your men and prepare to die.'

'I will speak. A wise man knows when his luck is played out,' answered Kolanos, keeping his voice low. 'We can no longer win. The Fates were against us. We can, on the other hand, kill perhaps another hundred of you. I can prevent that. I can also offer my services to Troy, Priam King.'

Priam stood silently, observing the Mykene. 'How can you prevent your men fighting?' he asked at last. 'They know they are doomed.'

'I can tell them you have agreed to let them go – if they surrender their weapons. Once disarmed you can kill them at little cost to yourself.'

'A noble act,' said Priam, with a sneer.

'They are – as you say – doomed anyway. At least this way no more Trojans will die.'

'And you will live.'

'Indeed. I can be of great use to you. I know all of Agamemnon's plans for these eastern lands. I know where he intends to strike, and what kings he has won over to his cause. I know the names of all of Prince Agathon's allies in Troy, whom he was to promote, and whom he was to draw into his inner circle.'

'Valuable information indeed,' said Priam.

'Do I have your word that my life will be spared?'

'You have my guarantee that not a single Trojan will raise a weapon against you.'

'How about Dardanians?' asked Kolanos, flicking a glance at Helikaon.

'No-one who fights for me will harm you,' promised Priam.

'No!' said Helikaon. 'I will not be bound by this promise. The man is a snake, and deserves death.'

'In my palace you will obey me, Aeneas,' snapped Priam. 'Your feud with Kolanos can wait. I'll not lose a hundred more brave men for the sake of your vengeance. Do I have your word on this – or do I need to have you restrained?'

Helikaon looked into Kolanos' pale eyes, and saw him grin. It was too much to bear. His sword came up. Priam stepped between them. Two Eagles grabbed Helikaon's arms. Priam moved in close. 'You have fought well for me, Aeneas, and I am grateful. Do not allow your rage to ruin everything. Look around you. There are young soldiers here who could be dead or crippled in the next few moments. These young men have wives and families, or sweethearts, or babes. They do not need to die to feed your revenge.'

Helikaon relaxed. 'In your palace tonight I will not kill him. That is all I will promise.'

'That is good enough,' said Priam. 'Release him.' Helikaon

sheathed his sword. Turning back to the Mykene Priam said, 'Very well, Kolanos. Have your men surrender their weapons.'

Kolanos bowed and returned to his men. There was some discord when he told them they were to be disarmed. Helikaon saw a young man with a wound to his face urging the soldiers to refuse the order. Kolanos calmly assured them that the weapons would be returned to them at the beach, before they boarded their ships. Helikaon could see that many of the warriors did not like this turn of events. Their faces showed their indecision. These were fighting men, who did not give up their weapons lightly. Yet here was their general, praising their bravery, and offering them life. It seemed too good an offer to refuse.

Trojan soldiers moved in among the Mykene, removing shields, spears, swords and helms. Finally even the breastplates were unbuckled, and all the weapons laid at the centre of the *megaron* in a huge pile. Stripped of their armour the Mykene were no longer terrifying, merely a group of young men, awaiting their fate. Kolanos returned to stand alongside Priam.

The king called out an order, and the Trojans surrounding the Mykene levelled their lances. Realization hit the Mykene then. There was to be no release, and now, disarmed, they were to be slaughtered. Then Priam stepped forward.

'Men of Mykene,' he said coldly, 'I am Priam King of Troy, and I hate you all with a depth of loathing you could not begin to imagine. My daughter Laodike lies dead in the queen's apartments. Many of my friends and loyal counsellors walked the dark road tonight. Now your general has sold you to die, defenceless like sheep. To gain his own freedom he has betrayed you all.' Priam swung to Kolanos. 'You have any last words for your men?'

Kolanos shook his head.

Priam gazed at the grim, defiant faces of the Mykene. 'Now understand me. I would rejoice to see your bodies slashed, your throats open, your blood spurting. It would gladden my heart to hear your screams. Instead I am going to allow you to walk to your ships. I will return your weapons, and you will live.'

Helikaon saw the shock on their faces. 'Aye, you heard me right,' continued Priam, anger causing his voice to tremble. 'I will tell you why you are spared. A great man died here tonight, and, as he was dying, I asked him if there was anything I could do for him, or his family. He said he had no family, but that if he had the strength he would walk down to this *megaron* and rescue *you*. For *you* were his comrades. Yes, you know of whom I speak. Argurios wanted you to live. Now, make no mistake, I want you to die. The king of Troy wants you to die. But this is the Night of Argurios. On this night he is greater than kings. So you live.'

A silence fell, and Priam turned and pointed at Kolanos. 'Bind him!' he ordered. Soldiers leapt on the Mykene general, pinning his arms behind him.

'I had your promise!' shouted Kolanos.

'Yes, you did, and I will keep it. Not a Trojan will lay a hand on you. You betrayed these brave men, and you offered to betray your king. Yes, Kolanos, I would love to know the plans of Agamemnon. However, as I said, this is the Night of Argurios. I think he would like *you* to travel back with your men. Perhaps they will keep you alive to explain yourself to your king. Perhaps not.' Priam strode through the Trojan lines until he stood directly before the Mykene. 'Who commands now?' he asked.

'I do,' said a dark-haired young man, with keen grey eyes. Upon his face was a jagged cut, stitched but still leaking blood. 'I am Kalliades.'

'I shall send for physicians to tend your men. They will meet you at the beach. My soldiers will escort you there now, and carry any of your wounded.'

'We can carry our own wounded, Priam King.'

'So be it. Your weapons will be returned to you at your ships. We will bury your dead, and they will be given honour.'

'Argurios was my comrade,' said Kalliades. 'He gave me this cut to my face, and I will treasure the scar.'

'And Kolanos?'

'You want him taken to Agamemnon, Priam King?'

'No. I would like to stand at my tower as your ships depart, and hear his screams echo across the Great Green. I would like to think that his suffering will be long, his pain excruciating, and his death assured.'

'You have my oath on that, Priam King.'

Priam turned away and walked back to where Helikaon stood. 'Will your vengeance be satisfied now, Aeneas?'

Helikaon glanced over at Kolanos. The man was terrified.

'It is satisfied. That was an act of greatness. Argurios would have been proud of it.'

Surrounded by Trojan soldiers, the Mykene began to shuffle from the *megaron*. Helikaon walked to where Hektor stood. The golden-haired warrior gave a broad smile, opened his arms, and drew Helikaon into a crushing embrace.

'This time I really thought they'd killed you,' said Helikaon.

'Have you no faith, boy? You think a few Gypptos could finish me off? And how could I not come back, when father has taken such pains to find me a bride?' Hektor glanced up at the gallery. 'Is that her? By the gods, I hope it is.'

Helikaon gazed up at Andromache. She was standing there in her torn white chiton, her bow in her hand, her flame-coloured hair hanging free.

'Yes,' he said, his heart breaking, 'that is Andromache.'

Then he turned away, and walked from the palace.

He followed the Trojan soldiers as they led the fifty Mykene to the beach and the waiting ships. Weary now, both in body and soul, he sat down on an upturned rowing boat and watched as surgeons and healers moved among the wounded. Kolanos, his arms bound, was sitting alone on the beach, staring out to sea.

The light of pre-dawn began to glow in the east.

Several carts trundled down to the beach, bearing the armour and weapons of the Mykene.

It all seemed a dream now to Helikaon, the bloodshed and the horror, the battle in the *megaron*. It was hard to believe, in this quiet dawn, that men had died and that the fate of a kingdom had hung in the balance. And yet, despite all the drama and violence, it was not thoughts of battle that hung on his soul. All he could see was Andromache and Hektor. He was more than happy that his friend was alive. At any other time, though, he would have been exultant. Emotions warred within him. The return of Hektor had robbed him of the one joy he had fought for.

Anger touched him then. 'I will not let this happen,' he said, aloud, and pictured himself returning to the palace for Andromache. He could see Priam, and offer him anything to release Andromache to him. Reality blew across his thoughts like a chill wind. Priam would not release her. He had announced her to the Trojan multitudes. She was the price of a treaty with the king of Thebe Under Plakos.

Then I will steal her, he decided. We will sail across the Great Green, and make a life far from Troy.

And in doing so you will shame Hektor, cause strife and possible ruin in Dardania, and live your life in constant fear of reprisal and death.

Is this love, he asked himself? Is this the kind of life you would visit upon Andromache? To become a runaway, exiled from her family, an oath breaker, loathed and reviled? Helikaon felt as if all his strength had been leeched from him.

As the sky brightened the air became filled with the sounds of seabirds, swooping and diving over the bay, their calls sharp and hungry and full of life.

On the beach behind him the Mykene began to climb aboard their galleys. Injured men were lifted to the decks, then the weapons were hauled up in fishing nets. Helikaon saw the bound Kolanos propelled roughly towards a vessel. He fell to his knees. A Mykene warrior kicked him, then dragged him to his feet.

With the dawn breaking the galleys were hauled out into the water, the last of the crew scrambling aboard. Helikaon watched as the masts were hoisted, and the oars run out. The Trojan soldiers marched back along the beach, and then up the long hill to the city gates.

As the galleys sailed off into the west a piercing shriek came echoing across the water. Then a scream of agony. And another. The awful sounds continued, growing more faint as the galleys rowed towards the headland.

Helikaon heard soft footfalls and swung to see Andromache walking towards him, a long green cloak around her shoulders. Rising from the upturned boat he opened his arms and she stepped into his embrace. He kissed her brow.

'I love you, Andromache. Nothing will ever change that.'

'I know. Our lives were never our own.'

He lifted her hand, and kissed the palm. 'I am glad you came. I did not have the strength to seek you out in the palace. I would have committed some madness and damned us all.'

'I don't think you would,' she said softly. 'Laodike told me you love Hektor like a brother. You could do nothing to bring him shame. I know you, Helikaon. And you should know me. I would never bring disgrace upon my family. We were both raised to duty – above all else.'

'Such duty is a curse!' he said, anger flaring once more. 'There is nothing on earth I want more than to sail away with you, to live together, to *be* together.'

He looked up at the sky. The rising sun had streaked the clouds above with crimson and gold, but over the sea to the west the sky was brilliantly blue and clear.

'I must go,' said Andromache.

'A little while longer,' he urged her, taking her hand.

'No,' she said sadly. 'With every moment my resolve is weakening.' Drawing back her hand, she said, 'May the gods grant you great happiness, my love.'

'In letting me know you they already have. More than I have deserved.'

'Will you come back for my wedding in the spring?'

'Would you want me there?'

Tears fell then, and he saw her struggle to retain her composure. 'I will always want you close to me, Helikaon.'

'Then I will be there.'

Andromache turned away and stared out to sea. 'Laodike and Argurios died hand in hand. You think they are together now? For ever?'

'I hope so, with all my heart.'

Gathering her cloak around her she looked into his eyes. 'Farewell then, King Aeneas,' she said, and walked away.

'Goodbye, goddess,' he whispered. She heard him, and he saw her pause. Then she continued on without turning. He stood watching her until she reached the high gate.

She did not look back.

EPILOGUE

The Golden Torque

BY THE ARRIVAL OF SPRING THE LAND OF DARDANIA WAS AT PEACE. Helikaon's soldiers had eradicated the more persistent of the outlaw bands, and with greater communication between towns and settlements grievances were dealt with swiftly, before they had a chance to fester. Community leaders, with access to officials at Dardanos, no longer felt isolated, and the Feast of Persephone, welcoming the new season, was a happy one.

Queen Halysia had led the sacrifice procession to the cliff-top shrine, wearing the golden laurel crown, and carrying the Staff of Demeter. King Helikaon had walked beside her. The queen's pregnancy was pronounced now, but no-one commented on it. The silence was hard to bear, for Halysia believed she knew what lay behind it. Either they pitied her, or they were hiding their revulsion.

Once the dancing and the singing began she slipped away and walked back up to the fortress, and the cliff-top gardens. They were unkempt and overgrown, and she decided she would spend more time here from now on, in quiet solitude, reshaping the flower beds, and cutting back the shrubs. However, today she merely sat, looking out over the shimmering sea.

A servant brought her a cool drink. She thanked the girl and sent her away. Down in the bay she saw the *Xanthos* had been refloated, and men were working upon her decks, ready for the voyage to the west. The first ship of the new season had docked here only yesterday, carrying copper and tin. It had also brought a gift for Helikaon that had caused him to laugh aloud. A friend on Kypros had sent him an ornate bow, decorated with silver thread. There was a short message. 'Now you can truly be the Lord of the Silver Bow,' it read.

Halysia had asked him about it. He told her about a half-starved child who had mistaken him for the god Apollo. 'It seems a long time ago now,' he said.

'And you helped her?' She laughed then. 'A foolish question. Of course you helped her. It is your nature.' There had also been messages from Troy, which he had shared with her. The rebel prince Agathon had been seen in Miletos, taking ship for Mykene. Prince Antiphones had been promoted to the king's inner circle, and given a new palace for his part in foiling the plot on Priam's life. This last news had pleased Helikaon. 'He is a good man,' he said. 'I like him greatly.'

A light breeze blew across the cliff top. Halysia strolled out from the garden and along the cliff path. She could still hear the music of the pipes in the distance, and the laughter of the guests. Such a good sound. There is too little laughter in the world, she thought.

She sat in the shade of an overhanging rock, and watched the seabirds flocking over the *Xanthos*. Then she dozed for a while in the heat. When she awoke the afternoon was waning towards dusk. Glancing back along the cliff path she saw Helikaon emerge from the gardens, some way in the distance. Her breath caught in her throat, and her heart began to beat faster. He had changed from the royal robes he had worn for the sacrifice to Persephone. Now he wore a simple white knee-length tunic, edged with gold.

And she remembered the visions of that dreadful night, when the Mykene had raped her and murdered her son. She had almost come to believe they were inventions born of her terror. But there had been a vision of Helikaon, dressed in this tunic, seeking her on a cliff top.

Her mouth was dry, and she felt like hiding from him. He had seen her, though, and waved.

Easing herself to her feet she waited for him. He was carrying a small package, wrapped in muslin.

'I thought I would find you here, lady,' he said. 'There is something we must speak of.'

'No!' she said sharply. 'You must not! I know what you have there. You must not give it to me.'

He looked puzzled. 'How can you know?'

'My dreams, Helikaon. You remember? The sea full of ships carrying blood-hungry men, a great city burning. Terror and despair! I saw the sky aflame and the sea rise up. I also saw you, coming to me here, and in your hands a golden necklace, decorated with lapis lazuli. You understand? If you give me this then the other visions must be true also.'

He stood quietly for a moment. 'I do understand,' he said. 'But listen to me, Halysia. If the visions were true, then they will come to pass whether you accept the gift or not. For I am here, and the gift is in my hand, just as your vision showed you. And, yes, one day the enemy will cross the Great Green. They will bring war and tragedy to these eastern lands. Such is the nature of vile men. Yet we cannot live in dread of them. We cannot hide behind high walls, our hearts trembling. For that is not life. We must accept the needs and the duties of each day, and face them one at a time. You are the queen of Dardania, and the people love you. I am the king, and they fear me. Soon you will give birth to a child – a son, if your dreams are true. It would be better for him, for you, and for the realm if we were to be a true family. We should be wed, Halysia.'

She turned away. 'You do not love me, Helikaon. And you promised yourself to wed only for love.'

He took her hand and smiled. 'You are wrong. I do have love for you. Yes, and respect and admiration. If the gods will it we will find happiness together. Or at least contentment.'

A cool breeze rustled against her gown and she shivered. 'When would we do this?' she asked.

'Tomorrow, while everyone is still gathered for the feast days.'

'I am so frightened, Helikaon.'

He drew her to him, his arms around her. 'Be my wife, and I will be a shield against all your fears.'

She felt the strength of his arms, and the warmth of his body, and she snuggled in even closer, feeling safer than she had in months. She sighed and closed her eyes, wanting the moment to last and last.

He stroked her golden hair, then eased her away from him, offering her the wedding gift. Halysia took it with trembling hands, and opened the cloth wrapping. The necklace was exquisite, made of scores of tiny golden squares, many of them embellished with brilliantly blue lapis lazuli. Lifting it from the cloth Helikaon draped it round her slender neck. The metal felt warm against her skin.

'It looks beautiful,' he said, with a wide smile. 'Now let us go inside, and announce the news.' Taking her hand he led her back along the cliff top. As they reached the garden she glanced back once more at the sea.

Yet again, in her mind's eye, she saw the massive fleet of enemy ships, bearing down upon the eastern lands.

But for this one, glorious moment, she no longer cared.